GETHSEMANE REVISITED

About the Author

James Brophy grew up in Belfast during 'The Troubles', but most of his working life has been spent in Dublin, where he currently lives with his wife Martina. Deeply involved in Irish politics, he has a lifelong fascination with history and travel, which influenced this novel.

GETHSEMANE REVISITED

JAMES BROPHY

Matador
9 Priory Business Park,
Wistow Road, Kibworth Beauchamp,
Leicestershire. LE8 0RX
Tel: 0116 279 2299
Email: books@troubador.co.uk
Web: www.troubador.co.uk/matador
Twitter: @matadorbooks

ISBN 978 1838595 395

British Library Cataloguing in Publication Data.
A catalogue record for this book is available from the British Library.

Printed and bound by CPI Group (UK) Ltd, Croydon, CR0 4YY
Typeset in 11pt Adobe Garamond Pro by Troubador Publishing Ltd, Leicester, UK

Matador is an imprint of Troubador Publishing Ltd

Grateful acknowledgement is made for permission by 'The Dylan Thomas Trust' to
reproduce excerpts from the poem, 'After the Funeral'.

Many thanks to all my family and friends who contributed so generously of their time in helping me to write this story. Particular thanks to my wife Martina and daughters Catherine and Jenny, and also to Jane Adams for her insightful guidance. And a special mention for my sister Maura for her unflagging support and amazing confidence that I could complete a novel.

Introduction

It could be that every message has its time, and perhaps mine is not now. Or maybe it's the understanding and acceptance of the message that require patience. We will see. I have done what I believe was asked of me. This is my story; only I know what happened, and I *know* what happened.

Chapter 1

Nuremberg, Germany;
5th August 1929; 11.05am

"Dr Goebbels, may I speak with you a moment?"

He turned and stared at Jerome; a politician's face, inscrutable but ready, if necessary, to alter to a smile of recognition. Slowly, his small eyes narrowed. "Do I know you?" He walked cautiously towards Jerome, who was clutching a light-brown envelope in his left hand.

"No, but I want to speak to your *Führer* and..." Jerome raised his left hand slowly. "I need to give him this envelope. It contains photographs that I think will be of great interest to him."

Men – many in their brown, *Sturmabteilung* (SA) military-style uniforms – continued to pass in and out of the sunlit entrance hall, oblivious to this conversation.

Goebbels's eyes narrowed to slits. "Is this some sort of blackmail attempt?"

"No, not at all," confirmed Jerome.

Goebbels moved very close to him, much closer than necessary for normal conversation. It was almost as though he were sniffing

Jerome to get as much sensory information as possible. "Who are you?" he asked slowly. Goebbels was small in stature, but, if anything, this seemed to add to the edge of menace in his voice.

"My name is Jerome Black. I'm not from this country and…" he lowered his voice before continuing, "of much more relevance, Dr Goebbels, I am not from this time. I can be here for only a few hours, and I need to speak to your *Führer*." Jerome offered the envelope to him; they were so close that he needed to step back to make it clear the offer was being made.

Goebbels said nothing, but looked him up and down briefly, and then stared directly into his face.

Jerome feared he was about to be dismissed or worse. "Dr Goebbels, I'm someone unique. This is the only opportunity your *Führer* will have to talk to me." Jerome stared back at him. "I assure you I'm not mad."

Without looking at it, Goebbels took the envelope and called over two men who had been standing patiently behind him. "Watch this man; I'll be back soon." He was about to go when he said tersely, "Search him," then, looking at the smaller of the two men, he added, "thoroughly."

Jerome was ushered into a quiet, windowless room with pale-blue walls from which the paint was beginning to flake in places. It smelled of disinfectant and reminded him of the nursing home where he had visited his grandmother, Helga. He thought of her at that moment, remembering her passion and defiance, even when she knew she was dying. The image reassured him, and he felt his resolve strengthen.

The body search was thorough and, in Jerome's view, unnecessarily intimate. They showed an interest in his watch, but returned it to him without comment. Their check of his passport was careless and did not even extend to a comparison of the photograph with his face. He was, however, questioned about the contents of the second envelope, which he had in the inside pocket of his jacket, but Jerome had taken the precaution of writing in German on the envelope, "STRICTLY PERSONAL, FOR THE EYES OF ADOLF HITLER ONLY". He pointed to this and said firmly that he could not divulge its contents. The smaller man squeezed it carefully and, satisfied that it contained nothing dangerous, returned it. Surprisingly, Jerome's silver ring was the object that aroused most interest, and he was sure it was interest rather than suspicion. They wanted to know the significance of the design on the ring; though when he explained it was the national emblem of Scotland, they seemed to lose their curiosity. He noticed they also were wearing silver rings but with a swastika rather than a thistle design on the front.

The three men sat and waited, saying nothing.

"Do you think he'll be much longer?" asked Jerome eventually, more to break the uncomfortable silence than with any realistic expectation of a helpful reply.

The guards shrugged their shoulders and made no further response.

Jerome looked at his watch and did not try to hide his agitation. Ten minutes more elapsed before he spoke again. "Would you inform Dr Goebbels *immediately* that I cannot stay much longer?"

The two guards moved their heads together to converse quietly. "You'll have to wait here until Dr Goebbels returns," said the smaller one with smiling conviction.

His colleague tugged a cigarette from the breast pocket of his brown shirt, lit it and stared distractedly at the concrete floor, as the smoke drifted upwards to the two bright light bulbs and across the cool room. Jerome inhaled the polluted air deeply and felt some of his tension ease.

Shortly afterwards, the door opened. Goebbels came part way into the room, scanned it, then walked purposefully towards Jerome and stood over him. "Where did you get those photographs?" he demanded.

"The originals were in newspapers. The photographs are printed copies," Jerome replied.

"What newspapers?"

Jerome began to stand up, but Goebbels's firm hand on his shoulder arrested his progress. "Please remain sitting, *Herr* Black. What newspapers?"

Jerome breathed hard before replying, "German newspapers. The details are on the bottom of each photograph."

"But the dates are in the future. Are you telling me these are from German newspapers in the future? Is that what you're saying?"

"That's exactly what I'm saying, Dr Goebbels."

Goebbels turned to the two men and gave a dismissive smile. "Well, I'm afraid you'll have to do better than that, *Herr* Black. I ask you again, where did you get those photographs?"

The two guards moved forwards in their seats, their faces alert with anticipation.

Tilting his head back, Jerome looked directly at the sallow, menacing face just above him. "Dr Goebbels, I've come a long way – an unimaginably long way – to see Adolf Hitler, not you. In just under four hours, I'll be gone, never to return. This one time only your *Führer* has an unparalleled opportunity to know about the future. Not crystal-ball gazing about what might happen, but details about exactly what *will* happen. So, are you going to deny him this unique chance to know the future?"

For a few moments, Goebbels did not move. Then, unfolding his arms, he smiled benignly, sat down and brushed a few flecks of dust from the knees of Jerome's pinstriped trousers. "Indulge me for a while longer, *Herr* Black. Tell me, where are you from?"

"I'm from Scotland; the city of Glasgow."

"Scotland; you are British?"

"Yes."

"May I see your papers?"

Jerome handed him the passport.

For a moment, Goebbels seemed taken aback as he stared at this unfamiliar document. Then, frowning with suspicion, he rubbed his fingers gently over the stiff, burgundy-coloured outside cover, as though assessing a delicate piece of material, before opening it slowly. "You speak very good German; how come?"

"My father is from Germany."

Goebbels's eyes lit up as he continued to scrutinise the passport. "Yes! Which part?"

"Berlin."

"Excellent. Well, then, you are one of us. Nationality passes through the paternal line, you know." He glanced briefly at Jerome. "It says in your papers you were born in 1996."

"That is correct."

Goebbels sighed irritably. "Ah, of course, in the future; so you have yet to be born." He continued to examine the passport, turning each page with a calculated slowness that unnerved Jerome. Eventually, he handed it back. "It's a marvellous forgery. That quality could only have come from an official source. I don't believe some backstreet forger could have produced it. Do you work for British Intelligence, *Herr* Black? Is your role to try to make our *Führer* look a fool?" He moved closer to Jerome. "Because Adolf Hitler is many things, but a fool is not one of them."

"I know that, Dr Goebbels. I admire Adolf Hitler tremendously for what he's done and what he will achieve," lied Jerome.

Cocking his head slightly to one side, Goebbels carefully scanned Jerome's face. "I'm not so sure I believe you. Tell me why you want to talk to him."

"To get his insight into the tumultuous events that will happen between 1933 and 1945." He paused for a moment and looked directly at Goebbels. "And to give him *my* opinions on those same events."

"Tell *me* about them."

Jerome shook his head apologetically. "I'm sorry Dr Goebbels, but I've come to talk to your *Führer*."

Goebbels pulled down the cuffs of his own suit jacket. "What about one of the photographs? For instance, the one with our *Führer* and me, among others, with the Eiffel Tower in the background. What is the occasion?"

Jerome, with calculated deliberation, looked at his watch and then at Goebbels. "We're running out of time. I'll be gone by 3.30pm. That leaves three hours and fifty-five minutes."

"Yes, you've mentioned that before, *Herr* Black. What do you mean you'll be gone? Will you disappear in a puff of smoke like Cinderella?"

The smaller guard laughed out loud. His companion grinned. Goebbels continued to stare wide-eyed at Jerome.

"Cinderella didn't disappear; she just left. But I will disappear," stated Jerome.

Laughing softly, Goebbels stood up and patted Jerome on the shoulder. "Quite right, *Herr* Black; I bow to your greater expertise on fairy tales. But let me see if I understand you." He paused and then spoke coldly. "If we are all in this room three hours and fifty-five minutes from now and you disappear suddenly, then you will have been telling the truth, but if you're still here, then we'll know you're a fraud and probably a spy who should be shot. Am I correct?"

"Your question's academic. I'll be gone, and you'll have denied your *Führer* the opportunity to know the future."

"Maybe so, maybe so, but I'm attracted by the idea of waiting to see what happens in…" He looked at his watch. "Three hours and fifty-three minutes. After all, it is not often a man is willing to bet his life in the way you are doing."

Still smiling, Goebbels left the room.

Jerome stared at the guards, but he knew he could do nothing except wait and hope that Goebbels's interest, or self-interest, would overcome his wariness.

Twenty minutes more elapsed before the door opened slowly. Goebbels, standing in the doorway, beckoned Jerome with the index finger of his left hand. "The *Führer* has generously deigned to meet you for a few moments." He turned to go and then abruptly turned back. "*Herr* Black, if you show any intent to harm our *Führer*, you will be dealt with ruthlessly and then you really will disappear. Do you understand?"

Jerome nodded silently.

All four men left the room and walked down a high-ceilinged corridor. Goebbels, limping noticeably, was slightly in front of Jerome, with the two guards endeavouring to walk together in military fashion a couple of paces behind; their footsteps echoing clearly from the smooth stone floor. They arrived at a set of double doors with two large, circular, crystal handles.

Jerome recalled Helga's encouraging words: "*Be careful Jemi, but don't be afraid.*"

"You can wait here," Goebbels instructed the two guards. He knocked lightly on the door and, without waiting for a reply, pushed it open. "*Mein Führer*, this is the young man."

Jerome followed Goebbels into the room as the door closed noiselessly behind him.

Chapter 2

Easterhouse, a suburb of Glasgow, Scotland; 10th August 2008

In the late afternoon of that warm, still Sunday, Jerome was lying on the sitting-room sofa. It was a habit his father disapproved of, feeling it looked slothful for a twelve-year-old boy, but Pieter Black was dozing gently in one of the two dark-green armchairs. Patricia Black, Jerome's mother, was sitting upright in the other, watching the television over her reading glasses, while flicking distractedly through a magazine. The only other living thing in the room was the old, ginger cat, which was purring contentedly at Jerome's father's feet.

"Shift, wee man," said Karl Black, coming into the room and pushing his younger brother's legs off the sofa.

Jerome gave an irritated groan. "I'm gonna kick you in your sore leg," he mumbled as he tried returning to his comfortable lying position.

"Well, I'll drop kick your scrawny arse like a rugby ball through the window and down the garden," replied Karl, picking up a newspaper.

"Well, then," Jerome began after a short pause, "I'll get Dad's saw and start sawing off your—"

"Stop it you two!" interrupted his mother. "You know I don't like that talk."

The three males in the room shook with silent mirth.

"Don't mind them, Mum; they're just talking their usual nonsense," said Jerome's father, who had been woken by his sons' banter.

"Well, I don't like it; and, Karl, you should know better at your age."

"Oh! It's all *my* fault now! Thanks, Ma," responded Karl in mock indignation.

Jerome gave his brother a beaming, triumphant wink and extended the middle finger of his right hand slowly so that only Karl could see it.

"You wee rat bag," shouted Karl with a laugh as he tickled his brother affectionately. "We indulge this child, Ma. We surely do."

The room returned gradually to its pre-interruption calm. Jerome was relaxed, though not asleep. He was aware of things going on around him: the general background noise of life; the three clocks – this was the maximum number of items for his father's hobby, or obsession, that his mother tolerated – were steadily ticking and humming; his father's breathing had returned to a gentle snore; and the volume on the television was low, creating no real disturbance. Even Karl's rustling of the newspaper seemed soothing. Later, Jerome would recall watching the cat arise and move languidly towards his mother and a warm lap. He remembered glancing at the electric clock on the mantelpiece, then, suddenly, his world stopped. It only lasted for a moment, but everything in the room froze. The picture on the television stopped, with the actors trapped momentarily in odd, awkward positions; his mother's hand halted in the middle of turning a page of her magazine; and the cat poised, frozen in the moment before take-off as she prepared to leap onto his mother's lap. Even the clocks fell silent. Then, just as suddenly, it all started again, the movements continuing quite smoothly, as though nothing untoward had happened.

During that very brief period, Jerome had experienced a silence more complete than he had ever known, but, just then, he was once again aware of the three clocks and their mismatched ticking, the rustle of pages being turned, his father's gentle snore and the murmur of the television.

Jerome, disconcerted, opened his eyes wide and gave a startled, involuntarily cough. At first, he thought it was some sort of practical joke instigated by his brother, who must have tampered with the television deliberately to make him think something odd had happened, but he realised quickly that this couldn't explain all the strange phenomena he had just witnessed.

"C'mon, Jerome, sit up properly and give me some room," said Karl, again pushing Jerome's feet onto the ground.

Jerome let them fall without his usual moan of protest and stood up abruptly, feeling confused and alarmed.

His mother, ever alert to any unusual nuance among her brood, looked up sharply. "Are you OK, Jerome?" she asked.

"Yep, yeah," he lied, fashioning a casual scratch of the head for emphasis. Jerome left the room, hurried upstairs to the bathroom and locked the door quietly. Leaning over the washbasin, he stared closely at his blue eyes in the mirror, but, aside from an unusually furrowed brow, nothing looked odd. He then opened his mouth, lolled out his tongue and made a soft "ahh" sound. In truth, Jerome had no real idea what he was checking for, but he was somewhat reassured not to discover anything horrendous. He flushed the toilet and went to his bedroom.

Lying on top of the green-and-white Celtic football club duvet that covered his single bed, his memory of the incident remained crystal clear, as though a photograph had been taken at the exact moment when time had seemed to stop. In his mind's eye, he could recall the entire scene, but he had no idea what had happened. The noise from outside of a ball being kicked disturbed his reverie. He knelt on his bed and looked out in the evening sunshine at his friend Paul Gambon, who was kicking a ball against the big oak tree that stood directly across the street. He watched pensively for a few minutes before Paul noticed him. The two friends then exchanged their pretend-gun-firing hellos.

"Are you coming down?" mimed Paul, pointing to the ball under his foot.

Jerome shook his head and pointed behind him in a gesture that could signify any number of reasons why he could not play football at this time. His friend gave a farewell wave.

The door to his room opened slowly, and his mother's strawberry-blonde hair and gently enquiring face appeared. "Are you sure you're OK?" she asked, seeking the reassurance his earlier response had not quite provided.

"Yeah, honestly, Mum, I'm fine."

She raised one eyebrow. "You're certain sure?"

"Yeah, it's just a wee bit of a headache, but it's going away. I think it was the smell of Karl when he came in."

Smiling, she ruffled his brown hair. "Well, your tea will be ready in about ten minutes, so you'll come down for it." She left the room, sufficiently comforted to let the matter go.

Jerome understood his mother well. She was the family's main problem-solver and was always approachable. And although he was only twelve years old, he recognised that while she loved all three of her children, she indulged him – Karl was right about that. He wasn't sure why he had decided not to tell her about the strange event, but he felt instinctively that he wanted to work it out for himself before mentioning it to anyone. *After all,* he thought, *it was probably nothing more than an unusual one-off incident and not worth making a fuss about.*

***

The rest of the summer holidays came and went, and although his memory of the incident had not faded completely, his concern had. He now believed it was nothing more sinister than a dream. He had been lying down at the time, so perhaps he had simply dropped off to sleep for a moment. That, he felt sure, was the obvious explanation.

But then it happened again.

***

Glasgow; 15th September 2008

It was a fresh, bright Monday morning as Jerome, together with Paul Gambon and his other good friend Paul Lennox, walked unhurriedly towards the school. Lennox was tall for his age, and, with Gambon being relatively small, they looked like three boys from different years. Tall Paul and Small Paul was how Jerome's sister Geraldine referred to them any time she met them. It was always said in Geraldine's no-nonsense-though-friendly manner, but Jerome sensed it sometimes irritated his smaller friend. The three boys ambled up the broad, tree-lined lane that led from the main road to the entrance to St Peter's.

As they rounded the last bend and joined the hundreds of other students making their way into the school, Jerome heard a loud clicking noise, followed by a strange buzzing sensation along both sides of his head. Immediately, everything was silent. People, who had been talking and walking one moment earlier, were completely still. Jerome too had come to an involuntary halt, and surveyed the scene for a few seconds with a mixture of awe and alarm. On either side of him, his two friends were both looking forwards, Lennox with his mouth open, giving him a strangely fish-like appearance. Ahead was a girl with three books apparently in mid-air just in front of her; above him, a stationary aeroplane hung in the sky. Everything was utterly silent. Then the noise and movement started again as suddenly as they had stopped. Paul Lennox finished his sentence, and the girl's books fell to the ground, despite her scrambling efforts to catch them. Jerome, in a state of shock, didn't move quickly enough and was barged into by a boy coming from behind.

"What the fuck you stop for? You bampot," the boy shouted.

Jerome's two friends looked round to see what had happened, and he caught them up quickly.

"Any problems there?" asked Paul Lennox.

"No, it was my fault; I tripped," stated Jerome.

* * *

Jerome went through the routine of that school day in a dazed state of anxious confusion. This incident, while similar to the first one, was much more worrying to him. For a start, it had seemed to last for five or six seconds, which was longer than the initial, momentary freeze. Second, it had happened out of doors and involved hundreds of people, not just his family. Crucially, it had happened while he was wide awake. He knew by then that this was neither a dream nor a one-off event, and he would have to tell someone. Briefly, he considered his grandmother Helga, before realising that this was a problem requiring a solution rather than unquestioning understanding; his mother was the obvious choice.

Frightened that it might happen again, Jerome was hugely relieved when the leaving bell sounded at 3.30pm. He had already determined to skip football, a decision that surprised and annoyed his friends, but he could deal with that later. Right then, he needed to unburden himself.

***

He and his mother sat either side of the large, glass-topped table that occupied the middle of the kitchen. There were papers and envelopes scattered around the salt cellar and sauce bottle as the pleasant smell from a lamb casserole drifted warmly from the oven. It was an everyday scene that was about to host a far from everyday conversation. Patricia Black was tired at the end of a day's teaching and, initially, displayed mild irritation as Jerome began telling her about the incidents. However, this turned quickly to concern as the unusual fear in her child's voice made her realise that this was not a joke. When he finished, there was a brief silence as they looked at each other, with him seeking reassurance, and her trying to hide a growing alarm.

"What do you think it is, Mum? It's nothing bad, is it? I feel fine now. I don't feel sick or anything." His big eyes looked encouragingly at her.

"Well, I'm not sure, but I don't think it's anything bad." She scrutinised his face and then began quizzing him gently in detail on the actual incidents, all the time trying to think of some innocent explanation. His answers provided no comfort. Finally, she asked, softly but firmly, "Jerome, have you been smoking or drinking at all?" As he began to shake his head, she continued, "Before you say anything, I'm not going to shout at you. I just need to know."

"No, Mum, I haven't," he confirmed.

"Or any drugs? You know, Jerome, I see it all the time at school; young people are given drugs and they don't even realise it. Could that have happened to you?"

He realised that if he had taken drugs, he was being given an easy out, but he answered truthfully.

"Are you absolutely sure?"

He found her tone surprisingly plaintive, as though pleading for a positive reply. "Honestly, Mum, I know what drugs are. I haven't taken any." The fear had gone from his voice and, just for a moment, it seemed like the roles of parent and child were reversed.

Then Patricia unfolded her arms, placed her palms on the table and said resolutely, "OK. Well, we'll go to Dr Sterling's tomorrow to get it checked out. That's what we'll do before anything else."

"Do you think he'll be able to give us something to stop it happening again?"

"Let's see what he says. I'm sure it's something simple." She smiled at him. "And, yes, that does mean you can have the morning off school."

However, Jerome was getting to know his mother as well as she knew him. He saw that the smile didn't reach her eyes and realised that she was far from certain it was something simple.

Chapter 3

Glasgow;
16th September 2008

Alastair Sterling was the Blacks' family doctor. His surgery, on the ground floor of an old town house that was a short walk from the Blacks' home, was dull, though not unwelcoming. The waiting room was full of magazines about houses and gardens, and other subjects that held no interest for Jerome. His mother picked one up and flicked through it, but her mind was elsewhere. Jerome was wearing his "lucky" Scotland socks. These were white with a royal-blue thistle emblem on the ankles, and they stood out against his dark trousers and shoes. He had been surprised that his mother allowed him to wear them that day.

Dr Sterling was a softly spoken man in his early fifties, and he had the comfortable appearance of someone who lived a contented, sedentary life. He welcomed them into his surgery with an old-world courtesy that put Patricia Black more at ease. For a few minutes, she conveyed accurately the information Jerome had given her, while her son sat calmly by her side and said nothing. Sterling listened attentively, alternating his gaze between Mrs

Black and the computer, into which he made some entries. When she had finished, he got Jerome to sit on his couch and shone a small torchlight into each eye. Jerome stopped jiggling his feet immediately.

"Did you notice any feeling or anything unusual just before they happened, Jerome?" The doctor's voice was gentle and encouraging.

"I felt a click noise in my head before the second one and a kind of prickle here." Jerome indicated the sides of his head shyly.

"Anything else? Any smell or odd sensation?"

Jerome thought for a few moments. "No, I don't think so. It was just like everything was frozen. I don't mean like cold frozen, just that it was stopped."

Sterling sat down and typed more into his computer before moving forwards in his seat. "Jerome, I just want to ask you a few questions. Do you mind if your mum stays here or would you prefer if it was just us two?"

Jerome shrugged his shoulders. "Mum staying is fine."

Making his voice even quieter, Sterling spoke to Jerome in what seemed like a conspiratorial voice, man to man, as though he was ignoring Patricia's presence. "Now, I'm going to ask you a few things, Jerome. Just answer honestly; don't worry about getting into trouble over anything. All your mother and I are interested in is finding out what is causing these episodes, so we can sort them out." He turned to Jerome's mother, who smiled nervously and nodded her confirmation.

The doctor continued, "Would you have been smoking any cigarettes before the episodes?"

"No," Jerome confirmed.

"Would you have been taking a wee drink, such as a beer or something, with your pals? You know, just trying it out."

Jerome looked quizzically at his mother then back at the doctor. "No, Dr Sterling, I hadn't taken anything like that."

"OK, that's fine, son." He gave Jerome a warm smile. "I don't think it's anything to worry too much about. Would you mind just sitting in the waiting room for a few minutes, and I'll have a wee chat with your mum."

Jerome left the room, feeling irritated that he was being excluded from a discussion concerning him, but he was still young enough to want the adults just to sort out the problem.

Shortly afterwards, his mother emerged, looking tired, and they headed for home.

"Well, Mum, what did he say?" asked Jerome as soon as they were outside.

"He's not sure what it is, so he wants us to see a Professor Walsh in Glasgow hospital."

Jerome felt she sounded deliberately casual. "It took him five minutes to tell you that? Did he get a stammer since I was in?"

For the first time that day, Patricia smiled. "He's a slow talker, so it takes him a long time to say anything." She looked distracted. "A bit like that character in *The Lord of the Rings*. What's his name, the old tree?"

"Treebeard," said Jerome. "Who's Professor Walsh?"

"I don't know. Dr Sterling says he's an expert."

"An expert on what, Mum?"

They were crossing a busy road and Mrs Black was focusing on avoiding the traffic. When they were back walking on the pavement, Jerome repeated his question about Walsh.

"He's just an expert, Jerome," his mum reiterated.

Realising he would get no further information, Jerome let the subject drop.

***

Later that evening, shortly after her husband had arrived home from work, Patricia Black ushered him into the kitchen. Jerome knew he was not meant to hear what they were saying, but he couldn't resist sitting on the stairs, at the point that was just above the kitchen door, and listening. He had missed the beginning of the conversation, but then he heard his mother's voice, which was quiet and oddly strained.

"He's not sure what it is. He still thinks it's probably something Jerome's taken." She paused, and then continued, softer than before, "He didn't say it, but I think he suspects drugs."

"But Jerome told him he hadn't taken anything, didn't he?" asked his father.

"Yes, and I believe him."

"Well, so do I."

Nothing was said for a few moments until he heard his mother's voice again. "I'd blame myself if there was something wrong."

Jerome leaned out from the stairs, getting closer to the kitchen door.

"What are you talking about?" asked his father.

"I was too old."

"Oh, don't be ridiculous, Trisha." His father's voice was impatient yet gentle. "Let's not get ahead of ourselves. We'll see what this Walsh guy has to say."

"HEY! WHAT ARE YOU DOING?"

Jerome almost hit his head on the banisters. He turned to see Karl coming down the stairs towards him.

"I think you were eavesdropping, weren't ya?" continued Karl, chuckling as he arranged his tall frame on the stair beside Jerome. "Am I right?" Jerome grimaced sheepishly as Karl affectionately shook his shoulders. "So, big guy, tell me, how did it go today?" enquired Karl.

"OK," said Jerome, his embarrassment passing rapidly. "I've got to see another doctor in the hospital. He's supposed to be an expert."

"Yes, so Mum was saying; a big doctor. Well, he should be able to sort you out. How do you feel anyway?"

"Fine," said Jerome, shrugging his shoulders nonchalantly. "Like I don't feel sick or anything."

Karl nodded, as though in understanding, then produced two pieces of coloured paper and held them out in front of his younger brother.

"What are they?" asked Jerome.

"What are what?"

"Those," said Jerome, nodding in the direction of the papers.

"Oh these!" said Karl with exaggerated surprise. "They're just two tickets to the Rangers game on Sunday."

"Really! At Ibrox?"

Karl nodded again and said nothing.

"Who are you gonna take?" asked Jerome eventually.

"I was thinking of taking Mum. I figured she'd enjoy the genteel atmosphere of a Celtic—Rangers game. What do you reckon?"

Jerome's face slowly broadened to a huge grin.

"Unless you'd like to go," continued Karl casually.

"I'd love to go! That'd be fantastic." For a moment, Jerome cautioned his beaming smile. "You're not messing, are you?"

"Nope, we're really going," said Karl, levering himself up.

"That's great. Fucking magic!"

"And less of the cursing in the house; you know I'll only get the fucking blame."

***

That night, after Jerome had gone to bed, his father came into the room. Angling himself so that his "good" left ear was towards his son he said, almost shyly, "I got you a nice wee clock."

Jerome smiled, knowing this was his father's way of showing genuine concern, even though he must have realised by then that Jerome was not going to inherit his obsession with these timepieces.

In fact, his father lavished so much attention on his clocks that, as a very young child, Jerome came to think he resembled one. His father's small mouth – which was set in a bright, circular face – was where Jerome imagined the key could be inserted at night when his father began to slow down. As his childhood mind developed, he realised that if there were any similarities, they were in his father's calm, consistent and reliable nature.

"Don't you worry, Jerome; you'll soon be right as rain," his father declared.

"I'm not worried, Dad," Jerome answered, smiling.

Pieter Black sat down on the edge of the bed, shifting uneasily. "Have you mentioned your turns to anybody outside the family?"

This was a new word for Jerome; "episodes" was preferable. "No, Dad."

"Well, I think it would be best if you didn't. Growing up can be tough enough without giving folks stones to throw at ya." He paused. "Is that OK?"

"I hadn't intended telling anyone anyway."

"Right, well, that's fine." He got slowly to his feet and then, for a few seconds, held the gold-fringed, rectangular clock barely above the cabinet top before gently placing it down. "I'll just leave it here so."

After his father left the room, Jerome gazed contentedly at his new clock as the second hand ticked out its discrete and reassuring clicks.

Chapter 4

Glasgow;
30th September 2008

"There are some very slight abnormalities showing up in one of Jerome's tests," began Professor Walsh.

He was a slight, fair-haired man, with small, silver-rimmed glasses and a boyish appearance that accentuated his obvious youth. His surgery, or "rooms" as they were more grandly called, was in a new, circular, white-brick building that stood on the site of an old church on Kelvin Way, which was one of the quieter, more upmarket parts of Glasgow, close to the main university.

For this visit, Jerome had been forbidden to wear his lucky socks.

Walsh sat behind a walnut desk, which seemed unnecessarily large in the tight, square room. The opaque window behind him let in some of the remaining afternoon sunlight, though the room remained cold. Jerome and his mother occupied the two black, plastic chairs in front of the desk.

"In the absence of anything else," continued Walsh, "I wouldn't be suggesting any treatment, but, as Jerome has had two episodes, it's probably an indication that they were, what we call 'petit mal' attacks."

Well, that doesn't sound too bad, thought Jerome, *Petit mal means little sickness.*

"Is that a form of epilepsy?" asked Patricia softly, almost apologetically.

Jerome thought she looked uncomfortable, almost shrunken in the low chair.

"It's just a brief lack of consciousness or awareness that can last from a few seconds to maybe half a minute. Quite often, people will be unaware of it. It's more of a nuisance than anything else. But let's begin Jerome on the medication. We'll start with two tablets a day, shall we? And see how we get on," suggested the doctor.

Patricia was hugely relieved. The episodes had been given a name; they weren't serious and could be easily treated. Jerome was less relieved, but only because he'd become less concerned. He had just wanted the adults to sort out the immediate issue, and they had. The potential longer-term problems had never entered his mind.

On their way home, his mother bought him the new Celtic football top.

***

The following Saturday, Jerome, as usual, called on his paternal grandmother, Helga. Ostensibly, these weekly visits to her small, ground-floor apartment were to check if she needed any little jobs to be done, but they were really an opportunity to chat. Jerome never considered it a chore, but quite the reverse. He looked forward to enjoying her sharp, bawdy humour, her disrespectful attitude to virtually everything, and her boundless admiration for anything he did. When he had first told her about the episodes, she had appeared interested rather than concerned.

At that moment, when he told her about the diagnosis, she was openly dismissive. "What do doctors know? They just guess about everything. Most of them don't know shit." She shook her head indignantly and glanced around the warm, cluttered room while Jerome beamed with amusement. Helga poured tea from her white-china pot and grimaced briefly at her unsteady hands. "So, what was this professor fellow like anyway?"

"Er," began Jerome, "he was just OK; a small, young guy. I thought he was a wee bit too proud, if you know what I mean."

"I know the type," suggested Helga, "a bitter, little, jumped-up prod."

Jerome laughed so suddenly that some of the tea he'd begun drinking came down his nose.

"I bet he put on his mason's apron as soon as you and your mum left the room," she continued.

"I don't think so, Gran." He paused to let his laughter subside and wipe his face. "His name is Walsh."

"OK," she smirked, "we'll give him a pass then."

Helga placed a box of milk chocolates in the centre of the coffee table and positioned two packets of potato crisps carefully on either side. Only then did she lift the bottle of reserve port from the sideboard, pour herself a generous glass and sit down. "Now, Jemi," she said, smoothing out her blue-pleated skirt and adjusting her pearl necklace gently, "tell me again about these special episodes you had. They sound amazing."

Jerome selected one of the strawberry chocolates and smiled sheepishly. "To be honest, Gran, I was a bit frightened, especially the second time."

"But you were able to see people frozen in time; that's incredible."

"Ah, I don't think anyone else thinks that."

"Really? Why not? Have you ever heard of anyone else who has seen that, because I haven't? I think it might be a gift of some sort."

Jerome scrunched up his face. "I really don't think so."

"Well, I do. I think you might have been chosen for a special gift; a blessing."

"Hmm." Jerome lifted one of the crisp packets and pulled it open. "Do you *really* think so?"

Helga's wide-eyed face nodded slowly. "Tell me, what did you hear during the episodes?"

Jerome swallowed his mouthful of crisps hurriedly. "That's one of the strange things. I couldn't hear anything. It was just so quiet. I think that's what scared me the most."

"Well, if it happens again, you'll be ready for it and I'm sure you won't be frightened."

"I'll try not to be."

Later, when he was leaving, Helga pushed a £20 note into his hand. "That's for your birthday."

"But my birthday was weeks ago. You already gave me money for that, Gran."

"Ah, yes, I forgot. Well, you'll have to keep it now anyway." As usual she held Jerome tightly, and he hugged her with warmth and affection.

***

Despite his mother's concerns and his grandmother's apparent delight, it would be many years before Jerome had a recurrence of the episodes, but, when it did happen, he knew immediately that things would never again be the same.

Chapter 5

Glasgow;
19th April 2014

It was an early Friday afternoon in the last term of Jerome's final year at school. The unseasonably warm weather, combined with the end-of-week-wind-down atmosphere, had created a relaxed, almost soporific mood in the classroom. George Bennett, the history teacher, was reading aloud a paragraph from a thick, red book. A bee droned lazily just outside an open window, bringing a welcome distraction for some of the students. The scene could scarcely have been less portentous.

There were eighteen pupils in the class. Jerome was sitting at the back, beside the window. From there, he could see everything and everyone in the classroom. He was gazing languidly at the board behind Bennett's head, when he felt something suddenly like a surge of electricity along the sides of his head, just above his ears. The surge, while extremely disconcerting, seemed somehow not unfamiliar, and it spread quickly over the top of his head, increasing in frequency and volume. Then there was a click – a definite and familiar click – and everything was still.

Jerome was seized with panic. What was happening to him? He tried to move his hands, but they wouldn't respond; he then tried to move anything, but he found it impossible. It was as though his entire body was being held in a vice. He attempted to swallow, but found he couldn't even do that, and when he tried to cry out, no sound came. He was petrified; for a few moments, Jerome thought he was going to die.

Directly ahead of him, he could see the backs of six students. Given the ennui in the room, their lack of movement was hardly remarkable, except for one girl who had her arm partly raised at a very awkward angle, and a boy who was looking across at her, his furtive glance frozen in a prolonged unblinking stare.

At the front of the class, George Bennett was standing with his head bowed and his closed fists positioned on the table to give him balance as he read from the book. But his reading had stopped, and there was no sound. There was only absolute silence. Further seconds went by, and Jerome realised he could move his eyes. Then he heard a noise: the sound of his own breathing. The sensations reminded him of snorkelling, when he could see under the water and hear only the steady in-out rhythm of his respiration. He could also clearly hear his heart beating and took some comfort from that.

On the clock above the board to the right of Bennett, the time was 2.17pm. The second hand had stopped just as it was approaching the number six. Jerome stared at it for a few seconds. It did not move. Further to the right, the door in the far corner of the room was slightly ajar, and a figure seemed about to enter. Through the large windows, Jerome could see a group of boys playing football. The ball was suspended in the air, with the laws of physics apparently on hold. In the distance, the sun shone. *Has it stopped moving too?* he wondered.

Jerome estimated that at least a minute had passed since the episode began. Feeling terror gathering again, he made a determined mental effort to jolt himself free. To his enormous relief, it worked.

"The signing of the pact came as a great blow to both governments, though it was less of a surprise to the French," continued Bennett.

The noises from outside returned, distant but distinct through the partially open window. The girl raised her hand to ask a question, while her secret admirer averted his gaze. Geoff Probert, the mathematics teacher, came into the room, caught Bennett's attention, and they both went outside.

Jerome, breathing heavily, glanced anxiously around the classroom. No one was looking curiously at him. In fact, no one was looking at him at all. They hadn't noticed. Whatever had just happened to him had been invisible to all of them. Tentatively, he moved his hands and then clenched his fists in heartfelt relief.

***

As when the first episode happened, almost six years previously, Jerome told no one and retreated that evening to the sanctuary of his bedroom to try to come to terms with what had occurred.

He assumed initially that it was a return of the petit mal. It was, after all, the same type of episode as the two previous ones, but there were differences. They had all started unexpectedly, although, on this occasion, the electrical surges had given him a brief forewarning that something may be about to happen. Also, this episode had lasted much longer: at least a minute, possibly more.

Apart from his eyes, he hadn't been able to move, and yet he had heard his breathing and his heartbeat, so his vital organs must have continued to function. Most importantly, he had willed the episode to end – and it had ended. It was possible that that was just an accident of timing, and his efforts to break out had merely coincided with the natural end of the episode, but he didn't think so.

Was it definitely petit mal? he thought. *If not, what else could it be? Shouldn't I tell someone?* These questions whirled through his mind as he sipped the mug of piping-hot tea his father had brought him.

"Don't study too hard now," was Pieter Black's unnecessary advice to his son.

"There's no chance of that, Dad," replied Jerome, blowing gently on the tea.

"Ah, you're lucky anyway. You'll sail through your exams."

Jerome raised his eyebrows. "Unfortunately, I'll have to do some work. I'm not *that* good."

As he was leaving the room, Pieter half turned and asked his son, "Would you fancy going to the game tomorrow? Francie can't make it, so you could take his seat."

Jerome was surprised and pleased at this suggestion. "Yeah, that'd be great, Dad. I'd really like that. Will Karl be coming over for the game?"

"I don't think so. He's on baby-sitting duty again."

"So, he won't be allowed out to play; that's a pity. The joys of married life, eh?"

"It has its compensations," said Pieter with a smile. "So, anyway," he continued while rubbing his hands together briskly, "shall we leave at around 1.30pm tomorrow? You know I don't like those last-minute rushes to get your seat."

"Yes, that's perfect." Jerome placed his mug on the bedside locker. "Dad…"

"Yeah?"

Jerome glanced away from his father. "No, nothing; 1.30pm is fine."

"Are you sure?"

"Yes, I'm sure."

Although Jerome and his father were both supporters of Glasgow Celtic, they rarely went to games together, with both preferring to go with their own friends, hence Jerome's surprise at being asked. But the timing seemed good, perhaps propitious. The prospect of an afternoon watching football with his dad seemed reassuringly normal. Jerome went back to his deliberations in brighter spirits.

***

Professor Walsh's original diagnosis seemed like a lifetime ago as Jerome googled "petit mal". Within a few minutes, he had obtained information from reputable websites on health. The details were consistent. A petit mal seizure was then more commonly called an absence seizure. It is brief, usually less than fifteen seconds. It occurs without warning and sufferers are unaware that a seizure is happening. This can lead to confusion when they come out of it.

There's nothing new there, he thought, recalling his previous searches as a curious twelve-year-old. He listed in his mind the reasons why it had to be this condition: it had been Walsh's diagnosis; he had responded to the medication; the episodes had come on suddenly; and he had certainly been in a strange state for a short period, although he wasn't certain he would describe himself as staring or absent – it was more like everything else was absent. Nor was he confused when he came out of the attack, though he was definitely perplexed. Probably, the strongest argument for petit mal was the far-fetched nature of the only alternative he could consider. Time stopped for everything and everyone, except him. That was not really believable.

Jerome was comforted by the thought that the tablets had stopped the episodes last time. Four years had passed since he had been taken off the medication, but there seemed to be no reason why the tablets couldn't control the episodes again if necessary.

Gradually, he realised that he was not feeling particularly concerned and was not experiencing the same initial level of unease that he had as a twelve-year-old. He was not sure why he felt this way, but he was conscious of certain other emotions: curiosity about this strange phenomenon and an element of pride that, even if this was petit mal or some other exotic condition, he was experiencing something most people would never know.

In order to get a better understanding of what was really happening, Jerome reasoned that he needed to know two things. First, how long an episode lasted, and, crucially, did time continue while he was having the episode or did it *really* stand still? He realised that the duration of the episode could not be measured by a clock or other external device as, presumably, based on his previous experiences, these would stop. He wondered if his own watch might continue to work as it was, in a way, connected to him, but he thought this would be very unlikely. It would be necessary to measure the duration of the episode using something that continued to move while it was happening. He thought for a while and then, closing his eyes, he smiled. His heart had continued to beat; the duration could be measured by the number of heartbeats.

He knew that his own pulse varied from about seventy beats per minute when relaxed, to well over 100 when he was doing strenuous exercise, but he couldn't be sure at what rate his heart would beat during an episode. So far, the three episodes had all happened when he was relaxed, so seventy beats per minute would seem a good indicator. He had no way of knowing if the onset of the surges had led to a release of adrenalin or another chemical in his system that could result in a much higher pulse rate, but, at the very least, he would have an estimate of the duration.

This left the second question. Did time *really* stand still? He felt that if he could observe something specific, just at the beginning and immediately after an episode, he should be able to determine if there was continuity. What this specific thing would be, he did not know. It would depend on where he was and what could be seen at the time, but it should be something where the continuity of the action or motion could be easily determined.

Jerome stood gazing out of his bedroom window at the solitary, still oak tree across the road, and he realised that, far from being concerned about these episodes, he actively wanted them to recur. And, until he fully understood them, he would tell no one.

* * *

The following afternoon, he and his father walked together from Glasgow city centre, up the increasingly busy London Road towards Celtic Park football stadium. They had made this trip together many times before, although not for a number of years. They passed the rowdy bars where the good-natured supporters spilled out onto the pavement, the enthusiastic flag-sellers, and the packed takeaways where the smell of fried food followed the boisterous customers as they rejoined the growing crowd that was moving like a green river flowing towards the stadium: their cathedral. Jerome glanced protectively at his father. He had always considered him to be old. Indeed, as a child, he had been embarrassed that his father seemed so much older than the other dads. He recalled this embarrassment just then with a sense of guilt.

"Hasn't changed much round here, has it?" suggested Jerome.

"Nah, it's still a disgrace, son. None of the politicians are interested in cleaning up the east end of Glasgow." He shrugged his shoulders. It was a point he had made on a number of previous occasions. They were on comfortable ground. "You know something? I think we'll win today."

"You think we'll win every day," replied a grinning Jerome.

"I know; I know, but you've got to be positive." He took a handkerchief from his pocket and, smiling, wiped his eyes.

It was an end-of-season game, and, as Celtic had already won the league, there was nothing much at stake. However, it would be an occasion to celebrate, and both were looking forward to it. They arrived at the stadium forty-five minutes before the match was due to begin and found their seats in the fifth row back in the bottom deck of the north stand. This was where Pieter and his close friend Francie had their season ticket seats, and it was where they met every fortnight. Jerome felt the position of the seats was too close to the pitch, but he made no comment.

Although the match was a sell-out, there were few other people in the stadium at this time. At 2.45pm, fifteen minutes before kick-off, the stadium began to fill quickly. A number of the men in the seats nearby acknowledged Pieter, who informed some of them, with what seemed to Jerome more than a hint of pride, that this was his son.

"You've fair grown, son," said one heavy man as he levered himself into the seat directly behind Jerome. "Did you lift your dad over the stiles and get him in for free? Or slip him into your pocket, maybe?" The man wheezed a contagious laugh.

"Well, he'd need a hell of a giant's overcoat to fit *you* into his pocket anyway, Jimmy," retorted Pieter good-humouredly.

"Aye," replied Jimmy, "you'd be talking 'Fee-fi-fo-fum' there all right." He wheezed again as he patted his ample midriff. "Anyway, how are you doing, Jerome?"

"I'm great thanks, Mr Davy. It's good to see you." Jerome reached back and shook hands with him warmly. "I suppose you guys will all be wanting your pies at half-time?" he continued. "Do you want me to get them?"

"That'd be magic son. Here…" Jimmy passed Jerome a £20 note. "Here you go."

"It's OK; I'll sort the money out later."

"No, take it, son. We couldn't have a young fella subsidising us rich old bastards."

"But that's £20," said Jerome as he turned smiling to look at Jimmy Davy. "I'm guessing you want more than one pie, right?"

"Well, a bird never flew on one wing." The older man winked at Jerome.

It was a time of celebration and everyone was in fine form. The match preliminaries ended with the crowd singing the Celtic anthem "You'll Never Walk Alone". It always stirred the emotions of both father and son, and singing it together added a certain extra poignancy for Jerome.

The first half of the game was uneventful. Indeed, for Jerome, most of the entertainment came from the comments around him. In the second half, Celtic played towards the goal, close to where they were sitting. With twenty minutes of the game remaining, the crowd had become relatively quiet. Celtic were attacking through the centre of the field. The Celtic full back had made a run towards the left-corner flag. As the ball was floated towards him, Jerome felt the surge begin just above his ears and move rapidly over the top of his head. Then came the familiar click sound, and everything became silent.

The feelings of the previous afternoon came roaring back: panic, fear and even bewilderment that he had actually wished for this to happen again. However, even though the feelings were strong, they were less intense than previously and they passed quickly.

Jerome knew he would be unable to move and so made no attempt to do so. On his right, his father was staring in front of him, his mouth slightly open as though about to say something. Others near him had been caught in similar frozen poses. The combination of the 60,000 people, and the total silence and absence of movement was awesome. Swiftly, Jerome began to regroup. *Start counting,* he thought. He was able to discern the beating of his heart: one, two, three... He knew he had missed a number of beats between the onset of the episode and beginning of the count, but he continued. Twenty-four, twenty-five; the beats were regular and, if anything, sounded slow to him. He was amazed at how relaxed he felt. Jerome knew he needed to concentrate on something specific, while continuing the count, though he remained mesmerised by the scene around him and was finding it difficult. He tried to focus on the pitch again.

The Celtic left back seemed no more than thirty metres away. When the episode started, the player had been positioning himself to chest the ball, which was in mid-air, coming towards him. Jerome concentrated on the ball, while continuing the count. When he reached 110, he decided to try to break out in the same way he had done in the classroom. He reasoned that, even if his heart were beating at 100 beats per minute, the episode had lasted at least a minute. At 112, he successfully broke out.

The ball completed its arc and reached the player.

His father's voice could be heard amid the other noise from the crowd, "Cross it now, for God's sake."

The left back controlled the ball and dragged it onto his right foot to avoid the on-rushing defender. The cross was put in but sailed harmlessly over the bar to sighs of exasperation and some howls of derision. Jerome glanced at his father, who was shaking his head. He had noticed nothing. The match had stopped for 112 heart beats; at least a minute and probably more, and the action had continued exactly as though there had never been any stoppage.

The world just stopped, thought Jerome. *The world just stopped, and I'm the only person who knows it.* He felt triumph and exhilaration; there was no fear.

Celtic finally scored with ten minutes to go. The crowd around them rose and roared their celebration. For the first time in years, he hugged his father.

Chapter 6

Nuremberg;
Monday, 5th August 1929; 11.35am

Adolf Hitler stood side-on to Jerome, talking animatedly to two other men. Herman Goering was one; Jerome did not recognise the other. All three wore beaming smiles and continued their conversation, paying no attention to the approaching Goebbels and Jerome.

"*Mein Führer*, this is the man," repeated Goebbels.

Hitler turned and stared at Jerome, his expression remaining bright. "Ah yes, *Herr* Black, the young man with the photographs. How do you do?"

"I'm well, thank you," Jerome said softly.

"Dr Goebbels tells me you have a very strange story. Tell us where you're from."

"I'm from Britain, *Herr* Hitler."

"Ah, I meant the strange part of your story. When do you claim to be from?"

"I was hoping to talk to you alone." Jerome was uneasy.

With an expansive gesture, Hitler indicated his three colleagues. "I trust these men with my life."

Jerome hesitated before replying, "I come from the future."

Hitler's full smile returned, and the others followed suit. "Far in the future?" continued Hitler in a casual tone.

"The next century."

Goering's large frame shook with laughter, long and loud.

"You're Herman Goering," said Jerome, looking directly at him.

Goering nodded, looking pleased that he had been recognised.

"Would you like to know *your* future?"

He gave a more cautious nod. "Yes. Why not? I've never been to a fortune teller before." He smirked at the others. "Do you read tea leaves or palms?"

For a few moments Jerome said nothing. He noticed Hitler's eyes wide with amusement while Goebbels remained watchful. "It will not be a pleasant ending, *Herr* Goering," Jerome spoke quietly.

Goering had stopped grinning. "Well," he stated loudly as he raised his heavy shoulders, "let's hear it."

"You will die in this very city. You will take a cyanide pill to avoid being hanged."

There was an uncomfortable silence in the room as Goering's face darkened rapidly. "I don't find that remotely funny."

"It's not meant to be funny, *Herr* Goering, but I assure you it is your future."

Goering looked to be on the point of physically attacking Jerome when Hitler intervened suddenly, "You will not come here and insult my comrades. Any more outbursts like that and I will have you dealt with immediately. Do you understand?"

Jerome nodded his silent assent. Throughout the exchange he noticed that Goebbels looked quietly pleased.

Hitler turned back to the two men, reigniting his smile. "Now, gentlemen, back to serious matters. Our meeting this afternoon is… at what time?" He glanced briefly at Goebbels, who replied immediately that the meeting was scheduled for 4.00pm. "Yes, let's regroup then. We have a lot to talk about and a lot to plan. And you know…" his face had abruptly taken on an almost ecstatic expression, "I think this was the greatest congress we have ever had; four wonderful, magnificent days. Don't you think so?"

Both men nodded their full agreement with his sentiments.

"And thank you for your heroic efforts." Hitler placed his right hand gently on the shoulder of each man in turn, as though giving them a blessing.

They saluted him, and the unnamed man and Goering left, with Goering staring fury at Jerome as he marched to the door.

"For someone so eager to talk to me, *Herr* Black, you have not started very cleverly." Hitler moved to sit behind a large, mahogany desk.

The room was big, with the same characteristic high ceiling as the corridor. In contrast, however, it was bright, with sunlight coming through the three vertical sections of window onto a light-brown, dusty, wooden floor. The walls were a faded yellow colour. Overall, the ambiance, if not overtly welcoming, was certainly not menacing. Jerome was not sure of the room's normal function. In size, it was like a classroom but without the normal array of desks or any sign of a blackboard. Hitler's desk was on the left-hand side of the room as Jerome looked towards the windows. In front of it stood two cream-coloured, open, wooden chairs; both appeared to have been painted recently. Behind it, looking very out of place, was a large armchair.

It was occupied by Hitler just then; his head was bowed, looking at the photographs arranged in two columns symmetrically before him. He picked one up and brought it very close to his face, like someone suffering from long-sightedness. Looking up at Jerome with a benign, almost kindly expression on his face, he indicated the chair to the front and right of his desk. "Please sit down. These are very interesting photographs. How did you create them?"

Jerome sat down before replying. "They are *real* photographs,

Herr Hitler. They are of events that have yet to happen." Jerome coughed to try to clear the slight tremble he detected in his own voice. "I know it seems impossible to believe that someone can be from the future, but I am."

The benign expression changed to a quizzical one. Hitler had picked up a silver pen, and he was holding it between the middle and fourth finger of his left hand, flicking the top of it with his thumb. "They're very good." It was almost as though he hadn't listened to Jerome speaking.

Just then, Jerome noticed Hitler's chair in more detail. It was a light-golden-coloured armchair with two matching cushions, and it looked out of place in the sparsely furnished room. Goebbels, who had seated himself on the chair opposite Jerome, craned his neck to look at the photograph currently engaging Hitler's attention.

Jerome looked at his watch. "*Herr* Hitler, in less than four hours, I'll be back in my own time, but, for now, I can talk to you, tell you how the future will turn out and answer your questions. In return, I'd like to get an insight into you and your decisions. In my world, you remain the most intriguing world leader of the twentieth century." Jerome paused. "If you want, I can start by telling you about the events in that photograph."

Hitler stopped flicking his pen. With the diagonal fringe of black hair tracing across his forehead, and his small, neat moustache, he looked exactly like the many pictures Jerome had seen, but with the exceptions that he wore an engaging smile and his eyes, while suggesting incredulity, remained calm.

"Who took the photographs?" asked Goebbels.

"I don't know who took the originals. These were taken from archive copies of German newspapers. The dates are on them," explained Jerome.

"To manufacture a date is hardly difficult," said Goebbels.

Hitler raised the photograph of him shaking hands with

President Von Hindenburg. "The date on this is 1933, four years from now. I seem to have aged well, but our president doesn't, although he's seemed like an old man since the end of the war." He smiled thinly before pointing to the photograph. "Do you know who these other people are?"

Jerome leaned over to look at it. Hitler was wearing a long, dark overcoat and looking almost boyishly deferential, as he shook the hand of the tall, austere Von Hindenburg, who, wearing a similar coat, was standing erect and nodding his head, his white hair still army-regulation tidy. The date was 31st January 1933, one day after Hitler had been asked to become chancellor. "One is Field Marshall Goering. I don't know the others," replied Jerome.

"Field Marshall Goering." Goebbels laughed. "When did he achieve that rank?"

"1938. He received it for being head of the Luftwaffe."

Goebbels smile widened. "The Luftwaffe! I don't think so, *Herr* Black. You can only achieve this rank of field marshal in the army, not the air force."

"It was a special title, Field Marshal General of the Luftwaffe." Although true, Jerome knew this sounded a weak answer, but it was his fault for giving them unrequested information, and he was annoyed with himself.

Hitler exchanged a glance with Goebbels before demanding, "Tell me about the circumstances of this photograph."

Jerome explained the background of the inconclusive elections of 1931 and 1933, and he ended by saying, "Your National Socialist Party, after the 1933 election, did not have a majority to govern, but no party had. Von Hindenburg, apparently with reluctance, asked you to become chancellor, and this is the occasion of your inauguration."

"Why do you think Von Hindenburg would not want me to be chancellor?" Hitler's voice was challenging.

Jerome noticed his gaze would flicker in an unusual way from

Jerome's eyes to his forehead. He was not sure if this was a nervous reaction, perhaps to meeting a stranger, or maybe a deliberate disconcerting tactic. If it was the latter, it was effective.

"It might have been to do with your background. You're not from the Prussian aristocracy." Jerome was about to add that Hitler had only been a corporal in the army, but he felt it was too early in the conversation to risk provoking him.

Hitler shook his head firmly. "Your intelligence is interesting, but inaccurate, *Herr* Black. Our president admires what we are trying to do. He knows Germany needs order and discipline, and, after the humiliation of Versailles, Germany needs her honour restored. Both of us want, above anything else, to give Germany back her honour." The words, though blunt, were spoken without menace. The four-day Nazi Party congress, which had ended the previous day, had been a great success for Hitler. He was obviously in good form, as Jerome had anticipated.

Goebbels shifted in his seat and then stood, appearing to be increasingly uncomfortable with the discussion. He placed his hands flat on the desk, with the cuffs of his suit jacket covering most of his fingers, and he spoke very quietly out of Jerome's earshot. Hitler nodded in response, but his interest seemed to be aroused as he looked at Jerome.

The picture of the burned-out Reichstag was the next one Hitler picked up. The date was 28th February 1933, one day after the fire. The headline below the picture read, "REICHSTAG GUTTED IN FIRE, COMMUNISTS SUSPECTED."

Jerome began, "The fire was important as it permitted you to govern by decree, without a parliament." He looked at Hitler. "You were effectively a legally appointed dictator."

As Hitler continued staring at the photograph, Jerome noticed that there appeared to be a very slight tremble in Hitler's left hand, which had again picked up the silver pen and begun flicking it as before. He knew that, in film, taken close to his death, Hitler had a pronounced tremor. It had been assumed that this was a result of the bomb attack on his life in 1944; just then, Jerome wondered if perhaps it was the final stages of something that had begun years earlier.

Hitler sat back in his armchair and laughed. It was a slightly high-pitched but, nonetheless, hearty laugh, and surprisingly infectious. Then he shot forwards again to look at the photographs. "These really are excellent, *Herr* Black. How on earth did you make them?"

"I've already told you that they're genuine. They're from real events in the future." Jerome felt his irritation rising, but he checked it quickly.

"So, you say the communists will burn down our Reichstag, eh? And how do you think we would deal with that?" Hitler rubbed the front of his nose vigorously.

"Many of the communist deputies were arrested and imprisoned," replied Jerome.

"And would that not be right, *Herr* Black?" Hitler asked casually.

"It was never proven to be them," Jerome began quietly. "It was never proved that the communists did it. The information came from your ministry, Dr Goebbels." Jerome glanced at him briefly. "The ministry of propaganda, which didn't, under your leadership, develop a reputation for the unbiased reporting of the truth."

It was clear immediately that Goebbels had taken no slight from Jerome's remarks, but quite the opposite. He grew visibly at the suggestion that he could be an important minister in his master's government. His response was thoughtful and, although delivered to Jerome, seemed solely for his audience sitting behind the desk. "You have the common misconception that propaganda is dishonourable." Goebbels spoke as a teacher to a dull student. "Good propaganda leaves nothing out, but does not add anything that is not necessary. Therefore, if we believe something, then that is what we must say, and we should not confuse the message by adding that we're not certain or it could be someone else. Anyway," he added in an irritated voice, "this is all purely hypothetical."

Hitler was looking at the third photograph by then, which showed him in an open-topped car, being driven through crowds in Vienna. "March 1938," he read, "the Anschluss. Tell me about this."

"Yes, that was when Germany absorbed Austria into a greater Germany. The picture shows your welcome in Vienna, which, as you can see, was euphoric. What would your feelings be about Germany and Austria coming together?" Jerome felt it was opportune to ask a question at this point.

Hitler frowned at him and adjusted the leather strap on the right shoulder of his neatly pressed, light-brown shirt. "You are asking me what I would think about Germany and Austria coming together." He seemed to relax again. "Germans and Austrians are one people. It's not the borders but the people that define a country. I am Austrian and I am German. The coming together of our two countries would be no threat to anyone." He showed no real emotion, but stared intently at Jerome.

Jerome continued, "Prior to uniting with Austria, Germany reoccupied the Saar region and marched troops into the Rhineland."

Hitler folded his arms, with the Nazi swastika on his left sleeve prominently to the fore. "*Herr* Black, tell me more about yourself. Where do you get all this knowledge and these opinions?"

Jerome replied assertively, "My answer is the same, *Herr* Hitler; I'm from the future, and the information I am giving you is fact, not opinion. It really happened." He stared, though he tried not to glare.

Hitler clapped his hands. "*Herr* Black, you're unbelievable but an interesting fellow, and your photographs and stories are interesting too." He paused and gazed through one of the three window sections, each one containing a long, oblong window at the bottom and a smaller, fixed one above it. "So, you say we reoccupy the Saar and the Rhineland. How do you think Britain and France would react to that?"

"They took no action."

Goebbels continued to look uncomfortable. "*Herr* Black, may I see your passport again?"

For the first time, Jerome noticed the thin stripes in the dark-grey suit Goebbels was wearing, which was perhaps to make him appear taller. Jerome handed him his passport reluctantly.

Goebbels left the room momentarily and said dismissively on his return, "Don't worry, we'll return it before you go."

For a few moments, as Jerome watched Hitler frown intently at the photographs while Goebbels stood sentry-like beside his *Führer*, Jerome was aware of how incredibly surreal this all appeared. Here he was in 1929 Germany, actively engaging with these people! And while Goebbels remained very suspicious, Hitler was definitely interested; he felt sure of that. His initial nervousness seemed to have eased, and Jerome wondered fleetingly, *Do I have the measure of this man?*

"So, what is this Kristallnacht photograph?" asked Hitler, picking up another one.

Jerome paused before responding. "A German attaché was shot in France," he began. "A Jew was suspected. This caused an outbreak of violence in Germany against Jews and their property. It was known as Kristallnacht because of the shattered glass. The night itself was not so momentous, but it did mark the beginning of something much more sinister. It was a clear signal from your government that violence against Jews was not just accepted but encouraged, and would form part of government policy."

Hitler sat back in his seat, with the photograph still in his hand. For the first time, he eyed Jerome with something approaching suspicion. "Are you a Jew, *Herr* Black?"

"No, I'm not." Jerome tried to appear calm.

"But I sense you're sympathetic to them. Am I not right?"

"I'm neither sympathetic nor unsympathetic."

Hitler paused before asking, "Do you know your history, *Herr* Black?"

"Yes, I know it very well. And don't forget, *Herr* Hitler, much of my history is your future."

Hitler ignored this comment. "Then you must be aware of the damage done to Germany by Jewish criminals." Before Jerome had a chance to respond he continued, "The crushing and humiliating terms of the Versailles Treaty were imposed by Jews, and they continue to try to destroy Germany. My position is clear on this. I will not tolerate any group, within or outside Germany, trying to destroy our great nation." He paused before wagging a finger at Jerome. "And now I ask you, *Herr* Black, why do you show me pictures of some broken synagogue windows? Why do you try to make an issue of the Jews? Are you suggesting that we forget their unconscionable crimes? Are you representing them?"

"No, I'm not." This time Jerome made no attempt to hide his glare.

There was silence in the room, though it seemed to resonate with the force and menace in Hitler's words.

Jerome felt he had to pursue this; it was so fundamental to the person. "Even if what you say is correct, *Herr* Hitler, and the terms of the treaty were influenced by some Jews, is it right to blame all Jews for this?"

Hitler removed the top of his silver pen and clicked it slowly back in place. "*Herr* Black, I'm finding this conversation increasingly wearisome and irritating. I've given you the chance to talk to me, to get my views on the major issues, on Germany's future and on Europe's future, but you prefer to talk about the treatment of a small criminal minority."

For the first time, Jerome noticed it was a beautiful day. The scene outside was one of bright sunshine and a large expanse of grass. Men were talking and laughing together as they packed up their tents and gear prior to departing for various parts of Germany. And it was all men; he could see no women. Most of them wore uniforms, but some were in lederhosen. In different circumstances, the view would have been reminiscent of a scout jamboree, but Jerome recognised the SA and Schutzstaffel (SS) uniforms, and he knew this was a much more sinister gathering.

"What is this Munich Agreement?" Hitler asked in a strong, composed voice. If there was any residual anger following his diatribe against the Jews it was well disguised.

His question jolted Jerome out of his brief reverie. Goebbels moved behind his leader and was trying to read over his shoulder. Hitler moved the index finger of his right hand over the wording in the photograph and read aloud, like a child being taught how to read, "Peace in Europe. War averted."

Jerome explained the build up to the Munich Agreement and its signing in September 1938 by Hitler, and the leaders of Italy, Britain and France, and how, subsequently, Germany occupied all of Czechoslovakia. "It marked the end of what the British and French called the policy of appeasement."

There was a soft knock on the door, and, on turning, Jerome saw it open slowly, and a distinctive face gradually filled the gap.

"Excuse me, *Mein Führer*, I'm terribly sorry to interrupt, but the men; would you be able to see them before they go?"

Hitler stood up immediately, his face beaming. "Julius, Julius, please come in." He walked around the desk, with his eyes fixed on the newcomer, and welcomed him, shaking his hand with great warmth and vigour. "Julius, my trusted comrade and friend, the last four days have been a huge success, and that is due in no small way to you. Thank you."

Julius Streicher was a squat man, though not particularly short, with a totally bald head and a neat moustache that was very similar to that of his leader. As Hitler's praise swept over him, his head blushed and his demeanour changed from nervous intruder to excited child.

"Of course I'll see these men. I'll go now," said Hitler.

Jerome became alarmed, thinking he could lose his opportunity. "*Herr* Hitler, I only have limited time left."

For the first time, Streicher seemed to become aware of Jerome's presence.

"Oh, I think you can make time, *Herr* Black. You've come a long way to interview me. You can stay a while longer. Julius and Josef will look after you while I'm gone." It was unmistakably a command. "This young man predicts interesting things for us, Julius. Take him outside for something to eat." Hitler smiled coolly at Jerome as he left the room.

Chapter 7

Glasgow;
19th May 2014

"Hi Gran, sorry I'm late." Jerome closed the front door behind him and, bending down, kissed Helga on a dry cheek.

"Oh, you feel cold, Jemi," she declared.

"Yes, it's fresh out there. Let's get you back into the heat."

Helga shuffled slowly along the short hallway in her apartment, using her white-painted, hawthorn walking stick for support. Jerome moved patiently beside her until she was back in the dining room, seated near the fire.

"I'll put the kettle on." He moved into the small, tidy kitchen. "I've something I want to tell you."

"Good news?" she called back hopefully.

"Yes," he nodded thoughtfully to himself, "I think so."

Jerome got them each a drink, walked back into the dining room, and placed the cup of tea and glass of port on the coffee table.

"So," began Helga, "what's this good news? Is it about that wonderful girl you keep mentioning?"

"Stancia? No, it's not about her. It's something completely different." Jerome sat down and paused for a few moments. "Gran, something unbelievable has happened to me over the last month, and I just need to tell someone. Well…" he smiled shyly, "I need to tell you. Do you remember those episodes I had when I was about twelve, when everything seemed to stop for a few seconds?"

Helga's bright eyes narrowed marginally. "Yes, of course I do. I remember them well."

"About a month ago, they started again. It happened first in school and then when I was at a Celtic match with Dad. It was just incredible." Jerome moved further forwards in his seat. "Time just stopped, and I could see everything. I could see Dad and his pals; I could see the players on the pitch. Gran, I could even see the ball stopped in mid-air; in mid-air! Isn't it unbelievable?"

"Wow." Helga's mouth had dropped open as she tried to absorb this information. "Did that really happen, Jemi?"

"It really did. I swear to God. And there was no sound; none at all. I was in the ground with 60,000 other fans, and there was total silence."

Helga swallowed a sip of port and brushed a tiny crumb from the side of her mouth. "And were you worried at all or frightened?"

"I was a wee bit at first, but then I learned that I could end the episodes at any time. It's like…" Jerome picked up his cup for the first time. "You know when you're having a daydream, you're staring at something and you gently jolt yourself out of it? Well, it's just like that, and it works every time. And then, Gran, do you know what else I discovered?"

"No." She had a slightly startled look on her face.

Jerome leaned over and touched her hands. "I'm sorry; I'm going too fast. I'm probably alarming you a bit, aren't I?"

"No, you're not, Jemi." She shook her head in a kind, reassuring manner. "Now tell me what else you discovered."

"I found out I could start the episodes at any time I want."

"How?"

"I was working in the bookies shop last Saturday – and I know you don't like the place – but, anyway, I'd started hiccoughing, and the women in the shop started slagging me, so I held my breath – you know the way you do to stop hiccoughs – and, after about twenty seconds, I took a big breath in and the episode started."

"What did you see there?"

"Oh! Nothing much really; I thought the women looked a bit odd, sadder somehow, though that might just have been the point in time when everything froze. But when I got home, I tried holding my breath and then breathing in deeply to see if an episode would start and it did." He gazed and her and said softly, "Gran, it did!"

"So, you can start and end these incredible experiences anytime you like?"

"Exactly; any time I want. And it's incredible. Do you know what I did last night?"

"No." She smiled bemusedly.

"I'm going too fast again. I'm sorry. I sound like a kid at Christmas." He paused for a few moments. "I propped open a history book on my lap, then triggered an episode, and I was able to read the two pages in no time; literally, no time. Then I ended the episode, turned over the page and did the same thing again. I was able to read a 300-page textbook in under an hour."

Helga shook her head in joyful disbelief. "And were you able to take it all in?"

"Yes, I even answered the test questions on it afterwards and scored well. And I'd never read the book before."

"Didn't you feel tired after all that reading?"

Jerome paused. "Yes, a bit, I guess. I felt like I'd been reading for a good while, and my eyes were getting tired. But what do you think, Gran? It's amazing, isn't it?"

She leaned forwards and took his hands gently. "Jerome, ever since the moment you took your first breath, I just knew you were special. You've been blessed in some way; in some miraculous way."

"You've said that before. What makes you think that?"

She squeezed his hands tighter and nodded gently. "I can't really explain it. I just feel so strongly that it's so." Slowly, Helga released his hands and sat back in her seat. "And you haven't told anyone else?"

"No, just you."

"Will you tell anyone, such as your mum or dad, or that girlfriend?"

"No, I don't think so; not yet anyway. I'd like to find out more about this… whatever it is. What do you think?"

"Yes, I think that's just fine. But don't do anything dangerous or anything that could damage your health; you're sure you won't?"

"Don't worry; I won't."

Helga stared silently at the unlit gas fire with a wide-eyed expression of delighted surprise. She said nothing for a few minutes. Jerome was happy to share this quiet interlude. He had told someone about his incredible secret, and had been believed.

Gradually, Helga's gaze moved back to him. She joined her hands in front of her face as though praying. "And when are you going to bring this girl to meet me? I won't be around forever, you know."

"Don't say that, Gran. Anyway, Stancia's not really a formal girlfriend as such; we're just very good friends."

She delicately picked up her glass of port and took a small sip. "Would you like her to be your formal girlfriend?"

Jerome raised his eyebrows and smiled. "Yes, I suppose I would. But we've been friends for so long, and I've kind of grown up knowing her so well that, you know…"

"It's tricky to move from friend to girlfriend?" continued Helga.

"Yes, although now that you say it, it does sound a bit wimpish, doesn't it?"

"Tell me what she looks like?"

"Well…" Jerome looked at the ceiling as though trying to capture a picture of Stancia. "She has blue eyes; lovely, dark hair; and she's very funny."

"Does she have curves in all the right places?"

"Jesus, Gran," Jerome responded with a laugh. "She is slim, actually, and very attractive."

"In that case, make her your girlfriend. Sweep her off her feet and then bring her round here so I can check if she's good enough for you."

"OK." Jerome smiled fondly at his grandmother. "You've never been someone who beats around the bush."

"No, I never saw the point."

"And thanks for listening to me today."

"It's my pleasure." She shifted in the seat and moved her neck as though massaging out some discomfort. "You know, Jemi, I haven't always loved some people as much as I should have, so never leave things too late."

Chapter 8

Glasgow;
12th August 2014; 1.15pm

Jerome's summer job, working in Ladbrokes bookmaker's, had been very relaxing and enjoyable. At that moment, he was sitting on a high stool behind the counter, gazing out contentedly at the people in the betting office as they stood around concentrating quietly on the pinned-up newspapers and television monitors, occasionally talking to one another in quiet, unhurried tones. The room was illuminated softly by artificial light, as the narrow, darkened windows successfully limited the daylight's attempt to enter this domain.

***

For the past three months, Jerome had been exploring and exploiting his new-found gift; for he had come to believe that's what it was. His A-level examinations became so much easier, as not only could he study for much longer than his peers but, during the actual examinations, he was under no time pressure. He could stop time to reflect on the question, consider his response and read his answers back to review them. He got A grades in history, German and English. His parents were delighted, though not surprised.

However, there were other opportunities that were much more fun. In pub quizzes, he never seemed to be flustered in answering the ten questions on each subject. As long as he knew the answer, he would have as much time as he wanted to recall it. He had been good at chess in school, but he had become formidable; he pondered crucial moves for fifteen or twenty minutes, but only used up a few seconds on the timer. Playing poker on a Wednesday night became increasingly lucrative, as he could stop time at crucial moments to look at all the shown cards and assess the bets. All of these experiences were reported back to Helga, who responded with a mixture of wonder and delight. On occasion, Jerome would also stop time to look at a girl he felt was particularly attractive, but he felt slightly embarrassed about this, as though it were too voyeuristic. In any event, he didn't share these experiences with Helga.

***

He put a betting slip through the machine and, as he took the punter's money, he felt his phone ringing. It was his mother's number.

"Hi," he said quietly.

"Hello Jerome, it's Mum here." There was an unusual pause. "Jerome your father has had a stroke, but he's stable now. Karl and I are with him in the hospital: the Royal Infirmary." There followed a further pause. "We're with Dad now in the Lomond ward. Jerome, can you hear me?"

"Yes, is he going to be OK?"

"Yes, the doctors say he's not in any danger."

"I'll come right away."

Jerome apologised to his manager and hurried from the shop into the bright, sunlit afternoon.

***

Forty-five minutes later, he stood outside the Lomond ward. With some trepidation, he pushed open the heavy, rubber doors. His father lay in bed, his hair unusually dishevelled. Pieter Black's eyes appeared open, though they looked unfocused. Jerome's mother sat by the bedside, while Karl stood opposite her, his arms folded, watching his father. Then, suddenly, Jerome heard the familiar click noise as he entered his first unplanned episode in months. He didn't try to come out of it immediately, but he gazed at his father. Jerome wondered if he was awake. His left eye appeared to be looking directly at him; the right one was more scrunched up. The fingers of his father's left hand seemed raised slightly, as if in recognition. He looked small – tiny, even – under the tightly tucked, white bed sheet.

Jerome felt a real sadness, but no tears came; not even the choking sensation that preceded them normally. During the event, he could feel emotion, but not physically release it. He brought the episode to an end.

Karl noticed Jerome and went over to him. "Hiya kid," he uttered softly as he put his arm around his younger brother. "He was awake a minute ago, although I think he's dozing now. The doctors say he's not in any danger."

"Jerome," his mother said quietly as he bent to kiss her and placed his hand very gently on top of her head.

"When did it happen?" asked Jerome.

"Around ten this morning," said Karl. "He was having his breakfast and he just passed out at the table. I happened to be there. We called an ambulance right away. He was conscious by the time it arrived and for most of the time in the hospital. He knows he's had a stroke."

Jerome nodded and gazed at his father.

"Geraldine knows about it; she'll be over later," continued Karl.

"What about Gran?"

"I'm driving over to tell her now. I don't want to shock her with a phone call," continued Karl.

"I could go and tell her. I don't mind."

"It's OK, Jerome, I'll do it. You stay and look after mum."

When Karl left the room, Jerome sat across from his mother; two sentinels guarding the sleeping man.

"Do you want to take a break, Mum? To go for a smoke or anything? I'm fine here with Dad."

Patricia thought and then nodded. "Yes, I'll just go to the bathroom."

Shortly afterwards, Pieter awoke.

"How do you feel, Dad?" asked Jerome.

His father raised his eyes in resignation.

Jerome noticed the left eyebrow reached higher. "Stupid question, eh?" He sat down on the bed, holding and stroking his father's hand. "Mum's just nipped out for a minute. Do you want me to get you anything?"

Pieter shook his head slightly in response, before asking weakly, "What time is it?"

Jerome scanned the room quickly, but seeing no clock, glanced at his watch. "It's nearly half-past two." He removed the watch and put it on his father's wrist, beside the hospital identity tag. "You hold onto this."

Jerome sat for a while, feeling helpless and saying nothing initially, just occasionally patting his father's hair back to its more usual position. Pieter's expression remained gently submissive.

"Well, fuck this anyway, Dad, eh?" Jerome smiled

sympathetically at him. The left-hand side of his father's face smiled, and Jerome squeezed his hand. "Strokes aren't contagious, are they?" asked Jerome suddenly, pretending to withdraw his hand.

The half-smile broadened in response to his son's black humour. Eventually, Pieter fell asleep, with the familiar, gentle snore bringing some reassurance to Jerome and his mother.

***

One week later, Pieter was allowed to return home. The stroke had left him frail; his right side remained partially paralysed, causing breathing difficulties. Patricia converted a downstairs room into a temporary bedroom, although she resisted stubbornly her children's pressure to hire a part-time nurse, feeling affronted by the mere suggestion. The new bedroom was bright, warm and welcoming, with none of the hospital's sterility.

"Look," his father declared, nodding at the oxygen cylinder in the corner of the room; it had a green woollen scarf draped discretely over it. "Your ma's put a bloody tea cosy on it."

His words sounded slow and strange, but Jerome was reassured to realise that the humour – and so, in his view, the person – remained intact.

Chapter 9

Glasgow;
25th August 2014; 10.30pm

Jerome and a number of his friends were at an eighteenth birthday party. For many of them, it was the last big get-together of school friends before they left Glasgow for university or work elsewhere. The venue was a noisy function room situated above a Greek restaurant whose management were relaxed about the drinking-age law. Jerome had just picked up a bottle of beer when he noticed Stancia Kennedy arriving. Craning his neck to catch her eyes between the revellers' heads, he smiled a warm welcome and waved.

"Hi," she mimed back through the din from the music.

Five minutes later, seeing that she was apparently on her own, Jerome left his friends to join her. "Did nobody get you a drink?" he asked.

She nodded energetically and pointed to a glass of white wine on a table beside her.

"Well," continued Jerome, "could you get me one? I'm nearly finished." He shook the almost-empty beer bottle and smiled playfully.

Stancia laughed and pushed him gently as the sound from the music quietened. "How's your dad?" she asked, touching his arm.

"Oh, he's recovering. It'll take a while and he'll need a lot of physio, but the doctors are hopeful that he'll get back close to where he was before it happened."

"That's great." She smiled as the music came back on full volume. "I like your father."

"Yes, he's not the worst. Anyway, how're your plans for Manchester going?"

"Fine, I've got the accommodation sorted; it's near the university. I just need to buy clothes and stuff, and pack about fifty suitcases. What about you? When do you head to London?"

"I go in a couple of weeks. I'm staying in the halls of residence for the first year, near Westminster."

"Oh, that sounds very cool," she said, looking genuinely impressed.

He nodded, making an exaggerated smug expression. "So, do you think you'll keep in touch?"

"What with *you*?" she said disparagingly. "No chance." She looked away disdainfully and then turned back smiling. "Only kidding! Of course I'll stay in touch."

They clinked glass against bottle.

"Have you any plans before you head to Manchester?" he asked.

"No, nothing special," Stancia confirmed.

"Do you fancy going to Paris this weekend?"

Tilting her head quizzically, she looked at him. "What?"

He said softly but clearly, "Would you like to go to Paris with me this weekend?"

Stancia's brow was furrowed. "You're not serious?"

"Totally serious. There's a flight out at ten past nine on Friday morning and one back at four o'clock on Sunday. I can book the flights and the hotel rooms."

"How did you know the times of flights to and from Paris?" She continued to look unconvinced. "Did you just check them out on the off-chance of meeting someone you could ask to go?"

"No, I checked them out in the hope I'd see you and could ask you to go."

"Oh, good answer."

"Shall I get you another drink while you're thinking about it?"

"Well, you can get me another drink, but I don't need to think about it. I'd love to go. But I'll pay half the costs."

Jerome smiled and shrugged his shoulders. "Whatever."

* * *

Jerome spent much of the intervening four days organising the trip. Though he had some money, he needed to borrow, and did so from Helga. When he explained what it was for, she wanted to fund the entire trip; his efforts at limiting her generosity were only partly successful.

* * *

They arrived in Paris late on a glorious, blue-skied Friday morning. The small hotel Jerome had booked was in the Pigalle district, just north of the city centre, and it lived up to its description of being, "Friendly, intimate and resonant of the cultural diversity that is Pigalle."

The afternoon was spent exploring the narrow, cobbled streets in the immediate vicinity of the hotel, enjoying the bustle and noise, and the smells of baking bread, roasting lamb and dark tobacco, before venturing further afield to see the Arc de Triomphe.

Jerome, at Helga's suggestion, had booked an evening meal on one of the cruise boats that sail up and down the River Seine. Their youthful excitement was still evident as they were shown to a linen-clothed table close to the side of the boat.

"Well, this is something else," said Stancia, looking around, her blue eyes flashing in the early evening light. "What a fantastic day."

Jerome beamed back as he took the wine list from the waiter.

"I have to ask you," began Stancia quietly after removing her short, white jacket, "When did you first get the idea of asking me to come to Paris?"

"Now, let me see…" Jerome scanned the wine list, recognised the word Beaujolais and ordered a bottle from the waiter. "If I said about two seconds before I asked you, would you believe me?"

"Nope, because you couldn't have known the flight times."

"Ah, that's true. Well, actually, I decided that I'd ask you just before I went out that evening."

"Really?"

"Really."

"That's still very impulsive. Are you often like that?" She was leaning her chin in her right hand, in a coquettish pose, and grinning broadly.

Jerome reflected for a moment. "Only when it's important."

"Oh, another good answer," concluded Stancia with a laugh.

"Yes, I thought it was a good one too. Anyway, what made you agree to come?" Jerome now had his chin in hand, mirroring her body position.

It was Stancia's turn to pause before responding. "I thought it was such an unusual and crazy thing to ask, and if I were to say no, I'd always regret it."

He smiled thoughtfully as the waiter reappeared and poured a sample of the Beaujolais. Picking up the glass, Jerome sniffed the wine slowly and deeply. Then, taking a sip, he swished it around his mouth before swallowing. "That's fine," he said with forced confidence, looking up casually at the expressionless waiter. "Please pour it." Jerome indicated Stancia's glass and smiled broadly as her eyes sparkled with delight.

They ordered French dishes from the menu, with Stancia deciding to experiment with snails for her hors d'oeuvres. "Here, try it." She offered him one, just prised from its shell.

Jerome shook his head, keeping his mouth closed firmly.

"Oh, go on, be brave. You'll only taste the garlic butter anyway," cajoled Stancia.

Grimacing, he opened his mouth slowly and accepted the snail reluctantly, but he made no attempt to chew or swallow it.

"You can't just leave it there; it won't melt." Stancia laughed.

Closing his eyes, Jerome chewed quickly three times and swallowed.

"Well?" she asked.

"Gross! No more slugs thanks. I think I'll stick to eating things with legs in future."

When the meal was finished, they stood at the side of the boat as the water slurped against its sides, and the Parisian skyline drifted by. Stancia had her arm through his, and her jacket buttoned tightly against the increasing night chill. Classical music was coming from somewhere on the riverbank.

"My dad once told me," began Jerome, putting his arm around her and pulling her close, "that hearing music on water is like hearing heavenly music; the music of the angels, he called it."

"Jerome Black, I think you're an old romantic at heart," she suggested.

"Oh, I'm not so sure about that."

"It's a compliment. Look!" She pointed to a large building that was beautifully illuminated by ground level floodlights. "Notre-Dame Cathedral; stunning, isn't it?"

Jerome rubbed his cheek gently across the top of her thick, dark-brown hair. "Yes, it certainly is."

***

Despite the wonderful time they had in Paris, Jerome's enduring memory of this weekend was an unpleasant one.

Late on the Saturday afternoon, they were returning to their hotel after visiting the Champs Elysees. The Metro train was crowded with tourists as they boarded it, and, in the crush, Stancia lost hold of his hand. When the train pulled out, he smiled reassuringly at her, over the heads of the two people sandwiched between them. The train was hot and clammy, and Jerome dreamily watched the stations go by, swaying gently with the movement of the train. As they were approaching Pigalle station, he noticed that Stancia was looking flushed and anxious.

"Are you OK?" he mouthed, catching her eye.

She nodded unconvincingly.

The doors opened, and he followed her onto the platform. "Are you sure you're OK?"

"Yes." She was breathing deeply. "It was just that guy beside me...he kept pushing himself into me."

Jerome turned abruptly, scanning the passengers remaining on the train.

"Oh no, Jerome," cried Stancia suddenly. "He's taken my purse." Disconsolately, she held the straps of her open handbag. "He's opened the bag and taken my purse."

As the doors of the train began to close, Jerome dashed between them and blocked their movement. For a few seconds nothing happened, then they opened again. Jerome pointed to one of the men who had been standing close to him.

Stancia nodded, ashen faced. "Yes, that's him."

He was a small, young man of Scandinavian appearance, dressed neatly in a light-coloured suit. Grabbing him by the back of his neck, Jerome pulled him into the doorway. "Purse!" Jerome shouted, gesturing with his open left hand. "Where's the purse?"

The man shook his head feebly, feigning ignorance. Again, the doors attempted to close, but they were blocked by the two bodies this time. The other passengers and people on the platform stared, but made no move to interfere.

"We can stay here until the police come," Jerome yelled into his ear.

Again, the doors tried to close unsuccessfully. Suddenly, the purse was tossed from somewhere within the carriage and landed on the platform beside Stancia.

"I've got it," she said picking it up. "It's all right; my credit card is here."

Jerome released his grip slowly and moved onto the platform. This time, the doors closed. He saw the man's face as the train pulled out and thought he was smiling at him.

"Shit! They've taken my money," cried Stancia staring at the purse, then added quickly, "but it doesn't matter; it doesn't matter. We've got the card, and that's the important thing." She linked her arm tightly in his and rested her head against his shoulder.

***

The week after they returned from Paris, Helga did get to meet Stancia finally when Jerome brought her to his grandmother's apartment unannounced. The older lady was thrilled, though she chided him immediately for not giving her advance notice.

"Come in, come in, my dear. You are most welcome." She linked her arm through Stancia's. "But I have *sehr wenig*, ah, very little to give you. Jemi, you really should have told me you were bringing a special guest; now I'm flustered and speaking German again." She stopped and looked into Stancia's eyes, then, putting one hand on each side of the girl's face, she kissed her forehead. "Come in and brighten up an old lady's room."

As Jerome expected, the visit went extremely well with both females being suitably impressed by their new acquaintance.

***

Later that evening, he received a text from Helga; it read, "She's lovely, Jemi. A keeper."

"A goalkeeper?" he texted in response, with a smiley emoji attached.

She replied with a further smiley emoji and her standard three kisses sign-off to him.

***

Manchester, England; 10th September 2014

Jerome went with Stancia to Manchester on a crisp, early autumn morning to help her move into her new home. It was a small, terraced house, close to the university, which she would share with four other students. Stancia had packed three large suitcases, which he thought was endearing but completely unnecessary. They knew this was their last time together for a while and, having spent so long in each other's company over the previous two weeks, there was an undercurrent of sadness running alongside the excitement of that day.

In the evening, they thought about going to one of the numerous restaurants on the famous curry mile for their final meal, but both agreed it didn't seem appropriate for the occasion. Instead, they choose a small Italian restaurant, in a basement just off Oxford Road. There, they reminisced over photographs from Paris, and smiled willingly for the enthusiastic waiter who insisted on taking another of them.

"Are we crazy, Jerome?" asked Stancia as they were walking arm-in-arm back to the house.

"What do you mean?" He looked slightly puzzled.

"Well, we get involved just as we're moving to different cities. You should have asked me to go to Paris a year ago."

"You mightn't have gone."

"Oh, I would have," she said tugging him closer. "I would have."

Chapter 10

London, England; 21st June 2015

In his room at the halls of residence, Jerome read the instructions carefully and, satisfied he understood them, decided to experiment with the oxygen that evening. It was midsummer's night, and London was uncomfortably hot. Most students had already left the halls for the summer, and so it was in a silent room in a quiet building that Jerome sat down to carry out the test.

Earlier that day, he had removed the oxygen dispenser from its black, canvas protective cover and placed it on the table beside his bed. He had been surprised at its compact size and, right then, looking at the neat, silver canister, he drew unfavourable comparisons with his father's large bulky one. For a few moments, he felt pangs of guilt. The oxygen mask was an opaque, colourless plastic. Slowly, he placed it over his nose and mouth, and pulled the elastic strap tightly over his head to hold it in place. Adjusting the dial to the open position, he positioned his left index finger above the on/off button. Suddenly, Jerome felt agitated and claustrophobic. He removed the mask hurriedly and walked around the room trying to relax. Going to the bathroom, he switched on the cold tap and let the water run over the backs of his hands before splashing his face.

"Why am I doing this?" he asked half-aloud. He gave himself no answer as he turned off the tap and watched the remaining water drain away. He then put on a CD by Ennio Morricone, which was a soothing piece of music that he felt would help remove his unexpected unease. Jerome did not really anticipate anything would happen with this experiment. He believed it was not a premonition of something dramatic that was causing his anxiety; rather, he felt it arose simply from a feeling of agitation when the mask covered his nose and mouth. He resumed his position, sitting on the edge of the bed and insisting to himself, almost angrily, that everything would be fine. Carefully, he replaced the mask.

***

The nine months since Jerome had first taken Stancia to Manchester had passed swiftly for him. Their relationship had not just survived the obstacles of living in different cities, it had blossomed. Every third weekend they would meet in either London, Manchester or, occasionally, Glasgow when it suited them to travel home. And the forced separation time between visits kept the desire burning brightly for them both.

Jerome had found the academic work surprisingly easy in his first year at King's College, where he had continued to benefit from his unique studying and examination abilities; although he would never admit it, he did take pride in the appreciation of his work shown by the tutors.

He had made a number of friends at university, some studying the same politics and history course, and others who lived in the halls of residence. One in particular became a close friend. Chris Grabowski was from Leeds in the north of England. Like Jerome, he was also in his first year, though he was studying physics. They had agreed to move into shared digs for the next term, which would be the first of their second year.

Each time Jerome travelled back to Glasgow, he would stay with his parents, and he would visit Helga every time. She was becoming much frailer physically, but retained all of her mental sharpness as she devoured his stories about London, and she always wanted to know about his "gift".

And it was Jerome's "gift" that dominated his thoughts increasingly as the months slipped by. He still derived tremendous satisfaction and, at times, great excitement when using it, safe in the knowledge that no one apart from Helga knew. But he had begun to feel that, somehow, he was cheapening or in some way misusing a truly incredible ability, and that bothered him. He read and researched anything that seemed similar to his episodes – time freezing, time moving slowly, time warps and wormholes – but it all seemed in the realm of science fiction. On two occasions, he emailed individuals who claimed to be able to halt time. Both times, he realised quickly that he was dealing with a crank. This disheartened him briefly, and he wondered if this would be the reaction of others to his story, but Jerome remained convinced that his was not a random, freak gift. He had it for a purpose and, eventually, he would learn what it was.

It was then he decided to experiment. He knew he could trigger an episode by starving his brain of oxygen for a short period, and then suddenly inhaling quickly and deeply, infusing oxygen into his brain. He also realised, from testing, that both the initial withdrawal of oxygen and the suddenness of the infusion were necessary. If he were breathing normally and suddenly inhaled deeply, nothing happened. Similarly, if he held his breath and cut off the oxygen supply for as long as he could – which was about one minute – and then, through shallow breaths, gradually restored his normal breathing pattern, no episode occurred. So, he wondered what would happen if he increased the effectiveness of either part of the process? One option was to use some mechanism to cut off the oxygen supply for a longer period than he could achieve by simply holding his breath; some manner of controlled asphyxiation. This undoubtedly held dangers. If the oxygen were cut off for too long, then he could die or, worse in his view, suffer permanent brain damage. At the same time, he was also considering how he could accelerate or intensify the rush of oxygen to the brain. Pure oxygen seemed to be the obvious answer. Instead of breathing normal air, containing just over twenty percent oxygen, if he could inhale one hundred percent oxygen it should improve the effectiveness significantly.

He was pleased to discover that obtaining an oxygen dispenser was, with one exception, surprisingly straightforward. The oxygen company representative helpfully answered all his telephone queries and confirmed they would be pleased to provide the required model for his father's visit to London on receipt of a medical prescription. On his next visit to Glasgow, Jerome "borrowed" his father's prescription and was then able to order, and subsequently collect, a lightweight, portable oxygen dispenser.

***

At that moment, he sat on the edge of his bed in the room in London on this midsummer's evening as the theme tune from *The Mission* was playing soothingly in the background on the old CD player Helga had given him many years ago.

He held his breath; twenty seconds passed, then forty. At fifty, he inched his finger in a gentle arcing movement towards the on/off button only this time he pressed it. The vibrating motor noise from the dispenser interrupted the music as the gas was released into the mask. He looked away from the machine to the clock on the wall as he continued the count. After fifty-five seconds of holding his breath, he inhaled deeply. There was no smell from the oxygen. He felt the familiar click and the vibrations along the sides of his head as the room froze. The red digits on the clock showed "23:11:48", and the display remained fixed.

Then, suddenly, there was black nothingness. This was not like any darkness Jerome had experienced before; it was absolute. And the nothingness was not just a complete absence of light. There was no sound, not even the reassuring noise of his heartbeat. Nor could he feel anything; there was no cold or hot or air on his skin. He could not move, and he was aware that his senses were not being deprived – they had gone. Everything seemed to have gone, except his mind. Jerome tried to quell the rising feeling of panic. He tried to think pleasant thoughts – of Stancia, his family and his mother smiling – but he could not hold them. Then he thought reassuring ones; this would soon pass. But what was soon? His sense of time had disappeared. He had no idea how long he had been in this darkness. Was it seconds, minutes or years? A dread fear that he had induced a coma in which he would be permanently trapped overwhelmed Jerome, and with a soundless primal scream, he pleaded with the God of his childhood, "Dear Jesus, help me."

A tiny, white dot, far in the distance, was followed by a searing, blinding light. He tried to avoid the stunning brightness, but it was everywhere; it was everything. At first, it overwhelmed all his senses, and only gradually could he hear a gentle wind-like noise; then came silence or the relative silence of sensory calm.

Staggering from the bed, he gulped rapidly at the air in the room and let the relief of normality wash over him. Gradually, he began to recover from the shock and fright of the experience. For a while, he could do nothing but stand by the bed and be hugely thankful it was over. He vowed never to try it again.

It was the light outside that interrupted his thoughts. Walking delicately to the window, he pulled back the curtain. It was daylight.

The road below, usually busy during term time, was quiet, but he could see three people walking on the far side, and cars were also passing. From the shadows, he knew it was evening. He glanced at his watch; it said 7.15pm. Had the episode lasted an entire night and day? Had he been asleep or unconscious for almost twenty-four hours? Again, he looked at his watch and then switched on the CNN news channel. The time on the screen was 7.16pm and the date 21st June. Confused and increasingly anxious, Jerome sat down. CNN might be showing North American time. He switched to the Sky news channel, which showed 7.17pm on 21st June.

It had been after 11.00pm when he had started the experiment; he was sure of that. Maybe he had got the date wrong? Maybe it had been the 20th June when he started? But, no, he was certain it had been midsummer's day: the 21st June.

Jerome, by then very alarmed, tried to recall everything he had done that evening prior to the experiment. He had returned to the apartment at around 7.30pm, and prepared and eaten lasagne and salad. But there was no sign of the meal. Rushing over, he opened the dishwasher; it was empty. Where were the plates he had used? He had drunk a coffee afterwards, but there was no used cup. What else had he done? Jerome's mind was whirling at this point. He had watched part of an old movie, *On the Waterfront*. He flicked the television control to check the evening's programme schedule. The film didn't begin until 9.00pm.

In the silence, Jerome remembered the CD. It was not in the machine but was still in its cover, neatly stacked away in its slot. The oxygen dispenser lay silent on the table. He checked the switch; it was in the off position. Had he accidently switched it off? Is that what had stopped the process?

Footsteps in the corridor outside startled him and, without knowing why, he became fearful, watching in growing alarm as the key was turned in the lock and the door began to open.

Suddenly, Jerome felt that he was being smothered. Reaching up, he tore away the object on his face frantically; it was the oxygen mask. He was back sitting on the edge of the bed. Turning around sharply, his heart pounding, he saw that no one had entered the room. The only noise was from the machine and the final haunting bars from *The Mission*. After switching off the oxygen dispenser, he again looked around the room for possible intruders. Satisfied that he was alone, Jerome checked his watch; it was 11.12pm. Although the curtains were closed, he could tell it was no longer daylight outside. The used coffee cup was back on top of the refrigerator, and the smell of lasagne was still evident. He was back in his room in normal time.

Hugely relieved, though still highly confused, Jerome walked slowly up and down the room. *It must have been a dream,* he thought, *a vividly clear and frighteningly realistic dream.* He went into the bathroom and threw water on his eerily pale face before crawling into bed.

The terror of the journey remained fresh in Jerome's mind, and that night he vowed never to repeat the experiment. For hours, he lay awake, anxious that falling asleep could induce the darkness again. Eventually, exhaustion lulled him to sleep.

***

When Jerome awoke the following morning, he checked his watch immediately; it was 8.07am. On jumping out of bed, he could feel his heart racing as he switched on the television. He held his breath until the screen also showed 8.07am on 22nd June. He gave an audible sigh of relief. Everything was OK; it must have been a terrible nightmare. Lifting the oxygen canister, Jerome wrapped it tightly in a dark-coloured T-shirt and packed it at the bottom of his suitcase, placing other clothes on top so he would not be reminded of it.

***

22nd June 2015; 4.30pm

As the heat of the day increased, it seemed to melt away Jerome's remaining anxiety, so that, by late afternoon, as he approached the Covent Garden area in warm sunshine, he believed his concerns had largely disappeared. He had arranged to meet his friend Chris for a farewell drink before they went their separate ways for the summer. Chris was sitting in his usual place at a table outside one of the cheaper restaurants. He gave his normal, barely perceptible nod of hello as Jerome sat down. The place was buzzing; it held a vibrant throng of tourists, students and workers who had left early to steal an extra hour in the sun.

"See that bloke there?" Chris inclined his head in the direction of one of the street entertainers, who was riding a tall unicycle. "He's been riding that bloody thing for half an hour. I'm not moving until the fucker falls."

"Same again?" asked Jerome as he pointed to Chris's half-empty pint glass.

Chris nodded and continued staring at the unicyclist. "Anyway…" He turned to Jerome. "Guess who's a bloody genius then?"

"Albert Einstein," replied Jerome.

"No." Chris shook his head with an exaggerated weariness. "I'll give you a clue. His initials are CG." Chris raised his arms and pointed both thumbs at his back.

"I give up."

"God protect me from imbecility. Anyway, I've got us a house for next year."

"Really!" said Jerome with genuine enthusiasm. "Where is it?"

"Not so fast." Chris put up a broad, calming hand. "There'll be four in it: you, me and two gorgeous women."

"*Really?*" Jerome laughed.

"Would I lie about something like this?"

"No, and, yes, you are a genius."

"Thank you." Chris nodded as though taking a bow before an audience. "It's not far from here. I know one of the guys moving out. We can move in in September, and, better still, you can move in right away so you don't have to spend the summer in those crappy halls."

"That's magic. How gorgeous are these gorgeous women?"

"Absolute stunners."

"So, you haven't met them yet," replied Jerome, smiling.

"No, but I'm assured all eight limbs are in place."

"Eight limbs each?"

"Jesus wept." Chris shook his head in mock despair. "Although…" he paused and looked into the distance, "a woman with four arms and four legs; I wonder. I'd like to think about that a bit more."

Jerome grinned broadly. He caught the waiter's eye and indicated they'd like two more pints of beer. "So, what time are you heading off tomorrow?" he asked.

"When I wake up. Then I'll get the train to God's own country: Yorkshire! I reckon I'll need a summer to recharge the dour, bloody-mindedness. I feel I've lost my edge a bit. I'm getting too nice." He placed his empty pint glass on the waiter's tray. "When does the beautiful Stancia arrive?"

"The day after tomorrow," said Jerome.

"Say hello to her for me."

"Will do."

"It's good that you're smiling again," said Chris, looking again at the street entertainer.

"Why, what do you mean?" asked Jerome.

"Well, you've seemed a bit distracted over the last few weeks. Are you OK?"

"Yeah, of course I am; it's too much studying. I'm my normal, entertaining self again. But thanks for asking."

"No problem, bud; no problem. And the good news is that I think I spy our drinks coming."

Chapter 11

London;
22nd June 2015

Later that evening, Jerome stood in his room in the halls of residence, gazing contentedly at the warm street below. Two young women wearing bright-coloured summer tops walked unsteadily along the far pavement, linking arms with each other and laughing. He smiled at them and, closing his eyes, took a long, lingering draw from the remains of his cigarette before blowing the smoke downwards away from the smoke detector.

The sudden buzz from his doorbell made him start. He was not expecting anyone, but was surprised at how edgy he felt as he moved cautiously towards the door. On opening it slowly, he saw no one outside. He leaned forwards to check the corridor when she bounded suddenly into his arms, almost knocking him over in the process.

"Surprise!" said Stancia as she kissed his ears and cheeks while continuing to cling tightly to him.

"Christ almighty, you almost scared me to death," replied Jerome breathlessly as a huge wave of relief washed over him.

Stancia lowered herself from his arms and started kissing his neck. "Oh yes, I can feel your pulse now. It's incredibly fast. Sorry about that; I just wanted to surprise you. Did I nearly kill you?"

"Yes." Jerome laughed. "But it's great to see you."

"Here, let me make you all better." Stancia kissed him passionately on the lips. "Oh, my favourite taste."

"What?"

"Marlboro cigarettes."

"Well, I didn't expect you until tomorrow," he said before picking her up and carrying her over the threshold.

***

It was early evening on the following day when the taxi dropped Stancia, Jerome and their suitcases outside the three-storey, red-brick town house in Westminster, which was the place that would become Jerome's home for the next few years. On opening the unlocked front door, he called hello up the stairs to alert Mary Clarke and Ser Armitage, the two resident tenants. They could hear a television but got no response, and so they climbed the carpeted stairs leading to the shared dining and living rooms.

"Hello," repeated Jerome to the two women sitting in armchairs either side of an empty sofa. "We're your new housemates."

"Oh hello," they replied together, both smiling.

"Sorry, we didn't hear you come in. You're very welcome," said Ser, standing up and warmly shaking hands with them both.

Mary, who was sitting in the chair closest to the television, raised the tray of food from her lap gingerly. "Sorry, I'm just finishing my dinner."

"Oh, don't let us interrupt," began Jerome, "please finish it."

"Coffee or tea?" asked Ser, playing hostess, as Jerome and Stancia arranged themselves on the sofa.

Mary turned back to the television, her long wavy hair partly hiding a thin, attractive face. "It's *Coronation Street*, and it's nearly over. I hope you like soaps." She turned briefly to them. "We're big soap fans in this house."

"We don't tend to watch much television," replied Jerome, smiling reassuringly at Stancia.

The end of the programme coincided with Ser bringing in coffee and a plate of chocolate biscuits.

"Did you just come down from Glasgow today?" Mary asked Stancia.

"No, Manchester. I'm at university there," explained Stancia, leaning closer to Jerome.

"Oh, that's a great city; I love it," said Ser. "What are you studying there?"

"Law."

"I wish I'd done something useful like that. I did sociology," said Ser, briefly scrunching up her face. "But, hey, I'd a great time."

Mary took out a packet of cigarettes and offered them around. There were no takers. Lighting one, she sat back in her chair and blew the smoke expertly towards the opening in the lightshade above her head.

"Will you both be around all summer?" asked Jerome.

"Yes, we're always here," stated Mary resignedly. "When's your buddy Chris coming? I hear he's a great laugh."

"At the end of summer," replied Jerome, "and, yes, he is very funny."

Mary's phone rang, and she went to the other side of the room to have the conversation.

"Are your suitcases downstairs?" asked Ser.

"Yes, I'll get them now," replied Jerome.

"We'll give you a hand," said Ser, smiling indulgently at them both, although she was only a few years older.

***

The day after they moved in, Jerome and Stancia went in search of summer jobs. Getting work proved relatively easy for them both. At the third place she tried – a large, two-storey, cavernous bar near Piccadilly Circus – Stancia was hired immediately and informed she could start the following day.

The manager of Jermaine's poker club told Jerome that he was too young to act as a dealer. "The punters like to see a few grey hairs when they're playing; a bit of life experience under the bonnet."

Jerome persisted and was told eventually that he would be taken on to do some general tidy-up work and perhaps work in the bar during the day, when the club tended to be quiet. Depending on how he worked out, they might revisit his dealing request. But, for the time being, night time work would remain the domain of his elders.

***

On the following Sunday, Stancia's first day off work, she decided to clean their room thoroughly. She had been assured by Mary that all the bed linen was new, but some doubts remained, and she insisted on buying new, bright-coloured sheets and pillow cases. She worked hard, putting her stamp on the place. In the process, Jerome's suitcase was pushed under the bed. It never crossed her mind to look inside, although he had taken the precaution of locking it.

That evening, they went to a busy Chinese restaurant in Leicester Square.

"So, what do you make of our new housemates after a week with them?" asked Jerome as he began eating from the mixed platter of starters.

"Ser's a lovely girl; a real sweetheart," answered Stancia.

"And Mary?" asked Jerome, smiling ruefully.

"No, I've had difficulty warming to her," she replied with conviction.

"Yeah, she's a bit of a strange fish."

"She's selfish," continued Stancia. "She believes that, just because she's the oldest and has been there the longest, she has proprietary rights in the house."

Jerome nodded in agreement as Stancia warmed to her task.

"She's also predatory," Stancia declared.

"Do you think so?" Jerome gazed into the distance.

"I know so," she said with surprising certainty and an unusual coldness. "I just know the type." Stancia picked up one of the spare ribs and started nibbling its side. "Anyway, let's move onto more pleasant topics. Is there any chance you'll be allowed to deal cards at that club of yours?"

"Not yet, but I think I've a good relationship with Paul, my boss, and I'm going to keep nagging him." Jerome pointed to the last spring roll on the plate. "Mind if I have that?"

"Yes, I want it."

"Really?"

"No." Her bright smile returned. "Of course you can have it."

Later, as they were finishing their main courses, Jerome asked Stancia if she would like to see the club where he worked.

"Sure," she replied. "Can anyone just walk in?"

"Well, it's for members only, but I'm certain I'll get us in."

"Oh, you're my hero," she batted her eyelids rapidly in pretend adulation, which made them both laugh.

***

Jermaine's poker club was on the first floor of a cream-coloured Georgian house just off Regent Street. They had no difficulty getting in and decided to sit at the bar, nursing two expensive glasses of Pinot Grigio wine. As a guest, Stancia was not allowed to play and, indeed, had no desire to do so, but she was intrigued watching the players, a surprisingly high percentage of whom were women. The fun and banter she had assumed would accompany the games were absent. Instead, quiet, unsmiling concentration enveloped each of the tables.

"I assume we're allowed to talk in here," said Stancia in a stage whisper.

"Of course," responded Jerome with a smile.

"It's just that I feel if I speak out loud or, heaven forbid, laugh, I'd get daggers looks from everyone, especially the women. Where do they come from anyway?" Stancia nodded at a nearby table. "Those women."

Jerome shrugged his shoulders. "I've no idea; probably from around here somewhere."

"Are they on their own? I mean, do they come here on their own or with friends?"

"Mostly, they come on their own." Jerome grinned. "Did you think they'd be chaperoned?"

Stancia furrowed her brow and gave a slight shake of her head as she continued looking at the women. "I just don't understand that."

Jerome clinked Stancia's glass and, leaning towards her, said, "I'm kind of glad you're not interested in it."

"Anyway," replied Stancia, "I don't think my mum would like the thought of her only child playing poker in a den of inequity in London. She'd be clutching her pearls in horror." She mimicked her mother by grasping an imaginary necklace and raising her eyes in a swoon-like manner. "Serious smelling salts would be called for."

***

"That's a very solitary place; almost lonely," said Stancia as they were walking home later. "It's like they were all sitting an exam.

I thought it would be full of noise, with a smoky atmosphere, whiskies on the table and some wee man in the corner playing a piano."

"You've been watching too many westerns." Jerome laughed.

"But it *was* odd. I don't understand how people could enjoy all that quiet, nervous tension with no fun to lighten it up."

"You should try supporting Celtic!" said Jerome.

"Yes, I suppose I never did understand that obsession either." Smiling, she linked her arm in his and pulled him closer.

That night, when they went into their room, Jerome noticed for the first time the bright-yellow bed sheets. "Wow," he said pretending to shield his eyes from the glare.

"You'll appreciate sleeping in nice, clean sheets. I never believed the ones her ladyship gave us were new," replied Stancia with a hint of indignation.

"Well, at least we'll save on electricity now. There's no need to turn the lights on."

She gave him a gentle push and went to the bathroom. When she emerged, she took one look at him and laughed spontaneously and loudly. He was sitting up in the bed, inside the bright-yellow sheets, wearing sunglasses and a sun hat.

Chapter 12

Towards the end of August, as their summer together was drawing to a close, Jerome and Stancia had travelled up to Glasgow to spend a weekend with their families. It was Saturday morning. Jerome had arranged to meet with Karl later to watch a Celtic match, but, before that, he wanted to check in with Helga.

He let himself into her apartment with the key his mother had given him and called out loudly as he closed the front door. "Hello Gran; it's me, Jerome." On getting no response, he knocked lightly on the living room door and opened it slowly. The television was on, but Helga was reading. A hardback book in large print rested on the lap of her red, woollen dressing gown. Her face lit up instantly with childish delight when she saw Jerome.

"Jemi, give your old grandma a hug," she said, as she struggled to sit upright in the armchair.

He embraced her warmly as the cold and bony but loving fingers caressed the short hair at the back of his head. Jerome was saddened to see how frail she appeared.

"You're not ashamed to be hugging an old woman?" she asked, sure of his answer.

"Don't be daft, Gran." He held her hands. "Anyway, you're not really old, just approaching your prime."

"Tsh." She flicked her hand in a "what nonsense" gesture. "Now tell me about your adventures in London."

Jerome did, though he ensured her glass of port was topped up first. He told her about the wonderful time he had spent with Stancia, and he relayed the many funny stories she always seemed to love. But, gradually, he noticed that her attention seemed to be elsewhere. "You're lost in thought there, Gran." He took hold of her hands again. "What are you thinking about?"

"Ach," she gazed sadly at him, "just about when I was a girl, a *Fraulein* in Berlin. I seem to remember my childhood better than yesterday. It was good when I was little. There was a beautiful park near where I lived. I used to play there a lot. And there was a zoo in the park with every exotic animal you could ever imagine."

"I don't really know much about your childhood."

She looked at him with an intense curiosity that puzzled Jerome. "Did your papa never tell you about me growing up in Germany?"

"No, not really. He just said it was very hard for you all."

"You know, Jemi," she began suddenly, "we didn't deserve Hitler. Germany deserved noble, strong leaders, but look what we got: a jumped-up little army corporal and his gang of dysfunctional shits." She made an attempt to spit contemptuously, causing the port to dribble down her chin.

Jerome wiped it away tenderly.

She took a firm grip on his forearm; her once-elegant hands had become too thin but were still surprisingly strong. "He used to prance about and boast that his *Reich* would last a thousand years. Bah, it didn't even last a thousand weeks." She looked around as though to check if anyone was listening. "But do you know what will last a thousand years?"

He leaned towards her in response to her beckoning eyes.

"Hatred and the thirst for revenge; that lasts forever. If I meet him in the next life, the one after that or the one after that…" the grip on his arm became greedier, "I will put my hands around his scrawny, Austrian neck and squeeze, slowly, slowly, until his eyes grow huge with fear." She had spoken to Jerome before about her contempt for Hitler and the Nazis, but, on this occasion, the passion was much more raw than usual. She seemed to relax and then moved in the chair with an agility that surprised Jerome. "Did your father ever tell you about your grandfather?"

"Just that he died during the war," replied Jerome quietly, alert that they could be moving to a sensitive subject.

"I wish he had." She sucked in air. "Your father was born Pieter Blackmann. Did you know that?"

"No," said Jerome staring with curiosity.

"Hmm, they didn't tell you much." She beckoned him closer. "He was born in January 1946 in the British-controlled sector of Berlin. Helga Blackmann was my name at the time. I was seventeen years old and lived, if you could call it living, with my mother." She paused and looked at him intently. "Your grandfather was Russian."

"*Russian!*" Jerome repeated softly.

"Your father, Pieter, was one of the *Russi Kinder* born to thousands of German women in the spring of 1946 after the Soviet armies overran eastern Germany in 1945."

Jerome looked at her, astonished. Whether her desire to tell him was a result of the senility loosening the ropes binding previously taboo subjects, or just a desire that her story be known and no longer hushed up, he didn't know. She told it in a calm, clear way that suggested she did not want the story to die with her.

She continued, "They would come for my mother and me most nights. They weren't brutal as such, but they just insisted on taking what they believed was theirs. The most surprising thing was how shocked they were when we cried, pleaded and tried to resist. It was almost as though they had paid for us and couldn't understand why we were reneging on the deal."

She continued in a matter-of-fact voice, totally at variance to the horrors she was describing. With the same nonchalance and clarity, she told Jerome how her mother had met a kindly British officer who took pity on the two women and baby. He was Scottish and a captain in the army. He had arranged the paperwork to allow them to come to Britain and had even given them some money to pay for the journey. "And," she had added pointedly, "he sought nothing in return."

They arrived in Portsmouth and stayed there for a short while. But her mother, possibly influenced by the kindness of the soldier, decided they would all move to Scotland. They had settled in Glasgow, shortening their name to Black in an attempt to avoid the anti-German feeling that remained strong; together, mother and daughter brought up Pieter. "You didn't know that story, did you, Jemi?"

Jerome shook his head and gazed in astonishment at this wonderful little woman with the horrific secret.

She reached out and stroked his face tenderly. "I'm sorry if I upset you, but I think you had a right to know. I'm tired now, Jemi."

***

It was just after 2.00pm that afternoon when Jerome walked into Babbity Bowster's pub, where he had arranged to meet Karl for a pre-match drink.

Karl hailed him from a table near the bar.

"Perfect timing, Jerome; I've just got the pints in. It's Belhaven Best, not that pish you drink down south." He hugged his younger brother warmly. "Do you want something to eat? I've just ordered a Cullen skink; will I get you a bowl?"

"No thanks," said Jerome quietly as he sat down on the free seat opposite his brother.

"So, how's life in the big smoke these days?"

"Karl," Jerome spoke softly, "I've just been with Gran."

"Aye, she's not great, is she? It's sad. I'm not sure how much longer she'll be able to live on her own."

"She told me a terrible story."

Karl eyed his younger brother closely as a bowl of thick fish soup was placed in front of him.

"She told me this story," continued Jerome, speaking quietly and almost inaudibly amid the raucous noise in the bar, "about dad's father. Do you know it?"

Karl Black's face registered compassion. "I think I do, Jerome."

"That he was Russian. That Gran was..."

Karl nodded slowly. "Yes, I know that."

"When did you know?"

Karl breathed long and hard. "Mum told me a few years back. I think she regretted telling me. She said Dad never wants to talk about it, which you can understand. It must be very painful for them all."

A group of supporters at the bar started singing "The Ballad of John Thompson", which is a Celtic favourite.

Jerome had heard and, indeed, sung this song many times, but, on this occasion, the shock and sadness he felt from his conversation with Helga seemed to emphasise the poignancy of the words.

"Why didn't you tell me, Karl?" Jerome leaned towards his older brother.

Karl shrugged his broad shoulders in a gently apologetic way. "I didn't see the point, Jerome. It would only have caused you unnecessary pain. And you and Gran have such a special closeness, so—"

"I'm not a kid."

"I know that."

"You should've told me, Karl. I'm your brother. You should've told me."

"The Ballad of John Thompson" song ended with both brothers looking sad and not at each other.

***

The following evening, back in London, Jerome and Stancia went to the local wine bar for their Sunday evening bottle of Rioja red wine. This had become their traditional wind-down treat before starting work on Monday. As usual, they ate some cheese and bread with the wine, although, unusually, Jerome picked distractedly at the food.

When he suggested a further glass of wine, Stancia agreed and then asked him, "Is there something wrong? You've been oddly quiet since we got on the train in Glasgow."

Jerome required no further invitation and he told her Helga's story.

"My God, that's awful," said Stancia. "I mean, it's awful what happened to her and her mother. Do you think it's definitely true?" she asked hesitantly.

"Yes, I do. I spoke to Karl about it. We didn't go into detail or anything, but, yes, he said it was true and that Dad didn't want to talk about it. He said it was just a taboo subject."

"How do *you* feel, Jerome?"

He took a long drink from his wine glass. "I feel lots of different things. I'm horrified by Gran's story and a bit confused about why she told me. I feel very sad for her and poor Dad. He looks so tired these days, though his form is great, which is incredible. But the two of them have been carrying this secret all these years, and it must have been such a painful burden. And I was angry at Karl for not telling me – which probably isn't fair – but that's how I feel."

"That's all normal, Jerome. You've just been told a terribly sad story about your family."

"And there's another thing," Jerome gazed at her, with a slightly confused expression on his face. "I'm intrigued by her story; absolutely fascinated. I sense that, in some way, that's just not right, but I can't help it. I can't get it out of my mind."

"Jerome, your emotions are bound to be all over the place. That's all normal. I think you should let things settle down and I think you should talk to Karl again during the week if you feel the need to discuss it." She looked caringly at him. "In fact, I think it would be a good idea to talk to Karl anyway."

Jerome nodded slowly. "Yes, that sounds like good advice." He reached out and stroked his fingertips gently down the side of her face. "Thanks," he said with a slight smile that started to smooth out his lines of uncertainty.

***

As the following days passed, things did start to settle down for Jerome, and he felt less angst about Helga's revelations, but he remained intrigued by them and found he was regularly dwelling on the subject. Not, he felt, obsessively, but he was conscious of being quieter in company, particularly Stancia's, and he made determined attempts to talk about other topics when he was with her. But, when on his own, he did think about it, and he also began researching on the internet for more information about the Battle of Berlin in 1945, and the German refugee situation shortly after the war ended. He found a lot of horrific stories confirming the appalling behaviour of many Soviet soldiers towards the German women after the fall of Berlin, though there were scant details about German refugees subsequently settling in Britain. He reasoned that Helga, her mother and his father must have been extremely fortunate to have met this Good Samaritan British soldier. Through all of this research and reflection, Jerome felt a strange sensation of being tugged gently by an invisible thread in a direction he was not unhappy to travel. And that path seemed to be connected to both Helga and his "gift". He decided not to contact Karl, telling Stancia that he would prefer to talk to him in person rather than on the telephone. She accepted his rationale, though she remained uneasy.

***

Chris returned on 29th August and overlapped with Stancia for three days. It turned out to be a hugely enjoyable time, highlighted by them all attending the Notting Hill Carnival on the final Monday of August. Stancia was delighted that Jerome seemed to be right back to his normal largely carefree self, and her previous concerns evaporated. They parted for the summer on 1st September at Euston train station. Jerome insisted on carrying her suitcases onto the train, even though he wasn't travelling with her.

"OK, I think that's everything," he said as he hoisted the final small case onto the luggage rack above Stancia's seat. "So, I'll see you in two weeks' time." He turned and hugged her tightly.

She reciprocated and wouldn't let go.

"Eh, I better go now. It'll only be two weeks," he consoled.

"Jerome Black, you take care of yourself," commanded Stancia.

"This is like that film *Brief Encounter*," he whispered into her ear.

"How did that end?" asked Stancia, looking into his face.

"I'm not sure I ever saw the end. Happily, I think."

Chapter 13

London;
Wednesday, 2nd September 2015

It was shortly before 12.30pm, and Jerome was finally alone in his room and alone in the house. He sat on the bed with his hands placed firmly on his thighs and gazed around the bedroom. It had an emptier and slightly lonelier aspect given that Stancia and her belongings were no longer there. Outside, he could see the small, narrow back garden with the unkempt lawn and the residual evidence of a recent barbeque. He looked at the little cuckoo clock on the wall; this was his father's parting gift when he had left for London and something Stancia particularly liked, for some reason.

But Jerome was not feeling nostalgic at this moment. Instead, he felt a growing excitement. For the final time, he debated with himself whether he should experiment with the oxygen cylinder again, but, in truth, this was a decision he had made already. Indeed, he had stayed out of the house all morning deliberately to avoid the possibility of his presence altering the experiment.

He retrieved his suitcase from under the bed and brushed off a thin layer of dust. Placing it flat on the floor, he unlocked it and opened it tentatively. The oxygen dispenser in its neat, canvas holder was lifted out from below the clothes covering it, and placed on his bed. He plugged it in to recharge the battery and sat watchfully as it recovered its power.

At 1.10pm, he opened the bedroom door and put a plastic bag of books on the floor. Quickly, he positioned the oxygen dispenser on the table and sat in a chair. Continuing to move rapidly, he put on the mask, noted the time on both his watch and the digital clock on his bedside table as being 1.13pm, and pressed the on button.

The experience of total darkness followed by searing light was the same, though not nearly as terrifying as the first time. As calm returned, he squinted around the room from his position in the chair. The mask and oxygen cylinder were no longer there. The clock now read 10.13am, exactly three hours from when he had left – assuming it was the same day. The television news channel confirmed the time and date. It was the same day.

Jerome could feel his heart racing, and he took a few deep breaths to try to calm himself. If this was a dream, then it was stunningly real. His reflection, as he glanced in the mirror, appeared mesmerised.

"Is this really three hours earlier? Have I really travelled back three hours?" he whispered to himself while touching his face for reassurance.

He waited quietly in the room for a few minutes, trying to absorb the realisation that he might have travelled back in time. His watch read 10.17am. The bag of books was no longer on the floor. Slowly, he opened the door to his room and stepped hesitantly but with growing curiosity onto the silent landing.

Outside, the day was dull, though warm. As he left the house, he saw two people who were standing and talking. Jerome kept his head down. If they knew him, he didn't want to engage at this point; not yet. He had no idea what he should say. Walking unhurriedly along the pavement beside the main road, he began to look covertly at the passers-by, wondering if they could see him. He smiled awkwardly at two girls, but got no reaction. A young couple were walking towards him, hand in hand. Jerome altered his path slightly to be directly in front of them, and, adroitly, they moved to one side. His shoulder brushed the girl's as they passed. Jerome felt the contact and knew he was no ghost.

Recognising none of the faces passing him, he went into the nearby supermarket. The familiar shop assistants were there. He picked up a newspaper and advanced to the checkout till where the slim Polish girl smiled at him in recognition.

"Oh, hello," she said. "No cigarettes today?"

For a few moments, Jerome said nothing and stared at the girl with unsuppressed excitement as though entreating her to speak again. She continued smiling.

"No, I think I'll try to give them up," he answered eventually. "I'll take a bar of chocolate instead," he added, trying unsuccessfully to sound casual.

She scanned it through and he paid. He had interacted and spoken with someone in a different time!

He moved to a busy shopping mall and stopped at a photo booth. He took four photographs of himself and stared at them for a number of minutes, looking for some strangeness or something different, but he looked exactly the same, if a little drawn.

Later, in the quiet of a nearby park, he sat and watched two young women pushing buggies, each containing an excited and animated toddler. They stopped at a pond and gave each child a small bag of bread to throw to the quacking ducks that had appeared suddenly. These were normal people doing normal things. Nothing seemed odd or false. This was real, but in a time that had already passed!

***

It was 1.00pm when Jerome stood outside his room. As he began opening the door slowly, he found himself suddenly in the chair, pulling the mask from his face. Breathing rapidly, he looked at his watch. It read 1.13pm. For a few minutes, Jerome did not move from the chair. He noted the open door, the bag of books on the floor and the sound emanating from the oxygen cylinder. He put his hand in his left jacket pocket, but there was no sign of either the photographs or the chocolate bar. And yet he had purchased them. He was certain of it. This had been no dream. Rising from the chair, he switched off the oxygen and closed the door gently. Everything remained silent in the house.

Jerome felt exultant. He had achieved the impossible, the thing of fantasy. His first inclination was to tell everyone he knew; to open the window and yell out, "I've just travelled back in time. *Can you believe it?*"

Quickly, however, caution began to exert its influence and temper his enthusiasm. Yes, of course he would announce it, but *he* would need to understand it better first. Further experiments, tests and journeys would be required. His mind felt like it was exploding with the possibilities opening up. Tomorrow, he decided, he would travel back again.

* * *

Later that night, Jerome tried to identify what he didn't yet know about his incredible powers. He took out an A4 sheet and began writing:

> *What would happen if I went back in time and met myself?*
> *If I go back in time and change something, would it remain changed?*
> *What would happen if I met someone I know?*
> *Could I be trapped in the past?*
> *Why do I have this power?*

He wrote down a number of further questions, and it developed into a much longer list than he had anticipated originally.

***

Jerome had planned to travel back at 1.00pm on Thursday, 3rd September, but, as noon approached, his impatience won out and he decided to go earlier. Ideally, he wanted to go back around four hours. Sitting on the increasingly cluttered floor of his bedroom, with the oxygen container beside him, he checked his watch, which showed 11.55am. After inhaling the oxygen and starting his third journey back in time successfully, he looked at it again; it said 7.55am, four hours from his start time, and exactly what he had wanted.

Jerome confirmed that the oxygen container was then on his bed, where he had placed it at 7.30am. After opening a drawer in his bedside cabinet, he removed a box of matches and then a steak knife. He took the ten remaining matches from the box, broke them all in half and placed them on his bed. Then he boiled a kettle of water and poured it generously over the blade of the knife to sterilise it. Tensing against the expected pain, he drew the knife quickly across the ball of his right hand. The cut was not deep, but he was able to squeeze a few drops of blood onto his bright-yellow pillowcase. At 8.10am, Jerome left the house and walked slowly towards The Red Onion cafe, about 500 metres away. As he approached it, he began to feel nervous. He had been in the cafe that morning, having breakfast between 7.45am and 8.30am. Twenty metres from the glass-fronted cafe, he stopped. What would happen? Would he see himself? Would there be an eerily unnerving moment when he met himself? Taking a deep breath, he moved forwards. Abruptly, just as his hand rose to open the door of the cafe, he found himself back on the floor of his bedroom. It was 11.55am again as he switched off the oxygen.

It was clear to Jerome that the time-travel episodes ended if he came into close proximity to himself. This had happened on both of his previous journeys when he was opening the door to his room while he was still inside, and the same thing had happened when he reached the cafe, so it was consistent. He checked quickly for the broken matches. As he expected, they were no longer on his bed, but were all back in the drawer, inside their box, and all unbroken. His right hand showed no sign of any cut, and the blood had vanished from the pillow case. Jerome had got some answers: he couldn't meet himself when travelling back in time, and if he changed something while back in time, it did not remain changed. He took out his list of questions and drew a neat, black line through the first two.

Chapter 14

Nuremberg;
Monday, 5th August 1929; 1.00pm

In his research for the journey back to meet Hitler, Jerome had come across Julius Streicher, who was described as a particularly unsavoury character but not a member of Hitler's inner sanctum. He was influential in the Nuremberg area and, Jerome felt, probably of temporary additional importance when the rallies were held there.

Outside, a different side of Streicher's persona was immediately obvious, as he barked orders at a couple of young men wearing light-brown shirts similar to his own. They promptly cleared a space at the end of a long trestle table, and Jerome, Goebbels and Streicher sat down. Three tin plates, piled high with small sausages, were soon brought, together with separate bowls containing mashed potatoes, carrots and what looked like shredded cabbage. Jerome looked at the food and thought how odd it was that he was eating virtually the same meal on two consecutive days, but almost a century apart.

The eating habits of Goebbels and Streicher mirrored their

respective builds. Goebbels took sparingly of the vegetables and picked at the food on his plate. Streicher ate largely and quickly, although it did not interfere with his ability to talk.

He asked Jerome a number of questions, though in a conversational rather than interrogative way. Not surprisingly, he was effusive in his praise of Hitler. "He truly is a wonderful fellow. Five of my men were arrested for fighting with the local police and were held overnight, but the police wouldn't dare charge them." He stabbed his fork at Jerome. "They're frightened of us, you know. Anyway, although my men got out, they missed the passing-out parade and were distraught, but the *Führer* has agreed to meet them personally. Isn't he a marvellous fellow?"

Jerome raised his eyebrows in a non-committal response and looked at his watch. It was 1.00pm. He had just two and a half hours left.

Streicher was a genial, attentive host and certainly warmer than the circumspect Goebbels, who said little. During the conversation, Jerome was able to avoid making any reference to being from another time. He felt this was the right course of action, but, towards the end of the meal, Goebbels determined otherwise.

"This man says he's from the future, Julius," Goebbels declared.

Streicher continued eating and showed no obvious surprise when he replied, "The future of what?"

"No, the real future; he says he's from the next century," clarified Goebbels.

"Oh! Is the next century a good place?" He looked at Jerome as though asking if he would like some more potatoes.

"It's quite different," said Jerome quietly.

Goebbels persisted. "He says we will come to power in 1933 and take back all our occupied lands without a war. What do you think of that?"

"That sounds wonderful. What will my future be like?" enquired Streicher.

At the time, Jerome could not understand Streicher's nonchalant responses to what could only be considered surreal questions. In hindsight, he believed that Streicher thought there was some private joke between Goebbels and Jerome, and did not want to be seen to rise to the bait. So, he answered in a matter-of-fact way, but he looked at Jerome for a response.

"You will prosper in Nuremberg and you will survive the war," said Jerome. He saw little to be gained in telling him he would be executed for crimes against humanity when the war was over.

"I thought you said there would be no war?" Streicher asked, almost playfully.

Before Jerome could reply, there was movement and noise from beyond the far end of the table, and, suddenly, the men who had been seated began to stand to attention. In the distance, between the rows of tables, he could see Hitler walking slowly in their direction. Just behind him was a man in a black uniform carrying a flag. There was an increasing volume of cries of, "Heil Hitler," as the men sought to outdo each other in the passion of their acclaim. As Hitler got closer, Jerome could see that he had added a tie and an Iron Cross medal, which hung from the left breast pocket of his shirt. The black, knee-high boots and jodhpurs moving slightly in the gentle breeze would, in other circumstances, have looked slightly comical; they didn't right then.

Hitler continued the slow procession, seeming to look directly into the eyes of each man as he arched his right hand back in the familiar salute. Emotions were high, and the outpouring of adulation was unmistakable and startling. Jerome could now see that Hitler was holding a piece of the flag in his left hand. It was a red flag with a black swastika in a white circular centre.

"IT'S THE BLOOD FLAG FROM THE 1923 *PUTSCH*," Streicher shouted above the noise. "I was with him," he added with undisguised pride.

Jerome felt his arm being tugged by Goebbels, who then spoke into his ear. "So, what about my future?" he asked mockingly. "What do you say will happen to me, *Herr* Black?"

Hitler was almost beside them as Jerome cupped his hand and whispered to Goebbels, "You'll be the only one who'll stay with him in Berlin until the end. The others will all desert him."

Hitler saluted Streicher, with a show expressive of gratitude. It was reciprocated passionately. Then his gaze moved to Jerome. His eyes did not appear manic or snake-like, as they had been described in some of the books Jerome had researched; instead, they were piercing and seemed hypnotic. And although it was clear who was in the superior position, the look did not make Jerome want to avert his eyes; in fact, the effect was quite the opposite. Jerome wanted to keep looking at him and, in the circumstances, felt it was best to give a silent salute.

Hitler nodded his acceptance and then, leaning in, spoke directly to Jerome. "You have an unusual stamp about you, *Herr* Black. We will continue our conversation presently."

Hitler moved on to Goebbels and saluted his disciple with a gentle smile of acknowledgement. After he had passed, Jerome thought he noticed tears in Goebbels's eyes.

Chapter 15

London;
4th September 2015

It was mid-afternoon the day after Jerome's third journey back in time. He stood in the main room of Jermaine's poker club and reflected again, with increasing excitement, on some of the events of the past two days: seeing and talking to the slim Polish girl in the shop, and watching the women and the toddlers feeding the ducks. They were inconsequential events, except that he had travelled back in time to witness them.

No one had come into the club to play cards in over two hours. "Paul, would you mind if I knocked off early today?" he asked his manager. "It looks like nothing's going to happen here until tonight."

Paul – immaculately dressed as always in a black tuxedo, with his short, grey hair combed neatly – looked up slowly from his newspaper and scanned the tables with an appearance of surprise, as though he was only just realising that the room was empty. "Christ, what's up with you today? You're like a cat on a hot tin roof. Anyway, what happens if some customers come in? Who's going to serve them?"

Jerome raised his eyebrows and cocked his head slightly in an expression meant to convey that this scenario was extremely unlikely. Paul's expression remained unchanged.

"OK," said Jerome, "if anyone comes in this afternoon after I go, I'll pay you my wages for the week; how about that?"

Paul scratched his chin thoughtfully, as though weighing up the proposal carefully. "You're very keen to go. Are you on a promise or something?" He eventually smiled. "All right," he conceded, "but be in early tomorrow. I'll need you to help tidy the place."

***

It was quiet when Jerome arrived back at the house; the only sounds were the distant cries of children playing somewhere beyond their back garden. Hurriedly, he opened his suitcase and withdrew the oxygen container carefully. He had made no specific plans for this journey, beyond intending to go back a few hours to when the house would still have been deserted.

As the machine was switched on, its familiar humming vibrations swirled around his bedroom. In the sticky afternoon heat, Jerome felt the rapid beat of his heart as he held the mask to his face and began counting, but another familiar sound interrupted him. It was the noise of the front door being opened and closed. Someone had come into the house.

The bedroom door wasn't fully shut. Quickly, he closed it and switched off the machine. The footsteps had climbed the first stairs and had reached the main room. They stopped as Jerome breathed quietly.

"Is anybody home?" It was Mary's voice.

He sighed with relief. "YES, JUST ME," he shouted down before returning the oxygen container speedily to the bottom of his suitcase and leaving his bedroom.

Mary was in the kitchen making coffee when Jerome came downstairs. "You gave me quite a start when I came in," she said. "What the hell was that noise?"

"What noise?" Jerome sounded calm.

"You know, the machine-like noise that was there and then, suddenly, wasn't there."

"I dunno. It was probably somebody using their lawnmower."

Mary stared hard at him. "I hope you're not doing anything dangerous up there."

"Would you like to come up and check?" Jerome returned her stare.

She took a first sip of her coffee and, smiling slightly, raised her eyebrows suggestively. "You're a fast worker."

"I didn't mean that, and you know it." Jerome also raised his eyebrows, but for different emphasis. "So, what brings you home early?" He fetched a mug from the cupboard.

"I had a splitting headache. I hate work," she replied with passion.

They sat down in the main part of the room. Mary took out her cigarettes and offered them to him. Jerome shook his head.

"Go on, I know you're a closet smoker."

"What makes you think that?" asked Jerome.

"We smokers know each other. It's the desire in the body language when cigarettes appear."

Slowly, Jerome took one from the packet.

***

Saturday, 19th September 2015

Following this near discovery, Jerome changed his plans and decided to start his next journey back in time from somewhere outside the house, feeling this would offer greater anonymity and remove the danger that he would appear suddenly among people he knew. He bought a medium-sized, blue-and-black rucksack and, with the oxygen dispenser comfortably packed inside, headed for the Underground. It was lunchtime when he arrived in Hyde Park. Even here, in the wide-open spaces, it was difficult to find somewhere where he would be sufficiently alone to use the oxygen. Eventually, however, he found a secluded spot close to some trees and not far from The Serpentine lake. He glanced at his watch; it was 12.13pm. Preferably, he wanted to go back about four hours to the early morning. Taking the dispenser from the rucksack, he started the process quickly and furtively.

Suddenly, Jerome could feel the cool morning air on his face. The lunchtime crowds strolling around the lake had disappeared and had been replaced by a few early morning joggers. His watch showed 8.15am. He had travelled back four hours, again, exactly as he had hoped. Getting slowly to his feet, he could hear the excited sound of his breathing as he moved from the secluded spot cautiously but with intense curiosity towards the broad green environs of the park. Once more, he felt the incredible thrill of watching, listening and engaging with people in a time he had already lived through. He was experiencing life twice! Jerome walked for hours before stopping eventually at an expensive restaurant to have lunch. He ate well and intentionally ate a lot. It was approaching 12.15pm, the time when he had initiated this latest journey. He was deliberately lingering over a coffee, waiting and wondering what would happen when he passed this 12.15pm time. As he raised the almost-empty cup of latte to his lips, Jerome was back in the park suddenly in normal time. Removing the mask from his face hastily, he packed the cylinder in the rucksack and made his way home, thrilled with this new adventure and, interestingly, hungry.

* * *

During the following week, Jerome made three more journeys. They all started away from the house and, on each occasion, he was thrilled by his ability to live life twice in the same time. He was also able to confirm to himself that he could travel back to the exact time he wanted. He had no idea how this worked, but then the whole idea of travelling back in time was so absurd that this additional piece of knowledge seemed simply plausible rather than fantastically unbelievable.

Jerome had chosen to travel back in time by twenty-four hours on his third trip of that week. It was on that journey that he first encountered a limit to his power. When he had been back in time for a period of just under five hours, his journey ended automatically. At first, he was unsure why this had happened. However, two subsequent journeys, both starting from a nearby park, confirmed the crucial information that, indeed, there was an upper limit on the duration of his time travel. It was four hours and forty-nine minutes, as accurately as he could calculate. He took out his list and after the question, "Could I be trapped in the past?", he wrote a confident "No" before drawing a black line through it.

While this knowledge did confirm a restriction to his powers and rule out some of his more extravagant plans, it did not really concern Jerome. In fact, he drew comfort from it and felt reassurance that he would always be brought back automatically to normal time. It also meant he could consider travelling much further back in time without the concern of being trapped. It was another step to fully understanding his powers. Maybe, when he had taken enough of those steps, he might finally understand the purpose of his strange gift.

***

London; Thursday, 15th October 2015

He had been trying to avoid meeting with anyone he knew on his journeys back in time. This was partly because he did not know how they would behave, but, more importantly, Jerome was unsure how he would react. It was on this particular day that he decided to find out. At 7.45pm, exactly as he had planned, Jerome entered the house. Chris, Ser and Mary were in the living room watching television. After exchanging brief hellos, Jerome went straight to his room and closed the door. He moved the oxygen dispenser into the far corner of the room and wrapped two jackets around it to muffle the noise before switching it on.

It was 7.30pm when, carefully, he descended the stairs leading to the main room. The television was on. Mary was watching it, Chris was reading a paper, and Jerome could hear Ser in the kitchen.

"Where'd you come from?" asked Chris.

"I was asleep in my room." Jerome had anticipated his sudden appearance from upstairs would cause a surprise.

"I didn't realise you were home. Did you climb in through the bedroom window?" continued Chris.

Jerome smiled in response but said nothing.

Ser shouted something from behind the kitchen partition, obviously continuing a conversation that Jerome's entrance had interrupted temporarily, and then joined the others. As Jerome was then occupying the chair she had been in at 7.45pm, she had to sit in a different one.

Jerome engaged each of them individually, though their enthusiasm for conversation seemed low. At 7.42pm, he walked to the kitchen, took a glass jar of beetroot from the refrigerator and deliberately dropped it on the terracotta-tiled floor. It landed with a loud crash, the contents spreading out and causing a generous purple stain, and glass scattering across the room.

"What the fuck was that?" asked Chris.

"Just dropped a glass; I'll clean it up," offered Jerome.

Ser popped her head around the door, grimaced at the mess and gave Jerome a sympathetic smile before returning to her seat. Jerome remained in the kitchen, listening carefully. Shortly afterwards, he heard the front door opening and recognised the sound of his own footsteps on the stairs. Suddenly, he was back in his bedroom, removing the mask; he was back in normal time.

When he returned downstairs, Ser was back in her original chair and all three were watching television. In the kitchen, the jar of beetroot was still in the refrigerator, and there was no mess on the floor. He went back to the main room, sat down again and engaged each of them with the same questions he had recently asked them. The answers were very similar, though not identical, and there was even less enthusiasm; everyone appeared more interested in the programme. But, clearly, they recalled nothing from the previous conversations. For them, it was as though Jerome's visit to the past had never happened. He mentally crossed another question off his list.

***

Friday, 23rd October 2015; 7.30pm

Jerome spotted her before Stancia had seen him. She was making her way along the crowded platform at Euston train station, pulling her wheeled suitcase and scanning ahead for a sign of Jerome. Stancia was wearing a beautiful, long, white coat, which made it easier to follow her progress as she approached the ticket gate. Jerome watched with growing delight as she neared him, still oblivious to his presence, with her face a picture of joyful anticipation.

"Hello blind person," he said as she was almost alongside him.

She let go of her suitcase and ran the few yards to hug him passionately causing the other passengers to channel around the embracing couple.

"Let me grab your case before someone steals it," he suggested, moving towards the case while still holding her hand tightly.

"Thanks. It's heavy as usual. I packed the whole kitchen this time and not just the sink."

They moved happily through the crowds in the station concourse, heading towards the entrance to the Tube trains.

"You look fantastic in that coat," he said.

"Oh, do you think so? Thanks. I have it for the whole weekend," she responded.

"Why, what happens after the weekend?"

"I have to give it back to the shop. They let you borrow it for a couple of days to see if you like it. So, I'll just leave it back on Monday."

"Would you not buy it?"

"Are you kidding? It costs almost £200. We don't all have an indulgent gran who gives us lots of money."

"You're something else," he said, laughing and pulling her closer.

***

One hour later, they were sitting in their favourite wine bar, close to home. It was crowded and so, unable to get a table, they sat at the bar and ordered the cold-meat platter. It soon arrived, with pieces of freshly-cut bread roll and assorted dips in small, china-blue ceramic dishes.

"Oh, don't you just love the food in this place," said Stancia, smiling with enthusiasm as she picked an olive from the plate with her slim fingers and popped it into her mouth.

When Stancia had left London for the summer, they had agreed that they would continue the previous arrangement of spending two weekends together out of every three weeks, alternating between London and Manchester. So far, it had worked well, and Jerome had spent the previous "free" weekend in Glasgow visiting his family.

"So, how were the clan last week?" asked Stancia as she drizzled some of the olive oil onto her plate and added a few drops of the balsamic vinegar.

"Ah, generally good, though getting a bit older. I think Dad's still frustrated that he can't get around the way he used to. Mum tries to look after him like a mother hen, which sometimes drives him crazy. It's hilarious to hear them arguing like two kids at times." Jerome picked up two slices of the chorizo sausage and placed them on a piece of bread. "Last Saturday afternoon, the doorbell rang and Dad said, 'I'll get it,' then Mum said, 'No, it's all right I'll get it.'" Jerome mimicked his parents' voices as he told the story. "Then Dad added, 'Can't a man answer the bloody door in his own house?' And Mum half-whispered, 'By the time you get there, they'll be gone.' But Dad heard her and replied, 'Oh that's charming, that is.' And then he said half-aloud, 'If you're not careful, I'll deliberately soil my pants.' And Karl and I were almost crying with laughter at this stage. It really was hilarious."

"They sound like they really love each other, though," said Stancia as she took her first sip of the Rioja.

"Yes, they certainly do."

"And how are things with you and Karl?"

"Ah, they're right back to normal; it's good again. Although poor Gran is getting very frail. She's still sharp as a pin, but really struggles to get around. It's just part of getting old, I guess." He gave a resigned look and shrugged his shoulders. "So, how's your mum?"

"She's fine; she doesn't seem to miss me at all."

"I don't believe that."

Stancia glanced down at the counter. "Well, you know I always worry a wee bit about her being lonely on her own, but she doesn't seem to be. Or if she is, she's disguising it very well." She smiled shyly at Jerome.

"You worry about her, and I'm sure she worries about you. You're well matched," he said lifting his glass to hers. "It's really great to see you again."

***

Monday, 26th October 2015

All of Jerome's journeys had taken place in London. He wondered if, in addition to the time limit of four hours and forty-nine minutes, there could be some sort of geographical limit or barrier to his journeys.

Taking the oxygen dispenser with him, he boarded the Eurostar train at St Pancras station in London, late on this Monday morning. After getting off at Gare du Nord in Paris, he went straight to his hotel room and, switching on the machine, journeyed back six hours. The time travel worked. He went out into early morning Paris, before it was properly awake. He loved being in a city at this time of the day, before people came to claim it. Just then it was owned, temporarily, by the birds and four-legged scavengers feeding unhurriedly on the debris of the previous evening. The only people around were the men driving their cleaning trucks, the early risers walking purposefully to open their shops or offices, and those lost souls who seem to wander aimlessly, rarely interacting with others, as though they too were inhabiting the same space, but were from a different time.

An old soldier with his medals on display was taking up his position at the entrance to one of the underground stations. Looking up, he rattled his tin at the passing young man. Pausing,

Jerome took some money from his pocket. He had €120. He dropped a €50 note into the tin. The old soldier looked startled rather than pleased.

"Spend it quickly, because I'm afraid it will soon disappear."

"*Monsieur?*" The smile did not hide the old soldier's confusion as Jerome walked away.

Chapter 16

London;
early December 2015

The first notes of winter had been struck, and it was growing colder. Jerome travelled back in time most days, spending an increasing amount of normal time sleeping to recover. As he was going back to times when the occupants of his house would have been different people and he would not have known if they might be in the house or, indeed, his room, he started most of his journeys from the nearby park.

Determining exactly how far back in time he could travel was something that intrigued Jerome. He just had to select a time, hold it in his mind and he would be transported there. Difficulties only seemed to arise when he was physically present at the selected time. In these circumstances, the journey did not take place and he remained in normal time. He discovered gradually that he could travel back, not just weeks or months, but years and decades. There seemed to be no limit. He often chose days of political significance, concentrating on the inaugural speeches of new prime ministers from the steps of 10 Downing Street. He watched Tony Blair and Margaret Thatcher, and even went as far back as Winston Churchill returning to power in 1951. Then he journeyed to days of state pageantry, witnessing the coronation of a queen and the funeral of a princess. On each such occasion, he dressed to avoid being conspicuous.

It was the day of the funeral of Diana, Princess of Wales. Jerome stood silently among the onlookers as the coffin was being carried towards the entrance to Westminster Abbey by eight red-uniformed soldiers. A woman standing alongside Jerome raised her hand to her mouth and said, to no one in particular, "I think one of those young soldiers is really struggling with the coffin. It looks like he might fall."

"It's all right," said Jerome, "he doesn't fall."

"Are you sure?" she asked, turning to him.

"I'm absolutely certain," he replied as he looked at the soldiers walking into the abbey.

Jerome had come to know for certain that, when he travelled back in time, only he remembered what happened. Those with whom he had interacted remembered nothing. It was as though, for them, it never happened. He also knew from the experiment when he had deliberately cut his hand that things that were done became undone back in normal time. Therefore, if, as a result of his interaction, someone was hurt, they would become unhurt when the time travel episode ended. Similarly, if he interfered to save someone from getting hurt, then the benefit would only be temporary; when the episode ended, that person would be hurt in the same way, as though Jerome had never interfered. He felt confident that saving people from death would be similarly futile, but decided he needed to prove this beyond any doubt.

***

Friday, 4th December 2015; 8.00pm

The three loud thumps on his bedroom door awoke Jerome.

"Hey, Rip Van fucking Winkle." It was Chris's voice. "Are you trying to break the world record for sleeping? We're supposed to be going out tonight for a few pints, remember?"

"I'm awake," replied Jerome trying to sound more alert than he felt. "I'll be down in fifteen minutes."

"What's with fifteen minutes? Do you have to put your make-up on or something?"

"OK, five minutes."

"Now that's more like it. Yeee hawww."

***

Shortly afterwards, Jerome and Chris were sitting at a table in Kent's, their local pub.

"I've been looking forward to this all hour," said Chris as he took a large gulp from his pint of lager and drew the back of his index finger across his lips. "Now I want to ask you a question and I want an honest answer."

"Fire away," replied Jerome with genuine interest.

"Do you think if I lost about five stone Mary would fancy me?"

Jerome grinned broadly. "She might, but how do you know she doesn't fancy you now?"

"Nah." Chris shook his head resignedly. "She's not giving off any of the right signals." He looked at Jerome before continuing, "Although she gives plenty to you."

"I don't think so," responded Jerome, smiling.

"Believe me, buddy, I've got a doctorate in recognising women giving the signals to blokes I'm with. And she does yours in bloody semaphore." Jerome laughed loudly. "Life's not fair. You have the beautiful Stancia, and Mary wants you."

"Do you like Mary?" Jerome sounded surprised.

"Of course not; I can't stand her, but what's that got to do with anything?"

"Fair enough," replied Jerome, shaking his head with laughter.

"Although…" Chris looked around in a slightly sheepish manner. "I did try to make a move last Saturday when you were enjoying yourself in Manchester."

"*Really?* What happened?"

"We were both sitting on the sofa watching television, and I moved my leg very subtly so it was just touching hers."

"And?" Again, Jerome was on the verge of laughing.

"She moved hers away like she'd been shot by a sniper."

"Ah, that's probably not a great sign. Were you pissed at the time?"

"Yep. You don't think I'd have mustered the confidence to make a move like that if I was sober, do you? Anyway, I'm going on a new health and fitness regime." He drank another third of his pint. "Not now, obviously, as we're coming up to Christmas, but in the new year; definitely in the new year."

The two friends sat in comfortable silence for a while, watching the other people in the bar, before Jerome spoke. "Do you remember that poor guy who killed himself last year when he jumped off the roof of the halls? What was his name?"

"Jesus, where did that come from? We were talking about my romantic failures, and then you bring up suicide. I hope there's no connection?"

"No, I was just thinking that it happened about this time last year."

"Yes, poor bastard. His name was Jay something or other. He was an American. Jay Goodman; that was it."

"Yes, you're right. That was his name. I remember now."

"Anyway, enough of the morbid conversation, do you see those two ladies over to your right?"

Jerome glanced in that direction. "Yes, I see them."

"Right, well, I need your help to get an introduction, so I want you to give them your best winning smile, I'll go over and ask if we can join them and then you can leave everything to me."

"Chris…" Jerome chuckled. "I have no interest in those women."

"I know that, but just get me an introduction. Go on."

So, Jerome turned and gave them his best winning smile.

* * *

The following day, Jerome arose early, as he had planned. He could feel the drop in temperature as he looked out the window to see frost glistening on the grass outside. Pulling on his heavy coat, he picked up the rucksack and left the still-sleeping house to begin his journey to his old halls of residence.

Jerome barely knew Jay Goodman. They had been in each other's company on a couple of occasions but had never conversed, or if they had, he had forgotten it. But Jay Goodman's suicide had shocked him. He had never known anyone personally who had died in this tragic way, and, even though Goodman was no more than a nodding acquaintance, it still disturbed Jerome. He recalled vividly being in his room on that Saturday afternoon almost a year ago when Chris rang his doorbell and told him that the American guy had jumped off the roof to his death. He replayed the conversation just then as he walked along the north bank of the slow-moving River Thames.

"But why would he have done that?" he had asked rhetorically.

Chris had shrugged his shoulders. "Who knows what goes on inside people's heads?"

"Do they definitely know it was suicide?"

"Yes, he left his shoes on the roof."

This information had added to Jerome's sense of horror at the incident. That someone – a young student like him – who was in a state of mind to end their life still took the step to remove their shoes before jumping to their death somehow made the action more planned and hence less understandable. Jerome had never forgotten his sense of tragedy about the American's death, and right then, as he approached the halls on this quiet Saturday morning, he wondered if he would be able to avert this tragedy.

He took the lift to the fifth floor and walked purposefully to the kitchen, which had been rarely used during his time there. Checking there was no one in the corridor, he pulled out the oxygen cylinder and began the process of journeying back.

***

6th December 2014

It was 12.30pm by Jerome's watch. Jay Goodman had died at around 1.30pm. There was no one in the kitchen, and he could hear no voices nearby. He made his way to the stairs and walked down to the third floor. Goodman's room was number 313. He knew this as he recalled it was exactly two floors above his own room, number 113. Jerome felt extremely nervous as he approached the door. The thought that he, Jerome, was also at this moment sitting in room 113 added to his sense of anxiety. He rang the doorbell to Goodman's room and waited. There was no reply. Again, he pressed the buzzer and added a few gentle knocks to the door. Jerome could hear movement inside. After another minute had passed, Jerome knocked again and said quietly, "Jay, it's Jerome Black. May I see you for a minute?" After another delay, he heard footsteps and the door opened slowly.

Jay Goodman looked tired but not distraught. He was a slim, young man with thick, wavy, black hair. Jerome noticed his shirt and trousers were both pressed neatly, and he wore no shoes.

"Hi Jay, I'm Jerome Black."

Goodman's expression didn't change.

Jerome continued, "I wonder if I could come in for a few minutes?"

"Oh, hi Jerome." His face registered a flicker of recognition. "I'm busy right now."

Jerome paused for a moment before saying, "Jay, I know you're in a very difficult place at the moment. I'd really like to come in and chat to you. Please."

At first, Goodman made no movement before he stepped back slowly to allow Jerome to enter the room.

It was identical to Jerome's former room, except much tidier. The bed was made, there were no clothes strewn about, and the desk had a row of books positioned neatly underneath with a laptop, a solitary pen and one hand-written page on the top. Goodman turned the page over and looked around the room in a slightly disorientated way.

"May I sit down, Jay?" asked Jerome, pointing to one of the two metal-backed chairs.

"Yes, of course."

"Jay, I can't really explain how I know, but I do know you are feeling very low and maybe thinking of doing something drastic." Jerome paused, awaiting a response, but he got none as Goodman remained standing. "Something drastic and irreversible."

Goodman, with world-weariness, eased himself slowly into the second chair and then looked at Jerome for the first time. "How do you know that?"

"I just do. I can't really explain how, but I do."

"Did somebody send you?"

"No, Jay; nobody sent me, and nobody knows I'm here. But I just want to help, if I can."

"You must have spoken to someone. I hardly know you."

Jerome gently shook his head, and Goodman's gaze fell to the floor. A minute passed.

"Is there anything you want to talk about?" asked Jerome.

"No," Jay replied softly.

"Are they your parents?" asked Jerome, pointing to a framed photograph on the bedroom cabinet of Goodman with an older man and woman.

Goodman looked at the photograph and nodded.

"Which part of the States are you from? I'm from Scotland, as you could probably guess."

"Just outside San Francisco," Jay said faintly.

"Was the photograph taken at home?"

"No," he shook his head, "near the Grand Canyon."

"Have you any other family, Jay?"

At this point, Jerome noticed the tears flowing freely down Goodman's face as the young man dropped his head and wept. Reaching out, he rested his hand on Goodman's right shoulder as it moved in involuntary spasms from his grief-laden sobs. Nothing further was said for a number of minutes.

Eventually, Jay Goodman raised his head and gave an embarrassed chuckle. "I haven't cried like that..." He left the sentence unfinished as he rubbed his cheeks briskly with the back of his fingers.

The two young men spent the next hour talking intermittently about important and irrelevant issues in a gentle manner that Jerome hoped would bring some solace to his new companion. At 1.45pm, Jerome got up to leave.

"Thank you," began Goodman, his face showing sincere appreciation, "just, thank you." He extended a hand, which Jerome took and shook warmly.

After leaving the room, Jerome decided to go to the roof of the building. Once there, he pulled his coat tightly around him against the cold wind, lit a cigarette and looked out over the clear London skyline. It was 2.05pm. In just over three hours his journey to this time would end automatically, and he would be transported back to the fifth-floor kitchen in December 2015. Jerome knew he could short circuit this process by going to his old room 113 and precipitating a potential interaction with himself. That, he knew, would end this journey back to December 2014 instantly. But the thought of knocking on a door where the occupant in the room was himself unnerved Jerome, and he decided to wait where he was. He was also aware that, as soon as he travelled back, Jay Goodman's life would probably end. Jerome did not expect anything to change as a result of his journey, but he thought, *Shouldn't I at least give him the next three hours of life, even if it is in this strange transitory time?* So, he hunkered down and waited, watching the door to the roof fearfully lest Jay Goodman should appear suddenly. But he didn't.

***

Saturday, 5th December 2015

Jerome returned to his house in Westminster as soon as this journey back in time ended. The risen sun had melted the frost, although the house remained quiet as he opened the door to his bedroom gently. Once inside, he threw his rucksack on the bed and, without removing his coat, sat down and switched on his laptop. For a few moments, he hesitated before looking up the report in *The Guardian* newspaper for 8th December 2014; a report he had read the previous evening before his interaction with Goodman.

"Student falls to death in Westminster" ran the headline. It was the same headline and exactly the same brief summary of Jay Goodman's death. Jerome's journey back had not changed anything. Jay Goodman had still died in the same way and at the same time in December 2014. Jerome leaned right back in the chair, his head swimming with different emotions. He had not expected his intervention to change anything and so was not surprised, but he did feel pangs of disappointment and a much more pronounced sense of loss, even though he had met this person for only a brief period of time. He realised that if he had spoken to Goodman in the same way, but in normal time, then he may have saved his life, though he felt little guilt as he couldn't possibly have known how depressed the American actually was.

Jerome also felt a sense of confusion. Why did he have this gift if, ultimately, he couldn't change anything and he couldn't help anyone? It seemed to make little sense. He recalled some of the conversation; in particular, Goodman's fond reminiscences of his parents, Jeff and Laura Goodman. For a few moments, Jerome considered contacting them to relay their son's warm, loving feelings, but dismissed the idea quickly, feeling it would only reopen a painful wound, and, anyway, they would almost certainly consider him a crank.

However, alongside all of these sad and negative thoughts, Jerome felt exhilaration. He had again travelled back in time and, even though he could not save this young man's life, he had been able to meet and talk with him, give him extra hours of life and make them much less painful than the final hours Goodman had actually experienced in real time.

By then, Jerome was certain that he could not change events. He could not change history. What happened had happened, and would always be so. He would never again try to interfere directly, but, while he could not change events, he *could* gain a better understanding of why they happened. He could talk to the people involved, not like the largely spontaneous conversation he had with Jay Goodman but in a carefully planned way. For the first time since he had discovered his remarkable power, he felt he was embarking on a definite path. The tug on the thread was getting stronger.

A buzz from his phone signalled the arrival of a text. He picked it up from his bed and saw it was from Stancia. "MISS YOU" it read. He smiled happily and lay back on the bed, looking up at the message before replying, "MISS YOU EVEN MORE". Another buzz came from the phone, and this time an emoji with heart-shaped eyes came through from Stancia. He held the phone tightly, as though holding her, and soon fell asleep still clutching it.

***

Sunday, 6th December 2015

It was on a phone call to his mother when Jerome first learned that Helga had to go into a nursing home. "She fell a couple of times recently, Jerome." His mother's voice sounded sad but definitive. "And then, last week, when Karl called, he found her asleep with the oven still on and the stew completely burned. We brought her up last Sunday. It's a lovely place. The staff are really friendly, although I know she'll miss her own home."

Jerome could almost see the resigned shrug of his mother's shoulders as he listened quietly. "So, how did she take it?" he asked.

"Not too bad."

He sensed his mother was painting a brighter picture than the reality.

"She sleeps a lot now, as you know," she confirmed.

"I'll come up to see her this weekend," he said.

"You don't need to, you know. We'll be visiting her this weekend anyway."

"No, I'd like to see her. I'll come up."

"She'd like that, Jerome. Thanks."

Chapter 17

Glasgow;
Saturday, 12th December 2015

Helga was sitting alone in her room, oblivious to his arrival. Jerome stood looking at her as she gazed out of the window. Although he had been forewarned by his mother, he was still shocked to see the deterioration in her appearance. Her grey hair, usually tied in a neat bun, had a number of strands hanging loosely down her cheeks and resting on her pitifully thin shoulders. Her skin was dull and papery, and an angry, red sore was visible just below her lips. He took a few moments to compose himself, knowing she was still unaware of his presence.

"Hi Gran." He moved in front of her, and, after a few moments of confusion, she smiled, and he bent down to hug her.

"Jemi, you've come back. Here, sit down beside me," she suggested.

He sat on the bed and held her hands as she stared longingly through the window at the two neat rows of young pine trees that flanked the avenue leading to the nursing home.

"Jemi, would you take me outside please? I'd love to be out in the sun for a while."

"Of course I will." He replaced one of Helga's slippers that had fallen off and tightened the cord of her dressing gown before helping her get gingerly to her feet. Then, in slow, small steps, they shuffled to the doorway of her room. From there, the sunlight could be seen shining through the closed french doors at the bottom of a long corridor. But just looking at the distance to the sunlight seemed to drain Helga.

For a while, she stood still and said nothing before turning forlornly to Jerome. "Not today, Jemi; we'll try another time when it's warmer."

"Are you sure, Gran? I could push you in one of those wheelchairs, and we could sit just inside the doors for a wee while if you'd like."

"*Nein,*" she shook her head sadly, "maybe when the summer comes again."

Her sense of disappointment fuelled his feeling of helplessness as they returned to the room. But, presently, she began to recover; colour reappeared on her cheeks and some brightness returned to her ever-watchful eyes.

One of the carers brought a bowl of chicken soup and placed it on a low table beside Helga. Jerome lifted the spoon and gently helped her take some.

Then, reaching out, she took the spoon from his hand tenderly. "I've got to try to feed myself, otherwise I'll never get out of this home for the bewildered." She glanced at him and winked. "Now, Jemi…" She was looking down at the soup. "You've something to tell me."

"Have I?" he enquired.

"Yes," she continued without looking up. "You have that excited look on your face. You know, like when you were a five-year-old and you couldn't wait to tell me that your teacher said how clever you were to be able to speak two languages. Do you remember that?"

He paused before replying, "Yes, I do."

"And you asked me if it was OK to speak German because someone in school had told you it wasn't."

"Jesus, Gran, you remember everything."

"Well, you have that look again, so what is it?" Her no-nonsense voice had returned, much to Jerome's delight, though her head remained bowed, as though she was deliberately not engaging in eye contact to make his task easier.

In a way, Jerome felt like he was in a confessional with a totally sympathetic ear waiting to listen and help. For a few moments, he said nothing.

"It's about your gift, isn't it?" she continued to look down at her soup as she slowly stirred it with the heavy, silver spoon.

Jerome chuckled. "I don't think I'll ever be able to hide anything from you. Yes, it is." He glanced around, but the only people nearby were other residents sitting in the lounge across the corridor.

"Don't worry about them." She was smiling reassuringly at him. "They're so drugged-up they wouldn't hear you if you yelled in their ears like a foghorn. Tell me about it."

"Gran," Jerome began quietly, "my gift has become unbelievable, literally unbelievable." He moved closer to her. "I can travel back in time; really back in time. And I can go to *any* time and *any* place I want." He paused to gauge her reaction, but she retained an inscrutable expression. "I can go back but only for a limited period, less than five hours. And here's the thing, Gran: when I come back to normal time, it's as if nothing happened. So, the people I met when I travelled back don't remember anything about it. It's as if it never happened; if that makes any sense to you?"

She nodded almost imperceptivity. "Who have you met in the past?"

"Oh, lots of people, mostly just ordinary people who I didn't know, and then others such as my flatmates." Jerome, conscious he was speaking rapidly, paused deliberately. "I've also seen well-known people." Again, he paused. "I went back this day last week to try to help a poor guy who had taken his own life."

"Oh, that must have been a very sad thing. Were you able to help him?"

"No, I was able to talk to him for about an hour, but…" Jerome shook his head. "It really was very sad."

"And, what did he say?" Her eyes narrowed with curiosity.

"Oh, we talked about his family and what it was like living in America. He was from a place called Sausalito just outside San Francisco. And, when I left him, he seemed in good spirits. But then, when I came back to normal time, I checked the newspaper reports and he had still died a year ago. It was as though my meeting with this young guy had never happened. At times, I find it difficult not to think about him and wonder if I could have helped him in real time in real life."

Helga tucked the loose strands of hair behind her left ear as she stared intensely downwards. "Could you be hurt going on these journeys, Jemi?"

"No, I don't think I can be. In fact, I'm certain I can't be. I cut my hand slightly on one of the trips, and when it ended, the cut had completely gone." Jerome held out an open hand as though providing incontrovertible proof of his statement. "It was like the cut had never happened. But it had," he added emphatically.

"Good." Helga nodded. "It's good you can't be hurt, but is it frightening going back like that?"

"No." Jerome moved back in his seat. "No, it's not frightening, Gran. Although the first time I did it, I *was* terrified." He recounted the story of his first experiment with the oxygen cylinder.

Helga listened attentively before responding. "Perhaps you were being tested."

"Tested? I don't understand. What do you mean?"

"For a unique gift like this, Jemi, there surely is a purpose, and maybe a burden. Maybe you were being tested to see if you wanted to carry that burden."

Jerome shook his head. "I still don't understand what you mean."

"Ach, sometimes I don't know what I mean either. Have you told Stancia?"

"No, not yet."

"Why not?" The question was asked in an unusually direct manner.

Jerome sighed audibly. "I don't want to lose her, Gran."

"And you think you might if you told her?"

"Well, she might think I'm crazy. I don't want to risk that."

"Do you still see her often?"

"Yes, we still try to meet at least twice every three weeks, although we can't always do that. And you know what else?" He shrugged his shoulders and smiled bashfully in a helpless gesture. "I'm always counting down the days until I see her again."

Helga turned her head and stared again at the row of pines, which were then looking more sombre as the sunshine faded. "You must love her dearly, Jemi."

"Yes," he replied quietly, "I believe I do."

"Do you think you could give up all these time-travel adventures? Just forget about it, settle down with that nice girl and lead a normal life?" She had turned again to look at him.

"No, I don't think I could; not yet anyway."

She nodded in an understanding way. "And have you plans for your next journey?"

"Yes." Jerome paused for a moment. "I want to go back and confront Adolf Hitler, but before he comes to power, when he's a younger man."

For a few moments, Helga said nothing, before responding quietly, "Jemi, is this anything to do with me telling you about my past?"

"Honestly, Gran, it probably is a bit, but I'm also fascinated by having the chance to meet him. Imagine being able to sit down and actually talk to him; I mean, years before he becomes the megalomaniac monster we all read about. It would be just phenomenal, wouldn't it? What do you think?"

"Oh, I don't know, Jemi. It all sounds so incredible. What will you ask him?"

"I don't know yet, but I will plan it all out in detail before I travel."

"You say you can't be hurt; are you absolutely sure?"

"Yes, I'm certain. If I am hurt, I become unhurt when I come back to normal time. I'm sure of that."

"Could you die?"

"Jesus, Gran." Jerome smiled broadly at her. "I wasn't planning on testing that. I'm not that crazy."

"You're not crazy; not in the slightest. And if you do go back to see him or his henchmen, be careful, Jemi, but don't be afraid."

"I will, don't worry." He moved the soup bowl off the table and held her hands as he always did on his visits. "Who would you go back to visit if you had the chance?"

"Oh, that's a question and a half." She turned her head to the side and gazed pensively at the floor. "At my age, even thinking about that is exhausting, although maybe visiting some of my childhood friends again would be fun. They were carefree, joyful times." She looked at him. "But I'd be going back as an old woman, Jemi. They wouldn't recognise me, and I suspect that could be tinged with sadness. But, anyway," she continued, opening her eyes wide, "it's *you* who'll be making the journey, and I'll help anyway I can."

***

24th December 2015

Christmas Eve, rather than Christmas Day, had always been the main time of celebration for the Black family. The tradition included attending the 8.00pm "midnight Mass" in St Peter's church, followed by the carol service, then home for the roast goose and plenty of mulled wine for the adults before exchanging presents. Christmas Eve 2015 was to be no different. Jerome and Karl had collected Helga from the nursing home in the early afternoon to get her settled in the house while Patricia, helped by her husband, prepared the mountain of food for serving that evening and the following day. Despite them trying to cajole her to stay in the warmth of the house, Helga insisted on going to church with the rest of them, including Stancia and Jerome's sister Geraldine and her family. Afterwards, back at the house, there was an atmosphere of noisy joy and excitement as the aroma from the mulled wine and the roasted goose enveloped the group; wrapping paper from opened presents was casually thrown on the floor; hugs with thank yous resounded around the room; and happy, gleaming eyes shone through the subdued light given out by the fire and the candles, all lit specially for the occasion.

"Jerome, you're letting Stancia's drink get low," said Patricia as she began putting freshly cut pieces of the goose on festively red-tinged plates. "Stancia, you can sit here between Gran and Jerome," she continued warmly. "Is that enough goose for you? There's lots more."

"That's plenty thanks, Mrs Black," responded a smiling Stancia as she showed Jerome covertly her large glass of mulled wine, which was still two-thirds full.

"Oh, call me Patricia, please," replied Mrs Black. "Now, Gran, I'm only putting one piece on your plate so let me know if you want more."

"May I call you Patricia too?" asked Karl as he pushed the bread and salads encouragingly towards Stancia.

"No, you may not," came the amused reply from his mother.

"We just call her the boss," explained Pieter, nodding knowingly at Stancia.

"Don't listen to them, Stancia," said Mrs Black.

"Yes, but Mum will kill us once you're gone," said Jerome, turning to his girlfriend and grinning broadly.

Patricia pretended to tap her younger son on the shoulder with the serving fork as she shook her head in mock exasperation. "Now, don't forget there are Christmas crackers to be pulled as well."

"I'll get them, Mum," offered Geraldine as she retrieved her two-year-old son from under the table where he had retreated to play with a new toy car. "Here, Gran, you get to pull the first one as usual."

"Oh, I don't think I'll be able to do that," said Helga, her bright smile darkening momentarily.

"Of course you will," continued Geraldine, picking up a green-coloured cracker and presenting it to Helga in a manner that brooked no refusal. "Here, I'll pull it with you, and Stancia can give you a hand."

The cracker came apart with a loud crack, which resulted in cheering from the adults, and shock followed by curiosity from the three young children, who all moved closer to their parents.

Everyone ate and drank their fill as the celebrations continued.

Then, as the conversation lulled towards the end of the meal, Geraldine said, "Gran, would you sing 'Silent Night' for us please?"

For a few moments, there was a hush around the table; even the children seemed to sense the appropriateness of keeping quiet.

Helga placed her hands nervously on the table and closing her eyes began in a thin quiet voice to sing: "*Stille Nacht! Heil'ge Nacht! Alles schläft; einsam wacht…*"

The other members of the Black family joined in, also singing in German, while the rest sang it in English. When it was over, there was a gentle silence as some wiped a tear from their eye.

"Happy Christmas everybody," said Pieter, raising his glass and beaming at everyone.

***

Later that evening, Jerome walked Stancia home to her mother's house.

"Your family are lovely. They're all so welcoming. I really like them," said Stancia.

"Well, as you might have guessed, they think you're great," confirmed Jerome.

She nuzzled her head into the side of his neck. "Aren't Christmases wonderful?"

"Yep, they sure are."

***

Jerome's decision to travel back to meet Hitler was not made on the spur of the moment. He had been thinking this through for a number of weeks before he mentioned it to Helga. At first, the idea that he could go back in time and talk to Hitler had seemed almost ludicrous. Surely it was ridiculous to believe that he could meet with this man, talk to him, and question him about events that had happened or were yet to happen? And, yet, as he considered each of the practical difficulties and how they could be overcome, he became rapidly more confident in the project. *After all*, he reasoned, *what problem could possibly be insurmountable to someone who can travel back in time?* He became convinced he would succeed.

Early in the new year, Jerome threw himself into the preparations. He had studied German while at school and had significant additional exposure to the language through his father and grandmother. But, wanting to prepare thoroughly, he enrolled in an evening class for advanced German.

He had already read widely on Hitler, but he then started to research in much greater depth, ensuring he covered the lesser-known period of Hitler's youth, the early political years and the term in prison. Hitler's book, *Mein Kampf* – which was written while he was in prison – was soon read and it proved to be just as turgid as the reports suggested, but it still added to his picture of the man. Jerome also researched Hitler's key associates: the spoiled Nazi princes, as his grandmother Helga had dismissed them sneeringly.

Determining when he should try to meet Hitler was not as difficult as Jerome had envisaged. He believed that the security around him after he came to power in 1933 would have been so tight that it would be impossible to get to him. His early life, before politics, was an option, but Jerome doubted that his thoughts and ideas would have been sufficiently developed by then to be meaningful. Eventually, he decided that the late 1920s would be the optimum period. The exact date would depend on where he would have the best chance of meeting him. After further research, he finally chose the occasion of the fourth Nazi Party congress, held in August 1929, three and a half years before Hitler's coming to power. Jerome decided that he would visit Hitler the day after the congress ended.

Jerome began his research of Nuremburg, the city where the 1929 congress was held. From Helga, he already knew that the name Nuremburg was symbolic of both the rise of Nazism in Germany and its ultimate fall. She had told him about the mass rallies held in the 1920s and 1930s; of the black-and-white newsreel, showing tens of thousands of uniformed men marching theatrically through the illuminated darkness, under their sinister flags; and how this remained a chilling spectacle for people who had lived through the subsequent cataclysm of horrors unleashed by this movement. The punishments of the remaining Nazi leaders following the post-war Nuremburg trials had been dismissed by Helga as totally inappropriate for the scale of their crimes.

Jerome's own research showed Nuremburg to be a city of 500,000 souls situated in the province of Bavaria in southern Central Germany. He read about the post-war history, learning that its geographical position meant that, immediately after the war, Nuremburg was in the American zone of control. Then, in 1949, it became a city in the new Federal Republic of West Germany. This fortune of geography was not lost on the people of Nuremburg, who embraced warmly their new masters, who were soon to be allies. Indeed, so keen were they to demonstrate their new loyalties that they embraced the notion of total German guilt for the war with a zeal that would have surprised even the Russians. In these circumstances, it was never going to be easy for Nuremburg to move on from the shadows of its past, and it was only after German reunification in 1990 that satisfactory closure could be achieved.

It was into this self-confident and prosperous city that Jerome arrived on Friday, 20th May 2016. The ten-minute taxi ride from the airport to the hotel was relaxing on this beautiful, still morning. Sitting in the back of the new, silver Mercedes, he watched a dense, green forest roll by and tried practising his German with some small talk to the taxi driver, which elicited cheerful responses.

The Holiday Inn hotel was situated near the centre of the old medieval town. It was a large hotel. Indeed, one of the reasons for Jerome choosing it was the anonymity that comes with size. In his fifth-floor room, he carefully unpacked the dark-blue pinstriped suit and black brogues he had bought three weeks earlier in London. A white cotton shirt and a red-and-blue striped tie comprised the other specific items he had selected to wear. He then took out the oxygen dispenser, and checked that it still worked before replacing it in its black protective covering and locking it in the suitcase. He hadn't sought permission to use it in the hotel and did not want any sharp-eyed hotel worker causing a problem if it was spotted.

As he examined the bathroom, he ran his hand over the new, short haircut he had received the previous day.

"You want to look like your granddad," the barber had suggested cheerfully as he started cutting.

And the short, neat style with a clear parting on the left-hand side gradually emerged. Jerome had got used to it quickly and, just then, as he looked in the mirror, his reflection smiled back. He sat down on one of the two large single beds in the room and, taking out his maps again, checked the location of the rally grounds, although he knew the details by heart by this time.

The remaining morning mist, still just evident during his taxi ride, had succumbed to the early summer sun, and it had become a hot day. Jerome put on casual clothes for his reconnoitre.

The area where the Nazi rallies had taken place is situated to the south-east of the city. He walked in that direction, following closely the railway line that also ran from the city centre to the old rally grounds and beyond. Jerome knew that trains taking people where they did not want to go were a dark feature of the third *Reich* and the symbolism was not lost on him. Although the distance to the rally grounds was less than two miles, his progress was slowed by the large number of gently ambling tourists and office workers enjoying their lunch breaks in the sunshine. He decided to join them.

The streets near the centre were lined generously with beech and lime trees, and flanked by tall, colourful town houses, all restored – after the destruction of the war – to their original medieval design. The cafes and restaurants were on ground level, many with awnings offering *al fresco* eating with protection from the increasingly hot sun. Eventually, he chose a small cafe where he could sit inside and watch the people go by.

There was a hum of enjoyment inside the cafe, as the waitresses

– in their smart, white blouses and charcoal-grey trousers – floated efficiently and cheerfully among the crowded tables, removing plates, taking orders and bringing food, all piled high on large, oval, white dishes. Jerome's waitress – a slim, red-haired girl – answered his questions about the fish of the day with encouraging patience and, sensing his indecision, suggested the small roasted sausages and sauerkraut, which was both a local and their own speciality. He agreed readily, but decided not to take her recommendation of a glass of local beer, as a very clear head would be needed for tomorrow.

Jerome ate the meal at a leisurely pace. He was feeling nervous, but he thought this derived more from excitement than apprehension. All of his energies were then focused on his meeting with Adolf Hitler. He knew it could go wrong – they could refuse him access to Hitler or he could be arrested, perhaps worse – but, ultimately, he felt in no real danger. He was increasingly driven by a conviction that he was doing the right thing, but perhaps more so by the riveting prospect of actually meeting with this man. Taking out his phone, he considered sending a text to Stancia. He hadn't seen her for two weeks and wouldn't see her for a further four. She had been offered a three-month placement at the University of Padua in Italy, based on her excellent first-year examination results. At first, she was adamant that she would not take it up, as it would be too disruptive, she couldn't really afford it and, anyway, she didn't want to be away from Jerome for that length of time. But he convinced her that it was a fantastic opportunity and that he would visit her halfway through the period. Finally, she decided to go and, from her phone calls and texts, she seemed to have settled in well by then. Jerome decided ultimately not to send any text. Stancia did not know he was in Germany, and, even if he were to send an innocuous text, he felt it would be in some way deceiving her and he did not want to do that. After one final cup of coffee, he left the restaurant as the crowds outside began to thin out.

He walked purposefully to the site of the rallies. On arriving, he was struck first by the wide-open, green spaces, which contrasted with the compactness of the town, and then by the monumental buildings, with the Colosseum-like Congress Hall being the most striking example.

He moved towards the hall, which was a never-finished building that then housed the documentation centre, and joined the queue beside a board indicating approximately twenty minutes from there to entry. At the large, glass entrance door, all rucksacks had to be searched. Jerome would be carrying one tomorrow, but would not be coming here. Inside the building there were numerous photographs of Nuremberg at the time of the Nazis. Jerome scrutinised closely those of the August 1929 rally, although he had already seen most of those pictures on his computer back in London.

After an hour, he left the building and walked over to where five large trees stood in a rough W shape at a spot well away from any buildings and from the crowds. He stood among the trees and, realising there was no one within 100 yards, let the pleasurable seclusion envelop him before, somewhat reluctantly, returning to his hotel.

Jerome's plan was to dress smartly for the meeting tomorrow. He also wanted to ensure that his clothes would not look out of place in 1929 Germany, hence the pinstriped suit and black brogues. He had considered dyeing his black hair blond to make his appearance more Aryan – and therefore perhaps more acceptable, or at least less suspicious – but the practical problems with passport photograph comparison and the absence of any knowledge on how to dye hair expertly persuaded him against it.

It was 11.15pm. There were some noises outside – cars moving, music from bars and occasional good-natured shouts – but it was quieter than Jerome had expected, and, as it grew late, the balmy night became increasingly still. He lay on the bed and stared up at the white, stuccoed ceiling. Absolutely no one knew he was here; not even Helga, who had been in a deep sleep on his previous visit and he hadn't had the heart to awaken her and tell her that, finally, he was travelling to meet Hitler the following week. For the first time in his life, Jerome felt alone, and a sudden wave of anxiety came over him. Jay Goodman again intruded into his thoughts, adding another level of unease. While Jerome had accepted that, rationally, there was nothing he could have done to help Goodman, he was still haunted occasionally by a sense of guilt about the young man's death. A sense of guilt that he reasoned was totally undeserved and yet, frustratingly, he couldn't fully shake off. Sitting up in bed, he looked at some pictures on his phone, particularly the ones of his family and Stancia that had been taken on Christmas Eve. He expanded the part of one photograph that Helga was in, looking frail but happy in her green dress and dark cardigan, with her thin fingers just resting on the mother-of-pearl necklace. He had kept her informed of his plans and progress each time he visited, and while never strongly encouraging him, she had always been supportive. Indeed, it had been Helga's suggestion to visit at the time of the rallies. Gradually, his feelings of apprehension began to ease as he steeled himself for the journey tomorrow.

***

At 7.30am, the alarm sounded. Jerome, who had been awake and reviewing his plans for at least half an hour, got up immediately. Dressing in casual clothes, he went down to the large breakfast hall, and had a buffet of orange juice, cornflakes, cheese, tomato and plenty of bread. It could be a long day, and he felt it important to be properly provisioned before heading out. Back in the room, he showered before changing into his 1929 clothes.

He took two light-brown envelopes from the zipped

compartment at the back of the suitcase, confirmed their contents and, after sealing them, placed one in the right inside pocket of his suit jacket. The other, together with his passport, was placed in the left inside pocket. Then he removed the oxygen canister and its protective container, placed them in the main pocket of the rucksack, and zipped it closed. Finally, and deliberately left to the end, he placed the silver ring with the small, circular thistle emblem onto the middle finger of his right hand.

Jerome took one last look at himself in the mirror. His face was showing lines of tension around the mouth, and his eyes lacked some of his previous confidence, but there was no way he was pulling out of this. He went to put his arms through the straps of the rucksack, then, feeling it might appear odd worn over a suit, decided to carry it using the soft handle at the top.

He left his room and went downstairs. Walking briskly through the hotel lobby, Jerome was reassured that no one seemed to notice him. It was now 8.45am, and another warm day had begun. He made his way quickly through the early morning tourists to the rally grounds, arriving at the five oak trees by 9.25am. Placing the rucksack at the base of one of the trees, he took out the oxygen cylinder cautiously. A further look around confirmed that there was no one near him. Carefully, he placed the mask over his nose and mouth, and he pulled the plastic strap over his head. Jerome then switched on the machine and began breathing deeply.

Chapter 18

Nuremberg;
Monday, 29th August 1929; 10.41am

The trees were smaller, and certainly thinner, but the W shape confirmed they were undoubtedly the same ones he had left recently. Jerome blinked a number of times as, gradually, he began to absorb his new surroundings. There were more trees in front of him, which had not survived into the next century, and the huge buildings were not there. At first, this startled Jerome, but then he remembered that most had been built after 1929. About 800 metres to his right was a construction that looked like a reviewing stand. A number of smaller, more permanent buildings were scattered around it in an apparently haphazard way. In the large, open spaces to the left of these, there were tents, hundreds of them, all set out in symmetric rows. Men, mostly in brown or black uniforms, moved around the tented area.

Perhaps surprisingly, it was not these initial sights that most intrigued Jerome. It was the small and faint differences that his senses were revealing. The light seemed different, or, rather, the colours in the light did. They seemed thicker or richer in some way.

Possibly, the journey had affected his eyes, and, conceivably, their ability to distinguish between shades of colour had diminished. Or maybe his eyes were unaffected, and the light was just different. There was a smell of smoke. Some of it was undoubtedly coming from the wood fires he could see burning at the top of each row of tents, presumably for cooking. He could also discern a heavier, slightly metallic taste to the smoke. The grass in front of him was a singular green colour, with no apparent shades, and it released a strong-but-pleasant odour, not unlike freshly cut grass, although he felt sure it had not been cut for some time.

Jerome began walking briskly towards the cluster of buildings, and, as he neared them, the hubbub of conversation and laughter grew. Instructions were being shouted by some individuals, but, despite this and the uniforms, the relaxed demeanour of most of the men was more suggestive of a holiday outing than a military gathering.

As he passed close to three men standing beside a wooden table, one of them turned to him and seemed to give a deferential bow.

"*Guten Morgen!*" said Jerome smartly.

"*Guten Morgen!*" came the staggered replies from the three men.

Jerome walked on, nervous and conscious that he looked conspicuous, though probably important, being dressed in his suit among all the uniforms.

As he approached the first and largest building, he saw it was single storey and rectangular shaped, with twelve windows running down the length of the longer front side. Inside were a number of rooms, which looked like classrooms; all appeared occupied. The entrance was in the middle – through a faded, blue double door – which had been jammed open to allow easy access to the many people going in and out.

At first, Jerome was relieved to see another figure in a suit moving towards the entrance doors. The dark-haired man was small and was walking slowly in front of two other men, who – although not beside him – seemed to be with him. Jerome watched them approach and paced his own steps, intending to enter the building just behind them. Suddenly, he recognised the small man as Josef Goebbels, one of Hitler's closest aides. For a second, Jerome froze, shocked momentarily at the sight of such a notorious figure moving calmly towards him. Regaining his composure, he hurried through the doors ahead of them.

"Dr Goebbels, *konnte ich Sie kurz sprechen?*" he said.

And Goebbels turned to look at him.

Chapter 19

Nuremberg;
Monday, 29th August 1929; 2.10pm

Twenty minutes after taking the salute, Hitler re-entered the room where Goebbels, Streicher and Jerome were waiting. He was in an ebullient mood, with the adrenalin rush from the parade still lingering. Streicher was treated to more praise, but he was made aware that his presence would no longer be required. He seemed to leave reluctantly. With the three of them alone again, Jerome deliberately said nothing.

"Well, *Herr* Black, you were telling us about this Munich Agreement, and how you predict that the British and French will agree to give us back what's already ours. 'Appeasement', is that what you called it?" Hitler sat on the edge of the desk beside Jerome.

"Yes," said Jerome.

"Yes, masterful, diplomatic language. When you steal something from someone and then agree to give it back, that's appeasement." Hitler smiled sarcastically at Goebbels. "But you are suggesting we could take back all territory where German people live without necessitating a war; would that be a common view in Britain?"

"It's what happened, *Herr* Hitler."

"That's not my question. Do you think it would be the view of influential people in Britain that this could be done..." Hitler paused. "If not amicably, then at least without interference?"

"I don't think many people would have considered it in 1929."

"Well, somebody has," Hitler added, seemingly more to himself than the others. There were two photographs left on his desk and his eyes flicked from one to the other.

Goebbels had returned to his seat and was looking at Jerome with a mixture of suspicion and confusion.

Hitler picked up the photograph of Foreign Minister von Ribbentrop on the steps of a small plane. The caption below it read, "SOVIET GERMAN NON-AGGRESSION PACT SIGNED". The date was 23rd August 1939. He showed it to Goebbels.

"Who is this man?" demanded Goebbels.

"Joachim von Ribbentrop. He was Germany's foreign minister at that time," said Jerome.

"I've never heard of him," continued Goebbels.

"I met a von Ribbentrop last year; he was a businessman," mused Hitler as he looked at the photograph again, "but he's not a National Socialist."

"Not yet," replied Jerome before explaining how both Britain and France had given a guarantee to Poland following the German annexation of Czechoslovakia. This pact with the Soviets then permitted Germany to carve up Poland with Soviet Russia, without having to worry about the possible war on two fronts. But this was a pact with the hated Bolsheviks, who were the arch-enemies of National Socialism.

Jerome watched the reactions of both men. Hitler was staring at the photograph, rocking slowly up and down, his face betraying no emotion. Jerome could see that Goebbels, his eyes raised in challenging disbelief and his mouth slightly open, wanted to give his opinion, but he was glancing at his leader, preferring to get some guidance on his view first.

Hitler said nothing as he picked up the final photograph and waved it back and forth. It showed him standing in uniform with the Eiffel Tower in the background. "Of all the photographs, this would have been the easiest to forge." He smiled thinly.

"Perhaps we are in Paris on our vacation," scoffed Goebbels.

Hitler grinned, encouraging Goebbels to continue.

He obliged. "Or perhaps we'll have our fifteenth party congress in Paris under the Eiffel Tower at the invitation of the French."

The grin turned into a laugh, and Goebbels beamed. Jerome was concerned that he was losing Hitler.

However, Hitler refocused quickly. "This is dated June 1940. Explain it."

Jerome outlined the build up to war and the subsequent stunningly rapid German conquest of France.

"So," began Hitler, "you *are* predicting war, *Herr* Black. You're suggesting that having agreed to Germany taking back her territories, Britain and France would go to war over Poland. Why? What's so special about Poland?"

"It was a cumulative effect; Poland was the final straw," Jerome explained.

"*Herr* Black, have you any comprehension of the state-sponsored terror that is being perpetrated on German people in Poland every single day?"

"I've read your book, *Herr* Hitler, and listened to many of your speeches."

"Then you know that German people in Poland, the Sudetenland and other places on our *newly imposed* eastern border are being systematically attacked, abused, stripped of their dignities and any rights, and treated like serfs. Is it not *reasonable* that we should want to restore these people and these lands to Germany?

And it's not just on our eastern border that these atrocities happen. The Saar region has been taken from Germany and handed over to the French to govern. And the German males are forced to work in the mines every day, to dig coal that goes solely to France to repay these pernicious war reparations. And when the miners try to strike, they are beaten like dogs treated worse than slaves. Is it not *reasonable* for us to want to take these lands back into Germany? Well, *Herr* Black?"

"Yes, they would seem like reasonable requests, *Herr* Hitler."

"Oh, you misunderstand me. These are not requests that I propose to make. If a thief breaks into my house, I will not *request* that he leave." Hitler looked wide-eyed at Jerome and then squinted again at the photograph of the Eiffel Tower.

"In your version of events, who declares war, *Herr* Black?" asked Goebbels.

"Technically, Britain and France declared war on Germany," confirmed Jerome.

"You do not technically declare war," responded Goebbels. "You either declare it or you don't. But, in your version, Germany would be fighting a defensive war against aggression."

Jerome saw no merit in getting into a discussion on this point. "I can give you details of the military campaign."

"You're a military strategist as well as a fortune teller. You're remarkably gifted, *Herr* Black," said Hitler.

Jerome took the second envelope from his inside pocket. After opening it, he removed one of the two maps and unfolded it on the desk. "In return, *Herr* Hitler, I expect a *quid pro quo*. I want your answers to some questions I have."

Hitler eyed him curiously. "I will answer questions if I choose to answer them. Is that clear?"

"I will trust you," replied Jerome, and he began describing in impressive detail the five-week military conquest of France, Belgium and the Netherlands in May and June of 1940.

An unusual silence descended. Hitler was again standing, looking out of the window, far into the distance. Goebbels had resumed the same impenetrable face he had worn when they first met, glancing from the floor to Hitler and, fleetingly, to Jerome. Jerome also gazed out the window, trying to avoid eye contact with either, and toyed with his ring. He wanted the conversation to slow down or at least move away from the detailed disclosure of actual events. He wanted Hitler's views on these events, but he felt that direct questions at this point could hinder this objective, hence his silence.

"So, *Herr* Black, you are suggesting that if there were to be a war, Germany could achieve in five weeks what she failed to do in five years after 1914. Rather unbelievable, don't you think?" said Hitler.

Jerome made no reply.

"The armistice with the French, where did you say it was signed?" asked Hitler, still with his back to Jerome.

"It was signed in the same railway coach in the forest of Compiegne where the 1918 armistice was signed."

Hitler's back seemed to stiffen, and he said nothing for a few moments. "The same coach. And what happened afterwards?"

"You ordered the site destroyed, and it was blown up."

Hitler stood, his arms akimbo, by then facing Jerome. "And what route did you say the victory parade took?"

"I didn't, but it followed exactly the same route as the French parade after the end of the First World War, or the Great War as you would know it." There was a long silence before Jerome spoke again. "Now I would like you to answer a question, *Herr* Hitler."

Goebbels promptly interrupted, "*Mein Führer*, you are scheduled to meet the committee shortly and you need to eat something. You've not eaten today."

Hitler shook his head as though wakening from a daydream. He stared at his watch, then, without looking up, said, "Josef, you start that meeting; I'll join it later. I want to spend some more minutes with *Herr* Black."

Goebbels looked uneasy, but saluted obediently and left the room. When they were alone, Hitler walked over to Jerome. His black boots had splashes of mud around their bases, but the rest of his uniform looked spotless and pressed smartly. A neat, little stud held his tie in place, and the armband displaying the Nazi swastika appeared to be sewn on to his left sleeve. Up close, Jerome was surprised to realise that Hitler's breath was extremely unpleasant.

"You're a very unusual fellow, *Herr* Black. You seem to have a remarkable gift of clairvoyance. Or else you, and whoever may be working with you, have mapped out cleverly in great detail one possible future scenario for Europe."

"I don't work with anyone or for anyone. I am totally alone."

Hitler screwed up his eyes as though reading Jerome's features.

"I'd like to ask you a question," began Jerome, "about the British withdrawal from France in 1940 when it seemed that German forces, if they had wanted, could have captured or destroyed their entire army. Do you think it made sense to let them go?"

Hitler continued squinting at Jerome. "Let me answer your question this way. Germany and Britain are not natural enemies. It is the opposite; we should be natural allies. If we had defeated a British army, it would make complete strategic and political sense to let them go. If you slaughter them, you create an action that must be avenged. Even if you capture them, there is a humiliation that must be expunged. No, let them go, defeated but with honour intact. It would make total sense."

He put his arm around Jerome's shoulder, leaving it there for just a few moments longer than Jerome found comfortable. "Walk with me. I often think more clearly when I'm walking."

They proceeded to amble slowly up and down the room. Hitler was a couple of inches shorter than Jerome and walked with a slight stoop, his head tending to point forwards and down. His boots echoed dully off the wooden floor. When he approached the yellow wall at the bottom of the room, he swivelled smartly on the balls of his feet, turned 180 degrees and began walking back, repeating the manoeuvre just before reaching the desk.

"Why have you come to see me?" Hitler enquired. He held Jerome's elbow gently as they walked.

"I've already told you. You're one of the most intriguing and influential characters of this century," answered Jerome.

He gave a small sigh of exasperation and increased the pressure slightly on Jerome's elbow. "No, *Herr* Black, you are not answering my question. Why have you come to see *me*? My sense is that it's something personal."

Jerome breathed hard and stared back at the face scrutinising his own closely. "It's not personal, but, *Herr* Hitler, you will be responsible for more death and destruction than any other human being throughout history."

There was no shock, surprise or even satisfaction on Hitler's face at this information. His eyes abandoned their brief intense assessment of Jerome's face and returned to focus on the ground; the pressure on the elbow relaxed. "Continue your story; I presume it doesn't end in Paris."

"No, it doesn't."

"Yes, I'd have been disappointed in your planning had you left it there."

The door opened, and two guards carrying trays of food and drink entered cautiously.

"*What's this?*" Hitler's anger wasn't even thinly disguised.

"It's your lunch, *Mein Führer*. Dr Goebbels told us to bring it," said one of the men.

They moved towards the desk but were halted abruptly and ordered to put it on the table beside the far wall. Jerome noticed they wore white gloves, just like the guard who had carried the blood flag.

"I'm forgetting my manners, *Herr* Black. Please help yourself." Hitler indicated the trays of food and drink. "Our food is simple German, but it's good food. And we have some of the best wines, from the Mosel region in southern Germany. I don't drink alcohol myself, but I'm assured the white is as good as the best French wines."

Jerome reminded him that he had already eaten.

"Personally, I find food has less and less attraction for me; it distracts me from work. I've virtually stopped eating meat altogether." Hitler glanced at the food before shrugging his shoulders and turning away. "It seems a waste of time. Dr Goebbels worries. He's not a medical doctor, but he fusses over me like one. He's a wonderful, loyal fellow." Hitler poured a glass of the white wine and handed it to Jerome. "I presume your story does not have a happy ending?"

Jerome shook his head.

Hitler continued, "No, that wouldn't be realistic, would it? Better then that only I hear this part; after all a dispiriting fairy tale is still dispiriting." He sat down opposite Jerome in the seat occupied previously by Goebbels, holding what looked like a glass of lemonade in his hand.

Jerome began again. "The following year, in June 1941, the invasion of the Soviet Union began. You then had a war on two fronts, even though the western one was stable."

"I thought you said there was an armistice."

"Not with Britain."

"So you're saying the British Army was defeated in France and then allowed to escape, and still Britain fought on! That's just not credible. Anyway, a war on two fronts wouldn't happen. I wouldn't allow it. You're mistaken in your conjecture."

"There's no mistake; it does happen and it preludes the greatest land battle in history."

For a while, Hitler said nothing. Then, pursing his lips and looking to the ceiling, he asked, "Does the invasion of the Soviet Union have a codename?"

"Yes, Operation Barbarossa."

Hitler folded his arms. "Go on."

Jerome took the second map from his envelope and opened it on the desk. "The invasion began with spectacular military success. Germany attacked in three army groups: north towards Leningrad, centrally towards Moscow and south towards the Caucasus. There were huge territorial gains and staggering losses inflicted on the Soviet forces. By early October, the German forces had advanced almost 2,000 kilometres and were only fifty kilometres from Moscow."

Hitler's eyes searched the maps. "And did we enter Moscow?" He sounded apprehensive.

"No, winter had set in and the Russian resistance was stiffening."

"What happened next?"

"The campaign ended for the year. It restarted in 1942 when the weather allowed the tanks and other equipment to operate again."

Hitler seemed somewhat buoyed by this statement. "So, it was only the end of the campaign for that year?"

"Yes."

"But, in your story, if we had started even a month earlier, we would have taken Moscow?"

"Perhaps, but, as I said, the Russian resistance was stiffening, so it would not have been a foregone conclusion. By the end of 1941, Germany had lost over one million men in the battle."

For the first time, Hitler appeared genuinely surprised. He soon recovered his composure and leaned back in the chair with his hands cupped behind his head. Small sweat marks were visible in the armpits of his shirt. "Do you think you could be mad, *Herr* Black?" The question was asked in the manner of a gentle enquiry about the weather.

"No, I don't believe so."

"But you have considered the possibility?"

Jerome made no response.

"Logically you're either mad or, as Dr Goebbels strongly suspects, a fraudster."

Again, Jerome remained silent.

"Tell me your story of 1942," said Hitler, slamming his hands on the desk suddenly.

Jerome looked at him. "Before that, there was another significant event. In December 1941, Japan attacked America, and, not surprisingly, America declared war on Japan." Jerome paused to let this information be absorbed. "You then also declared war on America. Germany was then at war with Britain, Russia and America. Many historians wonder why you did that, particularly as Germany was having its first major setbacks on the Russian front at that time."

Hitler had turned to his left and was grimacing slightly, more in thought than discomfort.

"Do you know why you would have declared war on America?" Jerome persisted.

"You are asking a ridiculous hypothetical question, and I have no intention of entertaining it. Continue with your story; what happened in 1942?"

Jerome began to describe the campaign in 1942. Hitler appeared annoyed that it again started so late in the year, in June, but remained silent as Jerome outlined the decision to send the bulk of the forces to the southern edge of the front and described in graphic detail the subsequent disaster at Stalingrad.

"Where is this? I cannot see Stalingrad on the map." Hitler's voice was soft.

Jerome scanned the map and then pointed. "There, on the Volga. It was called Volgograd until 1925 when its name was changed to Stalingrad, after Josef Stalin the Soviet leader and, ultimately, your nemesis."

"What happens next?"

"A slow, inexorable and brutal retreat before final capitulation and humiliating German surrender."

Hitler stared out of the window. "You're correct, *Herr* Black. Your story does not have a happy ending."

Outside the right-hand window, walking towards them in a slow and stately manner was a man leading a horse. The man was in khaki brown, and the horse was a dark chestnut. It was a magnificent creature; its head was held high despite the tugs of the lead rope.

Hitler's eyes lit up, and he hurried to the window immediately, his quick steps contrasting with the measured approach of horse and man. Opening the window, he called out, "Nordblitz. Here, Nordblitz."

The horse quartered his ears, as though searching for the voice, as he was led gently to the open window. Leaning out slightly, Hitler rubbed his hand softly down the horse's white blaze, while whispering the animal's name repeatedly, like a soft hypnotic chant. The horse responded by moving its proud head down and nuzzling into the left hand of Hitler, who stared at him with a look that was at once intense and affectionate. Finally, he gently pinched the side of its nose between his thumb and forefinger, and, after nodding a brief acknowledgement to the man, closed the window and walked back to his armchair, deep in thought.

"Isn't he a magnificent stallion?" Hitler asked, snapping out of his daydream suddenly.

"Yes, he is," answered Jerome. "A beautiful animal. Do you ever ride him?"

Again, there was a pause before the reply. "The emperor Caligula had a wonderful horse called Incitatus. He thought so much of it that he made it a senator." He grinned mischievously. "Imagine how outraged the old fool senators would have been. Alexander's horse Bucephalus was said to have had supernatural powers," he continued. "He tamed it when he was only a boy, and it served him as a valiant war horse and companion throughout his reign." He looked at Jerome, his eyes appearing to mist with emotion. "You know, I had a dog once, a German shepherd. I had her in 1921 in Vienna, but I was too poor to look after her and had to give her away. Do you know what that dog did?"

"No, I've no idea."

"She ran away from her new home and found me, even though I was then living in a different place, many miles away. You can depend on an animal's loyalty more than you can a man's. Do you like poetry, *Herr* Black?"

The question surprised Jerome. "Yes, some poetry I like very much."

"I like poetry and painting and music, especially Wagner. You know, I wrote a poem about my dog. How does that sit with your intelligence on me?"

"It surprises me, *Herr* Hitler. I knew about the painting and music, but not the poetry."

"They're all the same really. The poem is written from her point of view, when she was an old dog, near death."

"May I hear it?" Jerome sounded genuinely interested.

Hitler closed his eyes and began in a low, soft voice, "As I lie here my end draws close; I watch you with obedient eyes. I still recall the years gone by when I was always by your side. For I could run forever once; through summer fields of green and sky. And you were always in my eye. And you were always in my heart. Now I must go and you must stay. For I am old and you are young. But even as my eyes go dark, I will be loyal to the end. Always loyal to the end."

Hitler broke out of his reminiscing abruptly. "How old are you, *Herr* Black?" he asked. "Twenty-two, I would guess; no more than twenty-three. Certainly, too young to have seen any fighting in the war. You speak with such authority on military matters and yet you can have no experience of them. You have never needed to hunker down in a filthy trench and watch your comrades die from battle wounds, sickness or just despondency, while a reinvigorated and vengeful enemy spews fire all around you. How long have you been in Germany?"

"Just under two days," confirmed Jerome.

"And how did you get here?"

"I flew to Nuremberg airport."

"You flew!" He sounded surprised.

"Yes, in my time, journeys between Britain and Germany are nearly always by aeroplane; a commercial aeroplane."

"Where did you stay in Nuremburg?"

"In a hotel, in Engelhardsgasse. May I ask you a question?" Hitler made no response.

So, Jerome continued, "Do you find leadership lonely?"

"What do you mean?" Hitler's tone was abrupt.

"Carrying the burden of all these decisions with no one close to confide in, there must be times when you feel dispirited and would like to talk things over with someone close; a wife perhaps?"

"WHY ARE YOU ASKING THIS?" Hitler shouted.

"Well, you never got married, *Herr* Hitler, and I just wondered why not." Jerome deliberately ignored his brief marriage to Eva Braun just before his suicide.

"I will not tolerate these intrusions into my private life. These questions will cease." Hitler thumped the table melodramatically.

After a long and tense pause, Hitler spoke again. "Tell me, *Herr* Black, what did you hope to achieve by coming here today to talk to me?" His eyes were again focused on Jerome.

"I had hoped to get answers to some of the unanswered questions from the war."

"Is that the only reason?"

"It's certainly the main reason."

Hitler rose slowly to his feet, shaking his head slowly from side to side. "I don't believe you, *Herr* Black." He removed his jacket from a small coat stand in the corner, put it on and began buttoning it. "I must say farewell to my committee before they go; it would be discourteous to do otherwise. You will wait here. If you need anything, the guards will get it for you."

Jerome saw little point in challenging this instruction.

Chapter 20

Nuremberg;
29th August 1929; 2.40pm

Time was moving against Jerome. By his reckoning, the maximum he had left was just over forty-five minutes. In truth, however, he was glad of the break; the experience had been draining. He sat reflecting for a few minutes. Initially, he used the peace to clear his thoughts, then to reassure himself gradually that everything was OK and he was not in danger.

The two maps lay on the desk, with one draped untidily over the front edge. Apart from these, there was only a dark-blue ink well, a small note pad and blotter, and the silver pen. Jerome walked around to the back of the desk. There was one small drawer on each side, with elegant, golden-coloured handles. Without really knowing why, he tried each drawer in turn; both were locked. He moved quickly away.

Twenty minutes passed, during which he rehearsed the anticipated next section of the discussion while walking slowly around the room. He still could not guess its normal function. The sun remained high, although the east-facing direction of the room meant it was largely in shadow by then. He was glad, as the heat had been increasing towards an uncomfortable level. Jerome removed the jacket of his pinstriped suit and folded it neatly on his chair, rather than using the coat stand. The salesman from Brooks Brothers in London had been accurate after all; the material was indeed very crease resistant.

Outside, a distant buzzing noise disturbed his tranquillity. Looking out, he could see the field was emptying rapidly. He spotted the source of the noise: a single aeroplane was moving slowly from left to right across the clear, blue sky. It appeared to be travelling so slowly that, in the absence of noise from its engine, Jerome would have assumed it was far away. In any event, it was too distant to determine if it were a war plane. He watched it traverse the sky steadily on its level path and disappear from sight.

"Ah, *Herr* Black, you are still here." Goebbels sounded disappointed. "*Mein Führer* asked me to inform you that he will be along shortly."

Jerome looked at his watch; less than twenty-five minutes remained.

"Perhaps we could use this opportunity to have a brief chat," said Goebbels as he sat down and invited Jerome to do the same.

Sitting with his jacket resting on his lap, Jerome expected Goebbels to ask for further information on his own future, but he was wrong.

"*Herr* Black..." He paused, as though searching for just the right word, then leaned forwards, his hands pressed together, with his fingers apart, pointing directly at Jerome. "I don't trust you, *Herr* Black. My nose tells me there is something not right, and my sense of smell is rarely incorrect. Let me be quite open; I dislike you." He paused briefly, though Jerome was sure it was for effect rather than offering him an opportunity to respond. "Your presence here is not for our good; I'm sure of that. I sense you want to do damage to our cause and, in the process, upset the *Führer*; he is a truly marvellous man who should not be distracted by people like you who have no respect for his greatness. Your ploy in telling me that I would be the only one to stay loyal to the end was clever, but it was a ploy, *Herr* Black, and I am not stupid." He stood up. "So, as you keep looking at your watch, I assume you have other important appointments. I suggest you make your apologies to the *Führer*, leave quickly and…" again, a theatrical pause, "never return, *Herr* Black." Goebbels smiled and offered his hand. "Are we agreed?"

Had Jerome thought carefully about his reply, he would probably have politely declined the offer to leave and said no more, but he responded instinctively. "Dr Goebbels, thank you for being so frank with me. Now let me be equally blunt. I've come a long way to talk to your *Führer* and I intend to complete my discussions. I realise you are at a certain disadvantage, in that you don't know me, whereas I know you very well. I also know what you will become. How could I describe what you will become?" Jerome put in his own pause for effect. "An 'evil, twisted monster' would probably not be inaccurate. So, the fact that you don't like or trust me, I take as something of a compliment. By the way, you haven't returned my passport."

Throughout Jerome's tirade, Goebbels retained a look of benign indifference and kept his hand extended. "I think we know each other much better after our little chat. Good luck to you in your future, *Herr* Black, especially as I feel certain our paths will never cross again."

Jerome took Goebbels hand, but, as he did so, he added with slow deliberation, "You will have six children with your wife Magna. You will give them all names beginning with the letter H in honour of your leader. And, Dr Goebbels, you will murder each one of them before you commit suicide when Germany falls."

"Yes, I believe I would. We'll give you the passport when you're going." Goebbels smiled warmly and left the room.

The passport never was returned.

Jerome sat alone in the room and tried to take slow, deep breaths. He was aware that his voice had trembled during the confrontation with Goebbels and this, combined with the German's display of complete calm, had unnerved him. He was regretting his outburst and wondered if Goebbels would inform Hitler. The thought concerned him. He recalled Helga's question about whether he could die and, for the first time, he worried about this possibility. Jerome felt anxious unexpectedly and the option of just leaving seemed attractive. But he still had one set of questions for Hitler and was determined to ask them. He touched the envelope in his jacket pocket. The seconds were ticking by, but, for once, Jerome considered the diminishing time to be his friend. It would not be long before he was away from these people and back with his loved ones.

When Hitler eventually returned, it was without his previous menacing tones. "My sincere apologies; our meeting went on longer than expected. I hope you got anything you needed?"

"*Herr* Hitler, I have only until 3.30pm. In less than fifteen minutes, I'll be gone," answered Jerome.

"Yes, well, we must ensure you finish your story. When does the war end?"

"April 1945."

"So Stalingrad fell in January 1943, but the war didn't end for two further years?"

"There were many more battles with the Soviets, but none decisively in Germany's favour. The Red Army advanced inexorably westwards," continued Jerome. "Then, in June 1944, American and British troops landed in northern France, and the land war on two fronts was a reality."

"Where did they land?" he asked returning to the maps but with less of the previous interest.

"Normandy."

"Well…" he laughed softly, "if such a thing were ever to come to pass, the French would never forgive them."

"Would never forgive the Germans?" asked Jerome.

"No, no, no. They would never forgive the Americans and the British. They would never forgive their saviours. You don't seem to understand the psychology of a nation, *Herr* Black. Germans are proud, resilient and self-reliant. We depend on no one. The French like to think they are the same, but they're not; they're inferior. The shame of their defeat would only be magnified by the shame of having to be rescued by your friends. It would take generations to expunge that humiliation. Anyway, in your story, who captured Berlin?" He wanted details of the end, not the path to it.

"The Soviets, in April 1945." Jerome was about to tell him about his own death, but felt uncomfortable suddenly and hesitated.

"Was I captured?"

"No, you committed suicide." It seemed much easier to answer a question than just to offer the information.

"Good. A dishonourable surrender or death would be unimaginable for a true leader, don't you think?"

"Germany surrendered unconditionally in April 1945. The country was partitioned, with the eastern part remaining under the control of the Soviets, while the remainder was controlled by America, Britain and France. It was a humiliating defeat." Jerome's tone was deliberately cold.

"What is Germany like now?"

Jerome felt he was finally showing real belief in the story. "Germany is a strong, independent, prosperous democracy."

"And the German people, what are they like?"

"What do you mean?"

"Are they proud? Are they proud of their country and of who they are?"

"Yes, I'd say they are. But that is not how the generation of Germans who survived the war, or their children, felt." Jerome paused. "They felt a general culpability for the carnage of the war years that resulted in 50 million deaths. Shame and guilt were their overriding emotions, not pride."

Hitler moved closer, pulling his seat beside Jerome's, and fixed him with a wide-eyed gaze. "It doesn't have to be like this, you know. You don't have to be a spectator in life; you can be a player and make a real difference. I see great desire and potential in your soul; even the zeal with which you express your hatred of us can be harnessed in a different, positive direction."

Jerome stared at him, puzzled.

Hitler continued, "Grasp life, *Herr* Black. Join us in our historic mission, become part of the greatness. Who knows, you might soften some of our unnecessarily harsh edges, which seem to cause you such angst. Even if we are defeated ultimately, what a journey – what an incredible journey – it would be. We are going to Berlin tomorrow; why don't you join us?"

Jerome met his gaze inscrutably. "There was another chilling episode that took place during your leadership that I haven't yet told you about." Jerome again removed the envelope from his pocket, took out three photographs and passed them to Hitler. They showed bulldozers pushing wasted corpses into huge burial pits following the freeing of the concentration camps in 1945.

Hitler stared at them, but displayed no emotion.

"These are pictures of the concentration camp at Belsen in Lower Saxony, after the liberation by British troops in April 1945. There were a number of similar camps in Germany and in the occupied eastern countries. These camps were used to murder and dispose of the bodies of millions of Jews and other undesirables, including women and children," explained Jerome.

Slowly, Hitler rose to his feet. He continued to stare at the photographs as he pressed his clenched fists hard into the desk top. A short, dark-blue vein bulged in his right temple and, to Jerome's amazement, he noticed Hitler's eyes misting over as the Nazi leader moved his head back and stared at the ceiling with an expression like that of a supplicant seeking heavenly intervention.

Is he genuinely affected by the pictures? wondered Jerome.

"I could show you photographs, *Herr* Black," Hitler began still gazing at the ceiling. "I could show you photographs of German men, thousands of them, queuing to get bread and soup because they have nothing." He turned a colder eye on Jerome. "I could show you photographs of German mothers, broken and desolate because they can't provide for their children. And all because of the outrageously cruel and vindictive conditions imposed on Germany after the war. A war that was fought between soldiers, but now the so-called allies choose to punish German women and children to get their revenge. Have you any idea of the fury this causes in German breasts, *Herr* Black? *Have you?*"

Jerome averted his gaze.

Hitler went on, "I could show *you* photographs of German children starving and in rags; GERMAN CHILDREN IN RAGS! How would British people feel if this was being imposed on your children? And all because of a war that we did not lose; have you forgotten that, *Herr* Black? A WAR THAT WE DID NOT LOSE." Hitler jabbed his forefinger on the table to emphasise each word, his voice rising sharply. "Oh, I could show *you* photographs of the German criminals signing that treaty with your leaders and then marking the occasion by drinking champagne. They drank champagne to celebrate the destruction of the German people. Have you any conception of the anger and hatred that causes me? I suspect you have not, *Herr* Black. I suspect you have not." He picked up Jerome's photographs, ripped them in two and tossed them derisively on the floor.

The door opened, and three guards entered cautiously. Hitler nodded at their silent enquiry, and they moved to the far end of the room, where Jerome could see them clearing the table.

"From your first utterances when you insulted my friend *Herr* Goering, I sensed a certain inevitability about how this would end. Now you show me pictures of dead Jews, well, corpses you say were Jews, in blatant disobedience to my instruction not to discuss them further. Not only did you personally insult *Herr* Goering, but also Dr Goebbels," ranted Hitler.

For a moment, Jerome's face registered surprise.

"Oh come, come, *Herr* Black. Did you really expect Dr Goebbels not to tell me about your nasty, little outburst?" asked Hitler.

One of the guards began drawing curtains across the windows, while, out of the corner of his eye, Jerome could see the others moving the table towards the centre of the room.

"You invent a ridiculous story, and then you use every opportunity to demean our great nation and try to humiliate *me*!" Hitler declared.

Jerome resisted swallowing and stared back at him.

"Your purpose here is obvious. You want retribution: revenge for something personal. Well, I hope you feel you've got it, *Herr* Black, because you're going to pay a very high price." Hitler smiled at Jerome. "You have dared to challenge me about the Jews. Well, at this point, there's no harm in telling you exactly what I think. You don't know many Jews, do you, *Herr* Black?"

"No, I don't." Jerome knew he sounded fearful.

"No, I thought not. Well, let me educate you, even if it is a little too late. The Jews are not some scattered people connected loosely by a common religion. They are a close-knit family. They live together, they breed together, they conspire together and they steal together. You can never underestimate their avarice or their cunning. They do everything together. The Jewish financiers, who own their diamond shops in Manhattan and London, know the Jewish stockbrokers in Berlin, who know the Jewish pawnbrokers in Friedrich Strasse. They all plot together. So, if you ask me whether I blame the Jewish pawnbroker in Berlin for the terms of the Versailles Treaty? I do. Do I blame the Jewish shopkeeper for the destruction of the German economy, for mass unemployment and for starving German children? I do. And when you show me photographs of dead Jews, what do I do? I rejoice, *Herr* Black; I rejoice. Jews are the natural enemies of the German people."

"Even the children?"

"Children grow up. Anyway," he added casually, "wasn't it the Jews who wanted the sins of the fathers to be visited on the children when they killed Christ?"

Jerome turned around to see one of the guards standing on the table, throwing a small metal object over a beam in the ceiling. "What are they doing?" he asked.

"How well do you know me *Herr* Black? You and your associates have clearly done a lot of research, but how well do you really know me?"

"I don't know. I don't understand what you mean."

"Guess; guess what they're doing. Think about how we like to punish those who attack me personally."

Jerome had become extremely alarmed. "A few minutes ago, you asked me to join you. What if I'd said yes?"

"That would have added a certain frisson to the proceedings, but, ultimately, would have changed nothing."

Before Jerome could respond, the guards hauled him out of the seat and bound his hands tightly behind his back with thin wire. It cut deeply into his wrists as he resisted. He was dragged backwards to the table. They pulled him to a standing position on the table and yanked his head back. Jerome could see the wire looped around the beam. A noose of it was forced over his head and tightened around his throat. He could feel it beginning to cut into the soft tissue of his neck.

"Apparently, it's strong enough to withstand the weight of a

1,000 kilogramme shark without snapping, which is remarkable for something so thin," said Hitler nonchalantly.

The clock on the wall above Hitler's head read 3.27pm. By Jerome's estimate, the journey should be ending very soon.

A silence descended in the room before Hitler spoke again, beginning in a calm, almost reflective voice. "I feel I know you, *Herr* Black. I can see into a man's very soul; did your research tell you that? Did you think you could come here like some grim reaper, tell me about defeats, death, my death and the murder of some Jews, and Adolf Hitler would become dispirited, depressed, and perhaps break down and express remorse? That you could exact some sort of vengeance like the white angel who saved the Jews in Egypt? Well, you can't. The avenging angels will be wearing darker uniforms in Hitler's *Reich*." Hitler became quiet again; his mouth just open, lips dry from anticipation and eyes unmoving, as though he had decided not to blink lest he miss any of the spectacle.

Jerome looked down; his view obscured by his own cheekbones. "History has damned you as a perverted child molester. Your niece Geli's only escape from you was to kill herself." He had rehearsed these and other lines many times during the months of preparation, and he had fully intended that, if used, they should wound Hitler, but, at that moment, he just wanted them to act as a delay on these terrifying proceedings. "I have more to tell you…" he half-shouted, but his words seemed to tail-off and had no effect.

"Gag him," Hitler said softly. Then, moments later, his instruction having been obeyed, he ordered, "Remove the table."

Jerome stood on the balls of his feet, raising himself to ease the pressure on his neck. The two guards who had been holding him jumped down from the table leaving him alone, staring at Hitler. The clock on the wall had no second hand.

Slowly, they pulled the table backwards. Jerome, up on his toes by then, struggled desperately to remain in contact with the table, but felt it slide gradually away beneath him. He tried to scream, but the dirty rag jammed in his mouth caused the noise to reverberate inside his head like the plaintive wail of a dying animal. Jerome swung forwards like the pendulum of a clock. A searing, suffocating pain engulfed him as the wire began severing his neck.

Jerome was not sure if the look of shock he saw on Hitler's face came before or after he first felt the electric charges on the side of his head. Perhaps they happened simultaneously, but, suddenly, he was back among the W-shaped trees, alone and gasping for breath. There was no longer a stricture around his throat. He removed the mask and collapsed onto his knees.

Chapter 21

Nuremberg;
20th May 2016; 9.25am

Still feeling terrified, Jerome glanced at the W-shaped group of trees, which were returned to their 2016 size, and, further away, the snaking line of tourists queuing to enter the Congress Hall.

"Oh, thank Christ," he whispered as his rapid breathing continued. Reaching up, he touched his neck carefully and gave an audible sigh of relief as he confirmed there was smooth, unbroken skin. Jerome remained on his knees, clutching the oxygen mask in his right hand, as he scanned the area. There was no one close to him. Slowly, he rose to his feet and, still half dazed, pushed the mask and cylinder into the rucksack. He stood on this spot for some minutes, trying to process the events of the previous five hours and in particular the horrific final minutes. The members of the SA and SS, and their rows of tents, tables and camp fires were no longer there; neither was the rectangular building where he had been with Hitler and Goebbels. They were all gone; totally gone. Gradually, an almost overwhelming sense of relief washed over him as he began accepting that he was now safe.

He started to walk back towards his hotel through the morning sunshine, skirting deliberately close to the queue outside the Congress Hall as the gentle hum from their conversations gave him further reassurance that he was no longer in danger. As he made his way into the crowded city centre, his vice-like grip on the rucksack began to ease, and Jerome started to relax. He felt exhausted and, to his surprise, ravenously hungry, so instead of going directly to his hotel he made a path to the same cafe where he had eaten the previous day and sat outside, where the yellow-and-white awning partly shaded his small wooden table. Placing the rucksack underneath his chair, he spotted the red-haired waitress and raised his hand to attract her attention.

"Hello again." She glided over to him with a welcoming smile. "You must like our food. Shall I get you the sauerkraut again or something different?" She handed him a menu. "We still do the breakfast up to noon if you want that?"

"No, thanks." Jerome glanced at the menu and pointed to the chicken diablo pizza. "I'll have that please."

"It will be very hot," she said, raising a cautionary eyebrow.

"That's fine."

"Shall I bring you water as well or coffee?"

"No," Jerome blew out his cheeks. "But you know what I'd like? A draft beer; a large one, please."

He removed his jacket and, on spotting the two light-brown envelopes, he took them out. They were unopened. "STRICTLY PERSONAL, FOR THE EYES OF ADOLF HITLER ONLY", he read on one. He returned them to the inside pockets of his jacket, draped it over the back of his chair and took a satisfying first drink from his tankard of lager.

The shadows from the mid-morning sun shortened and left him sitting in pleasant shade as he finished the pizza. The waitress reappeared and with a questioning open hand enquired if he was finished.

"Yes, that hit the spot. Does that make sense in German? *Schlag auf den punkt?*" he repeated.

"I know that." She smiled. "Shall I get you another beer?"

"Yes, and a bowl of ice cream; vanilla, if you have it."

When the waitress left, Jerome watched the crowds of tourists ambling gently past his table. *These people have absolutely no conception of what I've done,* he thought. *I've just achieved something truly extraordinary, and they have no idea.* Jerome felt exultant and began playing out the conversation he would have with Helga. She would want him to go over every little detail, which he would be delighted to do. She would probably be thrilled by the insults to the Nazi princes, although he decided quickly to tell her nothing about the near-death experience at the end. That would be much too upsetting for her. Indeed, even in the brief time since it had occurred, Jerome determined it would be best to try to block that horrific memory from his own thoughts.

As he finished his third beer, the waitress brought the bill.

"You look a bit different from yesterday," she said, cocking her head to the side inquisitively.

"*Really?* In what way?" he asked, intrigued, as he took some euro notes from the outside pocket of his rucksack. "Better?"

She gave a slight shake of the head.

"Worse?" He pretended to look offended.

"No, I know you're the same person who came in yesterday, but, somehow, you seem to have changed. Maybe it's the suit. That must be it. Will we see you again tomorrow?"

"No, I'm flying back to London this evening."

"Ah, is your holiday over?"

"Well," he responded, smiling at her, "I'm not sure I'd call it a holiday, but my task here is over."

***

Jerome returned to his hotel room shortly before noon. He threw the rucksack and jacket onto a chair, and made a reassuring check in the mirror to confirm his neck was unharmed. Lingering at the mirror, he drew his fingers down his cheeks and peered closely at his reflection. The girl said he had changed in some way. *Have I?* he wondered. Turning his head slowly from side to side, he could see nothing unusual. There were some dark shadows under his eyes, but they were hardly sufficient to make a stranger notice and comment. Satisfied, he removed his brogues and lay back on the bed, staring again at the ceiling, but this time triumphantly; he no longer had any concerns or doubts.

His phone buzzed on the bedside locker. There was a "morning hello" text from Stancia and a missed call from Karl.

Quickly, he replied to Stancia: "And a very good morning to you too. Only a few weeks till I'm in Padua. Magic. "

Then he sat up on the bed and sent a text to Helga: "Gran, I did it! I actually did it! Love Jemi."

Soon afterwards, his phone started ringing; he hoped it might be Helga, but the screen showed Karl's name. He answered it with a, "Hi Karl."

"Hi Jerome, are you in London at the moment?" enquired Karl.

"Er, no, just outside. Why? What's up?"

"Jerome, I've got some bad news, I'm afraid. Gran died a few hours ago. She passed away in her sleep. It was very peaceful."

Nothing was said for a few moments.

"OK," said Jerome quietly.

"Dad's a bit shook up, though he has Mum. Would you be able to come home tomorrow? It would really help," suggested Karl.

"Yes, I'll do that."

There was a further pause before Karl spoke again. "OK, Jerome, thanks for that. I know Gran was very special to you.

Let me know when you're coming, and I'll pick you up from the station. Take care, and we'll see you soon."

***

Glasgow; 24th May 2016; 5.00pm

The funeral was over. Helga had been laid to rest in the small burial plot she had insisted on buying all those years ago, and the last of the mourners had paid their respects and left. It was just the family who remained, as it invariably is. Pieter and Patricia Black and their three children sat in the living room of their home. Small plates of food, and half-finished cups of tea and coffee lay about the room, as remnants from the final guests.

"Anyone hungry?" asked Patricia.

There was a general shaking of heads.

"I'll have a beer, Mum, please," said Karl, before adding quickly, "I'll get it. You sit there." He went and brought three bottles, and gave one each to his father and Jerome; his mother and Geraldine had declined his offer.

When he first heard of Helga's death, Jerome was numb with shock. Operating on autopilot, he had made his way back to London on the Saturday evening before getting the early morning train to Glasgow. It was only on this train journey that he began to allow his emotions to emerge. He felt painfully sad, but it was more than that. He had lost his special friend, his confidante and the only one who knew his secret. Jerome realised others would also feel the sense of loss, but, surely, he believed, his was much deeper and one that he could explain to no one. When Jerome arrived home, he behaved stoically, determined not to give the impression that somehow he was suffering more than others. And, gradually, as Sunday turned into Monday and then Tuesday, and Helga's body was brought home for the wake, he appreciated the grief of the others and felt much less alone. By the time of the funeral on Wednesday morning, Jerome had accepted that Helga had indeed led a full and mainly happy life, and was in a state of mind to join in the celebrations of her life, though he knew he would miss her terribly. Stancia had suggested that she come home for the funeral, but Jerome had convinced her it wasn't necessary. Right then, and more than ever, he was longing to see her again, and his trip to Padua couldn't come soon enough.

The five family members sat together, their presence and the absence of others was a comfort after the emotional and physical strain of the previous days.

"Well, we gave Gran a good send off," said Karl. "She'd have liked hearing Father Gerry say she was a feisty lady."

"Yes, she would," confirmed Pieter, cradling his bottle of beer with both hands. "I remember the first time I came home with drink on me, she was feisty then, all right."

"What'd she do, Dad?" asked Jerome, leaning forwards.

"She was hoovering when I came in the front door, and, of course, she smelled the drink immediately." Pieter started chuckling. "She charged at me with the Hoover. It was like a knight charging at you with his lance. I thought I was going to be impaled on it."

"What'd you do?" continued Jerome, smiling like the others.

"I ducked under her lance and scarpered up the stairs. She stood at the bottom of the stairs waving the Hoover and roaring up at me."

"She was probably trying to suck you back down," declared a laughing Karl.

"Do you remember the time, Dad," began Geraldine, "when you were taking us to the zoo, and the cop knocked on your car window?"

"Oh, I remember that OK. I thought I'd end up in prison." Pieter's eyes were bright with delight and mischief. "We were sitting in the traffic, which was hardly moving, and this big cop knocks on the window. You guys were teenagers." He nodded at Karl and Geraldine. "Jerome was only a toddler, and the three of you were in the back with Mum. Anyway, he indicates in this condescending way for me to wind down the window. So I did. Then he leans in and says in this pompous voice, 'Do you know what the speed limit is in this area?' And then Gran exploded, saying, 'How dare you try to intimidate us! There are children in this car. We want them to learn to respect the law, and then someone like you appears behaving like a bully. How do you think they're going to feel about the police after this, eh?'" Pieter laughed wheezily. "Then PC Plod got all flustered and started bumbling about. 'There's no need to talk like that, madam,' he responded, but he took his head out of our car and cleared off. Jesus, Gran was so proud of that."

"Yes, Gran never was a big fan of authority," said Karl. "You had to earn her respect; you couldn't just put on a uniform and get it."

"What was she like when you first met her, Mum?" asked Geraldine.

"Oh, I was a bit nervous of her. She had a reputation of being a formidable lady, but she was very kind to me. Though when you, Geraldine and then Karl came along, she used to watch me like a hawk to make sure I was doing everything right. It was a bit nerve-wracking. By the time Jerome arrived, I think she trusted me to do the mothering. But you knew she always had a heart of gold."

For the next half hour, they shared more warm and engaging stories about Helga as the family bond embraced them all gently at this time of common sadness.

"Well, I better be heading off if I'm going to catch this train," said Jerome glancing at his watch.

"I'll drive you," offered Karl, rising slowly from his seat and lifting the empty beer bottles from the table.

Jerome went to his room and, quickly, finished packing

his suitcase. As he turned round, his father was standing in the doorway holding an envelope.

"This is a letter addressed to you. It was found in Gran's locker in the nursing home." He offered it to Jerome, who took it tentatively. "I didn't want to give it to you while all the funeral stuff was going on. And I'm sure you'll want to read in peace anyway." He opened his arms, and they hugged warmly.

***

As they drove to the train station, neither brother said much; tiredness having caught up with them.

Karl parked the car very close to the station entrance. "OK, have you got everything?" he asked.

"Yes," said Jerome as he reached over and lifted his case from the back seat. "Karl, what time of the day did Gran pass away?"

"Oh." Karl looked surprised. "One of the nurses found her when she was bringing a cup of tea after breakfast. I think it was about half eight. Why do you ask?"

"No reason, really. I just was wondering what I was doing at the time she died."

Karl looked sympathetically at his brother. "Jerome, don't be down on yourself about this. Gran was old and she wasn't going to get any better."

"I know."

They shook hands above the suitcase that was perched on Jerome's lap, then he got out and went to board the train.

***

Jerome sat in a window seat, facing his direction of travel and holding Helga's light-blue envelope in his hands. As the train left the suburbs of Glasgow behind, he opened it. This is what it said:

Dear Jemi,

First of all, don't be sad.

I'm very, very tired these days and ready to cross over. In fact, I'd kind of welcome it. I just want to write in case I go before you complete your incredible journey. I feel certain it will all go amazingly.

And, Jemi, please don't come back to visit me after I've gone. I sense I would know you had come back and that would be much too sad.

You asked me once who I would like to visit if I could travel back. Well, I've given it a lot of thought and, you know, I think I'd like to visit Jesus – maybe when he's doing his Sermon on the Mount. That would be wonderful. Though it's strange that I'd want to travel back to see Jesus when I will probably be meeting him shortly anyway! In the meantime, I've asked him to look after you. Because if he doesn't, he'll have me to answer to, and he wouldn't want that!

Keep the faith, darling Jemi.

Your loving grandmother.

He turned his head to watch the flat, green and yellow fields stretch out towards the low, grey hills in the distance, with the sun still warming everything on this late May evening, as he blinked away the tears.

Chapter 22

Padua, north-east Italy;
Saturday, 17th June 2016

Jerome had flown to Venice, and was arriving in Padua by train on this stifling, hot day. As he disembarked, he saw Stancia standing at the ticket barrier holding a poster above her head. Written on it in broad, red letters were the words, "THE HANDSOME SCOTSMAN".

"You are definitely mad." He laughed as he hugged her tightly.

Stancia grabbed his hand. "Veronique, one of my flatmates, has her car outside, but it's parked illegally, so we'll need to hurry."

They moved quickly through the oven-like heat outside the station to Veronique's two-door, little, silver car. Stancia opened the passenger door, pushed his suitcase into the back seat and clambered in after it, leaving the front passenger seat for Jerome. The introductions were warm but necessarily brief, as Veronique concentrated on moving the car away from the hidden stares of two officials in blue uniforms and dark glasses.

"Sorry about all the rush," said Veronique in her clear Dutch accent, "but those guys would take pleasure in giving me a ticket."

"No problem, and thanks for picking me up," replied Jerome.

Stancia leaned forwards and ruffled his hair. "I like the new, short haircut; it's very cool."

"Thanks." He turned around to smile at her again after their six weeks apart. "Is Padua always this hot?"

"I know," Stancia replied, wide-eyed, "it's incredible today; it's almost 100 degrees Fahrenheit and it's not even midday, though Padua's not normally this hot. So, the plan is to drop off your bag at the apartment and then go for some lunch at a nice, shady cafe. How does that sound?"

"That sounds just perfect."

***

At the apartment, Jerome met Stancia's other flatmate, Pippa, who was also from Holland. Then he and Stancia began a leisurely stroll towards the little riverside cafe she had chosen. Jerome wore a dark T-shirt and grey chinos; Stancia was more appropriately dressed for the heat in a light-yellow cotton top, white shorts and a baseball cap, with her hair in a ponytail. On the way to the cafe, they passed close to the university where she was studying.

"Would you like to take a quick look?" she asked enthusiastically.

"Absolutely," Jerome confirmed.

They wandered through the main entrance doors, along a hushed, marbled hall and out onto a quiet cloister where the sound of birds singing was the only obvious noise.

"I like this," said Jerome, gazing around. "It has a real tranquil feel to it."

"I love it," she replied, linking her arm with his as they walked slowly. "It's quieter now, as most of the students are away, but the place has an attractive feeling of solitude to it even during term time."

Jerome nodded and nudged his sunglasses back into position.

"Yes, I can just imagine the generations of scholars doing circuits here as they tried to solve the problems of the world."

"Do you know who lectured here about 400 years ago and would have walked where we are now?" she asked, looking at the side of his face.

"No, I've no idea. Who?"

"*Galileo*," she half-shouted.

"*Really?*" said Jerome as he stopped walking.

Stancia burst out laughing. "Yes, really."

"Why are you laughing?" he questioned with a broad smile.

"Because I just knew that would appeal to the nerdy side of you."

"Yes, it does," said Jerome, a reflective grin remaining on his face, "It sure does. Imagine that, Galileo teaching here."

***

The cafe was one of a number alongside a straight stretch of the Bacchiglione River, where the dark-grey waters moved sluggishly towards the Adriatic Sea. The blood-red creepers covering most of the whitewashed walls were what distinguished this building from its immediate neighbours.

"Your flatmates seem very friendly," said Jerome as he gulped down some of the water brought by the young waiter.

"Yes. I don't know whether all Dutch people are this lovely or I just happened to meet the two nicest ones from Holland, but they're great fun, and so open and honest. And they never complain or make snide comments about anyone; they're perfect flatmates really."

"They sound boring."

"No, they're not," stated Stancia, hitting his shoulder playfully with her baseball cap. Her voice changed, and became quieter and more serious, "Anyway, I'm sorry I was away for your gran's funeral. How's everyone at home now?"

"Ah, everyone's very sad, but I guess it's just the way of things." Jerome shrugged his shoulders.

"You'll miss her a lot."

"Yes, I do," Jerome answered softly, "more than I thought I would. But, then again, this sounds stupid, but I never thought she would actually die."

Stancia reached over and rested her hand on his.

"It must have been very hard for you when your dad passed away," he said.

"Yes, that was ten years ago. I remember it was a huge shock to Mum and me. And, even now, I always feel a wee bit sad, but that's natural."

"Your mum came to Gran's funeral. She was very sweet."

"Yes, she told me. She's coming over to visit me here next week."

"*Really?* Good for her."

The waiter placed a plate of grilled sardines, and bowls of assorted bread and green salad in the middle of the table, and he poured the wine carefully from the bottle Stancia had ordered, before topping up the water glasses.

"So, how are things in London? How's Chris, Ser and the lovely Mary?"

"Ah, yes, talking of perfect flatmates – the lovely Mary." Jerome gave a wry smile. "They're all the same. Chris is heading home again for the summer, so I'll have the company of the two ladies until you come in August, though, to be honest, I see very little of them. No, everything is very much the same as usual."

***

But everything was not the same as usual for Jerome; far from it. On the night he returned to London from Helga's funeral, he had retreated to the sanctuary of his bedroom, and tried to make sense of the recent tumultuous and tragic events in his life. But the swirl of his emotions was too frantic to even understand fully all that had happened, never mind start the process of accepting and dealing with it. The sudden loneliness he had experienced on the night before his meeting with Hitler returned, but in a much deeper way; looking at pictures of Helga and his family would bring no relief on this occasion. Helga's message from beyond the grave, requesting that he not try to visit her on one of his journeys back in time, blocked an idea he had been nurturing almost from the moment he had learned of her death and left him feeling isolated. He wondered if he should tell anyone else his secret. He wanted to tell someone. If Stancia had been there, he would have told her. He considered phoning her, but decided he would leave it until tomorrow. Finally, he fell asleep at around 5.00am as the dawn chorus of birds began.

The following evening, at 7.30pm, Jerome awoke. He was astonished to discover that he had slept through the entire day; which was something he had never done before. And the extraordinary thing was that he felt totally refreshed. The intense feelings of the previous evening had gone.

Jerome felt as though he had been guided through the normal emotional recuperation that he would have had to experience after such traumatic events, except it had been done while he was asleep and in a hugely accelerated way. Thus, the fear and horror of the final minutes with Hitler were relived and accepted. All his conversations were replayed, analysed and neatly filed away. His sadness and loneliness from Helga's death were still there, but it was no longer a raw memory. It was like he was viewing all these events as though they had happened a long time ago. And he decided he didn't need to phone Stancia to tell her his secret; that could wait, at least until he was with her in Padua.

In the following days, Jerome's calm frame of mind remained, but what did undergo a gradual change was the importance he attached to certain things. His family and Stancia remained hugely significant in his life, but his primary focus was increasingly his power to travel back, and, as the days went by, the desire to travel back again grew stronger and stronger.

***

"I really love this place," said Stancia as she sipped her coffee at the riverside cafe, and the river's colour seemed to take on a brighter hue in the mid-afternoon sunshine.

"What, this cafe?" enquired Jerome.

"No, Padua. It's so easy-going, welcoming and *warm*," she added, emphasising the final word. "I'd like to settle down somewhere like this. What do you think?"

Jerome closed his eyes behind his sunglasses and raised his head sleepily. "Yeah, maybe someday."

"But you're not overly enthused by the idea?"

He removed his sunglasses slowly and looked at her. "Just as long as I'm with you."

"Is the correct answer again," said Stancia grinning happily.

***

By the end of Jerome's three-day stay, he too had begun to appreciate the charms of this city and was happy to agree that Stancia's flatmates were indeed very special. He never did tell Stancia about his powers, however. He did not recall making a specific decision not to tell her, but he no longer felt the overwhelming need to share his secret, and it just seemed easier to say nothing.

On the final day of his stay, Stancia included the Basilica of St Anthony on the tourist itinerary. She guided him up the cool centre aisle of the thirteenth-century church and then beckoned him towards a small alcove at the back-left corner of the high-ceilinged building.

"I know you're not religious, but come over here; I want you to see something," she whispered.

As they approached the alcove, she tugged his hand to stop him and nodded at the short queue of people. Jerome watched as each person in turn walked up to the wall of the alcove and appeared to speak beside the wall in a fervent way; many of them using their hands to emphasise the importance of their requests. He said nothing, almost not breathing, as he watched, in growing fascination, the passion of the supplicants.

After a little while, they left the basilica.

"What were they doing?" he asked as they emerged, squinting into the bright sunshine.

"They're asking St Anthony to intervene and help them with some very special needs," Stancia explained.

"Their needs must be very important. Some of those people were on the verge of tears."

"I know," said Stancia, "I feel like a voyeur watching them, but I keep getting drawn to it. There's something really spiritual about belief like that."

"Did you ever ask for anything?" said Jerome, inclining his head at the receding church.

"From St Anthony?"

"Yeah."

"I did once."

"What did you ask for?" he queried softly.

"Oh, you'd just laugh."

"No, I wouldn't."

"Well, I think you're supposed to keep it a secret anyway."

"Like when you make a wish at your birthday party and then blow out the candles; that kind of secret?"

"You see, you are laughing."

"No, I'm not," he said, again lowering his voice.

For a few minutes, they walked closely together in comfortable silence before Stancia spoke again. "I asked him that, whenever anyone I care about goes on a journey, they will arrive safely and they will come back home safely."

Jerome glanced at her. "Is that because of what happened to your dad?"

"I guess so."

"You know…" Jerome paused. "Sometimes I think you're much too good for me."

"Will you still be saying that when I'm nagging you to do more about the house and not to be going drinking again with your pals?"

"Oh, I think I could cope with a bit of nagging," he said smiling. "And, speaking of drinking, let's have a final one at that riverside cafe. Come on."

***

Jerome wasn't sure when he first got the idea of his next journey back: maybe it was when he read Helga's letter on the train; when he awoke feeling calm and untroubled the evening after he returned to London; or maybe it was linked to him getting away from the darkness of his meeting with Hitler, when he sensed a shadow had touched his soul. But he was sure of the time when he decided to act on this idea and make his next journey back. It was that afternoon when he watched the penitents ask for help in such a passionate way and learned about Stancia's secret prayer. Jerome was going to make the journey that Helga wanted to make but never could. He was going to visit Jesus when he gave the Sermon on the Mount.

Chapter 23

London
Summer, 2016

Jerome knew that the preparations for his next journey would be extremely demanding. A new language, Aramaic – assuming it was still known – would need to be learned. He would need to arrive at an exact time approximately 2,000 years ago, when there was no way of knowing this time with any great accuracy. He knew exactly where Hitler would be on 5th August 1929, but he would not have the same information on Christ. It seemed like an almost impossible task, and yet Jerome felt confident. He was sure that if he could identify an exact spot where Christ would be, then he could travel back and intersect at the precise time he was there. Something inside told him this would happen, and he never doubted it.

Back in London, with his second-year university examinations finished successfully, Jerome began planning for the journey. One issue he confronted immediately was the practicalities of money. He would need funds for this trip, and his regular gifts from Helga would no longer be there to supplement his income. The manager at Jermaine's was then prepared to hire him as a dealer for the night games during the summer months, but there was a stipulation: "Play or work, Jerome; you can't do both." Jerome chose to work in the club at night and use the days preparing for the journey.

The first thing he researched was the location of the place where the Sermon on the Mount was actually delivered. This proved reasonably straightforward. The sermon had been given on the Mount of Beatitudes, on the shores of the Sea of Galilee, in the north of modern-day Israel. A number of independent sources he read confirmed this, and although there were other possible sites suggested, he again felt a calm certainty that he had identified the correct place. He discovered that Aramaic, the language spoken in Galilee at the time of Christ, remained a modern-day language, though its use was limited to a few small areas in the Middle East. Jerome obtained what books were available and began learning the language intensely. He read and reread the New Testament from the Bible, together with many of the numerous interpretations, seeking information on both people and places.

His preparations came to a temporary halt during the final two weeks in August, when Stancia joined him in London. As was the case in the previous year, Chris returned to London and overlapped with the end of Stancia's stay. The three friends decided to share a few beers at the local pub on Stancia's final night.

"Here's to our last year in London," said Chris, lifting a fresh bottle of beer and wiping the top before taking a drink, "Well, my last anyway."

"Any plans on where you'll go when you finish university?" asked Stancia.

"Probably back up north, although I put on about five stone every time I go back." Chris patted his midriff, which had indeed expanded over the summer.

"Will you be able to get a job there?" she asked.

"I'm not sure, but three years in London will be enough for me,

I reckon, though I might try somewhere on the continent, if we're still allowed to move there by that time. What about you guys? Have you made plans for when you finish?" Chris questioned.

Jerome and Stancia glanced briefly at each other before Jerome responded, "Well, we haven't made any definite plans yet."

"Oh, sorry," began Chris, "I put you both on the spot a bit there, didn't I? That was unintentional. OK, let me rewind that question." He pretended to reel in an imaginary fishing rod. "And I'll ask a different one. Will you come to visit me in Yorkshire if I move back?"

"Try to stop us," stated Stancia with a smile.

***

Later that night, when they lay in bed together, Stancia said softly to Jerome, "We *haven't* made any plans for when we finish next year. Is there anything you'd like to do?"

"Yes," replied Jerome without opening his eyes.

"What?"

"Marry you."

Stancia levered herself up on one elbow. "Do you mean that?"

Jerome opened his eyes wide. "'Course I do. Will you marry me?"

"Oh, would I what!" She pressed her head on his chest and clung tightly to him.

"Shall I take that as a yes?"

She leaned up until she was looking bright-eyed into his face. "Yes, Jerome Black. I'll marry you."

***

The seasonal changes from summer to autumn to winter were largely lost on Jerome. He continued studying diligently and occasionally earning money from dealing cards, but his preparations for the journey were taking up increasing amounts of his time. He learned from his father that, in her will, Helga had left him £10,000. While he felt some level of guilt that he had been left much more than his siblings, he was still delighted, as this would more than cover the costs of his journey. Indeed, he wondered if that was the specific reason why she had left the money to him.

By early November, most of the preparatory work was complete, with the exception of the language. He felt he had reached a competent level of reading and writing Aramaic, but he had no experience of speaking it. He checked YouTube and, to his surprise, discovered there were tutorials in Aramaic, and while these proved useful, he also wanted to practice real-time dialogue. So, through an internet advertisement, Jerome arranged to have reciprocal sessions on an audio link talking to an Aramaic speaker who wanted to learn English. At first, he found the process slow and unsatisfactory, but he soon felt comfortable as the second tongue of both men improved. Indeed, so successful did he find it that he engaged two additional Aramaic speakers to cram in more practice ahead of his departure for Israel, planned for April 2017.

***

14th December 2016

Ser was enthusiastically outlining her idea for the evening when Jerome joined them. They had agreed the previous week that the four flatmates would have this night as their Christmas night out, although Jerome had given it little thought beyond agreeing to the date. The night was to begin with a bottle of inexpensive champagne – which, surprisingly, had survived in the house for almost a year – before moving to Sonny's restaurant. The planned ending was Kent's pub, which had the added attraction of being close to home; taxis were usually difficult to get at that time of the year and were never cheap.

The champagne helped prompt one of the not-infrequent exchanges between Chris and Mary. Chris had emerged from his room, wearing a pair of mirrored sunglasses.

"My God! Why are you wearing those?" enquired Mary almost immediately.

"Cos, they make me look cool," replied Chris, mimicking a high five.

"No, actually, Chris, they make you look like a perv," said Mary, sounding sympathetic.

"Yes, but a cool perv."

Mary shook her head in apparent exasperation.

"Don't you find me stunningly attractive?" he asked.

"You'd need to lose a bit of weight before anyone would find you stunningly attractive, Chris," she continued.

"Ouch, that's harsh, Mary. Did you ever think of taking a happy pill, something that might make you pleasant for an hour or so?"

"Or you could get a brand-new, fancy car," said Mary, "that always makes men far more attractive, doesn't it, Ser?" She placed her empty glass on the mantelpiece and, smiling, clapped her hands together briskly. "Come on, let's hit the town."

***

Sonny's pizza restaurant was crowded, noisy and great fun. All the Italian staff wore blue-and-black uniforms with colour-clashing, red-and-white striped aprons of a soft, silk-like material that was too flimsy to be functional.

"At least they match the table cloth," joked Mary as the atmosphere, alcohol and banter had the desired beneficial effect on the group.

"*You know what?*" Chris questioned loudly as they sipped

their second glass of sambuca at the end of the meal, "I wonder who decided clockwise was that direction and anticlockwise this direction?" He traced unsteady arcs in the air.

"What does it matter?" asked Ser, smirking.

"Well, if he'd decided it was the other way round, all our clocks would now be going backwards." Chris finished his drink and then continued. "And I wonder why the first guy who drew a map decided north was up. Just think, if he'd decided it was down, then Australia would be on top of the world, except it would be upside down. If you see what I mean." His voice trailed off.

"Whatever," said Mary, as she motioned for the bill to bring Chris's latest flight of fancy to an end.

Plans were changed; a nearby wine bar seemed a more attractive option than Kent's pub. After they had shared a bottle of rosé wine and one of white, Ser's boyfriend arrived, and the two of them departed for Leicester Square. Jerome, Chris and Mary stayed to drink a final bottle of white wine and then telephoned for a taxi.

"What's keeping Chris?" asked Mary, looking at Jerome across the empty glasses on the table.

"I'll go check. He's been in there a while."

Jerome walked wearily to the toilets and, on pushing open the brown half-doors, went in. The place looked empty.

"CHRIS, ARE YOU IN HERE?" he shouted over the sound from the piped music. The door to one of the cubicles was shut. "Chris?" said Jerome, knocking on the door, but he got no reply. Going into the adjoining cubicle, he stood on the toilet seat and looked over to see Chris lying slumped on the floor. "OH, FUCK ME! CHRIS, CAN YOU HEAR ME?" Jerome yelled anxiously as he began clambering over the side of the cubicle. Kneeling beside him, Jerome turned Chris's head to reveal blood trickling from a small cut on his left temple.

Chris opened his eyes drowsily. "Sorry, buddy, I must have fallen," he slurred.

"Here, let's try to get you standing." Gently and with difficulty, Jerome helped him to his feet. "Can you walk?"

"Not very well, buddy. I think the bastards must have amputated my legs."

"What did you have, Chris?"

"Too much, I think."

"No, what did you have in here, Chris?" There was an unmistakable note of urgency in Jerome's voice.

"A few lines." The voice was soft and apologetic.

"How many?"

"Two, I think; I'm not sure, bud."

Jerome helped him walk back to the table.

"What on earth happened to him?" asked Mary with alarm.

"He fell," said Jerome as Chris rested against his shoulder.

"Our taxi's here," said Mary.

"Good, it can take us to the hospital," said Jerome.

Mary nodded as Chris's mumbled objections were ignored.

***

The accident-and-emergency unit was crowded with other casualties of the night; all, it appeared, drink and drugs related. There was an air of weary regret about the place. For a while, Chris sat propped between Mary and Jerome, speaking occasionally but usually incoherently. Then he stopped and slumped against Mary. Jerome rushed to the white-coated, young doctor standing at the enquiry desk.

"This guy's taken drugs, and I think he's just lost consciousness." Jerome pointed urgently to where Mary was propping up Chris's slumped form.

At first, the doctor did not seem particularly concerned.

"*He's just lost consciousness after taking an overdose,*" ranted Jerome.

A few minutes later, Chris was in intensive care.

For almost three hours, Jerome and Mary waited. They talked little, with tiredness and concern weighing on them both. Jerome considered what would happen if he were to go back in time to the beginning of the evening, but he knew it would make no difference. This was a real event in real time and it could not be changed; the outcome was out of his hands. They were both sipping coffee from polystyrene cups when another, older doctor came through the door.

"Your friend's an extremely lucky man; he's going to be OK." The rest of his warning about drugs was greeted with relieved and sympathetic nods.

When he had finished, Jerome put out his hand. At first, the doctor looked unsure and then he shook it.

"Thank you," said Jerome.

***

At just after 4.00am, Jerome and Mary arrived back at the house. He poured them each a drink in the living room.

"Well, that was an eventful night," he said softly.

"Scary," replied Mary. "Why the hell does he do that? It's so stupid. Is it because he's a bit fat? Is that it, do you think?"

Jerome shook his head.

"I'm sorry I made that comment earlier on about him being overweight. Sometimes I just blurt out things without thinking. I don't mean it most of the time." She glanced apologetically at Jerome.

"Mary, I don't know why he took drugs tonight, but I'm certain it wasn't anything you said."

"Good; I hope so." She leaned back in the armchair and sipped from her vodka and Coke. "How are you and Stancia getting on these days?"

"Fine," said Jerome.

"I haven't seen her for a while, and you haven't been up in Manchester lately, have you?"

"No, I've had some studying to catch up on."

"You wanna watch that." Mary took a cigarette and offered the packet to Jerome, who hesitated before taking one. "You have to work at long-distance romances; I know," she confirmed.

"Why? Were you ever involved in one?"

She lit her cigarette and then his before replying. "Yes, with a guy from Sheffield. I met him when he was working here in London. Then he went back and..." She shrugged her shoulders. "He used to travel down every weekend. It was still great, better in some ways, because he was so eager to see me every time. It made me feel fantastic."

"But it didn't work out."

"No." Mary shook her head. "He started missing weekends, and then I probably became a bit suspicious and too narky. Things were said that you can't really come back from. Anyway, it was a couple of years ago and I'm well over it now."

After one further drink, they climbed the stairs. Outside Mary's bedroom door, they both stopped. She reached out and touched one of his hands, gently holding the tips of his fingers.

"Would you mind staying with me tonight? I still feel a bit upset," she said softly, her head bowed.

Jerome looked at her, his eyes tired though still alert. "I'm not sure that would be a good idea," he replied.

"I just want someone to hold me," she said tenderly. Mary opened the door to her room and delicately released Jerome's hand. As she walked into her bedroom, he followed her.

***

He awoke the next morning with Mary nestling against him, her long hair lying across his chest. He could feel the slimness of her body against him, which accentuated the fullness of her breasts. Opening her eyes dreamily, she gazed up as he traced a finger down from her forehead to her neck. He kissed her softly then; as she responded, with increasing eagerness, Jerome pushed aside the bedclothes before moving on top of her. Mary's eyes closed again as her head moved rhythmically from side to side with the pleasure of the moment.

***

Thirty-six hours later, as Jerome went to collect Chris from the hospital, he remained racked with guilt. "You stupid fucking idiot," he half-whispered to himself as he stood in the hospital entrance, waiting for his friend to reappear. The comment could have applied to Chris's behaviour, but it was only his own he had in mind. His feeling of alarm that Stancia might find out was beginning to ease as he recalled Mary's words when he left her room that morning: *"It was lovely, but one time only. It's not to be repeated."* Just then, he felt hugely relieved that *she* had said that, and he was also absolutely certain it would never happen again.

Chris emerged from the elevator and, with a sheepish grin, shuffled towards his friend.

Jerome gave him a reassuring smile and hugged him. "How do you feel?" he asked.

"Very delicate and a bit stupid," answered Chris.

"Well, let's focus on the delicate. Do you want me to carry that bag?" Jerome pointed to a large, dark-green, plastic bag that Chris held tightly round the neck.

"No, it's OK thanks. These are my medications, prescriptions and various support telephone numbers. It's funny, you go in with a drug overdose and you emerge with enough tablets to open a bloody chemist."

"Let's get you home," replied Jerome with a smile, delighted to see his friend back again.

***

That evening, the four flatmates sat drinking coffee and treading sensitively around the events of their evening out. For Chris and Ser, this meant being sensitive about his overdose, but there was an additional unmentioned issue to avoid for the other two. By 10.00pm, Mary and Ser had both gone out.

"Let's go and have a pint, bud," said Chris.

"Jesus, Chris, is that wise?" queried Jerome.

"Yes, just two pints. It'll be fine. It'll help me sleep."

"Are you sure?"

"Yes, I don't fancy going full cold turkey tonight."

In the pub, Chris sipped his pint uncharacteristically slowly, though he still seemed to savour its effect. "Oh, that's better. I feel more human now." He looked down at the top of his drink. "Listen, bud, thanks a million for the other night. I think you saved me, though, to be honest, my recollection of events is not laser sharp."

"No problem; you'd have done the same for me," offered Jerome.

"Well, I'd have tried. But I don't reckon I could have climbed over the wall of the cubicle. It would have collapsed under my weight." He smiled at his friend. "I don't really want to go over what I said before I passed out, but did I say anything nasty to anyone? Like to Mary?"

"No." Jerome shook his head reassuringly. "You said nothing offensive. You did talk rubbish at times, but, honestly, nothing remotely nasty."

"Good, I'm relieved. Cos, I thought Mary was oddly quiet tonight, and she seemed to be avoiding looking at me, so I was just wondering."

"No, she got a fright that's all."

"Are you sure that's all?"

For a few moments, Jerome did not reply. Then he exhaled and looked at Chris with a strained expression. "When Mary and I got back that night, we had a couple more drinks and then ended up in bed."

"Oh!" Chris rubbed his index finger across the bottom of his chin. "Well, that probably explains why she was a bit odd, all right." He looked at Jerome's pained countenance. "So that definitely means I didn't say anything wrong, so I'm in the clear."

Jerome half-smiled. "I feel so guilty, Chris. How could I be so fucking stupid?"

Chris nodded as though empathising with his friend and then said, "Hold on a second. I'm recovering from a drugs overdose, and you're shagging too many women and you want me to feel sorry for you. How the fuck did that happen?" He laughed and for the first time in two days his eyes sparkled.

"I know, I know," said Jerome, unable to share his friend's joviality. "I just feel so bloody guilty."

"Look, bud, you made a mistake. We all do. You're feeling guilty now, and maybe that's your punishment, but just let it go."

"Yes, thanks. That sounds like good advice. Hey, how come you've got so much wisdom after a drug overdose?"

"Maybe it's the drugs that give me the wisdom."

"I doubt it."

"Yes, I doubt it too. Oh, and by the way, next time you see Mary, would you put in a good word for me?" Chris's eyes continued to shine.

Chapter 24

Israel;
Tuesday, 16th May 2017

Ben Gurion airport was the first part of Israel Jerome saw. Named after the first prime minister of that country, it is situated twenty kilometres south-east of Tel Aviv on Israel's Mediterranean coast. The arrivals hall – with its striking, light-grey pillars towering to the high, lighted ceiling – was crowded and noisy, but it had a clean and efficient aspect to it, without any obvious overtones of the heavy security Jerome had expected.

Before boarding his El Al flight from London Heathrow that morning, the security had been thorough but not aggressive. They had checked carefully all the paperwork relating to the oxygen dispenser, which was to be carried in the hold. Lufthansa had done the same when he flew to Nuremburg. The only uncomfortable question was asked by the uniformed lady with the sympathetic smile: why was he going for just three days? Ultimately, his hastily made-up answer that he only had three days holiday available seemed to satisfy her.

It was just after 3.00pm on this warm afternoon. The car-hire attendant had been helpful, if slightly pushy, trying unsuccessfully to convince Jerome to upgrade the car. He was by then driving his small, blue automatic along Highway One towards Tel Aviv. Initially, he had considered going with one of the many tours, travelling "in luxury on air-conditioned deluxe coaches" as many of the advertisements trumpeted. After speaking to the Israeli tourist board, however, he had been reassured that travelling to the north-eastern part of the country in a hired car would not require any special security clearance.

It took just over thirty minutes, through heavy afternoon traffic, to reach the David Intercontinental Hotel. He duly completed a detailed form at the hotel reception, and was given the card for room 8003.

"It has a stunning view of the Mediterranean," the young man informed him cheerily, in what sounded like a nasal, New York accent.

Jerome went to his room, where he felt tired and lay down on top of the pristine, white duvet, intending to rest briefly. During the early months of 2017, he had been working intensively, balancing preparations for the journey with his university studies, while still maintaining his relationship with Stancia. His end-of-year examinations were finished, and, while his university work did not seem pointless, it had undoubtedly become much less important to him as the journey became his primary and passionate focus. When he was with Stancia, he was acutely aware of this huge part of his life that she knew nothing about, which he was keeping secret from her. Jerome often wondered whether she had any suspicion about what he was doing. He recalled her prayer to St Anthony in Padua to bring home safely any loved one who was travelling. *Could she have an inkling of what I'm doing?* he pondered, but he knew that was impossible.

He awoke in darkness, slightly disorientated. Gradually, he remembered where he was and looked at his watch to confirm it was 8.15pm, local time. He gazed down from the large, single window at the lights coming from the shops and traffic directly below and the more distant, glistening lights from the beach beyond. The steady hum of traffic, interspersed with agitated car horns, could be heard clearly.

Having showered and changed quickly, Jerome ventured eagerly into the Tel Aviv evening. It was an assault on his senses. Apart from the bright lights and cacophony of noise, magnified many times once he was at ground level, it was the differences of the people that first struck him. They were in Western business suits, in traditional Arab dress and in casual summer clothes, all jostling for space along the crowded pavements. While the predominant appearance of the people was dark-haired, olive-skinned Mediterranean, there were representatives of every other ethnic group known to Jerome. The cosmopolitan buzz of the city surprised and attracted him.

He had two purchases to make, and his plan was to get them first and then eat. However, as he walked down one of the streets jammed with small, lively restaurants, the warm wafts from cooking food became increasingly enticing. He was approached by an elderly man extolling the virtues of the wonderful food inside his Lebanese restaurant. The man had big, dark-brown eyes and luxuriant, white hair with a small, red cap perched neatly on the crown of his head. But it was his gentle, slightly sly smile and the enthusiasm in his voice that most amused Jerome and encouraged him to go inside.

He sat at a table close to an open window, overlooking the hot, busy street, ordered the *Musakhan* dish and thought of home.

***

During the previous three weeks, Jerome had spent increasing amounts of time in his detailed planning. So much so that he had experienced little contact with anyone else, as his preparations took precedence over everything else, even studying for his examinations. He realised his single-minded focus on the journey had become almost obsessive, but he felt it was not unreasonable for something as momentous as this. He hadn't seen Stancia during this period, which was their longest time apart since the previous summer when she had been in Padua. But she would be visiting him in London this coming weekend, and he was determined to make a fuss in case his recent distracted behaviour had created a false impression of coolness towards her.

***

For a few moments, as he ate his spicy chicken casserole, Jerome considered the issue of when he would tell Stancia about his incredible gift, but, as usual, he came to no definite decision.

His hunger sated, he went back outside to explore the hectic market stalls where the smell of well-cooked food, strong cigarette smoke and jasmine from the trees lining the street wafted pleasantly on the warm evening breeze. Occasionally, he engaged some of the more persistent hawkers in friendly banter, but bought nothing before finally reaching a corner stall that had a wide variety of men's shoes stacked on one side and ladies' on the other. Pointing to a pair of light-brown, leather sandals, he examined them briefly for size, bought them and asked that they be placed in a light plastic bag, rather than the large shoe box the young assistant produced.

For his final purchase, Jerome decided to leave the increasingly humid and frenetic market, and entered one of the nearby shopping malls. Many of the shops in this multi-storey building were deserted, and he took the opportunity to stroll around the air-conditioned floors. The clothes shop he found on the top floor had a small sign in Arabic, Hebrew and English proclaiming, "Best

Jordanian clothes for every occasion". The sign was lit subtly with a soft, candle-shaped light, and it was probably this as much as the merchandise in the window that enticed Jerome inside.

"Yes, sir, we have an excellent selection of *dishdashas*," the dapper assistant replied to Jerome's enquiry as, with his hands, he indicated smoothly a rack containing a number of the long-sleeved, one-piece garments.

"I'm looking for something more basic," said Jerome, as he saw the man prepare to select a navy-blue one with intricate thread designs around the neck.

"We have some in beautiful white cotton, which are perfect for the hot weather," the assistant said, stroking his moustache. Seeing Jerome's positive expression, he removed a garment from the rack and placed it, with exaggerated care, on top of the counter, so it could be better appreciated.

Jerome rubbed the fabric between his finger and thumb before nodding. "That's fine. How much?"

"Let me see." The assistant looked around, as though he had lost something. "We also have some excellent headwear, sir, which would match this very well. May I show you?"

"No, thanks," answered Jerome with a smile.

The assistant went through a practised routine of checking the labels and consulting a small brochure on the counter before confirming, "For that particular one, sir, it's $35."

"OK, I'll take it," replied Jerome immediately. Noticing the fleeting surprise on the salesman's previously impenetrable face, Jerome grinned. "You thought I was going to haggle, didn't you?" The grin broadened. "The garment looks good and the price seems fair, so $35 is OK."

If there had been any surprise, it was well buried by then. "Oh absolutely, sir, the cloth is top quality, and this is our sale price." He too was grinning. He reached for a thin, black, cord-like belt behind him, saying, "And, please, this will complement the *dishdasha*." He raised his hands in a pre-emptive gentle admonition of Jerome. "Sir, it is all in the price of $35."

Jerome smiled warmly as the salesman carefully wrapped the items.

"Are you sure you would not be interested in headwear?" the assistant enquired again, and, as if by magic, a selection of headwear appeared on top of the glass counter.

Jerome's momentary hesitation proved decisive, and he left the shop subsequently with three items, having come in for one. He had not intended to wear anything on his head, as he considered it would look out of place for the time. But whether it was a genuine change of mind or whether he was justifying the purchase, Jerome decided that wearing it might make him look more distinguished and thereby help achieve his goal of meeting Christ.

***

Once back in his room, he gazed out enviously at the flickering lights from the barbecues and parties on the beach. He liked this city, but it was necessary to get back to the business of his trip. Jerome tried on the new clothes. The *dishdasha* felt cool and looked surprisingly elegant. He struggled a few times with the headwear – laughing out loud at his initial, clumsy efforts – before replicating the salesman's instructions successfully. Everything was then neatly packed for the next day, before he sent Stancia and his mother further little-white-lie texts of no consequence, supposedly from his house in London.

Sleep did not come easily to Jerome that night. He blamed it on dozing too long earlier in the evening, but he was also aware of feeling a mounting excitement. His thoughts turned briefly to the waitress in the cafe in Nuremberg and her comment that he had changed in some way. Jerome had posed this question to himself a number of times in the subsequent months. He remained convinced that he had not changed physically, at least visibly. But he had lived longer than his twenty-years-and-nine-months existence in normal time. Jerome accepted that but did not dwell on its consequences. Eventually, he did drop off to the second repetition of the hourly news headlines on CNN.

***

The next morning, he paid his bill, confirmed his reservation for Thursday, declined politely the porter's offer of assistance with his suitcase, got in his hire car and drove out of Tel Aviv, heading north on Highway Two. Jerome decided to follow the coast road towards the city of Haifa and, from there, head east to the town of Tiberias, on the west bank of the Sea of Galilee. He would then journey the last fifteen kilometres to his ultimate destination, the Mount of Beatitudes, where Jesus delivered his Sermon on the Mount.

Traffic going north was busy but moved steadily. The good quality of the motorway impressed Jerome, though it did not surprise him. He guessed that any country in a semi-permanent state of war would place a high premium on having a road system capable of moving soldiers and machinery efficiently and effectively. When he was close to Haifa, he pulled in at a lay-by where one solitary wind turbine stood like a steel sentinel, looking out over the length of the Mediterranean to Gibraltar and beyond. Sipping water from the bottle he had taken from the hotel minibar, he gazed at the turquoise sea, which lay about fifty metres below him.

The memory of the meeting with Hitler had remained with Jerome. The experience had been deeply unsettling at the time. He recalled seeming to undergo a remarkable, calm acceptance of the events just a few days afterwards, but in his subsequent quieter moments, he realised it had continued to disturb him much more then he had expected. The almost tangible feeling of having been close to, and perhaps infected by, a heart of darkness had not disappeared with the passing of time. Jerome also realised how lucky he had been to be able to meet, and, indeed, confront and anger Hitler, and yet survive, unlike so many millions of others who had not sought to challenge him in any way and yet had perished. But if visiting Hitler had cast this shadow, then perhaps making this journey – the journey that Helga would have wanted – could help lift it in some way.

By then, it was almost 1.00pm, and the sun appeared to be close to its zenith. Shielding his eyes, Jerome looked up at the three massive, white arms of the turbine as they whooshed through the seemingly still air, like some modern-day giant waiting for its Don Quixote. *Father, Son and Holy Spirit?* he thought. *Maybe it's an omen.*

***

Tiberias is an old town and it has remained very popular with tourists throughout the centuries. He had booked into the Caesar Resort Hotel, which was another large and, he hoped, anonymous one.

The young woman at reception told him that his room would not be ready for about an hour. "But you are free to use our swimming pool. It is totally new, has three diving boards at different heights, and is wonderfully relaxing to swim in," she enthused.

Jerome was keen to continue his journey and so declined the offer courteously.

He then drove the final fifteen kilometres to the Mount of Beatitudes, on the north-west coast of the Sea of Galilee. As in Nuremburg, he wanted to reconnoitre the area before the actual journey, which would be tomorrow. He left the car in a small, grassy car park, and walked the short distance to the base of the mount.

"Hello." The greeting came from an elderly lady sitting on a bench close by. She was staring directly in front of her, and Jerome thought initially that she was blind. She wore a dark (not quite black) dress; had her hair in a tight bun, which Jerome thought was old-fashioned even for an elderly person; and was leaning on a brown walking stick.

"Hello," he replied warmly.

"I'm here with my grandson. He was determined to walk to the top, but I wouldn't be able to do that, so I've decided to wait here for him. My name is Angelic. What's yours, if you don't mind me asking?"

"Jerome." He thought Angelic was a young name for an old person.

"Are you travelling on your own, Jerome?" She was speaking English, but the accent suggested it was not her mother tongue.

"Yes." He relaxed as he sat down beside her. "I'm here on my own."

"Oh, I used to travel a lot on my own when I was your age, all over Europe. I felt very brave at the time. My father didn't like it, mind you; he used to say it was scandalous, but I loved it. Do you like travelling on your own?" Her voice was bright and unhurried.

"I don't mind. To be honest, I would prefer being with friends, good friends, but I have to make this journey alone." He was surprised by his own openness.

The old lady kept smiling peacefully. "Yes, being on your own can be, well, lonely at times, but I made many friends on my travels. I was a vivacious girl; at least, that's what they used to say about me. It's not a word you hear much these days. I'm not sure if being vivacious would be considered good or bad."

"It would be good."

For the first time, she looked directly at him. "Thank you." She blushed slightly. "Are you here to talk to Jesus?" She noticed the subtle tightening on his face and added quickly, "Oh, I don't mean to pry or anything; it's just that most people come here hoping to get closer to Jesus in some way."

"Yes, I'm hoping to speak directly to him," said Jerome. "Tomorrow," he added without quite knowing why.

"Well, I'm quite sure he would much prefer to talk to a young man like you than listen to an old person prattling on about her youth and how things were always better when she was young. They weren't you know." She turned again to him for emphasis. "Things are much better now. The world was a more dangerous and much darker place when I was growing up. Never believe old people who tell you different." She smiled again. "Anyway, I'm delaying you I'm sure."

Jerome stood up slowly, and then turned to her and offered his hand, which she took and held. "It was good meeting you," he said.

Still holding his hand, she looked up into his face. "When you talk to Jesus tomorrow, ask him to remember me, please."

"I will," he replied gently.

***

Jerome walked easily up the gentle lower slopes of the Mount of Beatitudes. To his left, he could see the blue, fresh waters of the inland Sea of Galilee, which sits at 200 metres below sea level. At various points around him were pilgrims making their journeys to or from the summit. He knew it was believed that Jesus gave his famous Sermon on the Mount somewhere on these lower slopes, and Jerome was looking for a possible site just then, hoping to see some obvious natural amphitheatre. In truth, the gradient was so slight that many places could have served that purpose.

He continued steadily to the summit, where there was a modern visitors' centre and a Franciscan church. The visitors' centre was large and crowded with pilgrims; Jerome did not like it. The church seemed to better reflect the quiet dignity he felt was appropriate for this place. Outside the church, a group of about twenty people – South Americans, he thought – were singing gently but with uninhibited passion. Jerome stopped to watch them, his face open and appreciative of the chance to witness their faith.

Going into the church, he sat down and made a wish rather than a prayer. "God, if you exist, help me on this journey tomorrow." He recalled Helga's question before his journey to Hitler: *"Could you die, Jemi?"* she had asked with concern. At the time, he had answered truthfully, saying that he had no intention of testing it, although now that response seemed almost flippant. Since then, he had wondered sometimes what would have happened had he been hanged before the expiration of the journey time saved him. He accepted that he would probably have died, but felt certain he would have returned to normal time physically unharmed. Any other outcome would have changed history, and that was contrary to the rules. Jerome had come to consider these rules of time travel to be as immutable as gravity or any of the other laws that govern everything else in the universe.

Outside, standing on the porch and leaning on the low, metal railing, he looked across the four-mile-long Plain of Gennesaret to the sea beyond. It was an ideal setting for contemplation. Jerome thought of Helga writing her final letter to him. She didn't want to visit anyone from her past because of the possible sadness it would bring. He understood that and felt it made her desire to visit Jesus all the more poignant. He would love to talk to her just then and had sometimes toyed fleetingly with the idea of travelling back to visit her, but she had requested specifically that he not do that, and he would never go against her wishes. Jerome wondered about his unusual encounter with Angelic at the base of the mountain. Was it a complete coincidence that, at a time when he wanted so much to talk to Helga, this kind, elderly lady had crossed his path? He thought again about the timing of Helga's death. It had been around 8:30am when she passed away. That would have been 9.30am in Nuremberg. So Helga had died at virtually the exact moment he had journeyed back to meet Hitler. Could that be a coincidence? Not for the first time, he wondered if someone or something was guiding him towards an unknown destiny. He remembered experiencing a similar thought when he awoke on the evening after Helga's funeral feeling remarkably calm, almost serene. How had that happened? But, then, how did any of this happen? Jerome resolved that, when this journey was over, he would no longer keep his remarkable gift a secret. Whether he had attained these powers randomly or they had been bestowed on him for a purpose, they should not remain a secret.

With his preparations almost over, Jerome began to think of the person he would be meeting tomorrow: the man who claimed to be God or, at least, about whom that claim had been made by others. What will he really be like? What will he say? What will he think of Jerome's story? Jerome no longer felt any doubt that he would meet Jesus.

***

Back at the hotel, he was given his room card by the same young woman on reception.

"We have a wonderful swimming pool, you know," she began as Jerome started smiling. "It has three diving boards, each of a different height."

"You don't remember me, do you?" he asked.

"Yes?" This was said more as a question than an affirmation.

"You told me about the pool earlier this afternoon."

"Ah, yes, sir. Would you like to try it? It is due to close in about ten minutes, but if you like, I can ask the attendant to keep it open for longer."

Jerome was about to shake his head, but instead said, "Yes, thank you very much. I'd appreciate that."

***

At 7.15am the following day, Jerome, dressed self-consciously in his Arabian clothes, was standing outside the back of the Franciscan church. The early morning sun was rising above the sea to the east, but it was still too low to be hot. Insects were beginning to stir, but it was quiet, peaceful even, and – most importantly – there was no one around.

He removed the oxygen container stealthily from the same soft rucksack he had used in Nuremberg. Hitler and Germany seemed a long time ago to Jerome suddenly; like another age. He made a final check to ensure he was alone before pulling on the mask and inhaling the pure oxygen.

He was still on top of the hill, the same hill, except there were no buildings any longer. He noticed that the ground was wet in places. The sun had moved; it was high in the sky and, if anything, had started down its westward arc. The air was hot and, here on top of the hill, breezy. Insects, perhaps the ancient ancestors of the ones Jerome had left behind, were confirming their existence by flight and sound. Down below, in the valley to the east, Jerome could make out groups of people. The rest of the hill appeared deserted and, being anxious not to draw any unnecessary attention, he began to make his way down to join them.

Chapter 25

Jerome stood in the valley, looking up at the people occupying the hillside. He had expected tens of thousands, but, in total, the crowd numbered no more than 2,000. It was densest at a place about fifty metres above him, where a clearing had been made on a flat, rocky spot by a number of men who had formed a circle. The sun was behind the mountain and made viewing difficult, though, by shading his eyes, Jerome could make out that the circle remained empty.

Around him, people – mostly men – stood together in small groups, talking quietly. Any noise came from the children playing and the women minding them. The women wore long-sleeved garments, typically wider than the men's, in an assortment of bright colours. The men all wore white, although of different shades, each probably reflecting the age of the garment rather than the type of cloth. Most of the people were smaller in stature than Jerome had anticipated.

Guardedly, he walked among the groups, partly to avoid any

possible suspicion that might be aroused by him standing on his own, and partly to hear the conversations. They spoke more rapidly and at a higher pitch than the people he had been engaging with back in normal time. But, even though there were some words that were new to him, he was delighted that he could understand most of what was being said. They seemed to be mostly farming people, and their talk about the weather and the price of livestock and grain reflected this. He overheard few talking about Jesus.

A crowd was gathered around what appeared to be a small market at the base of the mountain. On reaching it, Jerome saw merchandise, mainly clothes and jewellery, spread out enticingly on the ground. The sellers were sitting passively, watching their prospective customers examine the goods. Further on, there was food for sale: bread in large, wicker baskets; and fruit – grapes, oranges and pears – much of which looked overripe.

A woman was selling drinks, pouring milk and a clear liquid from two large, earthenware jugs. Jerome was surprised that all of the people buying seemed to have their own little cups. She was speaking softly in a language he did not understand while, behind her, a child struggled to hold the ropes tethering three goats. It wasn't clear if they were there to provide the milk or for some other purpose.

At the end of the market, Jerome came across a man hunkered down behind a makeshift stove, comprised of a thin, flat, circular stone that was balanced on three other stones, each the size of a man's fist. A fire was burning underneath the flat one. With his right hand, the man was taking small pieces of raw meat from a cloth on the ground, and placing them on the stone. Regularly, he would turn the pieces, using only the fingers of his right hand. He used his left hand to flick away the flies from the raw meat, rekindle and reorganise the fire, and to open the leaves that were used to hold the cooked meat when purchased.

The smoke from his fire drifted towards a small knot of fifteen to twenty people, standing about 300 metres away. As Jerome approached them, he noticed there was no one else anywhere near the group; they appeared isolated. Strangely, they seemed to be taking it in turns to walk clockwise around the group; when one person completed a circuit, another would start. It reminded him of the emperor penguins in Antarctica huddling together and taking it in turns to shuffle around the group in their attempts to stay warm. About fifteen metres from the group, some children were playing, and although they appeared oblivious to the adults, Jerome noticed it was as though an imaginary circle had been drawn, and the children knew not to go outside its circumference. He turned around and walked back, as a woman from the market screamed at her own child for wandering in the direction of the isolated group. Jerome was puzzled by this strange group of apparent outcasts.

Gradually, and almost imperceptibly, the crowd around him began to move up to the base of the mount. Jerome had heard no signal, but, as is often the way with crowds, the information had been picked up and conveyed with no obvious communication.

Although it was called a mountain, in reality, it was more of a large hill that stood around 200 metres high. The sun was sinking to the west behind it by then, allowing the green and brown hues of the hillside to be seen more easily. As Jerome ascended the lower slopes quickly, he could see, squinting into the sinking sun, that the circle above him was occupied by an elderly man, and he wondered if his entrance had been the prompt that caused the crowd to move. He kept climbing. The people around him, who were only men, were sometimes pushing and sometimes helping each other as they sought to get suitable vantage points, both to see and, more importantly, to hear. Jerome kept moving forwards, making his way through increasing resistance until he stood about thirty metres below and to the left of the figure.

"Have you heard Jesus speak before?" The question was asked

in a friendly tone by one of the two men standing very close to Jerome's left shoulder.

"No, I haven't. Have you?" replied Jerome.

"Yes, he's very good. Well, he's different." He pointed to the man behind him. "Baltha here prefers the preaching of John the Baptist, don't you, eh?" He turned to his friend. "His is more fire-in-the-belly stuff."

Baltha was more circumspect. "I like listening to them both."

"But you said Jesus was too full of himself," the first man continued.

Baltha winced slightly. "I said he was a bit too clever at times, that's all." He reached his hand across to Jerome. "As you now know, my name is Baltha, and this talkative one…" he pointed the thumb of the hand shaking Jerome's, "he's Gideon."

"My name is Jerome." He smiled warmly as he shook Gideon by the hand.

"Where are you from, brother?" asked Baltha. "Your skin suggests a colder place than here."

"Yes, I'm from a place far away, at the western end of the empire." He noticed the narrowing of Baltha's dark eyes and added quickly, "I've heard wonderful things about Jesus; his reputation has travelled far."

Their nodding agreement didn't disguise the element of suspicion the men seemed to have come to feel as they turned slowly away. Jerome decided to stay, though he was not going to engage with them further. At this point, he noticed that there were many people crowding above as well as below the circle.

After a few more minutes, the elderly man walked carefully towards the front of the circle. Unclasping his hands slowly, he raised them above his head in a gesture calling for silence. The crowd responded, and a murmur disappeared gently down the hill. Only the women and children at the bottom continued their activities, but they were too far away to cause any disturbance.

The elderly man began, "My brothers and sisters, you are all most welcome here today. We are here to listen to the words of Jesus, whom many of you already know. His message is one of love, not hatred or violence." He paused and, though thirty metres away, Jerome could make out the benign smile on his face as he continued his brief welcome to the crowd. He ended by asking them to sit down, so that more people would be able to see and hear, but only those very close to the circle chose to obey him. Finally, the white-haired man gave a deferential bow to the crowd, turned and left the circle.

Jerome could feel his heart beating faster than normal, and his mouth was uncomfortably dry. Inching forwards, he craned his neck, scanning the circle and the men surrounding it. He felt a gentle touch on his left arm.

"Are you well, brother?" It was Baltha.

"Yes, yes, I'm fine, thank you," replied Jerome, patting him on the shoulder in appreciation for his concern.

Jerome looked back to see a man, who was taller and slimmer than most of the others, enter from the back of the circle. He had brown, wavy hair down to his shoulders. His face appeared dark, although Jerome was still too far away to get a good view of his features. He was dressed in the same white *dishdasha* as the other men, although his had what appeared to be yellow squares just below both shoulders, and he was speaking to the men on his immediate right. Jerome was certain this was Jesus. He could not hear what was being said, but he noticed that Jesus appeared animated, almost agitated. Jerome watched intently.

At first, Jesus didn't move. He stood quite still at the rear of the circle. His head was held high, and he appeared to be gazing out over the heads of the people, towards the hill at the opposite end of the valley. The crowd remained quiet with just the laughter of children in the distance and the hypnotic noise of the crickets disturbing the silence. He walked forwards, with both arms hanging loosely at his sides. There was a soft, late-afternoon breeze that billowed his garment gently and caused his hair to move in front of his face. With a grace that was somewhat at odds with his earlier animation, he sat down so that his left arm was resting on a small rock and scanned the crowd near him slowly, with what appeared to Jerome to be an expressionless face. He said nothing and as the silence deepened so too did the anticipation. Then, lifting his right hand unhurriedly, he began: "Blessed are those who are low in spirit, for our Father awaits them in heaven. Blessed are those who seek justice, for they shall receive it. Blessed are those who forgive their enemies, for they shall have their sins wiped away."

Jerome blinked a number of times to clear his eyes, as he was briefly overcome by the emotion of the moment. He was listening to Jesus Christ delivering the actual Sermon on the Mount.

Jesus continued. His voice was soft and slightly high-pitched, and though Jerome could hear clearly, he doubted if those at the edges of the crowd could hear. The words were spoken in a conversational tone, as though talking to people in a room. Each time he spoke the word "blessed", he would lift his right arm and raise his index finger, but, apart from this, he moved little and the words were generally delivered in an even tone with little nuance beyond the shifts in volume caused by turning his head around. In spite of – or perhaps because of – the calm, quiet delivery, the crowd around him (including Jerome) were totally spellbound.

Jerome had noticed that some of the men sitting very close to Jesus were looking at the crowd and not Jesus. On occasion, they would turn in the direction of Jesus, but then return their gaze quickly to the crowd. It reminded him of the security personnel at a concert, ever vigilant for any danger to the performer. Once, when Jesus paused, some in the crowd stood up and began to ask questions, but the men protecting him intervened promptly by shouting, "No questions now, please." This managed response was supported speedily by others in the crowd, and the questioners went quiet.

This allowed Jesus to continue. "When you are giving, do not shout from the rooftops so everyone can see. Such people are vain hypocrites. If you can give, do so quietly and secretly. Your Father will see."

Jesus had moved, so that he was now sitting cross-legged. He had become more animated and appeared to be enjoying the lesson. There were some further shouts from the crowd, and, while not actively encouraged, they didn't meet with the same immediate response from his minders. It seemed to Jerome that this was similar to a performance, with the first part a lesson through verse and the second part through storytelling.

The final part of the sermon began. "When praying to the Father, you should pray like this. 'Our Father who art in heaven, hallowed be thy name. Thy kingdom come. Thy will be done, on earth as it is in heaven. Give us this day our daily bread. And forgive us our trespasses, as we forgive those who trespass against us. Lead us not into temptation, but deliver us from all evil. Amen.'" He paused before adding, "And remember, for all things, do unto others as you would have them do unto you."

He stopped, bowed his head as though in prayer, then got to his feet and walked slowly from the back of the circle, where he was surrounded immediately by four or five of his men. There followed a silence as people tried to come to terms with the teachings they had just heard. Then came a growing murmur as they began speaking to each other, in hushed tones initially, increasing in volume gradually and reaching a crescendo with a number shouting, "Rabbi, come back, please."

The cry was taken up by many in the crowd, and some close to Jerome seemed on the point of frenzy, but Jesus did not return.

Instead, the elderly, white-haired man reappeared and, after some difficulty, managed to get the crowd sufficiently calm to hear him speak. "My brothers, today we have heard Jesus teach us. Please think about his words and try to live them every day. It will not be easy, but it is the way to salvation." He paused and urged the crowd to quieten further. "Jesus has travelled far over the last few days and is very tired, so we must not demand more from him than he can give."

There were some groans from the crowd, but they were more in acceptance than complaint.

He went on, "He is concerned that many of you have travelled here and not had anything to eat. We have been able to gather some food, though it is not much, and this will be distributed to you. Please be patient while this is organised. Bless you all."

Chapter 26

Through the subsequent noise and jostling confusion, Jerome searched for Jesus. First, he climbed to where the circle had been. It had disappeared, and the area had been taken over by a number of helpers who were trying to organise the distribution of the food. As he moved higher, the crowd thinned out quickly. Above and to his right, on a flat, rocky part of the hill, he made out a group of about ten people; he was certain he recognised Jesus among them. As he watched, occasional bursts of laughter came from the group.

Suddenly, Jerome became unsure. Hunkering down some hundred metres from the group, he stared anxiously at the valley below. The hillside was then mostly in shade, and the early evening had become cooler. He placed his hand on the neck of his *dishdasha* and, making a fist, pulled it tighter to his chest. "Why am I here?" he whispered to no one. Fleetingly, he recalled Padua and his decision taken then to journey to this place and this time. There was the obvious connection to Helga's deathbed wish, and a tenuous link to his journey to Hitler, but he still couldn't fully answer his question: *why am I here?*

Every few minutes, he stole a glance over his left shoulder at them. By then, they were all sitting, and a thin trace of smoke indicated a fire had been lit. Taking a deep breath, he got to his feet and began moving towards them, in a steady and, he hoped, non-threatening way. When he was twenty metres away, one of the men stood up. Jerome stopped and looked at him, hoping in vain for some gesture of welcome. The man and Jerome continued to stare at each other, with the others seemingly oblivious to his presence. Then, just as he was about to move forwards again, the man began to walk across the hill towards him.

As he got close, Jerome said, "I've travelled a great distance to hear Jesus. May I talk to him, even for a short while? My name is Jerome." He held out his hand.

The man looked at it and then, with a smile, shook it. "You're welcome, brother. My name is Matthew." He put his arm around Jerome's shoulder and turned him gently so that they were both facing towards the valley. "Jesus is very tired and is planning to sleep now; perhaps you could meet him another time?"

"No, I must be gone this evening; if I don't meet him now, I never will. I've come a long way, and I must begin my return journey tonight." Jerome looked at him. "Please help me."

Matthew tightened his grip on Jerome's shoulder, and looked questioningly into his eyes. "Have you eaten?" he asked.

"No, not since morning."

"Well, if you've come a long way and you've a long journey home, then you'll need to eat. Come." He began walking down the hill.

Jerome had not moved. "But will I get the chance to talk to Jesus?"

"Let's eat first, and then we'll see," said Matthew as he continued down the hill.

Jerome followed him, feeling he had little alternative.

As they were approaching the front of the lines where the food was being distributed, Matthew stopped, looked around and said, mainly to himself it seemed, "She's here somewhere; I saw her earlier." Then, pointing to the furthest line, he beckoned Jerome to follow him. Matthew appeared paler than most of the other men, but, like many of them, he had a short, wispy beard, which Jerome noticed him tugging frequently with the thumb and forefinger of his right hand. Little downturns at the edges of his mouth gave him a slightly sad expression, which Jerome felt – without really knowing why – was not reflective of his personality.

"This man's come a long way to meet Jesus and hasn't eaten since morning. Can you give him something?" The instruction – for Jerome felt it wasn't a request – was issued to a woman standing beside six large baskets. She was taking food from the baskets and giving it to people queuing patiently in front of her.

"There are hundreds of people to be fed," she said, without turning or stopping what she was doing.

"Well, I'd really appreciate if you could do something for him," replied Matthew, glancing briefly at Jerome with a mischievous smile.

The woman turned and looked at Jerome. "Sit over there." She indicated, with her head, a spot a few metres behind her. "I'll bring you something over." Then, glancing at Matthew, she added, "I noticed that Jesus didn't have anything good to say about your friends today."

"He rarely does, but the important thing is that he likes me," stated Matthew, his face bright with good humour. Again, he put his arm around Jerome's shoulders before saying to him, "We'll talk later; in the meantime, eat."

Jerome sat watching her from behind. Her large, star-shaped earrings moved constantly as she worked. She was the only woman giving out food, but she seemed not to be inhibited by this. In fact, he noticed that she offered advice to the others on occasion, which was accepted without comment.

Eventually, she came and sat beside him, placing a small mat on the ground, then some bread and two brown earthenware cups of milk. "We have some fish as well, if you want. They're small and bony, but good if you're hungry."

"Loaves and fishes," said Jerome softly, staring at the bread.

"Was that a yes?" asked the woman curtly.

"Yes, I'd like some; thank you."

She rose and returned quickly with six small fish in her hands, which she arranged on the mat in a symmetrical pattern with one fish pointing to two o'clock, the second to four o'clock, and the others arranged at ten-minute spacings, with the last pointing to midnight.

"What's your name?" she asked, raising a cup to her lips. She had long, red hair, which was unusual, if not unique, among the people Jerome had seen. This appeared even more striking, as many of the other women had their hair covered with a headdress.

"Jerome. What's yours?" he enquired.

"Mary," she replied and added hurriedly, "where are you from, Jerome?" She had pale-blue eyes and small features. Her teeth also appeared small, like baby teeth, but the contours of her full breasts were not hidden by the blue garment that covered all but her head, and confirmed to Jerome that this was a young woman and not a child.

"I'm from a land at the far western end of the empire, a long distance from here. I heard of Jesus and his teachings, and I wanted to meet him. That's why I'm here today." Jerome bit off a piece of the bread, which was hard but fresh. "Are you from near here?" he queried.

"I'm from Magdalena on the western shore of the Sea of Galilee. It's not far from here."

"From Magdalena," echoed Jerome softly as he picked up the

fish pointing to eight o'clock and began to bite tentatively into its sides. It tasted like sardine and, to his relief, appeared to be well cooked.

"You eat politely," she observed. "But I don't understand how you could have come so far. Are you a rich man? You must have horses, camels and servants to help you travel. Where are they?"

"No, I travel in a different way. I have come alone." Jerome thought there was no point trying to explain further.

"What do you want from Jesus?" She had finished drinking and was no longer looking at him.

"I just want to meet him and talk to him. I believe he is an extraordinary man."

The subsequent silence was broken by Jerome as he leaned towards her. "I sense that you think I might be a danger to him, but I'm not. I mean him no harm at all."

She looked at him.

"I swear on my life I would never harm him," Jerome confirmed.

Mary said nothing, but her face had softened, and Jerome felt her concerns had at least eased, if not disappeared.

"Have you known him long?" asked Jerome.

"You ask a lot of questions." She glared at him momentarily before continuing, "Yes, I've known Jesus for more than a year."

Jerome waited for further information, which was not forthcoming, before asking, "What do you think of him?" Seeing the frown that furrowed her brow, he quickly added, "I'm sorry; it sounds like I'm interrogating you. I don't mean to. Please just ignore my questions if you think them intrusive."

"You use some words that I do not understand. And you speak in a manner that sounds strange to me." She paused, and the frown on her face relaxed.

Jerome felt relief that, despite the 2,000-year time difference, he was able to understand Mary and she seemed to struggle with only a few of his words. Before embarking on this journey, he had feared that he might not be understood at all.

"Jesus is a very special person," she continued. "I believe God has chosen him to save all of us, but he's only one man, and everyone is demanding time with him, including you. He gets so tired. I worry about him, but when I'm with him, well…" She sighed as her eyes welled up. "I cry very easily." She pointed hesitantly to where Jesus and his disciples were sitting. "Some of them think I do it just to get his attention, but I don't; it's just the way I am." She wiped her eyes swiftly, with a show of irritation. "He's not a danger to anyone and does not preach violence against anyone: Roman, Jew or Gentile." She looked at Jerome's food. "Don't you like your fish?"

"Yes." He shrugged and then added by way of explanation. "You were right; there are a lot of bones."

She picked up one from the mat, quickly and skilfully removed its head and tail, sliced the body with her thumb nail, and removed the backbone. "Here, you should find this easier." She smiled indulgently as she handed him the fish. "How did you get here?" she asked, as he began again to eat.

"I've told you that I'm from a long way away, but I'm also from a long time away. It's hard to explain, but, where I'm from, many millions of people know the story of Jesus, and his life and teachings."

"I don't understand. How do they know it?"

Jerome paused before replying softly, "Because it has already happened."

Mary stared thoughtfully at the cup cradled in her hands. "Tell me about you," she requested. "Are you married? Do you have children?"

"No, I have no children and I'm not married. I have one brother and one sister. My father and mother are both still alive, although my father is very ill."

"Do you want Jesus to cure your father?"

"I don't know. I had not thought of asking him to do that."

"Why not?"

Jerome reflected on this question for a few moments and said nothing.

"Don't you want him to be cured?" Mary persisted.

Finally, Jerome responded, "I don't believe that is the purpose of this journey."

She gave a bemused shrug of her slim shoulders before continuing, "Tell me more about you and what you do; are you a farmer, a soldier or what?"

"No, I'm none of those." Jerome smiled ruefully as he thought of what to say. "I'm still studying. I'm a student."

"Perhaps you too will be a rabbi. Perhaps that is what God has planned for you."

"Perhaps, perhaps," said Jerome quietly. "And you, Mary, do you think you will continue to follow Jesus?"

"Don't you already know?" Her tone was challenging, but not threatening.

"I know some things, yes, but not everything."

"But you do know the answer to your question?"

"Yes."

"So why did you ask it?"

"I'm not sure."

"You seem unsure about many things." Her face remained impassive and impenetrable.

Jerome glanced over his shoulder, but there was no movement from the group further up the hill. "Is it very tiring, travelling all the time with Jesus and his disciples?" he asked.

"No," she answered quickly. "We don't travel all the time anyway; in summer, it's too hot. Jesus stays in one place, and some of us stay with him. The others go back to their families. When we are travelling, it's not too hard. Most of the time, it's very enjoyable." She looked at him. "That surprises you."

"Yes, I suppose it does." Jerome pointed down to the valley. "There were a group of people there today. No one went near them and they were walking in a—"

"Lepers; they were lepers," interrupted Mary. "They have to stay downwind and walk like that to warn others away. The crowds coming to hear Jesus would be much bigger if they weren't there, but he won't let them be chased away."

"There were children in the group," said Jerome, sounding surprised.

"Yes." She looked at him, puzzled. "Lepers have children. Don't you have lepers in your country?"

"No," Jerome shook his head.

"What else do you know about me?" she asked, interest creeping into the corners of her eyes.

Jerome put down the remains of his fish and, speaking slowly, began, "Well, I know you are one of his very close disciples. I think you may be the sister of Lazarus and Martha, but I'm not certain. Also, there is a story about a woman who washed the feet of Jesus with her tears and dried them with her hair. I don't know if you are that woman." Jerome paused and looked at the then wide-eyed face. "I know that you will be the first person Jesus speaks to when he rises from the dead."

Mary stared at him, her mouth partly open, showing the little teeth, which were slightly prominent at the front. Her red hair was even more noticeable in the early evening glow. "Is he going to die?"

"Yes, but he will rise again."

She remained silent for a while before saying, "You know, I sometimes help him prepare for his teaching."

"No, I didn't know that."

"It's very little, but when he's preparing to give a lesson, he practices on me to see what I think. Last night, he told me the story of how you should love your enemies instead of hating them, and pray for those who persecute you. I told him I thought it was beautiful. That may sound a strange way to describe a story, but it's how I felt about it. I think everything he says is beautiful. Won't I die with him?" The question was sudden.

"No, you will live for a long time."

"He will die soon?" she queried quietly.

Jerome was not sure if this was a question, and he decided not to respond.

"The Martha and Lazarus you speak of are not my siblings. That is a different Mary. She is a rich woman." She looked away from Jerome before continuing, "Though also a good woman. I am an only child. My parents are both dead, so I have no family. I will remain with him as long as he wants me to." She began gathering up the remains of the food. "When you talk to him, don't tell him anything that could hurt him."

"I won't."

A noise above him made Jerome turn around. It was Matthew descending towards them. He moved quickly and with the agility of someone used to traversing hills. "Well, friend Jerome, have you eaten?"

"Yes, thank you." Jerome noticed Matthew raising his eyes questioningly to Mary and receiving a slight nod in response. "Mary here has been very kind."

"And you still want to speak to Jesus?"

"Yes, I'd like that very much."

"Very well, but, remember…" Matthew stared hard at him, "he's very tired, so it can't be for long."

As they walked away, Jerome turned to Mary to thank her.

She waved his thanks away dismissively before adding, almost as an unimportant afterthought it seemed, "Oh, the woman in your story who was crying – that was me."

For a moment, Matthew glanced quizzically at Jerome before continuing to climb the hill. When they were close to the group he turned around and said quietly but firmly, "You won't mind if I search you. There are people who want to harm him, even though he harms no one."

Jerome nodded his assent, and Matthew carried out an efficient and thorough body search. Jerome wondered at the similarity of such searches to those 2,000 years later, despite the changes in weaponry, but he realised that the places to hide the weapons hadn't changed.

Chapter 27

The twelve men in the group were all sitting when Jerome and Matthew joined them. The place had a smooth, grey, stone surface with an elevation at one side, forming a natural wall that would protect them from the wind when nightfall and cold set in. The men were arranged casually in a circle, with a glowing wood fire at its centre. There appeared to be a number of different conversations taking place, including laughter, all of which stopped when they arrived. Jesus, who was sitting with his back to them, turned around with his hand shading his eyes.

"Ah, the traveller; you are welcome." It was the same voice as before, and seemed more suited to conversation than to large crowds.

Jerome felt his heart racing again and his breathing became suddenly shallow. He tried not to appear nervous.

"Let's make some room for our guest," continued Jesus, and a man of stocky build who had been sitting beside him, arose and moved away quietly. "Here, you must have some food," said Jesus reaching towards a blackened pot that was simmering gently on the fire.

"I've already eaten, thank you. The woman, Mary…" Jerome indicated where Mary Magdalene was still moving below. "She kindly gave me fish and bread."

Jesus smiled reassuringly at Jerome. "Cold, dry fish and bread is not the most nourishing meal when you've journeyed far. This is good and it's hot."

Jerome took the wooden plate containing pieces of what looked like lamb in watery gravy and thanked him again.

The silence from the others continued, but it was not strained. It was like the comfortable silence between good friends, even though he knew none of them.

"I'm not sure what Matthew has told you." Jerome breathed deeply as his gaze flitted to Matthew and then back to Jesus.

"He told us just what you told him: that you've journeyed far to see us. Now, please tell us more. We like to hear news from distant places," requested Jesus.

Jerome rested the plate uneasily on his knee. "My name is Jerome Black. I'm from a place and time very different from here. I want to talk to you, because you've been a huge influence on the lives of millions of people, including me." His voice was sounding stronger and more confident. "I want to get your guidance, so I can bring it back to the people where I'm from." The words were directed at Jesus, but everyone listened.

"Tell us about this place where you're from. What do the people seek?" asked Jesus, looking at him with increasing interest.

Jerome's initial nervousness had gone by this time, and he looked closely at Jesus for the first time. His brown eyes were small and intense but not threatening. He had black facial hair that tapered into a wispy beard and partially hid the pockmarks on his cheeks. He seemed taller than the others, and, like most of them, was slim and dark in colour. The patterns Jerome had noticed below the shoulders of his *dishdasha*, were in fact diamond shaped, and their colour matched a white-gold crescent hanging from a thin, metal chain around his neck.

"I come from a place at the western end of the empire," began Jerome.

"Are you from Gaul?" asked one of the group.

"No, even further west," Jerome confirmed.

Jesus continued to stare at him and said nothing.

"The world I come from," continued Jerome, "is much larger than the world you know. Some places, or countries, are very rich while others are desperately poor. Even within certain places there can be great disparity. Generally, the very poor seek relief from poverty and illness. Others, who have more, try to better their position, while those with a lot…" Jerome paused. "They probably still want more worldly wealth, but almost everyone seeks spiritual guidance of some kind."

"That sounds just like here," responded one of the group with a laugh. "What's the difference?" The speaker was a young man sitting opposite Jesus. He had a bright, open face and was the only one who was clean shaven.

"Are you John?" asked Jerome.

"Yes." He looked taken aback. "How did you know that?"

"I know John is the youngest of the disciples, and I thought you might be him," Jerome explained.

"Do you know *my* name?" It was the stocky man who had moved to let Jerome sit down. He appeared older than the others.

"No, no, no, stop." Jesus raised his right hand and smiled indulgently. "Do not forget, he is our guest. It is not courteous to test him."

"I know the names of all your disciples, Jesus." Jerome whispered to him.

Jesus looked at him in questioning silence.

"Tell us more about your world. What is different about it?"

asked the stocky man in a tone that suggested interest and, to Jerome, some residual suspicion.

"Well, it's the same world, but I come from a different time when much more is known about the earth we inhabit. For instance, it's much bigger than the world is currently assumed to be, and more than 7,000 million people live in it. As to what are the differences between my time and now…" Jerome stopped to reflect. "Well, people have more knowledge. They know that the earth we live on is round. They know it circles the sun once a year and the moon circles the earth once a month. Men have flown to the moon and walked on it. People – well, people in rich countries anyway – live longer than people of today because they have better food and medicine."

"How old do they live?" asked another of the disciples.

"Many live to be 100 years old; some beyond that," stated Jerome.

"Methuselah lived to be almost 1,000 years old," replied the same voice.

"I know, but many people in my time find that difficult to believe." Jerome tried not to sound patronising.

"What do you mean you come from a different time?" asked the stocky man.

"I come from the future; 2,000 years in the future."

Apart from Jesus, the group appeared momentarily bemused by this answer.

"Go on, tell us more about your world," said John.

Jerome was happy to oblige. "People can see and talk to each other, even though they may be vast distances apart, and they can travel distances of thousands of leagues in a few hours. There are also many wars raging, particularly in the poorer parts of the world, and some armies have terrible weapons of destruction that are capable of killing millions of people."

No one in the group spoke. Some, such as John, wore

expressions of interest; most displayed barely concealed scepticism. All waited for Jesus to express a view.

"But for all their advances and greater knowledge, people, as individuals, do not seek anything different from people today, do they?" asked Jesus.

"No, they don't." Jerome leaned close to him. "I don't have much time. I must return to my own world soon."

"Let us walk awhile," said Jesus to Jerome in a voice loud enough for the group to hear.

"Rabbi, I'll come with you," said the stocky man, getting to his feet.

"No, Simon, this is not yet the time," replied Jesus enigmatically, then he took Jerome by the arm and guided him away from the watchful group.

"This is the site of an extinct volcano," said Jesus as they slowly climbed the steepening hillside. He picked up one of the dark-grey rocks. "These are lava rocks; you will find them all around the higher slopes. Very little can grow up here, but, down in the valleys and hills beyond, the lava has turned to good soil and made this one of the richest areas of farmland in all of Galilee."

At that point, they were both using their hands to help with the ascent. The well-marked path Jerome had walked the previous day was not there.

"Who are you?" asked Jesus, turning slightly to look at Jerome.

"I am who I said I was. I'm not trying to deceive anyone and I'm not mad. My name is Jerome Black and I come from 2,000 years in the future. When I said that to your friends below, I noticed their looks of disbelief, which I can understand."

"They mean no disrespect, but the idea of travelling from another time is incomprehensible to them."

"But, not to you?"

Jesus seemed to weigh up Jerome's question before continuing, "Why have you come to see me?"

Jerome stopped climbing. "I want to bring your message back to people in my time."

"Is there any other reason?" Jesus eyed him closely.

"I have no malign purpose to visit you, Jesus. I am not a spy."

"Why now? Why have you come at this specific moment?"

For the first time on this journey Jerome smiled. "Because of my grandmother," he began, "she had a dying wish to visit you giving the Sermon on the Mount. That's how your lesson today is known in my time."

Jesus folded then unfolded his arms before beginning to walk again. "Have you visited Rome?"

"Yes," replied Jerome following closely behind him, "but Rome two thousand years from now."

"What is it like?"

"A beautiful city; it's known as the eternal city. Many of the old buildings from today are still standing. It's like an open-air museum. But it's no longer the centre of the world. Other cities — some that don't even exist today — have overtaken it in importance." Jerome hesitated before adding, "I know you will never be there."

Up ahead, Jesus seemed to pause imperceptibly before asking Jerome, "If the people in your time have much better means of communicating and learning, they know the message I preach. That message will not change in two thousand years, nor will it change in two million. So why do you feel you could bring something from me that would change the way people live their lives?"

Jerome could hear his pulse racing, and he was not sure if it was due solely to the exertion of the climb. "Perhaps if they knew you were speaking directly to them, it would reawaken or strengthen their belief in your teachings."

"They already have the teachings and, most importantly, the free will to choose to believe or not. Besides, if my Father had wanted my message to be brought again, wouldn't he have guided me directly into your world?"

"I don't know, Jesus. I do know that if you were to come into my time, you would be able to speak to everyone. Your message is widely known, but it comes from this time when you could only meet a tiny fraction of all the people. The belief of all those who never saw you has been based on the spoken and written words of others, who give their own interpretations of what you said. And these interpretations may be very different from what you intended."

"This must be how the Father wants it to be." Jesus shrugged his shoulders and sat down. "Evil never rests. You must know that. Liars and thieves and charlatans will always exist to test us. They will twist words to suit their evil purposes, so good men must arise in every generation to combat them. It is an eternal battle." Carefully, he removed the worn sandal from his left foot and brushed some pieces of dirt from a gash just below the ankle, which had started to bleed. "I cut this on a stone yesterday; the climb has reopened it." Slowly, he began to redo the sandal strap. "Have you travelled before to see others?"

"Yes," said Jerome. "I have travelled back many times, but, somehow, I feel that this is *the* journey I was meant to make."

"Why?"

"I don't know, Jesus. Shall we stop here?" asked Jerome.

"No, we'll continue."

As they recommenced the climb, Jerome noticed Jesus was walking gingerly on his left foot, as though to protect it.

"You're wondering why I don't heal this the way I heal others," stated Jesus.

"Well, yes, I suppose I am," answered Jerome.

"I was sent to earth by God to live as an ordinary man. That means suffering the pains, however great or slight. If I were to cure myself of every ill, I would not be truly living as an ordinary man."

When they were within sight of the top, they stopped for a rest and sat down, both breathing heavily.

"May I see that?" said Jesus, pointing to Jerome's watch.

Throughout the day, Jerome had tried to hide it, wearing it high up on his left forearm, but it had come down in the climb. Removing it, he passed it over.

Holding it gently, Jesus turned the watch over a few times. "A small timepiece."

"You can keep it if you want," said Jerome.

For the first time, Jesus looked at him with disappointment, and Jerome immediately regretted making the offer.

"That could only be temporary," replied Jesus as he handed back the watch. "Maybe you will give me a more permanent gift sometime."

Jerome glanced at his watch as he fastened it to his wrist. "I can travel back in time for a short period only: less than five hours. I have been here more than four already and will soon be returned to my own time. Also, Jesus, no one except me remembers my visits, so I expect you will not remember meeting me or any of our conversation."

Daylight was fading as Jerome reached to an inside pocket in his *dishdasha*, took out a photograph and passed it over. Jesus held the photograph cautiously by one corner and gazed at it with frowning curiosity.

"It's called a photograph," said Jerome. "In my time, we can make a picture of something that is as clear and true as the actual thing."

"What is this?" asked Jesus, his frown lifting.

"I said that men had travelled to the moon. That is a picture taken from the moon, and it's a picture of the earth we live on."

Jesus stared intensely at the photograph showing the dark lunar landscape in the foreground with the stunning blue-and-white earth rising like a mystical ball in the darkness of space. "It looks beautiful," he began, "and yet it has a sad sense of loneliness." He gazed uncertainly at Jerome as he handed back the photograph.

"May I ask you about your sermon today?" asked Jerome after a brief interlude.

Jesus nodded slowly.

"You spoke about dealing with conflict between people. You said that if you are making an offering to God, but have an outstanding disagreement with someone, then you should leave the offering and go and try to sort out your disagreement. You also said two other things that, even 2,000 years from now, are very difficult to do; that is, to love your enemies, and if someone slaps you on the cheek, then don't retaliate, but instead offer him the other cheek. Don't seek revenge even if you think you've been badly wronged."

"Yes," replied Jesus, "our laws have always taught an eye for an eye, and taking revenge seems the just way. But if *you* feel you have been badly wronged, then your enemy may also feel that *he* has been wronged, so an eye for an eye will leave you both blind eventually. It is not easy to forsake vengeance, but the road to salvation is not easy."

"Yes, but, in my time, like now, many people die in wars between countries. What should you do when an aggressor's army invades your country and starts slaughtering, not just your soldiers but innocent people, including children? In those circumstances, do the people of the country being invaded not have the right, if not the duty, to take up weapons to protect the lives of their children? If they let their children die, is that not wrong?"

Jesus had taken the opportunity of the rest to remove the new collection of stones from his sandals and was tossing them gently down the hill, one by one, using his left hand. His fingers were long and slim, with nails that were darkened at the top where dirt had become lodged. "You could be referring to the Romans in Palestine or someplace else, but my answer would be the same. If you truly love your enemy, then you will not think him an aggressor. If you truly love your enemy, then you will never take up arms against him. And if you truly love your enemy, then you will not distinguish in importance between his life and the life of your child."

They sat quietly for a while, with the only sound being the noise from the wind that was gusting more strongly near the summit.

"That's very difficult to accept," said Jerome. "Everyone wants to protect their children; it's fundamental in all of us. Asking people to relegate that love to be below loving your enemy in some way is, I think, asking too much."

"Yet it must be asked, and we must strive to do it. If we can really strive to achieve this level of feeling towards our enemy, then, in the end, he will no longer be our enemy, and wars will become a thing of the past, as extinct as this volcano. Mankind has a narrow window to survive. You say there are weapons that can kill millions. If we continue to tolerate inequality and live as enemies, then such weapons will surely be used, and mankind will cease to exist. And perhaps your presence suggests it is very close to midnight." Jesus stood up and rubbed his hands together to clean them of the remaining debris. "Come, let us get to the top while there is still light."

As they approached the summit, the ground became less steep. By then, Jesus appeared to be moving without any obvious pain, and, in fact, had quickened his pace. Jerome did his best to keep up with him, but Jesus stayed ahead, scrambled up the final few metres, turned and smiled, offering his hand to help Jerome to reach the top.

"I didn't expect you to be so competitive," said Jerome, who was partly bent over and still trying to catch his breath after the exertion.

Jesus pointed to the valley beyond. "The light is not great, but I like to get to the top of a hill or mountain to see the view on the other side."

They both gazed down at the valley, where orange fires glowed near some of the small, white adobe houses. The outline of more hills in the distance was still just visible. They could hear the sound of a goat bleating; it was low and repetitive, suggesting hunger rather than genuine distress. The only other sound was their breathing, as it gradually returned to normal.

"Have you met your father?" asked Jesus.

"Yes, of course," said Jerome. "My father is a wonderful, gentle man, but he's very ill and will not get better."

Jesus frowned. "He doesn't know of your powers?"

"No, he doesn't."

"Have you discovered any other special gifts that you possess?"

"Other gifts? No, I don't know what you mean."

Jesus stared intently at him through the gathering gloom. "You say you're from the future, so you know my future and how my life will end?"

Jerome glanced away. For the first time, he was momentarily uncomfortable. "Yes," he nodded gently.

"And my family and friends, you know what will happen to them?"

"Mostly, yes."

"Will they suffer after my death? Will they suffer because of me?"

"No," replied Jerome. He knew some would suffer but felt there was no point conveying this depressing message.

But Jesus persisted. "I must ask you again. Will they suffer because of me, after I die?"

Jerome averted his gaze. "Yes," he began reluctantly, "but they will choose their fate knowingly and willingly." He looked again at Jesus through sympathetic eyes. "And joyfully. They will accept their fate joyfully because of their faith in you." He waited for a further response from Jesus, which didn't come. "Jesus, I will be gone soon. May I ask you something?"

Jesus turned away, making no reply.

"What do you want to achieve in this life?" queried Jerome.

He looked to Jerome again, with a harsh flash in his eyes. "That is a strange question from someone who claims to know the future. And if I tell you what I want from life, will you give me wisdom and knowledge? Is that what I'm being tempted with?"

"No," said Jerome, surprised at the reaction. "I can give you nothing. Even the timepiece I stupidly offered you will disappear when I go shortly. I can't even give you memories as you will recall none of our conversation when I'm gone."

"You know when I will die and how I will die?" Jesus asked softly.

"Do you want me to answer that?"

Jesus looked at the ground and smiled ruefully. "If the answer is that I will live four score years and die peacefully, surrounded by my grandchildren, then, yes, I would like you to answer it. But I sense that is not the answer, is it?"

Jerome shook his head.

"This winter will mark my thirty-third birthday. Your presence seems like a portent that I will not see many more."

Jerome made no reply, but he was aware that his silence signified confirmation.

"What will happen to Mary, the woman who fed you?"

"She will live to an old age."

"I can't imagine her as an old woman. Will she be alone?"

"She will have good friends, but she will never marry."

Jesus nodded in acknowledgement and asked no more questions.

The steep original crater at the summit of the hill had crumbled gradually into a gentle saucer-shaped top, covered in dark-green moss and, in some places, shallow puddles of water. As they walked across the springy vegetation, trying to avoid the cold water, Jerome said, "You taught today of the dangers of money.

How it is useless to store it up, and how you cannot serve both God and money. In my world, money remains very important to almost everyone. It's not that people are mean or selfish, most are not, and many give generously to the less fortunate, but they do seek to accumulate money for security or to have a better life. Are they wrong?"

At first, Jesus made no reply but continued looking down, choosing his footsteps carefully until they had reached the far side of the summit. Then, after sitting down, he began in a low, intense voice, "I despise the avarice of the rich. They accumulate wealth beyond measure while, close by, children die from lack of food. Their honeyed words pretend holiness, but their actions are wicked. They would be more honest if they shook their fists at the heavens and said, 'Do you see that child, God? Well, it comes from a poor family, so it must suffer and die so that I can buy more jewels to drape around the neck of my shameless wife.' Believe me, they will never see the kingdom of God." Jesus spat on the ground contemptuously. "If I had to stand at the gates of heaven and throw them down to the everlasting pit, I would do so without regret. But..." his face and voice softened, "they can always get redemption on earth by changing their ways. We must have infinite hope." He turned to Jerome. "You say this evil disparity continues in your time?"

"Well, yes," replied Jerome. "There are many good people who try to help the poor and hungry in our world, but there remains great inequality. Some people have thousands of millions of... gold coins... while others have nothing. And yet it is difficult to resolve."

"No, it is not." The edge had returned to his voice. "It is easy, but it just requires courage and an acceptance that you do not have to have more money than your neighbour to be happy. You do not need to display more baubles and trinkets to show you are superior to him or worthy of more respect. If you have more than you need of anything, then give it away with a generous heart to those who have less. That is not difficult to understand. And anyone who hoards wealth as you describe is an affront to God."

Darkness had almost fallen by this time, and the wind was getting stronger. It was coming from the desert in the east and, at this time of the evening, was still warm.

Jerome gazed up at the night sky, in which he had never seen so many stars so clearly. The broad band of the Milky Way was stretched across a dazzling, starlit sky. "I have never seen a sky like that. In my country, the light pollution from earth hides all but the brightest stars. It's amazing and beautiful."

"Yes, the heavens are special," confirmed Jesus.

Jerome looked up again. "Do you think there is life near any of those stars, or is this the only place where life exists?"

Jesus laughed out loud, and scratched his nose with his thumb and forefinger, "You should leave something for the future discoverers. The quest for knowledge is one of the great gifts from God, and we shouldn't take that from them." Then, in a serious voice, he asked. "What will you do when you return to your world?"

"I'll tell everyone about my journeys, including about this journey. I'll tell them about seeing you, hearing you give the actual Sermon on the Mount, and then talking to you man to man." He paused, looking slightly embarrassed, "Well, you know what I mean."

"You'll spread the word of God."

For a moment, Jerome glanced away and then looked into the face of Jesus. "Yes, I suppose I will."

"And what else will you do?"

"I'm not sure. I haven't planned beyond revealing the truth about my journeys. Maybe I'll just lead a quiet, normal life afterwards, although that may be naive."

"It would not be possible. And, anyway, you would not want to hide from your destiny."

"But I don't know what my destiny is. Do you know?"

"Our Father will guide you when you need to know."

"But do *you* know? Do *you* know my destiny?" persisted Jerome.

Jesus shook his head slowly. "No, I do not, though I sense it will not be an easy path. You may have to give up everything. Could you do that?"

For a while, Jerome did not answer. "I don't know about giving up everything. I've often felt sorry for the rich, young man in your parable when you ask him to sell everything, give the proceeds to the poor and come follow you. You don't seem to operate any halfway house. It's everything or nothing." As he said this, Jerome thought he noticed a look of surprise flicker briefly on Jesus's face, but he was not certain. It was only much later that he discovered the story of the rich man occurred after the Sermon on the Mount.

"Great sacrifices are sometimes asked of ordinary people. Do you not feel you are capable of rising to such a challenge? Could you not give up everything to follow your destiny?"

"You seem to have such certainty about everything," began Jerome quietly, "but, to me, life is never that clear. It's not all black and white. It's much more complex than that."

"All issues in life have a clear right and wrong answer. People deceive themselves for selfish or sometimes sympathetic reasons, but if you look into your soul, you will always find the one right answer."

"I don't know; I don't know..." Jerome's voice trailed off. "At the beginning, I wished I didn't have this power, but that changed and now I accept it, even welcome it, though it can be lonely at times."

"We all feel loneliness or fear at times."

"I struggle to imagine you fearing anything."

"I don't like to consider my suffering and death, but I know it will come, and soon."

Noises behind him made Jerome turn round.

It was three of the disciples, including Simon, who spoke in an apologetic voice, "Rabbi, we were concerned when you didn't return."

Jesus looked with exasperation at the men. "As you can see, I'm well. I already told you this was not the time. Go back down."

And they did.

Chapter 28

As they made their own way carefully down in the darkness, Jerome spoke to Jesus again. "These men, and Mary of Magdalena, have given up everything for you."

"Yes, and don't you know I'm aware of the sacrifices they have made?" Jesus responded.

"Jesus, I did not mean to suggest…" Jerome left the sentence unfinished, and, for the first time, an uncomfortable silence hung between the two.

Then Jesus went on, "Men can live this nomadic existence and return to ordinary life if they choose, but women cannot. Once marked out as different, they will not be accepted back into ordinary society. Mary has forsaken more than the others. I worry what will become of her and the others when I'm no longer here." Tiredness had replaced the edge in his voice.

Below them, one of the three men stumbled and was helped quickly to his feet, with some pushing and much laughter. Far below, Jerome could see the camp fire and the figures around it, whose numbers seemed to have increased. The sound of a woman singing drifted up and over him. Jerome brought his watch close to his face and could just see he had only a few minutes left.

"Jesus, I wish I could stay longer, but I will be taken back to my own time very soon."

"I sometimes feel I too am from a different time and place," Jesus mused, "and yet I have no memories of it." Then, as though snapping out of a trance, he said to Jerome, "Let me tell you a story before you leave. There were two young men, Lort and Nebal, who were close friends." His words were being delivered in a low, almost hypnotic manner. "They grew up in the same village and were inseparable as boys. When one was in difficulty, he could always depend on the other to help, and when one had something to celebrate, he could be sure that the other would be there to share the joy, as though it had happened to him. They both married and settled down in homes close to one another. Soon afterwards, they each had a son. Both were overjoyed at how happy they were.

"As time went by, their family responsibilities took up more of their time, and they did not see each other so much. One day, Lort decided to move his family to another house that was near the river, and so involved less-onerous journeys for his wife to fetch water. The river had flooded the year before, and so the price of a house in this area was not expensive, but it had made the land very fertile, and Lort was able to grow a good harvest in his first year.

"The harvest was even better the next year, when he invited Nebal and his family to a celebration meal. Nebal had also prospered, but the dryness of his land made it difficult, and, even with his hard work, he could not reap as much as Lort. At the meal, Lort, who was overjoyed to see his friend, served the best of his food and wine. His wife looked radiant in her bright-blue dress and thin, golden necklace. During the meal, Nebal began to feel irritated. He thought the display of food was unnecessarily extravagant, and he once caught his wife looking at the golden necklace, and was sure she gave him a look of reproach."

As Jesus spoke, Jerome watched him studiously. His teeth were very white; surprisingly so, thought Jerome, although he couldn't recall if it was the same with the other men he had met. He noticed that one of Jesus's incisor teeth was at a crooked angle, which pushed his lip up slightly and gave an impression of a sneer when he was silent; this was an illusion that was dispelled rapidly when he began to speak.

Jesus continued with the story, "In the years that followed, the pattern of harvests remained the same. Nebal toiled diligently in his fields and was able to make a good living, but the richness of Lort's soil meant he always had a better harvest. Nebal's resentment towards the man who had once been his closest friend grew bitter.

"Eventually, Nebal decided to sell his house and move very close to the river, to a house that his friend sold to him for a fraction of its real value. But, in the first year after they moved, the river flooded and all of Nebal's crops were destroyed. Lort did not suffer as much and gave generously to Nebal to help him. By this time, Nebal's resentment had developed into hatred.

"Then, one day, news came that Lort's son was very ill. Nebal and his wife called at Lort's house, and they found him and his wife distraught with concern for the sick child. Nebal uttered words of comfort and reassurance, but – although he would not admit it, even to himself – in his secret heart, he was glad that Lort was suffering. While he prayed with him, beseeching God to deliver the child from the fever, he secretly did not want Lort's suffering to be lifted. Nebal got his wish and the child died.

"Later that day, when the child was being buried amid the anguish and sorrow of his parents, Nebal thought of how he had let the envy and resentment against Lort distort his feelings to the extent that he had wanted an innocent child, who was dangerously ill, not to recover. His desire to have possessions at least as good as his friend's had become an obsession that had twisted all his judgements, even about the most fundamental element: life itself. He wept more bitterly than anyone else at the burial, but only he knew why."

Jesus stopped about fifty metres above the group, which numbered around twenty by then, and included women and children. "By focusing on increasing your wealth on earth, it is almost impossible to avoid the dangers of avarice. If you want to enter the kingdom of heaven, you should spend your time concentrating on what you can do for your neighbour, rather than what you can accumulate for yourself." He stopped and placed his hands gently on Jerome's shoulders. "Answer me this question: in your world and in your time, who do people say I am?"

Jerome hesitated before replying. "Many people say you are the son of God; others that you were a great prophet."

"And, *you,* who do *you* say I am?"

"You will put that same question to Simon, and he will tell you that you are the Messiah, the son of God." Again, Jerome paused. "As for me, I believe you're just a man, though a great philosopher."

Jesus gazed above Jerome as though staring into the distance. "Simon is a good man. But he is childlike in many ways and needs the reassurance of these beliefs that, somehow, I am all powerful and can solve every problem... which I cannot. And, anyway, if I were to say I am the son of God, then that would be blasphemy, and you could have me arrested." For a brief moment, he looked challengingly at Jerome before smiling. "Though I'm certain you would not."

As Jesus went to continue down the hill, Jerome reached out and grabbed his hand. He was aware suddenly that he was holding the hand of Jesus Christ, and, for a moment, he squeezed the hand as a child might grasp the hand of a parent who had been out of sight and was found. Whether this was due to feelings of security, recognition or something else entirely, Jerome was not sure, but the gesture was reciprocated. Jerome blinked back his emotion.

Jesus began walking the final few steps alone. Jerome could see Mary Magdalene advancing towards them. She had a warm-though-anxious expression.

Jesus turned abruptly and asked him with quiet urgency, "Will I suffer before my death?"

Jerome, surprised, did not answer but was immediately aware that his silence conveyed a clear message that he bitterly regretted giving.

Jesus nodded resignedly and said softly, "I sense we will meet one more time before I die."

"Jesus, come," Mary called. "The wind is turning and it will soon be cold. Come to the fire." Her glance at Jerome mirrored the changing temperatures.

As they rejoined the group, a number of them, especially the children, gravitated towards Jesus. He did not ignore them, but he listened closely to an old man who was staring up into his face with an expression that looked like deep gratitude. Who he was, Jerome was never to find out.

Chapter 29

Mount of Beatitudes, Israel;
Thursday, 18th May 2017; 7.15am

For some time, Jerome remained unmoved in the early morning sunshine; the oxygen mask was held loosely in his left hand as he stood, head bowed, staring silently at the dewy grass between his sandaled feet.

A distant voice, seeming to come from the direction of the Franciscan church at the top of the mountain, jolted him into action and, crouching down, he repacked the mask and oxygen cylinder into the rucksack quickly. Another voice could then be heard, gentle and clear in the still morning air. Two monks came into view. They were opening the gate to the church and were the source of the voices. Jerome gazed at them and then returned their waved salute before making his way thoughtfully down the mountain side.

Following the path, he looked keenly for the places where Jesus had given his sermon, and where he and his disciples had eaten and rested subsequently, but he found none that closely resembled either spot. Jerome checked his watch. It was 7.20am. Pausing, he removed the watch and, placing it gently in the palm of his hand, scrutinised it for some evidence that it had recently been held by Jesus, but, of course, as he knew, there was none.

* * *

On returning to his car, which had been left in the same grassy car park close to the base of the mountain where he had parked the previous day, he sat reflecting, trying to come to terms with the extraordinary events he had just lived through. His calm, almost serene outer appearance disguised a turmoil of thoughts as his mind flitted rapidly through the people and events of the previous five hours of his life: the noise and smells from the ancient marketplace; the lepers, with their bizarre circular walk to warn off others; Baltha and Gideon, the friendly and ultimately suspicious men; the actual Sermon on the Mount; meeting Matthew, who was helpful; Mary, who was intriguing and defensive, and yet so open; and, finally, the conversation with Jesus. What was he to make of all that? How could he distil and make sense of all these events?

In truth, Jerome hadn't thought deeply about how he might react after the journey. If asked, he would have guessed possibly feeling joyful, euphoric or even disappointed if he had not met Jesus. But, right then, he just felt overwhelmed by the events. He sat quietly, and largely oblivious to the other pilgrims parking their cars and beginning their trek up the mountain. Eventually, he started the motor and began to drive away slowly.

As the kilometres passed, he made the decision to try to rearrange his flight to later that day rather than spending another night in Tel Aviv. He felt the comforting draw of home. Pulling into a service station, he parked well away from the other cars and changed into his Western clothes. He had planned to leave the *dishdasha* behind, but he felt it had too many powerful memories and so it was packed into his suitcase. Two telephone calls later, he had rearranged his flight home for 4.00pm that afternoon and cancelled his one-night stay in the David Intercontinental Hotel in Tel Aviv.

***

By the time Jerome had checked his bag into Tel Aviv airport and gone through security, he felt exhausted. He was also ravenously hungry; this was something that reminded him of how he felt coming back from his journey to see Hitler. He bought two chicken sandwiches and a large Coke from one of the many food kiosks, and then went and sat down at a quiet table to enjoy them away from the bustling crowds. Afterwards, he made his way through to the departure lounge and – after sitting on one of the hard, grey-blue plastic seats – closed his eyes and gave in briefly to the tiredness washing over him. He fell into one of his short naps; after awaking with a start, he checked his watch to confirm his flight would not be for another hour.

Opening his eyes wide to force away the lingering remnants of sleep, he noticed a familiar face in the row of seats opposite. She was smiling warmly at him. It was Angelic. There was no one sitting in the seats either side of her, so Jerome moved across rapidly and, after getting her permission, sat down beside her.

"I thought it was you," she said breezily, "but you had your eyes closed, so I couldn't be sure. Then you opened them, and I was certain." She transferred her thin, dark walking cane to her left hand and placed her right hand softly on Jerome's arm. "You looked so peaceful when you were asleep that I didn't want to disturb you," she whispered to him. "But I was delighted when you woke up." Angelic smiled like a mischievous child. "It looks like we're on the same flight to London."

"Yes, that's great. I'm really glad to see you again." Jerome's face had brightened considerably. "Are you travelling alone?" he asked.

"Yes, my grandson drove me to the airport and checked in

my bags. He's very thoughtful. He even wanted to come through here to see me safely onto the plane, but I told him that would be nonsense. Anyway, my daughter will collect me in London. She's a doctor who specialises in geriatrics at St George's Hospital, so I'll be well cared for." She smiled with a hint to pride.

"Is that the same grandson who was with you at the Mount of Beatitudes..." Jerome paused, momentarily unsure about timelines, before finishing with, "yesterday?"

"Yes, I wonder if you passed each other on the mountain. I'd say he's about your age."

"We probably did." Jerome smiled.

A loud announcement from the public address system halted their conversation temporarily. The message was repeated in three languages and gave both an opportunity to consider what they would next say. Angelic remained quiet when it ended.

"Do you remember I said I was going to talk to Jesus?" Jerome spoke softly, his head lowered and inclined towards her.

"Yes, of course I do," she replied immediately. "But I didn't like to ask in case... well, in case you didn't want to talk about it. I know people like to keep some things private, and if that's what they want, then they shouldn't be pestered."

Jerome looked at her, his face reflecting the excitement of a child at Christmas. "Angelic, this morning, I met and spoke with Jesus in exactly the same way I'm talking to you now. I watched him deliver the actual Sermon on the Mount. And then I walked with him and spoke to him for over an hour. I was able to travel back in time to meet him, and I know that sounds crazy, but it happened just a few hours ago."

Her face mirrored his excitement. "But that's wonderful. What was he like? What did he say? Did he tell you anything special? He must have been amazed to speak to someone from the future; was he?" Her words gushed out, thrilling Jerome, who had feared a very different reaction to this genuine enthusiasm.

"He looked just like an ordinary man, nothing unusual. I don't think he believed me at first, you know, that I was from the future. He seemed a bit guarded, and some of his disciples were very suspicious. But, eventually, I think he did believe me."

"You met his disciples too?" Her tone betrayed no scepticism.

"Yes, I spoke for a while with Matthew."

"The tax collector?"

"Yes, but he didn't behave like one. He was very helpful and had a friendly, almost playful manner; although, like the others, he was very protective of Jesus. And, he introduced me to Mary Magdalene. I spoke with her for quite a while. She gave me food... bread and fish."

"I would love to have spoken to her. You know, strangely, I think about her a lot. I don't know why, but I do. What was she like?" Angelic placed her hand on Jerome's for emphasis and, staring straight ahead, closed her eyes as though preparing to conjure up an image of this woman from 2,000 years ago. "Tell me what she was like."

For the next half hour, Jerome described in detail his interaction with Mary Magdalene and his encounters with the others he had met. He went through the events in chronological order and spent the final ten minutes talking about Jesus. Angelic interrupted little, but her questions or comments, when they came, displayed a genuine fascination with the story and trust in its veracity. Jerome was overjoyed to be able to tell his phenomenal story to a listener who seemed to believe him without question. When he had finished, Angelic did not immediately speak, as though she were collecting her thoughts carefully.

"Jerome, I think I would give almost anything to have this gift you have. You must be the most fortunate person in the world. Is that how you feel?" she enquired.

"Well, I know I'm almost certainly the only person who can do this. So, yes, I guess I am very fortunate," Jerome pondered.

She looked at him with benign concern. "And, yet, I sense some worry around the corners of your eyes. Is there something about this journey that troubled you?"

Jerome looked at her with an impressed-though-rueful expression. "How are you able to tell that by just looking at the corners of my eyes?"

"Oh." She gave a gentle laugh. "Years of practice bringing up children and grandchildren... and understanding men."

"Yes, the journey was... well, I honestly struggle to put my thoughts into words, but, you're right, I do have some feelings of concern and feelings of guilt to be honest."

"Why guilt?" she asked quickly. "Why would you possibly feel guilty?"

Jerome intertwined his fingers and lowered his head again, with the enthusiasm of the previous half hour having dissipated by then. "I said things to Jesus that I think caused him pain. They caused him to fear what the future holds. I didn't mean to cause any hurt, but I think I did. And, really, I shouldn't have done that."

"But you didn't do it deliberately, did you?"

"No, but it was thoughtless or, at least, careless."

"But can't you just say sorry? After all, we make mistakes all the time. Can't you just say a prayer and say sorry?"

"That's not how it works." He smiled at her again, knowing that he was not going to try to explain to her the laws of time travel. "People never remember when I travel back to meet them, so maybe Jesus will be the same and remember nothing about me."

"Tell me, Jerome, do you have family and friends back home? No, I'm sure you do," she added quickly, shaking her head in apparent irritation. "That's a silly question. What I meant to say is do any of your family or close friends know about your gift?"

"No, none of them know."

"And do you plan to tell them?"

"Yes," he uttered in a voice that combined softness with a

degree of uncertainty. "I plan to tell my girlfriend – we're getting married next year – and my brother. He's my older brother."

"Well, just be careful."

"Why? What do you mean?" he asked.

"There are some things that people – people who care for you very much – may prefer not to know." She adjusted the dark-red handbag on her lap. "That can be lonely for you if you're forced to keep it a secret. But you'll be in the best position to judge, and I'm certain you'll make the right decision."

The announcement that their flight was boarding came loudly from the steward at the entrance to the gate. Jerome helped Angelic to her feet and walked with her as she moved unsteadily, but with her head held confidently high, down the narrow gangway and onto the plane. He lifted her case into the luggage compartment above her first-row seat before moving to his own, midway down the aisle. The last time he saw her was when she was sitting in a wheelchair on the ground in Heathrow airport in London, being pushed by an attendant, as Jerome descended the stairs from the plane. She had turned and, on recognising him, gave a warm, cheery wave. He beamed back and raised his hand to acknowledge her.

***

London; Thursday, 18th May 2017

It was after 9.00pm when Jerome arrived back at his London house. He climbed the stairs leading from the front door two at a time. When he entered the main living room, his expression changed rapidly from good-humoured to confused to deep concern. Sitting on one of the seats, leaning forwards and starting to get up was Karl. He walked purposefully to his younger brother and placed his hands on Jerome's shoulders.

"Jerome, I've some very bad news, I'm afraid." His voice sounded soft, almost apologetic and without the trademark Karl confidence. "Mum passed away." His voice broke to a tremble. "Our mum's gone."

For a brief period, Jerome struggled to absorb this message. He noticed Mary sitting on the sofa, her eyes red and downcast. *Why would she be crying?* he wondered. *And where are the others?* Then he looked again at Karl's compassionate face, which was unchanged and awaiting an indication from Jerome that he understood what had been said.

But all Jerome could utter was a quiet, puzzled word, "Mum?"

Karl nodded and hugged his brother closely. "She passed away suddenly during the night. She had got up to go to the bathroom, and Dad heard her fall. She just collapsed. The doctor says it was probably a massive heart attack." Karl's voice had recovered some of its normal authority. "Here, sit down, Jerome."

Mary stood and embraced him gently before he sat on the sofa, with a look of confusion rather than sadness registering on his face. Still Jerome said nothing.

So Karl continued, "Dad phoned an ambulance immediately and then me. I got there about fifteen minutes later, just as the ambulance arrived. But..." He raised his eyes in a show of resigned hopelessness. "She had already gone at that point. There was nothing anyone could do. It's just so sad. Geraldine is looking after Dad now, and I wanted to come down and tell you rather than just phone."

Jerome looked at his brother and nodded his appreciation bemusedly. "Thanks, Karl. That was kind of you."

"When I got here, Mary said you'd been away for a few days, so I was worried you wouldn't be back tonight. I was about to phone you when you came in. I'm just glad I was able to tell you in person," continued Karl, reaching out again to touch his brother. "Were you out of London for a while?"

Jerome made a non-committal movement of his head in response before asking softly, "Had Mum been unwell?"

"No." Karl shook his head and wiped his hands down his own drawn cheeks. "Dad said she'd gone to bed early complaining of indigestion, but he never thought it was anything serious."

"I'll make some tea," said Mary before getting up and moving towards the kitchen. "Or would anyone prefer a drink? Karl, would you like a beer or something?"

"Yes." Karl looked distractedly at her. "A beer would be great, thanks. Do you want a beer, Jerome? Or maybe a brandy; brandy is good when you've had a shock. Mary, do you have any brandy in the house?"

Mary shook her head apologetically. "Sorry, there're just a few cans of lager. I could nip down to the off-licence and get a bottle of brandy. It's just a few doors down."

"That would be very kind of you. Thanks a lot." Karl took two £20 notes from his pocket and gave them to her, despite her mild protests. "I think that should be enough. And thanks again."

Mary left them.

At the sound of the front door closing, Karl continued. "Well, I got to meet Mary at last. She seems decent enough."

"Yeah," replied Jerome vaguely.

After a pause, Karl went on, "It's hard to believe Mum's gone."

"I still can't believe it," said Jerome, putting his palms together with the tips of his fingers touching his upper lip, as though in a praying position. "Did she... I mean, like, did Mum have a heart condition or anything?"

"No." Karl shook his head. "At least, not that I knew of, but we won't know for sure until we get the autopsy results."

Jerome began to weep quietly. "That's an awful thought: some stranger performing an autopsy on Mum."

"Yeah... sorry, I shouldn't have said that."

"Ah, Karl, you've nothing to apologise for. You didn't do anything wrong."

"Nobody did anything wrong, Jerome. It's just life; it's bloody awful but just part of life."

"Does Stancia know?" asked Jerome, after remaining silent for a few minutes.

"I'm not sure. Her mother probably knows, so she might know. Do you want to ring her now?"

"Yeah, I'll ring her in a few minutes. How are Dad and Geraldine?"

"Shocked, just stunned. We can travel up early tomorrow. They'll be delighted to see you." Karl sounded tired, and he had already decided they would not be travelling back that evening.

Jerome nodded, his face remaining serious and questioning. "What time did Mum die, Karl?"

"Around 5.00am, I think. I got there about half five and, as I say, Mum had already passed away."

"Do you know the exact time?"

"I'm not certain, Jerome," he replied looking with sadness and concern at his brother. "I'd guess around a quarter past five. Why do you ask?"

"I just want to know what I was doing at the moment Mum left us."

For a while, neither brother spoke.

Then Karl asked gently, "Were you out of London over the last few days?"

Jerome paused before responding, "Yes."

"Anywhere interesting?"

"I'll tell you all about it soon, but not just now."

"Are you in some sort of trouble, Jerome?"

"No, it's nothing like that; I'll tell you all about it, but I just need some time to clear my thoughts. I'll tell you after the funeral."

Karl gave his younger brother a puzzled look as the front door opened, signalling the return of Mary with the bottle of brandy.

Chapter 30

The traditions and rituals surrounding all funerals tend to be similar, but the grief felt by the mourners can differ markedly, and so it was with the Black family following the sudden death of Patricia.

On the drive up from London, Jerome and Karl said little, with both wrapped in their own thoughts as they sought to deal with this tragic situation. At a service station midway to Glasgow, they stopped for a coffee. Karl made a phone call home to check how his sister and father were coping, and confirm what time they'd be arriving. Jerome went outside, lit a cigarette and phoned Stancia again. She was still as shocked as she had been the previous evening when he had told her.

"I'll come up tomorrow," she said.

"Thanks. We'd all appreciate that."

"Oh, Jerome. It's just so awful."

"I know," he replied, his voice breaking momentarily.

He noticed Karl emerging from the front doors of the service station. Raising his palms, Karl indicated to him to take his time on the call, but, for once, there seemed to be nothing further to say.

"I better go now," he said briskly.

"OK, well, you both be careful, won't you? It's a tiring drive at the best of times."

"Yes, we're splitting the driving. I'm taking the next bit. I'll see you tomorrow."

"Bye." Her voice carried the sadness she so clearly felt.

***

As they approached the southern outskirts of Glasgow, Jerome felt an increasing tiredness weighing on him. Karl and he had spoken more on this part of the journey, mixing reminiscences of their mother with the practical issues that needed to be addressed over the coming days before the funeral. The conversation helped fend off the fatigue.

"It usually takes about half an hour from here," said Karl as he turned to gaze at a large shopping centre. "You can smoke in the car if you want."

"Are you sure?"

"Yeah. Special treat."

Jerome gave a gentle chuckle of appreciation and, lowering the driver's window slightly, he lit a cigarette and blew the smoke towards the thin rectangular slit of air.

"You have my full permission to lower that window further if you want," said Karl as he fanned some smoke away with his hand.

Jerome lowered it right down, and the incoming breeze blew the smoke directly over Karl. The brothers looked at each other and laughed.

***

Jerome was shocked when he saw his father. Pieter Black – who was sitting hunched in a large, green armchair – looked completely overwhelmed by sadness. He made one unsuccessful attempt to stand and greet his youngest child before Jerome bent down and hugged his thin frame. He had the appearance of someone who had been crying for a long time and had reached a stage of hopeless resignation. Pulling up a stool beside him, Jerome put an arm around his father's shoulders.

"So, how are you, Jerome?" Pieter asked.

"I'm OK, Dad. How are you? Will I make you a cup of tea or something?" queried Jerome.

"No, thanks."

"Have you eaten today? I could make a sandwich for you." Jerome looked at his father, still astonished at the sudden feebleness of his appearance.

"No." His father shook his head. "But there's plenty of food in the kitchen. You help yourself."

At that moment, Geraldine came in, and Jerome stood to embrace his sister fondly. The three siblings stood in the middle of the room, looking with concern at their father, who was gazing distractedly at his open palms resting on his lap.

"OK," began Karl, quietly but firmly, "I guess we better start sorting out the arrangements."

Jerome pulled a coffee table in front of his father's chair, and the three children sat on stools around it. They then began the necessary and distracting task of planning for the funeral. Although nothing specific was said, all three of them were clear that their father would be involved in every decision and, indeed, his permission was sought. And although he contributed little, any of his suggestions were accepted readily.

At one stage, Geraldine turned to Jerome and asked gently, "Could you say a few words about Mum at the Mass, Jerome?"

Karl said nothing but looked affectionately at his brother. At that moment, Jerome was certain they had already agreed to ask him, and he felt a surge of gratitude towards his two siblings.

"Your mum would like that, Jerome," said his father.

Jerome briefly hooded his eyes with his left hand. "It would be a privilege."

***

The following days passed quickly for Jerome and his family. There was little opportunity for him to reflect on the recent dramatic and tragic events, as the practical demands of the funeral preparations absorbed his time. Stancia arrived on the Saturday morning and, from that moment, provided help in an understated and yet ever-present way: assisting with the flow of commiserating visitors, providing refreshments and chatting when necessary – as though she were part of the family and yet never in a manner that would suggest her grief was on a par with theirs. Throughout these days, she appeared on occasion like a quiet sentinel alongside Jerome.

Jerome's nephews and nieces, when they were around, provided an added welcome distraction. Most of them were aware of the sadness being felt by the grown-ups and, for a while, tried to reflect it. But they were too young, and their own immediate childish needs broke through regularly, often to the unspoken relief of the adults.

During these days, Jerome felt he grew closer to Geraldine than he could ever remember. He had always loved her as his elder and, indeed, only sister, but the age gap, and the absence of football and the other male-bonding points had limited their interactions as he was growing up. By the time the funeral day arrived he had begun to appreciate her kind and thoughtful qualities, which were often unfairly overlooked because of her brisk, no-nonsense demeanour, and which he realised he'd long taken for granted.

***

It rained on the day of the funeral; a thin, mizzling rain that sometimes suggested stopping, but it never quite did. Jerome gave his eulogy about his mother, trying all the time not to look directly at his family for fear he would become emotional. He succeeded in getting through it with without faltering, and he was relieved.

Afterwards, they gathered around the newly dug grave, shielded by dark-coloured umbrellas, and said their final farewells. As they walked away from the graveside, Stancia moved to Jerome's side and linked arms tightly with him.

"They were lovely words you said today." She leaned in to him as the rain pattered on his umbrella. "Your mum would have been so proud; so proud of all of you."

"Do you think so?" asked Jerome.

"Oh, yes; your mother adored you guys."

He nodded his silent appreciation.

"How's your dad today?" she continued as they approached the car park.

"He's struggling, but hanging in there. I was thinking I might spend some time with him to help him get used to Mum not being there."

"I think that's a lovely idea, Jerome. You should do that."

***

Later, family and close friends returned to the house, with a feeling of emotional tiredness enveloping most of the group. There was little further reminiscing as the reality of their loss held its silent grip on them all. By 10.00pm, everyone had left except Pieter and his three children.

"Right, I'm for bed, I think," said Pieter. Pressing his hands on the arms of his chair, he levered himself slowly to a standing position, ignoring the signalled offers of aid.

"I'll help you up the stairs, Dad," said Karl as he opened the door.

"No, thanks. I need to do it myself."

Karl didn't protest, but he left the door open as they listened in an uneasy silence to their father ascending the stairs and closing his bedroom door.

"Do you think Dad will be OK on his own?" Jerome asked.

Neither of his siblings said anything; both displayed a dubious look.

"Well, he says he'll be fine," began Geraldine, speaking more softly than usual for fear her father might hear. "But I don't know. I somehow doubt it."

"I'm going back to London tomorrow, but I could come back up on Saturday and stay with Dad for a couple of weeks." Jerome glanced from his sister to his brother. "To see how he settles down."

"Could you do that Jerome?" said Geraldine. "What about your exams?"

"No, they're all finished."

"That would be great," she continued. "It will give us a good indication of how Dad will cope."

"It's the least I can do."

"Yeah, we appreciate it," replied Karl, reaching out to touch his brother's shoulder.

"Well, I'd better go as well," declared Geraldine, lifting her coffee cup and two plates containing the remains of sandwiches.

"Leave them, Geraldine. I'll clear up later," offered Jerome.

And, unusually for Geraldine, she replaced the plates and cup without protest before, quietly and sadly, hugging them both and leaving.

The two brothers sat in silence for a while, listening to the still reassuring noise from their father's clocks.

"There'll be nobody to stop Dad from filling this room with clocks now," said Karl. "It'll be like sitting inside Big Ben when it hits noon."

Jerome grinned at the thought, before getting to his feet and tiptoeing quietly up the stairs. He soon returned. "It sounds like he's asleep."

"Good." Karl nodded. "He could do with a good, long kip."

Karl took a thoughtful sip from his can of beer. "What was that poem Mum always wanted us to learn?" he began wearily. "Something like, 'After the funeral, mule praises, brays, something, something, something.' It seems apt at the moment." He relaxed back into his seat and looked across at his brother. "I think it was by that Welsh guy, Dylan Thomas. Do you remember it?"

Jerome nodded gently and said clearly:

> *"After the funeral, mule praises, brays,*
> *Windshake of sailshaped ears, muffle-toed tap*
> *Tap happily of one peg in the thick*
> *Grave's foot, blinds down the lids, the teeth in black."*

Karl gave an amused chuckle. "That's it. How the hell do you remember that?" He smiled to himself. "Though maybe it's because I've had a few beers, and you're totally sober." He shook the half-empty can in his hand. "Are you certain you won't have one? I'm sure Mum would expect us to on the day we said our final goodbye to her."

"No, thanks," replied Jerome.

Karl glanced over at his brother. "Well, do you want to tell me where you'd been last week when I called at your house?" He raised his free hand, with palm outwards. "And if it's none of my business and I don't need to know, that's fine."

Jerome folded his arms and stared earnestly at him. "Karl, I have something to tell you, and I want you to just listen until I've finished. Will you do that?"

Karl squinted with curiosity at his brother. "Sure," he replied, shrugging his shoulders to emphasise his agreement.

"I have a very strange gift; a power, you might call it. I can travel back in time. And I know it sounds insane, but I can do it and I have done it a number of times. I've travelled back to meet ordinary people and famous people. But they never remember it; only I remember it. And nothing ever changes. The past always remains exactly the same."

Karl shifted uneasily in the seat as a cautious smile began to play at the edges of his mouth. "This is a joke, right?"

But Jerome's unflinching face halted Karl's smile in its tracks. "Please just listen until I've finished," requested Jerome.

"OK." Karl nodded uncertainly.

"I've had this power for a few years now. I first discovered it when I was in London. Gran knew about it, though I'm sure she never told anyone. And I wasn't even sure about telling you, but..." Jerome paused briefly. "I've been on two major journeys. The first one was when I travelled to Nuremberg to meet Hitler in 1929. And I know that sounds totally crazy, even as I'm telling you. But I discovered later that the exact moment I travelled to see Hitler was the moment Gran died. I assumed it was just a coincidence, because she was very ill at that time anyway. But then I went on the second major journey last week. I went to Israel and travelled back to meet Jesus as he gave the Sermon on the Mount. I travelled back at 7.15am on Thursday morning. Then, when I got back to the house in London, you were there to tell me that Mum had died. And that she died at around 5.15am. There's a two-hour time difference between Israel and Glasgow, so, again, it happened at exactly the same time. I've no idea why I've got this power or what I'm supposed to do with it. But, now, with Mum's death, it feels like I may have caused it in some way."

"Stop, Jerome; just stop for a second." Karl put his can down firmly on the small, dark, wooden table. "Is this a joke? Because if it is, it's not funny."

Jerome breathed deeply. "Karl, I swear on our mother's grave that it's the truth."

Karl moved forwards in his seat and twice adjusted his hands, as though in a prelude to speak, but on both occasions said nothing. Then, rising abruptly, he walked over to his brother and placed one of his hands on Jerome's shoulder. "I know I'm asking you this for the third time, but this isn't some sort of sick joke, is it?"

"No, it's not Karl," Jerome said softly and clearly, shaking his head as he looked up at his brother.

Returning to his seat, Karl sat down slowly, almost painfully, and stared momentarily at the floor. "OK." He glanced at Jerome with a look of confusion as he tried to sound decisive. "So, what do we need to do?"

"Karl, you don't need to do anything. I knew this would be upsetting for you, and I'm really sorry for that. But I just needed to start telling people, and you and Stancia are the people I trust most in the world. I know I'm unburdening myself, which is selfish. And I did think about not telling anyone, but with the timing of Mum's death I just... I just want to tell someone very close to me."

"But you can't just expect me to do nothing, Jerome. You can't just dump this information on me and expect me to just say ho hum and move on." He paused as both brothers sat in strained silence. "Have you thought of speaking to anyone about this?"

"Just you and Stancia."

"No, I didn't mean that."

"You mean like a psychiatrist?"

"Yes, someone professional."

"Why would I, Karl, when it's true? It's not caused by drink or drugs; it's not a figment of my imagination; and it's not some delusion. It's true."

"You said you were in Israel last week?" Karl asked suddenly.

"Yes, I went to Tel Aviv and then up to Galilee where the Sermon on the Mount was given."

"Do you have your passport here?"

"Yes, it's in my bag upstairs."

"May I see it?"

Jerome gave him a slight accusatory glance. "You want to check that I was actually there?"

"Yes, Jerome. I do."

Three minutes later, Jerome returned and handed the passport to his then standing brother. Karl stared in disbelief and then concern at the visa stamp. "Fuck me, Jerome; you actually were in Israel. What the hell were you doing there?"

"I already told you."

"OK, let's sit down and think this through." He handed back the passport and moved towards his seat, but he did not sit down. "So, what are your plans? What do you plan to do now?"

"I'll tell Stancia."

"No." Karl shook his head vigorously. "No, that wouldn't be a good idea. You'd devastate her."

"Karl, we're engaged to be married next year. I can't not tell her."

"So, when are you going to tell her?"

"On Friday."

"No, don't do that. Leave it, at least for a while. Jerome, I need to get my head around this, so don't tell anyone else for the time being. Will you do that?"

"Of course I will. Karl, I'm genuinely sorry this has unsettled you so much."

"Unsettled! No, when I have a bit of tummy indigestion, I'm unsettled. I'm majorly alarmed, Jerome!" He softened his voice. "I'm alarmed about your health. And I still hope I'll wake up tomorrow, and you'll laugh and tell me I'm a gullible idiot, and then I can kick your arse."

"Try not to be alarmed, Karl. I'm not alarmed, and I'm the one this has happened to. But I'd really appreciate your support."

"Let's sleep on it, Jerome. I need to think this through."

They stood in the middle of the room.

"Do you want me to tell you anything about my meeting with Jesus?" asked Jerome.

"No, I don't," Karl replied quickly. "Let's just talk in the morning."

***

It was windy, though not cold, when the two brothers met as arranged the following morning, at the eastern gates to Kelvingrove Park in Glasgow. They exchanged unusually formal hellos and began walking in the direction of the art gallery.

"So, did you sleep OK in your old bed?" asked Karl, his hands thrust deeply into the pockets of his black windcheater.

"Yeah, fine," replied Jerome. "How'd you sleep?"

"Crap actually," came the blunt reply. "Do you remember everything you said last night?"

"'Course I do." Jerome continued to gaze fixedly at the ground ahead. "Were you hoping I wouldn't?"

"Yes, I suppose I was." Karl gave a tired sigh. "Jerome, what're your plans for over the next few days?"

"I'll get the train back to London tonight and sort some stuff out. Stancia's coming down on Friday. I plan to tell her then, Karl." Jerome felt an increased rigidity in his brother's gait. "Then I thought I'd come back home for a couple of weeks and stay with Dad."

"That would be good, Jerome; you being back here and staying with Dad would be great. It would really help."

"Well, it's the least I can do. You and Geraldine have been here for him and Mum for so long."

"Yes, well, he says he wants to stay living on his own, but I'm not so sure he can cope. Anyway, if you're with him for a couple of weeks, it would, you know, be a big help. But, Jerome…" for the first time that morning Karl looked directly at his brother, "I wouldn't tell Stancia about the other thing."

Jerome made no response.

"Look, I've been thinking about it all night," continued Karl, sounding unusually nervous. "I reckon you shouldn't say anything for the next week or so. And then, if you still feel like talking about it, maybe you could have a chat with someone professional; I can investigate that in the meantime. Let's leave a bit of space after Mum's death, and then we can try to resolve it together. What do you think?"

"Karl, I understand how you want to protect me and how you hope I'll snap out of this madness after a few days, then a psychiatrist will help me understand these delusions and I'll just be your normal wee brother again. But that won't happen because what I told you last night is the truth."

"I'm not saying you're lying or making this up."

"I know," Jerome interrupted him. "I know you're not."

For a while, the brothers walked in silence as they approached the art gallery. "I don't suppose you want to go in?" asked Karl.

"No."

"Good; I can't stand the pretentious pricks in there."

They continued walking briskly along the path that curved away from the gallery. "Can we agree on what to do next?" asked Karl quietly.

"Well, I don't think we'll agree, but let's try."

"Jesus, Jerome." Karl placed his hand on his brother's arm suddenly and stopped him. "You seem totally normal. This all seems fucking mad. Why did you tell me that stuff last night?"

"Well," replied Jerome with a gentle smile, "you did ask."

"What do you mean?"

"You asked me where I'd been last week."

"Ah, for fuck's sake, you could have lied. I was hardly going to grill you."

"I needed to talk to someone, Karl."

Karl looked at a nearby bench, examined it for dirt and gave it a cursory wipe before sitting down.

Jerome joined him. "I have to tell Stancia, Karl."

"No, you don't." His brother was firm. "You don't have to tell her. Not now anyway. What harm can there be in leaving it for a couple of weeks, eh?"

Jerome gave an indefinite nod. "Because nothing's going to change."

"How do you know? How can you be so certain?"

"I just am."

After a pause, Karl went on, "You'll only terrify her."

"That's not fair, Karl."

"Isn't it?"

Jerome leaned forwards and spoke to the ground. "I will say nothing to Stancia in London, but I can't put it off forever. *That* wouldn't be fair."

"Thanks, Jerome. I think that's the right thing to do. And if I arrange for you to meet someone professional, will you talk to them?"

"No. I wouldn't waste their time or my time."

It was Karl's turn to give an indefinite nod. "Fair enough." He glanced at his watch. "Do you have time for a pint before you catch your train?"

"Yeah; that sounds good to me."

Karl looked at his brother. "I feel like I'm living through a bloody crazy dream."

Chapter 31

Jerome sat on the train, circling his finger slowly around the top of his coffee cup and staring absent-mindedly as the first drops of rain made their downward sloping path on the window. The heat had gone from the day, and the cooler late-spring temperature had returned with the rain. He was tired – dead-dog tired, as Helga sometimes characterised it when she became too exhausted to even listen any more. But he couldn't sleep. His mind remained stubbornly restless, demanding that he assess and try to understand, if not come to terms with, the events of the previous week.

His mother was gone forever. And the real grief at this loss remained raw. Even the gathering of his family had brought little solace on this occasion. The death had been too sudden, too unexpected. Stancia had been with him for much of the last few days, and she had been wonderfully supportive. She had sensed when to talk and when to just listen, and had watched over him like a protective guardian angel. He knew he had never loved her so much.

Jerome was glad he had told Karl about his powers. He knew his brother didn't believe a word, but then he had not expected him to, or not initially anyway. But to share this knowledge with someone so close provided a dam burst of relief. Stancia would be next to be told, although maybe Karl was right, and he could delay that for a while, but only a short while. It would not be right to keep her in the dark about this if they were to share the rest of their lives together.

And as for his trip to see Jesus, Jerome had experienced no real opportunity to reflect on this momentous journey. The sometimes tyrannical randomness of life events had dictated otherwise. Although, were the events random? He retained a strong suspicion that they were not unrelated. The exact timings of his journeys back and the deaths of Helga and his mother were too close to be considered purely coincidental. His initial feelings of guilt, or at least of complicity in the deaths in some way, had eased. These had been replaced by gnawing confusion and a small seed of anger that his use of these powers, which he had never sought, was resulting in the deaths of his loved ones.

Longing for a cigarette, he went to the train toilet cubicle, opened the narrow top window, lit a cigarette and blew the soothing smoke into the darkening-evening air. Some raindrops touched and refreshed his face as he closed his eyes and listened to the comforting, repetitive sound of steel wheels on steel tracks as the train arrowed its way towards London. Jerome wondered if this night's sleep would bring him the same comforting acceptance of events that had occurred when he returned after the death of Helga. Could his now hyperactive mind assess, compartmentalise, and bring acceptance and understanding to him in the remarkable way it had happened before? He hoped so as he began to reflect on his journey back to Galilee.

* * *

He awoke late the following morning, feeling slightly disorientated, before remembering he was in his bedroom back in London; his fourth different bedroom in just over a week. For a few minutes, he lay still; cautious about opening his mind fully before he had prepared himself emotionally for whatever would emerge. He felt like someone who had gone to sleep with a worrying physical wound and was then reluctant to touch it, in case it remained or, indeed, had worsened in the night. But, as he gradually opened the doors and allowed the memories to come back, he discovered that the incredible calmness and acceptance that he had experienced after Helga's funeral had indeed returned.

He showered and dressed in a slow, deliberate manner, as though wary that any sudden physical movement could disturb this wonderful equilibrium he was experiencing. But his caution proved unnecessary. He returned two missed calls: the first to reassure Karl that he was fine, and the second to tell Stancia that he couldn't wait to see her the following night.

Then, walking to the nearby park, Jerome sat on the same bench where he had watched the children feed the ducks in his first planned journey back in time almost two years previously. *That was a lifetime ago,* he thought. There were office workers strolling, chatting and eating their lunchtime sandwiches. Their presence injected a note of warmth into his calmness. He allowed thoughts of his mother to meander into his mind, but they caused only a gentle, poignant nostalgia rather than raw grief. Easing his head back to stretch the muscles in his neck, Jerome closed his eyes and let the sun warm his face. He did not feel angry, he did not feel guilty, and he did not feel grief-stricken. He felt peaceful and ready for the next stage of his life, whatever that may bring.

***

Later that evening, Chris was insistent that he take Jerome out for a drink. He had missed the funeral due to it clashing with his university examinations, and was apologising profusely for his absence, even when Jerome told him that he fully understood. So they took the familiar, short walk to their local pub, with little conversation being exchanged along the way. They sat at their usual table; a corner one that gave a full view of the other customers in addition to access to one of the big television screens, although neither paid any attention to it on this occasion.

"I must say, buddy, you seem remarkably stoical about your mum," began Chris. "If it were me, I'd probably be curled up in a corner somewhere just feeling sorry for myself."

"Yes." Jerome folded his arms tightly and rested his elbows on the top of the rectangular, wooden table. "It's a bit strange. I feel like I should feel a lot sadder than I do. But I don't know. It's just hard to explain. I loved my mum so much, and, to be honest, I can't really believe I'll never see her again." He moved his hand and, almost absent-mindedly, pulled one of the beer coasters closer. "Maybe if I believed I'd never see her again I'd feel, you know, like a normal sadness. But just not at the moment."

"I think the brain adjusts to these things in its own good time, Jerome. And…" Chris paused as the drinks were placed on the table and then paid the waiter, brushing aside gently his friend's attempts to pay. "We're all different in how we deal with things. That's just the way. And I'm still sorry I wasn't able to make the funeral. I do feel really bad about it."

Jerome smiled at him. "Chris, please forget about it. I completely understand. Honestly."

They clinked their beer glasses gently as Chris nodded his acknowledgement that further apologies were unnecessary.

"You know," said Chris, "even though we're the same age, I increasingly feel like you're somehow older than me."

"What do you mean? Do I look older?" asked Jerome, genuinely intrigued.

"No, well, actually, I think you do look a bit older for some reason, but that's not it. You seem to have a maturity beyond your years. It's as though you've put more into your years of life than I have." Chris took a further slug from his pint. "Although, come to think of it, it wouldn't be too hard to be more mature than me."

Jerome tilted his head slightly and glanced thoughtfully at his friend, but he decided not to pursue this point.

The two young men chatted genially about family and friendship as Jerome's accepting attitude, combined with the alcohol, helped relax Chris into his more customary warm humour.

"Do you remember the night I strong-armed you into chatting to the two women who were sitting over there." Chris pointed to a table close by.

"Yes, though I don't think you exactly strong-armed me," responded Jerome.

"Well, don't look now, but they've just walked in."

Jerome looked up as the two young women walked through the bar. One of them saw him, smiled and mouthed a hello.

"Did you see that!" exclaimed Chris in mock exasperation. "She smiled at you. Even after you made your pathetic excuses and left that night, she still says hello to you."

Jerome grinned at his friend.

"It's good to see you really smiling again." Chris then lowered his head and moved it closer to Jerome in an exaggerated, conspiratorial way. "You know, we could try again if you like? But no…" He moved back to an upright sitting position. "That's completely inappropriate now on so many levels. That was a ridiculous suggestion by me." A mischievous grin began to appear on his face. "Although, obviously, if you were interested, I'd feel obliged to help you."

Jerome shook his head, smiling warmly.

"I know; I was only kidding," said Chris. "Listen, Jerome." His voice took on a more serious note unexpectedly. "We'll be going our separate ways soon and making our own routes in the big, bad world. If you ever need anything, just ask me. I'll be there for you."

"Thank you." Jerome was surprised and genuinely touched by his friend's words.

"No, seriously; I owe you my life, and I'll never forget that. So if you ever need anything, you just shout out to me, won't you?"

"OK. Who knows, I might just take you up on that someday."

"It would be my pleasure, buddy," said Chris, raising his glass one more time. "It would be my pleasure."

***

The following night was to be Jerome's final evening in the house. Stancia was travelling down from her mother's home to mark the occasion and help him move his belongings back to his temporary home in Glasgow. It was just after 5.00pm when her train arrived. As always, he was there to welcome her. She had long ago given up telling him she could make her own way from the station to the house, but remained quietly pleased at his insistence on meeting her every time.

"Did you remember to rent the car?" she asked in a voice still bright with delight at seeing him again.

"No," he said, kissing the side of her head as they walked along the station concourse, "I forgot."

"Jerome." She looked at him with a hint of annoyance, which softened quickly to one of uncertainty. "Did you really? Because we might struggle to book one now."

"It's OK. I've booked it. We pick it up tomorrow morning. And it's got manual gears like you said, not one of those new-fangled eco-friendly automatics."

"And we can both drive it?" she asked, smiling as she clung tightly to his free arm.

"Yes, we're both named drivers, as per your instructions."

"You'll thank me for it when you want to sleep off your hangover tomorrow." She leaned even further into him. "Love you."

"Love you too," he replied softly as he raised her case, and they descended the stairs to the Underground station.

"They're all joining us tonight – Chris, Mary and Ser – for the final meal together," he said. They were then standing on the crowded Underground train as it made its brief, noisy journey between stations.

"Great; where are we going?" she queried, looking down to confirm her case was still wedged between them.

"Some bistro Chris is booking. I think it's mainly Italian food. You don't mind the full gang coming, do you?"

"Of course not; it's your last night."

The train stopped at one of the intermediate stations.

"Your Karl called over this morning," explained Stancia.

"Yeah? Why was that?" Jerome tried to sound casually interested.

"He was bringing something back that Mum had left in your house; an umbrella or something. He told me to look after his wee brother. He's very sweet, your Karl."

"Yes, he is, although I don't think he'd like being called 'sweet' somehow." Jerome gave a relieved smile.

The departing passengers had been replaced quickly by even more commuters as the train moved out from the station.

"How are you anyway?" she asked, not looking directly into his eyes.

"I'm fine, actually." He nodded confirmation of this statement with a pleasantly surprised look on his face. "I really am."

"Well, that's all I care about." She stood beside him, her wide eyes glistening, and asked no further questions.

***

The bistro was crowded but not too boisterous when they entered.

In a way, this suited the sense of fond farewell within their group, which, naturally, was tempered by the recent death of Jerome's mother. As the evening progressed, the reminiscences became more light-hearted, and everyone felt increasingly comfortable with the humour and the laughter. Jerome, conscious that Stancia may feel left out of these shared stories, tried to ensure she was never excluded from any of the conversations, but she just seemed happy to be with him.

"Shall we go for one final, nostalgic drink in the pub?" suggested Chris after they had finished the meal and were waiting for the bill.

His plan received no objections, and they soon headed to the pub, although the limit of one drink was breached quickly and they ended up staying late. Towards the end of the night, the noise became very loud, and, for each of them, it was only possible to converse with the person beside them. Chris and Jerome were leaning across the table, almost having to shout to each other, while Mary and Stancia, their heads inclined towards each other, were deep in conversation. Jerome noticed that Ser's eyes had begun to close from tiredness and so, with a combination of words and gestures, he agreed with the group that they should return to the house.

* * *

Once they had arrived back at the house, as Jerome and Stancia planned to leave early the following morning, final farewell embraces were exchanged in the living room before everyone retired to bed.

In their room, Jerome noticed that Stancia looked odd. "Are you OK?" he asked concernedly. "You look very pale. Do you feel sick or anything?"

"No." She undressed quickly and put on her nightdress.

"Are you sure?" he asked, unconvinced.

"Yes."

She got into bed, as he was still undressing, and lay on her back, looking at the ceiling. Jerome sensed from her uncharacteristically clipped responses that she was not OK. Leaving the bedside light on, he got into bed beside her and wrapped his arm gently around her midriff.

For a moment, Stancia made no response and then, suddenly, she sat bolt upright in the bed. "Jerome, this may not seem fair, but I've got to ask you a question." Her voice was cracking.

He looked at her in bewilderment. She was trembling and had a look of fear in her eyes. At first, he thought she was going to say that Karl had told her about his time-travel story and he began mentally preparing for that.

But her question shattered that illusion. "Have you slept with her?"

For a split second, Jerome was genuinely confused. "Who?"

"You know who I mean, Jerome." Tears appeared in her eyes as her hands clasped tightly onto the duvet cover. "I need you to be honest with me."

Jerome, very alarmed by then, sat up. "Do you mean Mary?"

"Yes, I mean her. Did you sleep with her?"

"What did she say?" he asked, panicking and struggling to know how to respond.

Stancia covered her face with her hands, and, after a few moments of silence, Jerome could hear her weeping bitterly, her shoulders shuddering. She appeared so delicate to him suddenly.

"Stancia, look, don't cry, please. I…" Gently, he touched the side of her hand, but she withdrew quickly from him. He looked on helplessly as the weeping turned to convulsive sobs before subsiding.

All of the time, Stancia continued to cover her face. Eventually, she withdrew her hands, and brushed her eyes and cheeks with the outside of her fingers.

"May we talk?" he asked softly.

She shook her head bitterly and lay down with her back to him.

He continued to sit up, looking at the hair on the back of her head where it just covered the top of her nightdress. "Stancia, please, we can't just leave it like this. It's not what you think."

"I don't want to hear about you and her. I don't want to talk. I'll go early in the morning."

After a further ten minutes had passed, he lay down and gazed at the ceiling in shock and dismay.

"Stancia, please let me explain," he asked.

"I do not want to hear." Her voice was angry and definitive. "I do not want to hear anything."

***

Jerome didn't sleep that night, despite the usual soporific effect of the alcohol, and he felt sure Stancia didn't either, although he felt he couldn't check. With the first shafts of sunlight appearing, he felt Stancia move and saw her sitting on the side of the bed, checking her phone.

"Stancia, may we talk please?" he pleaded.

He watched the back of her head shaking a no. She stood up and dressed quickly.

Jerome was so confused that he didn't know whether to get up too or remain in bed. "Where are you going?" he asked.

"There's a train at 7.00am. I'll catch that."

"For Christ's sake, Stancia, don't go like this." He got out of bed and, standing behind her, touched her shoulder softly. Again, he could hear the quiet weeping, and he removed his hand.

"You've broken my heart, Jerome."

He remained standing helplessly behind her.

Stancia's phone buzzed. "It's my taxi outside," she said, and she lifted her case, opened the bedroom door and closed it quietly behind her without turning around.

Jerome stood totally still, listening to the front door closing and the taxi being driven away in the early morning stillness. She had left. Stancia was gone. He felt physically ill and almost paralysed with confusion. He covered his eyes with his left hand and, breathing rapidly, tried to think what to do. His first reaction was to feel he had been a pathetic fool for just letting her go without trying harder to explain. And yet he also felt that, at this extremely raw moment, it would have done no good. He would have to wait until she was prepared to listen to him, assuming she would do so at some stage. Then he could apologise properly, unconditionally, and beg her forgiveness. He had to get her back. Fleetingly, he thought about going into Mary's room and demanding to know what she had said to Stancia the previous night, but realised quickly that this would be stupid. He could talk to her later in a more rational and calm manner. Jerome decided to text Stancia. Fumbling for his phone, he tapped on her name and, immediately, saw the last text she had sent yesterday. It read, "Just getting on train. Can't wait to see you. Love you lots."

Blinking at the screen, he considered what to type. Initially, he thought of starting with a sad-faced emoji, but he dismissed the idea quickly as totally inappropriate. It would be too much like diminishing the seriousness of her hurt. Finally, he typed, "Stancia, I just want to say I love you. Please contact me when you're ready." Then he added, "And I'm so sorry" before hitting the send button.

Jerome sat on the edge of his bed, placed his elbows on his thighs and cupped his hands over his face. It was 6.05am. They had planned to collect the car from the car-rental company at 8.30am. He decided he still would go there, although alone instead. His family were expecting him to move in with his father that evening. That plan was unaltered.

Chapter 32

London;
Friday, 26th May 2017

Distractedly, Jerome showered and dressed before strolling the half-mile to the premises of the car-rental company. He sensed they wouldn't be open this early, but he had felt suffocated staying in the room and needed to get out. He stood outside the office's glass front door and peered inside. There was no one there. A small, white notice on the door showed 7.00am as the opening time. Drawing his third cigarette of the morning from its packet, he lit it and inhaled the soothing smoke deeply. He walked around to the back of the premises, partly to look at the newly washed cars but mainly to keep himself occupied as he tried to coordinate his still-jumbled thoughts. His phone buzzed, and he pulled it from his jacket pocket immediately, but it wasn't Stancia; it was from Karl. The text read, "Hope you had a great night. See you later."

He thought of sending another text to Stancia or phoning her, but decided it would be better to leave it for a while. He needed to talk to Mary first.

Soon afterwards, a neatly dressed young man arrived to open

the office. He smiled a hello at Jerome, who followed him in.

"Just give me a minute to get myself sorted," the young man began as he switched on his computer and draped his blue suit jacket over the back of the chair.

"Yes, sorry, I'm a bit early. I wasn't sure what time you opened." Jerome fished out his driving licence and credit card from his back pocket and stood patiently. "It was to be two drivers, but it will just be one. It's booked in my name, Jerome Black."

"Oh." The young man's face tightened.

"That's not a problem, is it?" said Jerome.

"No." The smile had returned. "I just need to change the details."

Jerome looked distractedly at the bare, white wall behind the young man as he typed in the necessary information and completed the documentation checks.

"Right, you're ready to go," he began breezily. "Here's the key with the reg number attached to it and here's your copy of the contract. The car is in bay twenty-three. Is there anything else I may help you with?"

"No, thanks." Jerome took the key, stuffed the contract in his back pocket, and walked smartly to the car.

He drove quickly back to the house and parked outside. Returning to his room, he finished packing his remaining belongings and carried them down to the car before going back to the first-floor living room. It was now 7.30am, and there were no sounds coming from the bedrooms above. He sat down in the seat opposite the stairs and waited.

Even in his troubled mood, he respected the recently agreed no-smoking policy in the house and sat gnawing at the ball of his thumb as he waited for Mary to appear. At 7.55am, he decided to go to her room, but, as he stood up, he heard one of the bedroom doors opening. He watched intently as Mary descended the stairs, her long, pink dressing gown tied loosely at the front.

"Oh, I thought you'd gone." She looked surprised and stopped briefly on one of the stairs before continuing her descent. "What time are you heading off?" She widened her eyes inquisitively and appeared genuinely pleased to see him.

"What did you say to Stancia last night?"

Mary looked at him quizzically. "What do you mean?"

"What did you say to Stancia last night, about you and me? What did you say?" Jerome spoke quietly but his voice had an increasingly hard edge.

"I don't know what you mean." She swayed back slightly and put a hand to the neck of her dressing gown, with a look of concern appearing abruptly on her still-puzzled face. "What did I say?" She glanced at the floor; her brow furrowed as though trying to recollect the late-night conversation. "I don't really remember saying anything specifically. Why? Is something wrong?"

"Yes, there's something wrong." Jerome could hear the anger in his voice as he continued. "Yes, there's something fucking wrong. You were talking to Stancia last night, and then, when we went up to the bedroom, she knew we had slept together. Now, what did you say to her?"

"Jerome, I didn't…" Mary looked wildly at him. "I swear to God I wouldn't. I… I don't remember what I said, but I wouldn't have told her."

"What did you say to Stancia? I need to know. Think. What did you say?"

"I'm not certain. I think I said that I'd really miss you, but…" Tears had started to appear in Mary's eyes as she glanced upstairs with a look of bewildered fear.

Her appearance diffused his anger immediately and it was then his turn to gaze at the floor, this time with tired resignation.

"I swear, Jerome. I don't remember saying anything about us. I'm really sorry."

He nodded slowly without looking up. "Well," he began after a long sigh, "I'm not exactly blameless in this."

"Is there anything I can do?" she asked plaintively.

"I don't think so." He rubbed his forehead. "No, there's not."

Jerome took out a set of house keys and placed them carefully on the table. "OK, I'll be going now."

"Jerome, I really am so sorry."

"So am I." He reached out and touched the side of her face briefly. "Take care of yourself."

***

The drive to Glasgow took just under seven hours. He made one stop on the way to reply to Karl's text and then, with trepidation, he tried phoning Stancia but only got her voicemail. He didn't leave a message.

It was mid-afternoon when he arrived at his father's house. No one was there, and the place seemed eerily quiet. He unloaded his cases and carried them to his old bedroom. A room that he was fairly certain had been used by nobody else since he was a boy. Pulling the curtain back, he looked across the road at the big oak tree, now heavy with wet leaves, and drew a certain reassurance from its permanency. He watched for a while until Karl's car arrived, and he saw his brother help his father out of the car, along the driveway and into the house.

"Hi Jerome; you guys made great time. We didn't expect you for another hour," Karl said brightly as his father moved along the hall to greet his younger son.

"Yes, I've just arrived. The traffic was light most of the way," replied Jerome as they all moved into the living room.

"Is Stancia here?" asked Karl.

"No, she's not here."

"Did yis stop for anything to eat on the way?" asked his father, still standing beside his green armchair.

"Yes, we did, but I'm a bit peckish now. Shall I make you something?"

"Not for me, thanks, Jerome. I've got to rush back to the house. Dad, do you want anything to eat?" enquired Karl.

"I wouldn't say no," Pieter replied, sitting down finally.

"I know Geraldine left a ton of food in the fridge, Jerome, so help yourselves. I'll give you a call later." Karl turned to his father and spoke more loudly. "OK, Dad. I'll see you later."

"OK," said Pieter, and he raised his arm in acknowledgement as Karl left, closing the door behind him and leaving a sudden quietness in the room.

"Let me make us a cup of tea first and then I'll check on the grub," began Jerome. "How does that sound?"

"Perfect," replied his father. "Will Stancia be around later?"

"Er, no, not tonight."

Jerome went and busied himself in the kitchen, making the tea and checking the food provisions. He thought Pieter looked brighter than when he had left him two days ago, but he hesitated to say anything in case his father would consider it in some way inappropriate that he should look better so soon after the death of his beloved wife.

Thirty minutes later, they were sitting at the kitchen table in front of plates of smoked cod, boiled potatoes and peas – a favourite dish of his father. When his mother was alive, eating in the living room was forbidden, except for on special occasions, and both father and son were happy to keep up this custom, at least for the time being.

Pieter began eating slowly but with obvious enjoyment. "This is very good. Where'd you learn to cook like this?"

"Well, it's hardly Michelin-star standard," responded Jerome with a smile, "but you do learn to fend for yourself a bit when you're away from home."

"Well, it's very tasty. Pass us the HP Sauce there, would you?"

"So, Dad," began Jerome as he watched his father squeeze a large portion of sauce onto the side of his plate. "How're you getting on living on your own?"

"Sure, I'm not really on my own. Geraldine and Karl are like two mother hens fussing round me all the time."

"I don't think Karl would like to be called a mother hen." Jerome grinned.

"No, I guess he wouldn't. Well, a big St Bernard then."

Jerome cut into his fish. It did taste good. "And are you sleeping OK?"

"I don't sleep much at night."

Jerome nodded. "Is it a bit lonely?"

"No, even when there's nobody in the house, I'm not lonely." He widened his eyes to stress the sincerity of his words. "She's still here, you know; your mother."

Jerome paused in his eating but made no reply.

"I can sense her presence. And sometimes I'll hear her, just saying something gentle like she always did or humming a wee tune. I really do."

Jerome, blinking, watched his father continue with his meal, seemingly at ease with what he had just told his son.

Chapter 33

Glasgow;
Saturday, 27th May 2017

It was shortly before 6.00pm, later that day, when Karl phoned.

"Hi there," answered Jerome as he levered himself up in the seat in which he had been half-dozing in front of the television.

"So, how are you and the auld fella getting on?" Karl's voice sounded exaggeratedly upbeat.

"Fine, we had our dinner, and he's just gone to lie down."

"That's good. What's your plan for the evening?"

"I reckon we'll take it easy tonight. I'll probably order a takeaway, and we can watch something on the television. That film *Mississippi Burning* is on later."

"Oh, he'll enjoy that. Plenty of gratuitous violence and the good guys win."

"And he won't have Mum to tut disapprovingly at him."

"Yeah, that's right," replied Karl. "Are you sure you want to stay in all night? If you want to head out with Stancia for a while, I could drop over."

"No, thanks." Jerome paused. He didn't want to discuss

Stancia, and he didn't want to have to lie about anything. "I think an early night for both of us is a good idea."

"OK. I'll call over tomorrow morning, and maybe the two of us can have a chat about the other thing."

"Yes." Jerome was conscious of the discomfiture in his brother's voice and did not want to exacerbate it. "I'd appreciate that."

"Great." Karl sounded relieved. "I'll call over at around 11.00am. Enjoy the movie, and if you're getting a Chinese takeaway, Dad likes chicken chow mien."

"OK, thanks. See you tomorrow."

***

Father and son spent a gently companionable evening together. Pieter ate sparingly of the chow mien, despite Karl's recommendation, but he became engrossed in the movie. Jerome was pleased to see him leaning forwards in his seat, his partly squinting eyes focusing intensely on the screen. And, for a while, they could both forget their sadness.

***

Later that evening, lying on his bed, Jerome sent another text to Stancia: "Just thinking of you."

He wasn't sure if she was in Glasgow or Manchester, but he decided that if he hadn't heard from her by the following morning, he would call at her mother's house. Jerome also reflected on his father's words earlier that day about how he could still hear Patricia speaking or humming a tune. Jerome knew this was nonsense. His mother was dead, and while his father might genuinely believe he still could hear her voice, it was only a delusion; harmless, but a delusion. The irony that he could dismiss his father's claims so easily and yet somehow expected Karl to believe his story was not lost on him. And yet he looked forward to seeing his brother tomorrow.

***

Pieter was eating porridge when Jerome came into the kitchen the following morning.

"Morning Dad, did you sleep well?" Jerome enquired.

"Yes, I've only been up about ten minutes. I've made porridge for the two of us, so you just need to give that pot a wee heat." Pieter nodded at the small, silver pot on the hob. "That was a great film last night."

"Yes, I like Gene Hackman." Jerome looked into the pot, then added some milk and stirred the warming porridge. "Are you going to Mass today?"

"No, I think I might give myself the day off," replied his father as, tilting the bowl towards him, he scooped the remaining porridge onto his spoon.

"I'm going to nip out for a while after breakfast," said Jerome as he poured the steamy mixture into his bowl. "Karl's coming over around 11.00am."

"That's fine. Will you get the papers on your way back?"

"Will do."

***

Thirty minutes later, just before 10.00am, Jerome rang the doorbell of Stancia's mother's house. The door opened slowly, and her mother stood there looking uncomfortably at Jerome. Immediately, he knew that she was aware of a problem in the relationship.

"Hello Mrs Kennedy," Jerome spoke softly, his voice sounding almost frail in the quiet morning air. "Is Stancia at home?"

Mrs Kennedy opened the door a fraction further. "No, she's not, Jerome."

He thought he detected a note of sadness in her reply. Jerome turned away briefly and then back. "OK, would you tell her I called, please?"

"Yes, I'll do that."

Jerome nodded thoughtfully, said his thanks and returned home.

***

"Did you forget the papers?" asked Pieter as Jerome opened the front door and walked into the hall.

"Oh, shit. Sorry, Dad, I'll go and get them," offered Jerome.

"No, don't worry. I'm going out for a walk anyway. I'll get them on my way back." He motioned with his walking stick at the half-opened door to the living room. "Karl's here."

"You're early." Jerome smiled gently at his brother as he entered the room and sat down opposite him.

"See you guys later," called their father from the hall.

The brothers replied and then listened silently as the front door was pulled closed.

"So, how'd you both get on last night?" Karl asked cheerfully.

"Fine; Dad loved the film."

"Yes, he said he did. He looks brighter this morning, don't you think? He said he had a good night's sleep. How do you feel?" Karl spoke more quickly than usual.

Jerome sensed uneasiness in his brother. "Shall we talk about it now; my time travel?"

"Yes, let's do that. So how *do* you feel now?"

"You mean do I still believe that I travelled back in time to meet people? Yes, nothing has changed, Karl, and it won't. It happened, and I know it happened."

"OK." Karl averted his gaze briefly. "Listen, Jerome, I've been thinking about this since you told me. In fact, I've been thinking of little else, so just hear me out. I've spoken to a… a psychiatrist with expertise in grief counselling. And I haven't mentioned any names, but I gave her the general gist of what you told me. Now she'd be happy to sit down and have a chat with you; it would be totally confidential and it would be private. It's not on the NHS [National Health Service], so there'd be no formal record of it. You could just go along and chat to her. I found her really professional and very empathetic. It's worth a go, no? What do you think?" Karl looked encouragingly at his brother.

Jerome looked sympathetically in return. "Karl, look, first of all, thanks for what you're trying to do. I know you only want what's best for me. I also know, with complete certainty, that I have travelled back in time and so meeting with this psychiatrist or, indeed, any other psychiatrist would be a waste of everyone's time."

"But what harm can it do, Jerome, just to meet her once?"

"I know you might think I'm being unreasonably stubborn here, but I have zero interest in sitting down with a psychiatrist."

"OK." Karl nodded defensively and gave an accepting shrug of the shoulders. "But the offer is there any time you want it. Just let me know."

"I appreciate it. I really do." Jerome folded his arms. "And if you ever want to hear about my journeys back in time, just let *me* know. I'd be delighted to tell you about them."

Karl gave a wan smile. "I think I'll pass on that for the moment."

"Fancy a cuppa tea?" asked Jerome to break the ensuing silence.

"I'd love one. Actually, I'd prefer a coffee. I haven't had my morning fix yet."

"Do you know what Dad said to me yesterday about Mum?" Jerome asked when they were sitting drinking from their hot mugs.

"No, what?" Karl looked less tense and seemed relieved that the previous subject of conversation had ended. He sat up with interest at the question.

"He said he still felt Mum was in the house, and he could hear her singing and humming a tune."

Karl chuckled and shook his head with exaggerated resignation. "For fuck's sake, Jerome; at this rate, it'll be me going to the psychiatrist complaining that I'm the only person in the family who can't communicate with the dead. You don't believe him, do you?" asked Karl, checking his humour momentarily.

"Of course not, and, before you say anything, I know that what I'm asking you to believe is a lot stranger than what Dad said."

"You'll get no disagreement from me on that point."

"But, anyway, that's what he said. And I think it gives him comfort to think Mum's still around."

"Aye, I expect it does." Karl smiled reflectively, seeming to acknowledge suddenly the poignancy of his father's words. "By the way, do you want to go out with Stancia tonight?"

"Er, no, it's all right."

"Is she still in Glasgow?"

Jerome paused before replying, "I'm not sure."

"Is everything OK?" Karl looked at him curiously.

Jerome scrunched up his face. "No, we've had a bit of a falling out."

"You didn't tell her about the time-travel thing, did you?" Karl asked painfully.

"No, I didn't; it's much more mundane."

"Want to tell me?" Karl appeared genuinely relieved.

"I had a one-night fling with someone else, and she found out on Friday night."

"Ah." Karl grimaced, folded his arms and blew out his cheeks. "Jesus, you're on a hell of a roll at the moment! Is there any more bad news? You haven't developed Ebola overnight?"

Jerome shook his head, smiling jadedly. "I've had better weeks."

"Was it someone Stancia knew?" Karl asked with a wincing expression, as though anticipating more bad news.

"Yeah, Mary from the house in London."

"Hmm, yes, that's tricky. Did Mary tell her?"

"I'm actually not certain." Jerome closed his eyes briefly. "They were talking on Friday night, and Stancia confronted me afterwards. I'm not sure if she already suspected, and Mary said something to convince her… but, anyway, she knew."

"Well…" Karl gave a deep sigh. "I guess living in the same house can present temptations on occasion."

"I was dumb."

"You're right; you were dumb. I was just trying to make you feel better. Is there any chance of you guys getting back together?"

"I hope so. I'm certainly going to try."

"Absolutely, we all make mistakes, but that girl's good for you. My advice is to try very hard to get her back."

"Don't worry, I will."

Karl leaned back in the chair, looking at the ceiling as he tried to absorb this latest information from his brother. "Your head must be all over the place with all these things happening." He looked at his brother with concern. "You really need to look after yourself."

"Thanks, I will."

"One thing's for sure, Jerome: I could never accuse you of being dull."

***

By the time Pieter had returned from his walk, carrying the newspapers in a cream-coloured, cotton bag, Geraldine had joined her two brothers.

"Ah, you're all here; that's good," declared Pieter. Taking the newspapers from the bag, he placed them on the coffee table before removing his coat.

"I was going to put your dinner on, Dad," began Geraldine, "but Jerome won't let me. He says you two have it under control."

"What's for dinner?" asked Pieter.

"Roast chicken," answered Jerome.

"Lovely," said his father, easing himself into the vacant seat.

"What are you cooking with it?" asked Karl with a hint of mischief.

"Potatoes and veg," replied Jerome smartly.

"Even better," pronounced Pieter.

"And gravy?" queried Karl.

"Of course," Jerome said, "it wouldn't be the same without it."

"Well, I'm impressed, Jerome." Geraldine smiled.

"Let's see how it turns out before we hand out any medals," suggested Karl, grinning at his father. "Do you know how to switch off the smoke alarms, Dad?"

Pieter gave a contented smile. "I reckon Jerome and me will get it done."

***

Later, when his two older children had left, Pieter stood in the kitchen, watching closely as Jerome put the chicken in a roasting tin and placed it in the already-heated oven. "What temperature did you have that at?" Pieter asked.

"It's at 200 degrees," replied Jerome standing up. "We'll leave it for about half an hour, then turn it down to 100. It should be ready in about two hours."

Pieter retained a look of intense concentration as he repeated Jerome's instructions quietly, as though committing them to memory. "I must have seen your mother do that a thousand times, but I never paid any attention."

"There's not much to it, Dad. You'll get the hang of it fairly quickly. Although I've never made gravy before, so we'll need to keep our fingers crossed on that one."

"I don't mind having butter instead of gravy," suggested his father.

"Well, let's have a go at the gravy anyway. The butter can be our fallback position."

"Sounds good to me."

Jerome's subsequent attempt to make gravy turned out well, much to his satisfaction and his father's delight. Having eaten their meal at a leisurely pace, they moved back to the living room to relax. They both read the newspapers for a while before Jerome took his phone from his trouser pocket. There was still nothing from Stancia.

Quietly and thoughtfully, he typed the message, "Stancia, don't let it end like this. Can't we just talk?"

Then, after sending it, he returned the phone to his pocket.

Less than five minutes had elapsed when he felt the phone buzz. The text from Stancia read, "Can you meet me in the village cafe at 11.00am tomorrow? If so, we can talk briefly then."

Jerome stared at the message for a long time. At least contact had been restored, but the word "briefly" was both ominous and disheartening. On glancing up from the screen, he noticed his father had fallen asleep, and so – to the slow, rhythmic sounds of his father breathing and the clocks ticking – he texted his reply, "Yes, of course. I'll see you at 11.00am."

Chapter 34

Glasgow;
Monday, 29th May 2017

As he crossed the main road opposite the village cafe, Jerome peered through the large front windows. It was 10.50am, and, as usual at this time of the morning, the place was busy, mainly with young women with toddlers, taking their morning coffee break. He saw Stancia sitting side-on to the front window at a table near the back. Her head was bowed slightly as she appeared to be studying her phone. He opened the door, still wondering if she had seen him, and made his way to her table.

"Hi," he said quietly.

She glanced up briefly, showing neither surprise nor welcome in her face. He sat down beside her, facing the front of the cafe, and was careful not to make any physical contact. Stancia looked thin and extremely pale; her eyes had a stoic sadness about them as she put her phone into a neat, black handbag and wrapped her fingers around the bright-yellow coffee mug.

"How are you?" he asked.

She turned to look at him, her eyebrows raised above tired eyes, but made no reply.

"Stancia." Jerome leaned closer and continued to speak softly. "I hate to see you upset like this. I'm so sorry to have caused you such pain. I'd do anything to make it up to you."

She tightened her grip on the mug and stared down at the barely touched coffee. "Ah, you're sorry, so that makes it all OK, does it?"

Jerome moved back slightly in his chair.

"You can sleep with that bitch and destroy our relationship, but all you have to do is say sorry, everything will be forgiven and we'll just move on smiling as though nothing has happened. Well, that may work with others, Jerome Black, but not me. You have no idea how you've hurt me."

A young boy at a nearby table knocked over his carton of juice. It hit the floor with a gentle thud. Jerome glanced at it briefly as he took a deep breath. "I love you, Stancia. You must know that. I'll do anything to prove that, to get us back to—"

"No, I don't want to hear it." Her voice was coldly dismissive as she raised her eyes to look at him. "Something changed in you in the past few months. You were different: distant in some way. Now at least I understand why. I need to trust the people I love, and I can't trust you anymore."

Jerome lowered his head, then raised it slowly again and said, "I know what I did was stupid, idiotic and incredibly selfish. But it was just on one occasion, I swear to God, and I know this isn't an excuse, but it was the night of Chris's overdose, I just wasn't thinking straight and…" Even as he said the words, Jerome knew they sounded feeble.

"And you continued to live with her afterwards. With *her!* What does that say about you?" said Stancia.

He sunk in his seat, unable to answer this question in any way that could help his cause.

Stancia sat up straight and brushed the hair from her eyes in a business-like manner. "Well, I'm sure you'll enjoy your future life with her or whoever else you end up with. I've spoken to Veronique and Pippa. They're both still in Padua. I'm going to join them. I'll get a job out there, for the summer anyway."

"What can I say or do to make it up to you?" Jerome's voice had a hint of desperation.

"Nothing; our lives will go on, but we won't be taking the same path." Her eyes started to fill up as she stood.

"For Christ's sake, Stancia, don't go."

But she walked to the door and was gone.

A waitress came over to the table. "Would you like to order anything, sir?"

Jerome opened his mouth, but no words came. He looked up at the waitress and shook his head.

* * *

When he got back to the house, Jerome's father was in the hall with his coat on.

"You're back early. I thought you'd be longer. I was just heading for a walk in the park," explained Pieter.

Jerome didn't fully close the front door. "Shall I come with you?" he asked.

"Yeah, but only if you want to; I'm not going to fall into the duck pond and drown myself or anything daft."

He smiled at his father. "Come on, let's go. I think a walk would do me good too."

The park was normally a ten-minute walk from the house, although at Pieter's slower pace it took closer to twenty minutes.

"Shall we go in?" asked Jerome when they reached the entrance gates.

"Of course; at my speed, it would be a bit of a waste to come this far and then just stare through the railings," answered his father.

They sauntered along the tree-lined beginning of the path.

"Were you anywhere interesting this morning?" Pieter enquired.

"Ah," replied Jerome. "I just had something I needed to sort out."

"And is it sorted?"

Jerome paused for a moment. "Yes, it's sorted."

"That's good." Pieter stopped and pointed his walking stick at a kiosk further along the path. "Fancy a wee bun from that place?"

"You know what, I'd love a wee bun right now."

"Good; it's my treat," said his father winking at him.

Jerome sensed strongly that his father knew there were problems in his relationship with Stancia. He felt fairly sure Karl would not have mentioned it, and so he put it down to parental intuition. But, however Pieter had come to know of it, Jerome appreciated that he didn't press him for information. He did not want to talk to his father about this; not then anyway. They sat on a park bench and ate the buns, mainly in comradely silence. Jerome felt heavy-hearted, but did not want his father to sense this lest he be upset. So, occasionally, he made conversation to ensure the silences never lasted too long.

Karl had said he would call at the house around 8.00pm, and, just as the clocks in the living room were signalling the arrival of that hour, they heard the front door opening.

"Only me," Karl announced as he came into the room and, removing a newspaper from the sofa, sat down. "Do you fancy going out for a pint?" he continued, addressing both father and brother.

"You two go," replied Pieter quickly. "I want to watch something on the television."

"Are you sure, Dad?" asked Jerome.

"I'm certain; you guys go on. I need to digest that kebab we had for our dinner anyway."

"*You had a kebab for dinner?*" exclaimed Karl, looking in bemusement from father to Jerome.

Pieter laughed noiselessly. "We had lovely bacon, egg and chips. Made by your young brother, I should add."

Karl retrieved his jacket from the car, and the two brothers began walking briskly towards the local pub.

"I'll only have the one as I'll be driving afterwards," said Karl.

"One's fine for me too," Jerome confirmed.

"Any excitement today?" asked the older brother as he zipped his jacket to the top.

"I met Stancia this morning."

"OK." Karl nodded slowly in acknowledgement that some private information was about to be disclosed. "And how did that go?"

"Not good," began Jerome. "She's going back to Padua for the summer. Her two girlfriends are still there."

"Hmm, so she was not in the forgiving mood, then?"

"No, not at all."

"That's a pity."

"She said I've been different and distant over the past few months."

"And have you?"

"Yes, I think maybe I have. It was in the middle of all my preparations for the journey," Jerome paused, "back to Galilee."

Karl remained silent for a while before asking softly, "You didn't mention that to her, did you?"

"No, I didn't."

"Thanks, Jerome. You must have been tempted."

"There's no need to thank me Karl."

"Well, maybe 'thanks' isn't the right word, but I'm just glad you didn't mention it. And, who knows, she might come around. Was she angry?"

"Very."

"Angry's good. It may work out."

"You sound like you've got experience in this."

Karl gave a non-committal smile as they turned the final bend and could then see the yellow lights from the pub at the top of a gentle incline. "So, I assume that alters your plans for the summer," continued Karl.

"Yes, we'd been planning to go to Germany, pick up some summer work and then do a bit of travelling."

"Any thoughts on what you might do now? Although it's probably a bit too soon to know," added Karl.

"I'll spend this couple of weeks with Dad. Then, I don't know; maybe I'll try to get some work down in London."

"Well, I could ask around for temporary work in Glasgow, if you want? Although it's not quite the same as London. And, by the way, don't feel that you must stay these two weeks with Dad. If you want to take a break, and maybe go to London for a day or so, that would be fine."

"Thanks, Karl."

"There's no need to thank me, Jerome," Karl said grinning playfully at his brother as they pushed open the door to the pub.

Chapter 35

London;
2nd June 2017

Jerome took up his brother's suggestion of spending a day or two away from Glasgow. Early on the following Friday evening, he arrived at a Premier Inn hotel on the south bank of the River Thames, near Tower Bridge in London. It was a small but clean and reasonably inexpensive place to stay. He rested briefly before confirming with Chris by text the place where they had arranged to meet. Chris had already suggested that Jerome could stay in the house as no new housemate had yet arrived, but he declined. There were too many recent memories that he didn't wish to revisit. He wasn't sure how much Chris knew about the breakdown of his relationship with Stancia, but, as he had received no push back on his decision to stay in the hotel, he assumed his friend was at least aware there were problems.

**

It was a friendly-faced Chris who approached Jerome as he sat outside the cafe bar, with two pints of lager glinting in the still-warm evening sunshine.

"Well, buddy…" Chris patted Jerome gently on the shoulder and sat down. "I didn't think I'd be seeing you so soon, but I appreciate the beer." He drew the nearer pint glass closer as he turned around to gaze across the river. "That's some view from here; St Pauls and all those." He gestured vaguely towards the high-rise buildings defining the skyline in the City of London. "Bloody brilliant. I'm not sure I've ever been down here before." He turned back to look at Jerome. "You look like shit, by the way."

"Thanks," responded Jerome.

"Don't mention it." Chris took an unusually small sip from his glass. "So, I'm assuming things are not great between you and Stancia?"

As Jerome gave him the details, Chris listened quietly, attentively and sympathetically as the tourist boats passed smoothly behind him on the blue-grey-coloured river.

"You know what I think," proposed Chris when Jerome had finished his story. "I reckon you'll get back together again. You two are way too close to let something like this end it forever. My advice – although I admit it's from a guy who's never had a long-term girlfriend – would be to go over to Padua at the end of the summer and surprise her."

Jerome looked unconvinced by his friend's suggestion.

Chris continued. "Do you remember you told me you took her to Paris when you weren't even going out together? Now that was spontaneous and daring. I really admired you for that. So be like that again. What have you got to lose?"

"Well, I could surprise her and discover she's with another guy."

"OK, that wouldn't be great, but you'd have tried. And what woman wouldn't love that?"

Jerome smiled at his friend. "Actually, that does sound like good advice, thanks."

"*Really?*" Chris looked surprised and then affected a smug expression.

"Yes, really." Jerome looked away from his friend towards one of the small sandbanks dotted along the river's edge, where the lapping water turned to a muddy brown. "There's something else I want to tell you, Chris."

And this time Jerome told him a very different story. A story about a boy growing up who realised gradually that he had strange but incredible powers; who, step by step, had experimented with these powers and discovered finally that he could travel back in time; who had then used these powers to visit people, many of them long dead – ordinary people, famous people and infamous people; how two of his journeys had coincided with the deaths of loved ones; and how he still retained these powers.

And this time, Chris didn't listen quietly, attentively or sympathetically. At first, he kept interrupting Jerome to tell him to stop messing around. "Why are you telling me this stuff?" he asked at one stage, with pointed frustration. But, as Jerome continued, Chris became agitated, then annoyed, then concerned, then alarmed.

Jerome ended ultimately by telling him he had also informed Karl of his incredible powers.

For a long time, Chris said nothing, but gazed at his friend with deep worry. "And what did Karl say?" he asked eventually, with the frown remaining on his brow.

"He wants me to see a psychiatrist. One who specialises in grief counselling," explained Jerome.

"What do you think of that idea?"

Jerome shook his head. "I'm not mad, Chris. I know these things happened."

Chris leaned forwards on the table. "I don't know what you want me to say, Jerome."

"Nothing. It's just a relief to be able to tell someone close; someone who knows me well."

"Have you told Stancia?"

"No; I intended to, but the opportunity didn't come up. And I can't now. It would look like I'm trying to invent some crazy story to get her back." As Chris nodded, Jerome continued. "Look, Chris, I don't expect you to believe any of this; that's OK. I don't expect anyone to believe it. I can't prove any of it." He reached over and clinked his friend's glass. "But it's a real relief to be able to tell you."

"No wonder you look like shit, with all this stuff going on inside your head. Fuck me, Jerome; I need more drink," said Chris standing up, "a lot more."

* * *

There followed a strangely enjoyable, if highly unusual, evening for the two friends, as they drifted among a few bars just behind the waterfront. At first, Jerome was reticent to say much about his specific journeys back in time, but, as the alcohol took effect and he sensed a bemusement rather than alarm in his friend's demeanour, he opened up. Soon, he was revelling in the opportunity to be able to tell someone for the first time about all of his journeys. At times, he made himself stop, conscious he was hogging virtually all of the conversation, and ask Chris something about his own plans, but he would soon return with renewed enthusiasm to the fascinating task of telling him about Galilee, Nuremburg and even the tragic story of Jay Goodman, the sad American. Occasionally, Chris would ask questions, but they were non-threatening, never probing to test the veracity of his story. Jerome would have preferred the latter and was aware that Chris's questions sometimes resembled the way an adult would indulge a child who was telling a fanciful story, but he was still thankful to have this audience.

"Did you ask Hitler the key question?" asked Chris, shortly after the barman in their final pub had told them it was closing.

"What would that be?" Jerome's bleary eyes narrowed sluggishly.

"Did he really only have one ball?"

Jerome gave a delayed laugh. "No, I forgot to ask that."

"Ah, please, just one more round." The voice came from one of a group of young women at the bar, pleading in vain with the barman, who was studiously ignoring them.

Chris turned the top half of his body slowly to look at them. "Do you see that?" he said, turning back to his friend. "We could offer them half of our drinks or your drink anyway. What do you reckon? They're very attractive."

"I don't think their boyfriends would be too impressed."

Chris repeated his slow body turn to confirm that, indeed, the young women were in a larger group with a number of young men. "Two-timing bitches," he whispered, laughing heartily.

"You need to finish up here now, lads." It was another of the bar staff, as he removed empty glasses from their table.

"I wonder who I'd go back in time to see if I could do that?" Chris mused as he gripped his final drink tightly, lest the barman remove the glass.

"Maybe there's some old relative you'd like to see again?" suggested Jerome.

"Nah, nothing maudlin like that. No, you know who I'd go to see." He took a sip of his pint and wagged his finger as though preparing to delivering a lesson in wisdom. "I'd go back to see Albert Einstein in 1905, just after he'd published his theory of relativity."

"Why? Would you want to discuss it with him?"

"No, not at all. I'd tell him about quantum mechanics and elementary particles and all the other stuff that hadn't been discovered at that point. It would freak him out." Chris began to laugh again. "There'd be him thinking he was the smartest man in the world and then this fat bastard from Yorkshire tells him,

'Relativity is so old hat, Alberto. You're about a century behind, you thick fucker.' It would make his hair even frizzier."

The two friends were soon convulsing in drunken laughter as Chris continued his story of how he'd humiliate Albert Einstein.

***

Jerome's hotel was on the route back to the Underground station. They stopped outside it, with both slightly unsteady on their feet.

"Well, thanks a lot for listening to me tonight. I know you don't believe a word of it, but it did me a lot of good just being able to talk so freely to someone I trust," declared Jerome.

"No problem, buddy. No problem at all," replied Chris, looking uncomfortably at his friend.

"And I know you didn't believe a word, but that's OK."

"May I give you a bit of parting advice?"

Jerome nodded. "Of course."

"Your brother cares a lot for you. I'd be inclined to listen to him and maybe take his advice." Chris sounded very sober suddenly. "Anyway, for what it's worth, Jerome, that would be my advice. So take care of yourself, buddy, and I'll see you soon." He hugged Jerome warmly.

"See you soon."

Chris turned to go and then turned back. "Don't become a stranger now. Stay in touch."

"I will. Don't worry."

Chris gave a jerky wave and shuffled off under the red-brick archway towards the Underground station.

Jerome returned to his hotel room, replied to a text from Karl and then lay down. He had felt happy in Chris's company. His friend just had that effect. He smiled at the ceiling as he remembered some of the funnier stories. "Alberto Einstein," he said softly and grinned. But Chris had also said, "*Don't become a stranger.*" Jerome wondered why he said that. Was it just that their lives were unlikely to overlap much in the future or did Chris sense Jerome drifting away? The thought made him melancholy momentarily, but it did not stop him falling asleep.

Chapter 36

London;
Saturday, 3rd June 2017

The 6.55am alarm startled him awake. Edging slowly out of bed, he moved gingerly to the shower and let the warm water flow over his tired body. He felt groggy, and the enthusiasm from the previous night had largely gone. Jerome had told Chris he was heading back to Glasgow on the early morning train, but, even as he had said it, he knew in his heart that he wasn't going to do that. He had brought the oxygen cylinder with him to London. And while he had partly convinced himself that this was a precaution in case he might want to use it, he knew he would use it.

A plan had entered his head to go to Paris – encouraged, no doubt, by Chris's reference to it the previous evening. Those days spent there with Stancia remained poignantly clear to him. Checking out of his hotel, he travelled to St Pancras station, where he caught the Eurostar train to Paris, arriving at Gare du Nord station just before noon. Making his way to the Pigalle district, he found the hotel where he and Stancia had stayed three years previously. There were vacancies, and he checked in for one night.

Jerome sat still and silent on the bed, and he watched anxiously as the oxygen cylinder recharged on the floor. When the small, green light came on, he picked up the mask, pulled it over his face and switched on the machine.

***

Paris, France; Saturday, 30th August 2014; 3.00pm

There was no one in the room. Jerome realised he had been extremely careless to not anticipate someone being there, but he had been lucky. He checked quickly and confirmed there were no clothes or suitcases in the room. It was unoccupied. Quietly, he left the room, although he deliberately did not fully close the door, before walking outside. He remembered this August afternoon as being overcast and muggy, and so it was. He removed his jacket, folded it and carried it tightly in his left hand as he moved purposefully along the cobbled, hilly streets. By 3.25pm, he was standing on the platform of Pigalle station, where Stancia had endured her purse being stolen. He positioned himself about fifty metres beyond where he recalled the incident taking place.

As the first train pulled in, he lowered his head, as he did not want to risk catching sight of himself, lest he be transported immediately back to 2017. As the doors opened, he let the passengers exit and then, after getting on, he stood in the open doorway, glancing guardedly down the platform. There were no abnormal noises or indications of any disturbance. As the doors started to close, he stepped nimbly back onto the platform. He repeated this process for the second train. The third train arrived at 4.01pm. As before, the passengers hurried off and as those on the platform began to board, Jerome took up his position in the doorway. This time, he heard shouting and noticed people turning to look in the direction of the noise. He let his gaze move slowly up the platform. And then he saw her.

Stancia was standing alone on the platform, side-on to his view. He recalled then the white blouse and light-blue skirt she had worn. But it was the first time he had seen the fear on her face. She pressed her fists anxiously to her chin. The doors to his carriage began to close but then shuddered to a halt and reopened. Again, he could hear shouting. He saw Stancia turn around, her eyes wide with alarm as though seeking help. She looked so young. He gazed sadly at her. Again, the doors made an unsuccessful attempt to close. Then he saw the purse land on the platform, close by her feet, and he watched as she stooped swiftly to pick it up. Taking one final glance at her, he stepped inside the carriage and turned his back to the platform as the doors closed firmly behind him.

Abbesses Metro station was the next stop. Jerome hopped off the train immediately, and watched vigilantly as the passengers disembarked from Stancia's carriage. The small man of Scandinavian appearance wearing a neat, brown suit didn't recognise him at first, but then did suddenly, and he moved his arm instinctively in front of his shocked face.

"You didn't expect to see me again, did you?" Jerome stood in front of him, expressionless, blocking his progress.

He felt a twinge in his left side as though someone had prodded him hard with a finger. Turning, he saw a second man standing very close and staring aggressively. Looking down Jerome realised this man was holding a knife; its blade was short with specks of red on it. His hand went to his side and felt the blood trickling through his shirt. Jerome looked at his attacker and saw defiance but no fear. He watched helplessly as the two men moved rapidly through the crowded platform and began running towards the exit. No one was looking at him.

Shocked, Jerome made his way back to the hotel. He felt little pain, but he could see that the bloodstain had widened considerably and could feel the warm liquid on the top of his leg. He pressed his jacket to the wound to staunch the flow and avoid any passers-by noticing his bleeding, but it made little difference. By this time, he was genuinely alarmed, as the realisation that he had been seriously injured began to dawn on him. He knew he would be transported back in a few hours' time and the wound would disappear. He just wanted to rest in his room until that happened. As he passed the front desk of the hotel, he moved to the stairs rather than waiting for the elevator. But, as he climbed the two flights, he felt increasingly light-headed and had to pause three times before reaching his second-floor room. The door remained open as he had left it. He went inside and lay on the bed, exhausted, then looked down at his side with some trepidation. His shirt and the left side of his trousers were soaked in blood by then. He tried to press his coat more firmly into his side, but he did not have any strength. Jerome was getting cold. He managed to turn his head slightly and noticed the blood stains were also on his left shoe. He felt tired; very tired. He tried to move his head but found he couldn't.

Is this how it's going to end? he wondered. *Am I going to die in this friendless place and in this pathetic way? Will anyone even know or will I just disappear from memory?*

Jerome thought he heard voices, and he imagined people looking at him and pointing. Then, suddenly, he was back in the hotel room in 2017. Removing the mask, he raised the left side of his shirt tentatively and touched the place where the wound had been. It was no longer there.

***

Dumb, reckless and voyeuristic were some of words that came to Jerome as he reflected on this journey back in time. On the two trains, from Paris to London and then London to Glasgow, he sat alone and deeply regretted his decision. *What the hell was I thinking?* he asked himself on more than one occasion. The spur-of-the-moment decision contrasted badly with the meticulous planning he had put into his other journeys back. He had wanted to see Stancia. He knew that was why he had brought the oxygen cylinder to London. But seeing her in this way had been crazy. He cringed physically at the thought of her ever finding out. He felt the same about Karl; if he were to be told, it would cement his view that Jerome had mental problems. Even Chris would find this story bizarre in a disturbing way. Jerome determined he would tell no one about it.

But, despite the genuine regrets, he did learn a few things from this journey back in time. Jerome knew by then that even if he died while travelling back in time, he would return unharmed. He was certain he had died in that lonely hotel room and yet had returned with no physical scars, although he couldn't say there would be no mental ones. While others he met on his journeys back could never remember anything, he could never erase any memories: good or bad.

The second thing Jerome had learned was that he did not fear death. He recalled feeling something akin to anger at the pathetic pointlessness of his oncoming demise as his life-blood seeped away, but he did not feel fear. And he did not think this was born from any certainty that he would "rise from the dead".

Jerome's final learning from this ill-considered journey was that he did not want to stop using his powers. He remained puzzled and yet fascinated by them. And he knew he would use them again.

Chapter 37

Glasgow;
Friday, 23rd June 2017

Jerome had extended the stay with his father from two to four weeks. London, or indeed anywhere else, held no immediate attraction for him as he settled back into a temporary routine of living and working part-time in Glasgow. His old boss at the bookmakers was glad to take him back for a few days each week. The other staff had all changed since Jerome had last worked there, which made his rejoining easier in a way. Jerome had no definite short-term plans. His longer-term ones began with the consideration of travelling to Padua at the end of the summer. Beyond that, he knew he would have to start looking for a full-time career, although that could wait until the end of his last "free" summer. But, ultimately, it was his time travel that dominated his thinking. He had major decisions to make on that too.

***

And so it was that, towards the end of the fourth week, he was having his evening meal with his father; on this occasion, it had been prepared by Pieter.

"A working man deserves to have his food served up to him," said his father half-jokingly as they sat down in front of the piping-hot lasagne Pieter had bought in the local supermarket. "It happened again today, you know," continued Pieter as he lifted a portion from his plate and, without asking, added it to his son's already full plate.

"Are you sure you don't want that, Dad?" asked Jerome, in what had become a ritual at mealtime.

"No, I've plenty here, thanks."

"OK, so, anyway, what was it that happened again today?" Jerome responded to his father's earlier question, not expecting anything of importance.

"I heard your mum singing in the kitchen, but when I went in, she'd gone."

Jerome halted the movement of his fork. "You miss her a lot?"

"I sure do. But I love hearing the little snatches of song. I just wish I could talk to her again. Not about anything important, just, you know, an old chat about nothing."

"I know. I'd love to talk to her too." Jerome placed his fork on the plate. "Those episodes you have where you think you hear Mum, they're very common when loved ones pass away. I looked it up once. It even has a fancy name that I can't remember now. But it's nothing to worry about."

"Who's worried?" said Pieter as he continued chewing. "I hope they never stop."

***

As each day went by, Jerome felt increasingly the ache of his mother's loss. Living in the family home only brought constant reminders of the times they had shared and that would never come again. The unfairness of him not having an opportunity to say farewell gnawed at this pain, even though he knew this was not unique to him. At this point, his father's words had again raised a possibility that he had been trying to suppress. For Jerome knew that he had a power that would let him see his mother again, and that he could have a much more real contact than his father's post-bereavement hallucinatory experiences. But journeying back in time to see her just didn't seem right. He recalled Helga's written note asking him not to visit her after her death, and he felt that his mother, had she known of his powers, would have made a similar request. It was almost as though there was a spiritual bond that would be broken if he were to make such a journey. And, yet, despite these strong reservations, Jerome's growing yearn to see his mother once again, to talk to her and to ask her advice won out eventually.

* * *

It was just after 11.00pm the following evening. Pieter had been in bed for over an hour, and Jerome had just returned from confirming his gentle snoring. Closing his own bedroom door, Jerome took out the oxygen cylinder, wrapped it in a coat to muffle the noise, then pulled on the mask and began to breathe slowly.

* * *

Saturday, 8th April 2017; 6.30pm

Jerome looked around his bedroom with a mixture of relief and nostalgia. It had a tidy, unoccupied appearance, but yet retained its warm familiarity, as though it was just waiting for someone; this was a look he suspected his mother ensured was always there. Pulling on his jacket, he descended the stairs quietly before opening and closing the front door gently, with the intention of alerting his parents to his arrival. There was no noise inside the house aside from the television in the main room.

He had chosen this time on a Saturday as he was fairly certain his parents would be alone, and he was hopeful his father would be asleep. Walking quietly up the hall, he could see, through the half-open door to the living room, Pieter dozing gently, his face much calmer – and, in a way, more recognisably him – than when he was awake. He heard a noise from the kitchen and opened the kitchen door gently. "Hi Mum," Jerome said.

Patricia Black looked up from the kitchen table where she had been writing. Her soft eyes narrowed and then opened wide on recognising her son. "Jerome! What are you doing here? I thought you were in London."

"I just thought I'd come up for a few days to see me old ma." He sat down beside her and, suddenly, felt his eyes well up with emotion.

"There's nothing wrong, is there?" she asked, removing her reading glasses.

"No, nothing at all." He sensed his smiling reassurance was not convincing. "I see you're still writing instead of emailing." He pointed to the paper on the table to try to distract her gaze.

She glanced briefly at the letter. "Yes, I still think writing a letter is much more personal. But, seriously, there is nothing wrong?"

"Nothing at all, Mum. I just wanted to get your advice on something."

"OK. Well, you can start by giving me a hug, and then I'll put the kettle on. You must be hungry if you've come all the way from London at this time of night." She got up with a wince of pain.

"I'll put it on. Is your leg still getting at you?"

"It's just stiff. Old age, unfortunately. Where's your suitcase?"

"Oh, I left it in the hall," answered Jerome hastily.

She got some ham, tomato and mayonnaise from the fridge, and made a sandwich as he prepared the tea.

When they were seated back at the table, she looked at him with both her hands clasped tightly around the navy-blue cup. "Now then, tell me what's up?"

Jerome sighed deeply. "Let's see. Where do I start?"

"They say the beginning's usually a good place."

"The beginning, yes. I'm not too sure where that is."

At that moment, the kitchen door opened, and Pieter appeared. "I thought I heard voices in the kitchen." His voice was bright. "When did you arrive?"

"I just got here." Jerome stood and embraced his father.

"Great; that's great," replied Pieter as he sat down to join his son and wife.

Neither Jerome nor his mother mentioned the conversation they were about to start, and, for the next four hours, the three of them chatted and ate and drank tea and shared gossip in their usual, familiar way. They had moved to the comfort of the living room when, shortly before 11.00pm, Pieter rose slowly to his feet.

"Right," he began, "it's time for my bed. You don't have to head off early in the morning do you, Jerome?"

Jerome smiled at his father. "No, I'll be here for a while tomorrow morning."

"Good, see you then. Night all." He went to leave the room.

"Good night," came the joint reply as Pieter closed the door behind him.

For a while, mother and son sat in silence.

"He's still madly in love with you, you know," said Jerome quietly when he was sure his father was out of earshot.

"Oh," Patricia gave a pleased smile. "We know each other very well at this stage." After a further pause she continued. "So, do you still want to have our chat?"

Jerome hesitated and grimaced slightly.

"I think you should." She looked at him encouragingly.

For the second time that evening, he could feel his eyes filling with emotion.

"What is it, Jerome? There is something wrong, isn't there?"

He leaned forwards and said with as much conviction as possible, "No, honestly, there's nothing wrong. Mum, I have special abilities; a gift you might call it." Again, he hesitated before continuing, "I can go back in time, and see and talk to people; famous people." He raised his left hand in anticipation of her disbelief. "I know it sounds unbelievable, but it's true. And, before you ask me, I'm not taking drugs or anything else." He looked into her eyes. "It's true, Mum; I can do this, and I have done it."

She said nothing, but the look on her face prompted Jerome to speak again. "Don't be frightened. Honestly, I'm fine. There's nothing wrong with me." He took the cup from her hands and held them.

"But how can you travel back? I don't understand."

"It's very difficult to understand." Jerome breathed deeply. "Do you remember those episodes I had as a kid, the ones that were diagnosed as petit mal?"

She nodded meekly.

"Well, they weren't. I was able then to see the world where everything except me had completely stopped. Later, when I was about eighteen, they came back, but I was able to manage them. Eventually, I was able to control them, so that not only could I see things frozen in time but I could go back in time. I know it sounds unbelievable, but it's true." He stopped to await her reaction.

"Have you spoken to your father about this?"

"No, I haven't. I wanted to talk to you first."

"Is it dangerous or painful?"

"No, it doesn't hurt me or anyone else."

She nodded again, but her face remained alarmed. "What did you want to ask me?"

"One of the last people I went back to see was Jesus Christ."

Jerome closed his eyes. "I know this might disturb you, Mum, but I met him, and we spoke together for a while. I wanted to ask you whether I should tell people about what he said to me."

His mother's pained expression remained unchanged. "What did he say?" she asked quietly.

Jerome leaned back in his seat, and he began telling his mother about the Sermon on the Mount and meeting Mary Magdalene and Matthew. He tried to remain calm, but felt himself getting passionate as he talked about his conversation with Jesus. "Well, what do you think? Should I tell people about this?"

She was silent for a moment before replying softly, "I don't think you should tell anyone about this, Jerome."

"Why do you feel that?"

"Because I can see nothing but pain for you if you do."

"Don't you believe me?"

"I don't know, Jerome. It does sound incredible. Even if it's really happening to you, people will hurt you if you tell them about it."

"But how can I just ignore what I've been told, Mum? Why have I been given this gift if not to use it?"

"I don't know. I just think that if something is in the past, then maybe we should leave it in the past."

He looked away, trying to hide his disappointment.

"Jerome, ultimately, you have to follow your own heart. As a mother looking after her son, I would advise you to say nothing about this. But, as I say, in the end, you have to follow your own heart." She watched him, allowing the silence to hang for a minute before asking, "What did he look like?"

He looked up hopefully. "Jesus?"

"Yes." She smiled at him, encouragingly.

"He was tall – well, relatively tall; his disciples were smaller than him. He had dark hair down to his shoulders, a bit like the paintings of him, but his eyes were narrower and smaller, and his skin was a bit pockmarked. He had a crooked tooth here." Jerome pointed to one of his incisors.

"And can you go back and see anyone?"

"Theoretically, yes; anyone."

"You know, Jerome, you've always been full of surprises." She smiled. "The first surprise was when the doctor told me I was pregnant with you. I was forty-six years old. Did you know that?"

"I know, Mum; that's probably not the perfect age."

"We hadn't planned on having another child, but when you came along, you were wonderful, though demanding and exhausting," she told him, smiling at the memories. "The doctors didn't want me to go through with the pregnancy. They said it would be dangerous for me, and there was a good chance you could have some... well, you know what I mean."

Jerome nodded. He wondered if his father's view had been in accord with his mother or the doctors, but he would never ask.

"Anyway," his mother continued, "you arrived three weeks early. We nearly lost you, did you know that?"

"No, I didn't." Jerome was intrigued.

"It was shortly after you were born. You stopped breathing. I remember there was a great big panic. Bleepers were going off, doctors and nurses were rushing everywhere, and they were shouting at each other in their medical jargon. The whole thing only lasted a minute or so, and then, just like magic, they all calmed down again. Do you know something, Jerome?" She continued without giving him chance to answer, "During that minute, I felt serenely confident that no harm would come to you. Perhaps that was the result of the drugs they gave me, but I don't think so. I just felt that God hadn't asked me to bear another child at my age unless there was a very special reason. So it made sense that he wasn't going to allow you to die at birth. From that moment on, I just knew you were going to be someone special."

"Did you really?" Suddenly, he sounded like a child seeking parental affirmation.

"Yes, but I suppose every mother feels like that. Anyway, with drinking all this tea, I need to go to the bathroom." She got up slowly and left the room, but she returned almost immediately. "Jerome, you said your suitcase was in the hall, but it's not there."

"Oh…" He hesitated and looked flustered. "Dad must have taken it up."

"Dad doesn't carry anything upstairs. He's not allowed." There was a hint of concern in her voice as she looked at him, hoping for a simple explanation, which didn't come.

There was a further silence between the two, before she gave a sharp intake of breath suddenly and asked softly, "Jerome, have you come back in time to see *me*?"

His delay in responding seemed to heighten her fears.

"Oh…" She gave a little start, and looked anxious and confused. Then, sitting down, she asked in a whisper, "Does that mean I'm already dead?"

"It's OK, Mum," he said, vainly trying to repair the damage.

But it clearly was not OK. Her look of bewilderment turned hurriedly to one of fear. "You don't look any older than the last time I saw you, so it must happen very soon. Oh…" She put a hand to her mouth.

"Don't be frightened, Mum; you won't remember any of this." He tried again to allay her fright.

"Will I be alone when I die?"

"No. Dad will be with you, and it will be peaceful." Jerome was panicking by then and wanted to end what had turned abruptly into a nightmare. "Mum, I'll be going very soon. I'm only causing you distress. I'm so sorry; I didn't mean to do this. You won't remember any of this, so everything will be OK." He glanced at his watch. His time was almost at an end. He stood up, unsure what to do.

But she gripped his arm with surprising strength. "Don't go; this is the last time I'll ever see you."

"It's OK, Mum." He put his arm around her, his mind racing. "I'm not going anywhere."

And, suddenly, he was back in real time.

***

Saturday, 24th June 2017; 11.30pm

Jerome stared disconsolately at the grey, scudding rain as it whipped in from the coast and traced slow, diagonal lines down the bedroom window. He sat on the bed, motionless, with his hands resting flat on his thighs, feeling desperately lonely. The image of his mother that he carried with him was an unhappy one. She appeared almost reproachful, as if saying, "How could you do this to me?" Yet he knew that wasn't how she had really looked. She would never have made him feel guilty like that; she loved him too much. But this train of thought provided him with no comfort.

He was distraught to have caused his mother such fear and stress; it was unforgiveable. Maybe Karl was right, maybe Jerome always had been self-indulgent. He tried to comfort himself with the thought that his mother would remember nothing of the visit, but her sense of distress had been so palpable that he wondered how it could not leave an imprint in real time.

A knock on the door disturbed him. "Hi Jerome, are you all right in there?" It was his father.

Quickly, Jerome pushed the oxygen cylinder under the bed. "Yes, I'm fine, Dad." He went to the door and opened it to find his father looking frail in his red, woollen dressing gown.

"I just thought I heard a strange noise a few minutes ago, like an engine. Did you hear anything?"

"No, maybe you were dreaming," added Jerome uneasily.

"Aye, you're probably right. Sorry if I woke you."

"You didn't, Dad. I was wide awake."

"Ah, that's OK. I must have been dreaming. Sleep well."

"You too."

Chapter 38

Monday, 26th June 2017

The phone call from Karl early the following Monday evening was unusually cool and abrupt. He wanted to meet Jerome but not in their father's house. Karl also rejected the suggestion of a pub and said they could meet at Kelvingrove Park where Jerome had chatted to his older brother previously on the morning after first revealing his secret.

Jerome, filled with curiosity rather than concern, arrived at the park at 7.15pm. The wind and rain from the previous weekend had blown through, and lovely evening sunshine greeted him as he said hello to his brother.

Initially, Karl made no response as they walked along the path. After a while, Karl began, "I needed to talk to you."

"Sure. Is everything OK?" enquired Jerome.

"No, it's not. I was talking to Dad today."

"Yeah, what about?"

"He said he woke up on Saturday night and thought he heard a noise like a motor engine coming from your room."

"Yes, he knocked on my door. I said he must have been dreaming."

Karl stopped and pulled on his brother's arm. They stood facing each other.

"And was he dreaming?" questioned Karl.

Jerome made no reply and looked away.

"I went into your room to check the radiators, in case they were making the noise," Karl said slowly. "And I found an oxygen container with a mask attached to it under your bed. That's what Dad heard, wasn't it?"

For a moment, Jerome looked angry, but it passed quickly. "You didn't need to sneak into my room."

"Don't evade the fucking point, Jerome. That's what Dad heard, wasn't it?"

Jerome nodded resignedly. "Yes, it was."

"What on earth were you doing with that, apart from frightening the hell out of Dad?"

"It's how I travel back in time."

"Right." Karl glanced away for a moment. "You're going to see this psychiatrist, and I'm not taking no for an answer. I'm not going to let you destroy yourself. You've brought me into this, and I'm going to see that it's sorted out. So we're going to agree that you'll see the psychiatrist and, in the meantime, you won't go anywhere near that oxygen thing."

Jerome's mouth slackened. "Do you know who I travelled back to see on Saturday night?"

"No, and I don't want to know. Jerome, I'm not going to indulge—"

"It was Mum. I went back to see Mum."

"I DON'T CARE," Karl shouted. "I don't care what you think Mum would say to you if she were still alive. She's not. She's dead and she's not coming back." He paused and, to Jerome's surprise, he saw his brother's eyes begin to fill up. "Jesus, kid, you're killing me. Do I ever ask you to do anything? Do I? Well, I'm asking you now, for all our sakes, to see this psychiatrist. Is that too much?"

Jerome, perhaps worn down by the sadness and trauma of recent events and genuinely upset to see his brother's reaction, nodded his agreement. "OK, I will."

Karl turned, and they both began to walk slowly on.

"Thanks Jerome. I'll arrange it. It's the best thing we can do."

"OK."

"Is there anything else I can do in the meantime?" asked Karl.

"You could believe me a little bit."

Still looking ahead, Karl put his arm around his younger brother's shoulders and gave him a strong squeeze. "I always believe in you, Jerome. I always believe in you."

* * *

In the days that followed, Jerome reflected on how readily he had agreed to Karl's demand that he see a psychiatrist. Though somewhat surprised at his immediate acquiescence to his brother, he felt no regret or resentment for agreeing to something that, just a few weeks earlier, he would have rejected out of hand. But what Jerome found unexpected was how relieved he felt. It was as if the turmoil of the last few weeks – the momentous, tragic and frightening events – had almost overwhelmed him and left him feeling like he had been in a war zone. At this point, someone – a person he trusted totally – was stepping in and taking some control, and was easing the solitary burden that Helga had once referred to years ago. And he welcomed it.

Even the upcoming sessions with the psychiatrist caused him no angst. It would give him the opportunity to tell his story in a protected environment without having to deal with alarm or ridicule, and he was not concerned if he would be believed or not; in fact, he was certain he would not. There was a sense of freedom about that.

Chapter 39

It was on an overcast mid-morning when Jerome made his way towards the room of Sarah Wine, which was situated on the same Kelvin Way where he had been brought by his mother as a young boy to see Professor Walsh. He walked thoughtfully up the four stone steps and pushed open the heavy, unlocked entrance door to the two-storey building. The reception area was empty, except for the solitary woman sitting at a low desk behind a curved, wooden panel. She welcomed him, took his details unhurriedly and asked him to take a seat. He did so, comparing mentally the comfort of these soft chairs to the hard, plastic ones he and his mother had sat on all those years ago. Glancing at his watch, he confirmed it was 10.20am. He was ten minutes early. There was a distant sound of soft orchestral music floating in the air. Jerome wondered whether it was coming from the earphones of the receptionist, who had returned to her computer screen, but subsequent visits were to confirm that this music was one of the relaxing features of the waiting room.

"Jerome Black?" The question came from a woman standing where the waiting room joined a partly hidden corridor.

He recognised the southern-English accent he had first heard in the brief telephone conversation they had engaged in the previous week. Sarah Wine was a smallish woman with short, dark hair. She wore a neat, royal-blue trouser suit. Jerome guessed her age at around thirty. He was surprised to see spectacles hanging on a chain around her neck, which was something he would have associated with a much older person, though he did wonder whether it was an affectation to appear older and perhaps more experienced.

"Hi, I'm Sarah Wine." She shook hands warmly, and held him in a gaze of watchful curiosity, before indicating a door further down the corridor. "It's a drab, old day; isn't it?" she continued as she walked slightly in front of him to open the door. "We're in here."

The room had a full-though-uncluttered appearance, and it seemed to continue the warm and welcoming aspect that the then-silent music had helped create.

"Please take a seat." Sarah pointed to one of the two chairs either side of a low coffee table. There was also a desk in the room, and she moved briefly behind it to place a folder in one of the drawers before sitting down in the matching high-backed chair opposite him. Jerome noticed there was no couch in the room.

She looked at him, her lips pressed together, as though stifling any words from coming out too soon, and then began, "Well, I'm very pleased to meet you, Jerome. I know we had a brief chat on the phone last week, and your brother Karl had been talking to me prior to that. What I'd like initially, if you're OK with it, is just to hear from you about Jerome Black: what you do, what you're interested in, what you like and don't like, and who are your family and friends. This is just to learn about you. We can talk about your episodes later, but, for now, I'd just like to know about you in your words. How does that sound?"

Jerome said that was fine, and he began to talk about growing up in Glasgow, his school days, his move to London for college, his close-knit family, his friends in Glasgow and London, and how he was temporarily living at home due to the recent death of his mother. He spoke freely and thoughtfully, not rushing but pausing to reflect on her questions when asked.

When he mentioned the death of his grandmother Helga and his mother, she probed gently, asking him about his grief at the loss of people he described so lovingly.

Jerome began to explain how the times of their deaths had coincided exactly with two of his major journeys, and this had caused him bewilderment, alarm and, initially, guilt that maybe he had been instrumental in their deaths in some way.

But she moved him on from this adroitly, making further notes at the same time with a thin, elegant pen in her black notebook. "Outside of your family, is there anyone you are very close to?"

Jerome, aware he had avoided mentioning Stancia, proceeded to tell fully the story of their relationship and the recent break-up.

"And how do you feel about the break-up?" asked Sarah.

"I felt very down about it; I still do," he confirmed.

She nodded in a matter-of-fact way and went to make another entry in the notebook, but she paused. "Do you feel angry about it?"

"Angry? God, no. I did a very stupid thing and am paying the price."

"OK," she replied lightly, "that's fine."

Jerome looked at the clock on the wall behind her desk and was amazed to see he had been talking for thirty-five minutes. "Apart from our brief phone conversation, we haven't talked about my journeys yet; my 'episodes', as you called them."

"No." She looked at him intently. "May I ask you something, Jerome? Why are you here?"

"Why am I here?" he repeated. "That's a fair question. If you'd asked me that a week ago, I'd have said it was because my brother, whom I trust very much, wanted me to come, and I didn't have the heart to upset him. But now I feel I'd like to tell my full story to someone who is not emotionally connected to me, and who won't be upset or unnerved by hearing it."

"OK, let me ask a related question. What do you hope to get out of our sessions, if we go ahead with them?"

"That's another fair question," began Jerome. He thought for a while, looking at the hard-backed books stacked tightly in a glass-fronted cupboard on the wall. "Ideally, at the end of our sessions, I'd like to feel that you believe me to be a normal guy and..." he cocked his head slightly, "you just might have a tiny thought that my story isn't crazy. But I feel fairly certain that's not going to happen, so I'd settle for us agreeing to disagree on my special ability, but you accepting it is not in itself damaging me."

"That's interesting." She paused, which Jerome felt at the time was more for effect than required, though later sessions changed this slightly cynical view. "What you seem to want out of the sessions is that *I* would accept the reality of these episodes in some way, rather than *you* accepting the reality or unreality of them. Would that be right?"

"Yes, I think that's what I'd want. May I ask a question of you?"

"Of course."

"What do *you* hope that I will get from our sessions together?"

"That's a big question." Again, there was a pause. "I hope that you will come to understand what is real and what is not real, and to accept the difference. In the same way that, when you awake from a dream, you know it's not real. It may be extraordinarily vivid, but your brain can discern quickly that it's not real. Ideally, your episodes would stop, but, even if they continue, you could deal with them in the knowledge that they're not real. How does that sound?"

"That sounds honest, though I've absolutely no doubt that my journeys are real."

"Would you be open to being persuaded that perhaps they're not?"

It was Jerome's turn to pause as he noticed the clock showing the forty-five-minute session was drawing to an end. "Despite my extraordinary story, I consider myself to be a very rational person. If clear, indisputable evidence were produced to prove that my journeys never actually took place, then I believe I would be open to that. But I'd like to think that if the reverse happens, you too could have an open mind."

She gave her first warm smile as she slowly stood up. "OK, let's start exploring your journeys next week."

***

During the following week, Jerome worked at the bookmakers each weekday, with the exception of the Thursday morning. He explained to his employer that he needed this time off to take his father to physiotherapy. In fact, it was for his own visit to the psychiatrist. This was a pattern he would maintain as his weekly meetings with Sarah Wine continued and remained unknown to anyone outside the family.

"I mentioned to Geraldine that you're seeing a counsellor," said Karl in a confident voice, which Jerome suspected was hiding his unease. "I just said that you were feeling very low after Mum's death, and then you and Stancia splitting up. I didn't mention anything else. Hope you're OK with that?" It was the day before Jerome's second appointment, and the two brothers were standing alone in the kitchen of their father's house.

"That's fine," replied Jerome. "I don't like the idea of secrets within the family anyway. What about Dad? Have you mentioned anything to him?"

"No, I'd prefer not to; not yet anyway. What do you think?"

"Well, I don't like hiding things from him, but I guess it's probably best not to say anything at this stage."

And so he didn't, but Jerome always sensed that his father knew he was keeping something from him, though he would never quiz his son on it directly.

Geraldine raised the subject of his counselling the next time they were alone. She did so in a generous and caring manner. But he also sensed, from their lack of discussion on it in subsequent conversations, that his sister was uncomfortable, and he sometimes wondered if there were hints of irritation mixed with the sympathy. If so, he could understand it; after all they had all lost their mother.

***

As before, Jerome arrived for his second session ten minutes early. But, on this occasion, the waiting room was not empty. A heavy, middle-aged man wearing a pinstriped suit and tie was sitting, with his head lowered, reading from one of the magazines. He didn't look up when the receptionist confirmed Jerome's appointment time.

"Jerome." The voice came from Sarah Wine. She had the same warm smile that he recalled from when they had parted the previous week. "I'm just going to grab a coffee from the machine. Shall I get you one?"

He declined politely as she moved to the vending machine in the corner of the waiting room and returned with a plastic cup of black coffee. They walked briskly to her room.

"So, how was your week?" she asked when they were both seated.

"Fine, thanks," replied Jerome.

"On a scale of one to ten, where one is complete relaxation and ten is hyperactive, how would you rate it?"

"I'd say about a three."

"And how do you feel about that?"

"Fine," repeated Jerome. "I presume a bit of calmness will do no harm at this time."

"A bit of calmness is never any harm." Her smile had faded subtly. "So, you didn't have any episodes?"

"No," replied Jerome. "I didn't trigger any journeys back."

"OK." She moved the coffee in from the edge of the table, picked up her notebook and pen, turned over a page from her previous week's entries, and looked at him. "I'd like you to tell me about the first time you experienced any of these unusual events."

Jerome began to describe the day in August 2008 when, as a twelve-year-old boy, he was lying on the sofa at home, and the world suddenly stood still. He spoke slowly, trying to ensure he left nothing out.

"And you didn't tell anyone about that? Not even your mother?"

"No, not immediately."

"Why not?"

"I'm not certain. I think I just wanted to try to figure out myself what had happened."

"Weren't you a bit frightened? After all, you were very young."

"No, I don't recall being frightened. Not on that occasion anyway."

"Tell me about the next occasion."

Jerome recounted his walk to school a few weeks after the first event and how the world had again stopped suddenly, but this time for longer, and how he was frightened this time and told his mother.

"How did she react?"

He allowed his gaze to wander round the brightly painted walls as she took an opportunity to sip from the coffee. "At the time, I thought she was a bit shocked and possibly a bit frightened, but she was decisive. She was going to get it resolved. Now, looking back, I think I can understand better why she might have been frightened."

"Why?"

"I was a late pregnancy; she was forty-six when she had me. The doctors didn't want her to proceed with it, but she was determined. And if there had been anything wrong with me, she might have blamed herself."

"How do you know that about the doctors?"

"My mother told me."

"OK, so what happened next? Did your mother take decisive action?"

"Yes, we ended up seeing a Professor Walsh, and he diagnosed petit mal and put me on a course of medication."

"And did that stop the episodes?"

"Yes, for a number of years."

"And how did you feel about the episodes stopping?"

"Relieved."

"And were your family relieved?"

"Yes, I'm sure they were, although I don't think my grandmother Helga was bothered about the episodes at all. She seemed to think they marked me out as special in some way."

"You spoke very fondly about Helga last week. Tell me more about her."

He spoke with a wistful fondness of his earliest memories of his grandmother. "As a child, I never recall her not being there, and I always knew that, no matter what happened, she would always be on my side. On occasion, I recall my mum trying to persuade Gran not to over indulge me, but she never paid any heed; she was a strong-willed lady."

"And you say she didn't seem bothered when you had these time-freezing incidents?"

"No, she didn't seem concerned at all; she was completely

dismissive of the doctors." Jerome smiled inwardly as he recalled Helga's offensive comment about Walsh, but kept this to himself. "I think the time-freezing incidents just confirmed her view that I was special in some way."

"And how did you feel about that?"

Jerome glanced at a framed photograph on the desk, showing two young girls in maroon-coloured school uniforms. The older one looked no more than seven. "I'm fairly certain I liked it. Gran turned something to be concerned about into something to be proud of."

Sarah wrote in her notebook. The writing was quick and sketchy, and even if it was not upside down, Jerome would have struggled to decipher anything.

"When you were growing up, do you think you would have tried to please your grandmother?"

"Well, if you mean would I have made things up just to please her, the answer is no. Even if I'd wanted to, she'd have known immediately if I was making something up. But, yes, I did like to show my appreciation to her whenever I could."

"It sounds like you had a wonderful, honest relationship."

"Yes, I'm very lucky like that."

"When were the next incidents?" Sarah's expression had returned to a more formal and harder, though not harsh, appearance: her game face, as Jerome subsequently came to consider it. He recounted the incident at school as a seventeen-year-old and then at the football match shortly afterwards.

"And you told no one?"

"No, not then anyway; I did tell Gran later."

"Didn't you think about going back to your doctor or the professor who saw you before?"

"I thought about it, but I was too fascinated by the wonder of what was happening. I guess I knew that if things started to get out of hand, I could start the medication again; it was a bit like having a safety net. But I was intrigued and started to experiment, and then I discovered that I could initiate the time freezing and stop it at will. That was a revelation."

"What do you mean a 'revelation'?"

"I became convinced that this was not a medical problem but an incredible ability I had."

"And the only other person you told was your grandmother?"

"Yes."

"What was her reaction this time?"

Jerome closed his eyes momentarily, recalling sitting with Helga in the front room of her apartment and telling her about his new powers. "She was intrigued as well, excited even, though she wanted to be sure that I couldn't be hurt. And I reassured her that I couldn't."

"How did you know this couldn't harm you?"

Jerome shrugged his shoulders. "I just assumed it wouldn't harm me."

"So would it be fair to suggest that your grandmother reinforced your view that this was a special gift rather than something you should seek medical guidance for?"

"Yes, that would be fair. In fact, I think she may have used those very words: a special gift."

"Who from, do you think?"

"What do you mean?" asked Jerome.

"Who do you think she felt this gift was from?"

"Oh." Jerome shook his head. "If you mean did Gran think this was something religious or spiritual in some way, then, no, I'm sure she didn't."

"And what about you? Are you religious at all?"

"No, I'm not against religion, but it's not for me."

Sarah closed her notebook slowly and her face relaxed. "OK, Jerome, that's today's session over."

"Oh." He glanced with surprise at the clock, which confirmed that the forty-five minutes had elapsed. "Doesn't time fly when you're talking about freezing it? Who'd have thought?"

She started to grin but seemed to stifle it. "So, I'll see you again next week. Keep trying for that three-out-of-ten calmness level. I think we're making some progress."

Chapter 40

"You're up earlier than I expected," Pieter said brightly as his younger son entered their living room shortly after 10.00am the following Sunday. "I thought you'd lie in until noon. Did you have a good night?"

"Yes, it was a good laugh." Jerome stretched his arms above his head. "I met a bunch of the guys, and we ended up in some club. I think I can still hear the music thumping in my ears."

"Good for you." His father continued to smile. "Do you want me to fry some bacon and eggs for you? Would you fancy that?"

"No thanks, Dad. I'll just grab a coffee. We'll be well fed later at Geraldine's. What time are we due there anyway?"

"Around 3.00pm."

Jerome made his coffee and then, after opening the back door, stood just outside, sipping from the mug and smoking his first cigarette of the day as the sunshine covered their small back lawn. "Dad," he called back over his shoulder, "do you fancy going for a spin down to Largs beach later this morning?"

Pieter waited until his son had returned inside the house before replying, "Aye, that sounds good. You don't mind driving?"

"No, not at all."

***

Largs beach lies on the Ayrshire coast about a one-hour drive from Glasgow. It was a place where Jerome had spent many happy summer days as a child. He drove there this Sunday morning at a leisurely pace and arrived just after noon, stopping in a car park that overlooked the sand-and-shingle beach.

"Do you want to go for a walk or would you prefer to sit here?" asked Jerome.

"I'm happy to stay in the car, if that's OK with you?" replied his father.

"Sure." Jerome unbuckled his seatbelt and manoeuvred his seat back. "The sea looks very calm today, doesn't it?"

"Yes, it looks like glass, although I remember it can be really wild at times."

"And very cold," added Jerome.

"That didn't seem to bother you much when you were young. You'd just wander into the sea holding Mum's hand or Gran's hand."

Jerome continued gazing at the sea as the waves made a gentle lapping sound, barely audible through the half-open car windows. "I must have been a handful for you guys when I was born." He turned to his father. "You weren't in your early twenties anymore."

"Ah, it was your mother who did most of the rearing as you know."

Jerome turned back. "I think one of my earliest memories is building sandcastles on this beach, although I'm not certain if I really remember it or have just seen photos of it."

A gentle silence ensued. Jerome considered having another cigarette, but he decided against it.

"What's your earliest memory, Dad?"

"Mine? Oh, probably queuing up to start school with your gran waving at me through the school gates wearing that no-nonsense look she had."

"She must have had it tough."

"It was tough for everyone in those days."

Jerome squinted as the sunlight reached his eye-line. "Gran told me a tragic story about her life at the end of the war in Berlin."

Pieter continued to stare straight ahead. "Aye, they were terrible times."

"Did she ever talk to you about it, Dad?"

Jerome's father exhaled wearily as he turned his head away from his son. "Not really."

Jerome probed no more. If his father wanted to talk about these matters, he would do so in his own time. His son would not force him there.

***

"What do you think we'll get for dinner at Geraldine's?" asked Jerome as they began the drive back to Glasgow.

"Roast beef with tons of veg," suggested Pieter.

"Yes, I suspect Joe's gradually converting our Geraldine into a vegetarian."

"I reckon you could be right there."

"He'd never convert us, though."

"No way, Jose," replied his father.

***

"Jerome." Sarah Wine appeared slightly distracted as she called over to him in the waiting room. It was 9.10am and his third appointment had been scheduled for 9.00am.

"Sorry for the delay," she continued as they entered her room. "One of my daughters is ill and had to take the day off school, so I'm just sorting out minders for the day."

"I hope she's OK."

"She'll be fine. It's me and her father who'll be stressed." Sarah sat down and placed her hands either side of the notebook on the low table. She had small, delicate fingers, which Jerome was surprised he had not noticed previously.

"Is it your older daughter?" He pointed to the photograph on the desk.

She half turned. "Yes, it is. It's at times like this we miss not having a granny or granddad nearby." She breathed in audibly, and her usual controlled calmness re-emerged quickly. "So, on the one-to-ten scale, where one is totally relaxed, how was your week?"

"Oh, I'd say maybe a four."

"So, a bit less relaxed or laid-back than the previous week?"

"Well I went out a few nights with my pals so yes a bit less laid-back."

"That sounds good," she responded encouragingly. "Now, at our last session, you were telling me how you felt you could freeze time, but you decided to tell no one." She consulted her notes. "No one except your grandmother."

Jerome nodded his confirmation.

"OK, what would you like to talk about today?"

He was annoyed by the question, as it seemed to suggest a disinterest in his story. Disbelief, he could understand and accept, but this question seemed almost disrespectful. He waited before responding. "I assumed we were going to talk about my journeys back in time."

She nodded without looking at him. "Tell me about the first time this happened to you."

Slowly, at first, Jerome began to tell the story of the evening of 21st June 2015 in his room in the halls of residence in London; about how he hadn't realised initially that he had travelled in time, but he began to understand gradually what had really happened.

"You said you inhaled oxygen," she began when he had finished. "What made you do that?"

"Well, I knew I could trigger the time-freeze episodes simply by holding my breath for a short period of time and then inhaling. So, effectively, I was stopping my oxygen intake for a brief period. And I wondered what might happen if, instead of inhaling ordinary air, which only has about twenty percent oxygen, I inhaled one hundred percent oxygen."

"Do you do that every time you have one of these trips?"

"Yes."

"Where did you get the oxygen from?"

"I used my father's medical prescription."

"You do know that inhaling pure oxygen for a period of time can be dangerous?"

"Yes, but I only inhale it for a few seconds."

"Jerome…" She paused. "Jerome, inhaling oxygen like that can't be good for your health – either your physical or your mental health. And it could very well contribute to your belief that you go on these journeys. Do you understand that?"

He noticed the left side of her dark hair remained slightly unbrushed as she looked at him intensely. "I understand fully what you're saying. I considered not mentioning the oxygen at all because I guessed this would be your reaction. But I want to be totally open and honest in our conversations, so I decided I'd tell you about it."

"I appreciate that." She glanced away momentarily. "But will you undertake not to use the oxygen for the duration of our sessions?"

It was Jerome's turn to inhale audibly. "OK." After a brief silence, he continued. "That was my first experience of travelling back. And it was so frightening at the time that I decided never to do it again. But, eventually, months later, curiosity drew me back, and I tried it again." Jerome told of his initial journeys back and how, by experimentation, he began to understand the laws that governed his time travel.

Sarah listened patiently, though the appearance of the discomfort that had arisen abruptly when he mentioned the oxygen cylinder had not totally softened. "So you created these laws around your ability to time travel?"

"I discovered them gradually. I didn't create anything."

"How did you realise that you couldn't actually change anything?"

"There was a young man called Jay Goodman…" Jerome told, in slow detail, the story of the sad American, and how, despite being able to travel back and stay beyond the time when he would die, the American had still died at the exact same time. Nothing had changed.

"That is a very poignant story and terribly sad," said Sarah. "How did you feel after that?"

"Sad and a bit confused."

"Why confused?"

"I wondered what the point was of being able to travel back if I couldn't change anything."

"And do you still feel confused about it?"

"Not really. They are just the laws. I've learned to accept them."

She paused to write in her notebook again, and glanced at her watch. "You have a remarkably clear recall of that conversation with Jay Goodman."

"It was the first time after I'd journeyed back in time that I wrote down exactly what had happened."

"Why did you do that?"

"I think it just affected me deeply, and I wanted to note the names of people and places in case I forgot them."

"Did you ever think about contacting his parents?"

"I thought about it very briefly," said Jerome, shaking his head. "But it was never going to bring any comfort to them."

"What other journeys did you record in writing?"

"My two major ones: back to see Hitler in 1929 and then Jesus at the Sermon on the Mount. They were also the two journeys when my grandmother and then my mother died at the exact time I travelled back."

"Yes, you've mentioned before about the timing of their deaths coinciding with your journeys. And I'm not ignoring it, but I'd like to discuss it at one of our subsequent meetings, if that's OK? In the meantime, would you mind if I read your recollections of those journeys?"

Jerome sensed an increasing interest from Sarah and was happy to agree to her request.

"If you want, you can just drop them at reception in an envelope marked personal for my attention only. I'd like to read them before our next session," clarified Sarah.

"I'll do that," replied Jerome as the session came to an end.

Chapter 41

"That'll be him now," declared Pieter.

Jerome heard his father's voice as he closed the front door quietly after returning from work the following evening. He pushed open the door to the living room gently.

"There's a visitor for you," said Pieter, beaming at his son.

Sitting opposite him and smiling contentedly, was Chris. "Hiya, buddy," said Chris, still grinning as he got to his feet.

"What are you doing here?" asked Jerome as he shook hands warmly with his friend.

"Oh, I just thought I'd like to see Glasgow, so I decided to drop in."

"Well, it's great to see you," replied Jerome. "Have you just arrived?"

"Yes, I got here about an hour ago. Your dad's been looking after me very well."

"He said he was going to book into a hotel," began Pieter. "But I told him he'll do no such thing. He can stay here. There's plenty of room."

"Absolutely," agreed Jerome as Chris gave a helpless shrug. "How long can you stay?"

"Oh." Chris looked at Pieter. "Maybe one or two years." He still had not stopped grinning.

***

Jerome had already arranged to meet with two of his other friends in a city-centre bar at 9.00pm that evening: Tall Paul and Small Paul. Chris was happy to join the group, and, by 8.45pm, he and Jerome were standing at the bar ordering their first drinks.

"I like your dad," began Chris as he leaned against the bar, cradling a pint glass against his chest. "He's real friendly and has a great sense of humour."

"You mean he laughs at your jokes," replied Jerome, raising his eyebrows good-humouredly.

"An extremely discerning man."

"Yes, he's a good guy, all right." Jerome grinned. "Anyway, what made you decide to come to Glasgow out of the blue?"

Chris's face took on an unusually serious appearance. "Well, our last conversation in London was a bit…unusual."

"You mean surreal?"

"That'd be a better word, all right. And, as I wasn't gleaning too much information from your texts, I decided Muhammad was going to have to come to the mountain and check up on you. So how are you?"

Jerome looked fondly at his friend. "That's very thoughtful of you. I really appreciate it."

"So how are you?" repeated Chris.

"I'm fine," he began. "No, really I am," he added in response to the doubting look on Chris's face. Jerome leaned closer to his friend. "I took your advice about listening to Karl's suggestion. I've had a few sessions with a counsellor."

"That sounds sensible. Are they helping?"

"To be honest, I only agreed to go to placate Karl. The sessions are OK. They're not intense or traumatic in any way, but I sense she just wants to pigeonhole me. You know, 'delusions brought on by extreme grief', that sort of thing. I think I'll go to one or two more, but I feel it'll be a waste of time ultimately."

"Well, you seem remarkably sane. Not that I thought you were insane," added Chris hastily. "The sessions can't be doing you any harm. Why don't you just keep attending?"

"Because she's trying to convince me of something that I know is not correct, and I promised that I wouldn't try to travel back while I'm meeting with her."

Chris nodded in a non-committal way. "You said 'her'; what's she like?"

"I'd guess she's about sixty, but looks older and not very attractive."

"You're lying. She's gorgeous, isn't she?"

Jerome laughed. "Yes, I'm lying. She's much younger and very attractive."

"See, I can always tell when you're lying. I can read all the little giveaway signals on your face."

Jerome paused. "And when I tell you I have made these journeys back in time, am I lying?"

Chris averted his gaze momentarily and then looked intensely at his comrade. "Not that I can see, buddy. Not that I can see. Anyway, as far as I'm concerned, you look and sound healthy, so I can head back tomorrow and go on my own epic journey feeling reassured."

They briefly clinked glasses.

"What epic journey?" asked Jerome.

"I've bought my Interrail ticket, and I'm going to backpack across Europe for a month," Chris explained.

"That sounds great. On your own?"

"Yeah, I don't mind being on my own and just doing exactly what I want. Anyway, I thought I better do it now while my passport still operates in all these countries."

"Ah, it'll always operate," commented Jerome with a smile.

"I'm not so sure. It's a pity you couldn't travel into the future instead of the past, and then you could let me know. Anyway," continued Chris, "how's life on the romantic front? Have you had any contact with Stancia, or shouldn't I ask?"

"She's still in Padua, as far as I know."

"You haven't tried to make contact?" Chris probed gently.

Jerome shook his head.

"Are you going to try?"

"Yes, I will. But I don't know; it just doesn't seem to be the right time now."

"What about surprising her in Padua at the end of the summer?"

"Maybe," said Jerome unconvincingly.

"You're not saluting that idea."

"It just feels like I'd be stalking her. But I will make contact. I'm not giving up. I miss her too much." Jerome looked over Chris's shoulder and waved as he noticed the two Pauls arriving. "Here are the guys now."

Chapter 42

Glasgow;
10th August 2017

There was no one at the reception desk when Jerome arrived for his fourth session. Eventually, at 9.10am, he knocked on Sarah's door. She had been unaware that her receptionist was missing and invited him in, apologising for the delay.

Despite his comment to Chris about being pigeonholed, Jerome felt his interest rise as he sat down. He had immediately noticed his typed pages detailing the journeys to see Hitler and Jesus lying on the table in an open Manila folder.

"These are two extraordinary stories," she said, picking up her black notebook. "Really extraordinary."

Jerome was pleased with this comment and sought to glean further information from her face, but received none.

"As you can see…" she indicated some pages in her notebook, "I've made a few notes on them and have some questions. Would you mind if we explore them?"

"Not at all," replied Jerome as he unfolded his arms and sat more upright in the seat.

"My first question is why did you decide to journey to see Hitler?"

Jerome explained Helga's harrowing story and how that had been the primary reason for his decision.

"That is a horrific story," commented Sarah.

"Yes, it is."

"When did you find out?"

"My grandmother told me. She was in a nursing home at the time. It was towards the end of her life."

"Was this ever discussed within your family?"

"No, I did ask Karl after I'd heard from Gran. He knew about it but said Dad didn't want to discuss it; there were too many painful memories. I did try to raise it with Dad once, but..." Jerome shook his head.

"Do you find it a bit strange that it was never discussed with you?"

"No, not strange," began Jerome thoughtfully. "It's just a very painful memory that people want to... that is, it's better not being raised if it only causes hurt."

"But this hugely important information was kept from you. You would never have known of it if your grandmother hadn't told you herself. How do you feel about that?"

Jerome reflected on her question. "At first, I was angry that I hadn't been told, but that passed."

Sarah leaned back in her seat. "You mentioned before that your family are very close. Would it be fair to also describe your family as being secretive, in the sense that discussions on sensitive issues were never encouraged?"

"No. I don't think that would be a fair description," Jerome replied hurriedly. "This was the only time I can recall not being told about something important."

"I see. And your grandmother, how did she feel about Hitler?"

"She absolutely despised him and all the other 'Nazi princes' as she called them."

"So your decision to visit Hitler arose solely from the traumatic experiences of your grandmother?"

"Well, mainly, but I was also fascinated at the prospect of meeting him."

"What did you hope to achieve?"

"I wanted to get his view on some of the key events that were yet to happen. And also to make him uncomfortable and maybe insult him in some way."

"As revenge for what happened to your grandmother?"

"Yes, though I'm not sure that insulting him could be classed as revenge for what happened to her."

"But you felt it would be something that would please Helga?"

Jerome touched the outline of the cigarette packet in his jacket pocket. "Yes."

"How did you learn of Helga's death?"

"I got a phone call from Karl when I was in Nuremburg. Then, when I went back to Glasgow, I learned that she had died at the exact moment I travelled back in time to see Hitler."

"Why do you think that would have happened?"

"You mean why would my grandmother die at the exact time I went back to Germany in 1929?"

"Yes."

Jerome looked away as he wiped gently at an itch just below his left eye. "To be honest, at first, I thought it was really strange that she could have died at that exact moment, but then I convinced myself it was purely a coincidence. After all, she was an elderly lady who was quite ill. But then, when my mother died at the exact time I travelled to see Jesus, I knew these events couldn't be coincidences."

"So why do you think they would happen?"

"I don't know."

Sarah gazed at the notebook resting on her lap. The pen moved slightly in her right hand, but she wrote nothing down. "Would you have any idea why these deaths would occur at the exact time you travelled back?"

"I sense you feel that I should know the answer to that question, or perhaps that I do know but don't want to accept it. However, the fact is that I have no idea why my mother and grandmother died at those precise times."

"Do you feel responsible in some way?"

"For their deaths?"

"Yes."

Jerome shook his head. "No, I don't feel responsible. Why should I? That would make no sense."

"Well, responsible in the sense that if you hadn't travelled back, they may not have died at those exact times."

"Or not have died at all," replied Jerome, looking challengingly at her. "But, to answer your question again, I don't feel responsible."

"But," she persisted, "do you believe that if you hadn't travelled back, then they wouldn't have died at those times?"

Jerome puffed out his cheeks and then exhaled slowly as he stared pensively into the far corner of the room. "I don't know," he said quietly. "I honestly don't know."

She glanced at Jerome with a hint of bemusement. "Let's talk about your journey to see Jesus."

She turned the page in her notebook as Jerome sipped from his coffee. It was the first time he had accepted a drink in her room.

"Why did you decide to visit Jesus?" Sarah enquired.

Jerome explained the letter written by Helga shortly before her death.

Sarah listened attentively and did not respond immediately. "So, the destinations of your two major journeys were both at the suggestion of your grandmother. Would that be right?"

"Certainly, the journey to see Jesus give the Sermon on the Mount was because of Gran. The journey to meet Hitler…"

Jerome glanced out of the partially open window and reflected for a moment as the sound of cars passing on the road below interrupted the silence. "Would I have journeyed to see Hitler if it hadn't been for Gran? No, I don't think I would."

"By the way, did you keep that letter your grandmother wrote to you?"

"Yes."

"Did you ever show it to anyone else or tell anyone about it?"

"My father gave it to me on the day of her funeral. He gave me the unopened envelope and never asked what was in it. And I've never told anyone."

"Not even Stancia?"

Jerome shook his head. "She wouldn't have understood it."

"You've kept a lot of stuff to yourself down the years, Jerome." She looked at him, her eyebrows slightly raised.

"Yes, but only where it relates to my time travel."

"Would you mind if I saw that letter from Helga?" The request was spoken gently.

Jerome replayed the content of the letter in his mind before responding. "That would be OK. I'll leave it in the reception, marked for you. But please take care of it. It's my last contact with Gran."

"Don't worry, I will." She adjusted the spectacles on the chain around her neck.

"I've never seen you use them," said Jerome indicating the spectacles.

"Oh, I need them when using the computer screen." She pointed to the desk behind her. "I kept losing them, hence this," she added, lifting the chain. "My husband keeps nagging me to get laser treatment on my eyes, but the thought of it sounds terrifying, so I'll continue with these for the time being anyway."

"Getting back to your journey to meet Jesus, you say at one point that you felt this might be *the* important journey. What did you mean by that?"

"I think I had a sense that I was going to learn something profound about my powers on that journey," Jerome confirmed.

"And did you?"

"No, I didn't."

"Were you disappointed with that?"

"To say I was disappointed after meeting with Jesus and Mary Magdalene sounds crazy, but I did feel a sense that something was missing."

"I'm intrigued by some of the comments you say Jesus made." She consulted her notes. "Like this one, when he returned your watch and said, 'Maybe one day you will give me a more permanent gift.' What do you think is meant by that remark?"

"I've thought about that a lot and I really have no idea. What gift could I give that would be permanent to someone from the past? Everything ends in less than five hours, so nothing could be permanent."

"He must have had something in mind, don't you think?"

"Yes, I don't believe it was a throwaway comment. Maybe he had something specific in mind, possibly something to do with his death. Maybe he thought I could help him prepare for his death in some way or remove the suffering he would have to go through. He did express a fear of suffering. But I'm only guessing." Jerome looked at her. "He also asked me if I had any other special gifts. So he may have felt I had special powers that could help him."

"You've also written that he said, 'I sense we will meet again one more time before I die.' Why do you think he said this?"

"You are asking me questions that I ask myself continually. And, as yet, I have no answers. Again, it may be that he felt I could help him in some way before he died." Jerome could hear a door opening outside in the corridor and some indistinct words spoken, probably a greeting, before the door closed again.

"One thing I did wonder," began Sarah. "When you travel on these journeys, does everyone speak English?"

"Of course not." Jerome spoke in genuine surprise.

"So how did you converse?"

"I had to learn the languages. German wasn't difficult. My gran spoke it a lot."

"I did a German A level. I enjoyed it," she replied. "*Kannst du es flieband sprechen?*"

"*Ja, Ich kann. Aber Aramaisch zu lernen war jedoch viel schwieriger.*"

She averted her gaze briefly, while a gentle smile tugged at the corners of her mouth as though she had been caught out in some minor misdemeanour. "I'm afraid I didn't quite understand all of that."

"I was confirming that I do speak German fluently, but that learning Aramaic was much more difficult."

"Is Aramaic the language Jesus spoke?"

"Yes."

"How did you learn it?"

Jerome explained the various steps he had taken over many months to learn this language. "Would you like to hear some?" he asked brightly.

"Well, I wouldn't know whether you were speaking it correctly. I'm afraid my linguistic skills are not that good."

"I could translate something for you." He looked at her desk. "Do you have a voice-memo app on your mobile phone or an old-school Dictaphone? I could speak the translation into that."

"I don't have a smartphone, and I don't have a Dictaphone here. I think I may have an old one at home."

"Well, if you bring that for our next session, I'd be happy to translate something for you. And you could then check it."

Her face registered a vague uncertainty before she replied, "Yes, OK." She paused for a short while before continuing, "Tell me more about Angelic."

"Angelic?" Jerome looked confused momentarily as the question caught him by surprise.

"Yes, you included her in your account of the journey to see Jesus, although you weren't back in time when you met her, is that right?"

"Yes, Angelic is a person from our time. I met her twice: once before and once shortly after my journey back."

"She seemed like just the right person for you to meet at those times."

"What do you mean?"

She glanced above his head, as though gathering her thoughts. "Well, Angelic was someone you could talk to and confide in. And you seemed to know that implicitly." Her gaze lowered to meet his eyes. "She seems almost like a mystical figure: a guardian angel. She is aptly named." Sarah smiled gently. "Have you tried to make contact with her again?"

"No." Jerome opened his mouth slightly as though to continue speaking before closing it again.

"Did Angelic remind you of your grandmother?"

Jerome placed his open palm in front of his mouth momentarily before replying. "Do you think Angelic doesn't exist?"

Sarah made no response as the two sat in a still silence.

Jerome became aware of a faint rattling noise from the old-fashioned, gold-coloured radiator on the wall and a far-off, high-pitched sound of a siren. "Sarah, do you think I invented her?" He spoke more loudly than intended.

"I don't know, Jerome."

Again, he waited for the expected further comment, but none came. The siren had drifted away, and the radiator settled down to a faint humming sound.

***

Later that evening, Jerome sat in front of his computer screen, gazing pensively at an email he had drafted. He intended sending it to a list of physicians dealing in geriatrics at St George's Hospital in London. He had found it relatively easy to get the email addresses from the hospital's website. But, then, as he reread the email, he hesitated:

> *Dear X,*
> *My name is Jerome Black.*
> *Recently, on a flight from Jerusalem to London on 18th May, I met with a kind, elderly lady called Angelic. She told me that her daughter worked as a doctor specialising in geriatrics at St George's Hospital. I would very much like to speak to Angelic again and so, if it is possible that she is indeed your mother, would you please ask her to contact me.*
> *Kind regards,*
> *Jerome Black*

He sat back in the chair and folded his arms tightly, as though erecting an additional barrier to the process of sending the emails. Sarah's doubts about the existence of Angelic had shaken Jerome. Of course, he had expected that she would not believe his time-travel stories, but this was questioning the existence of someone he had met twice in normal time. Again, he replayed the conversation with Sarah. She had merely alluded to the unusualness of Angelic, which had resulted in Jerome asking the question about her existence. But it wasn't just her words, "I don't know, Jerome," that unnerved him. It was the look of sympathy as she uttered them. It was the same caring, almost sad expression he had seen on Chris when confronted with the revelation of his time travels. He had been so unsettled by the experience that he wanted to prove the existence of Angelic to Sarah. He also realised that he needed to prove her existence partly for himself and that was even more disconcerting. He wondered if sending these emails was a ridiculous idea. What would Sarah think of him sending them?

Although, ultimately, what did it matter what she thought or believed? But Jerome realised that it did matter to him. He clicked on the send button.

***

By the following morning, Jerome was regretting his decision to send the emails. Reading it again, he envisaged the recipients thinking this must be a message from a crank and deleting it immediately. He also considered the possibility that Angelic had made up, or at least exaggerated, the story about her daughter. After all, he hardly knew her, and she had accepted his story of time travel so matter-of-factly that it didn't require a huge leap of faith to believe she may invent stories.

In the days that followed, he received a few replies – always courteous but confirming they knew of no Angelic. He deliberately dwelt no more on the possibility of contacting Angelic. But Jerome did reflect, with growing intensity, on the questions raised by Sarah about his conversation with Jesus. The same questions he had previously been unsuccessful in understanding: What did Jesus mean when he said Jerome might one day give him a more permanent gift? Why did he say, 'I feel we will meet again before I die'?

But the question Jerome wanted an answer to more than any other was this: *Why did my mother die at the exact time I travelled back to see you?*

Chapter 43

Glasgow;
17th August 2017

Jerome's fifth session began with the familiar, friendly, welcoming conversation.

"Did you remember to bring the Dictaphone?" he asked, settling into his usual seat.

"Oh." Sarah grimaced slightly. "Sorry, I forgot. I'll definitely bring it next week." Slowly, she opened the Manila folder on the table. "I read the letter from your grandmother. Thank you for sharing it."

"That's OK."

"In her letter, she said that she didn't want you to make any journey back to see her. What did you think of that?"

"I respected her request. I never travelled back, although I wanted to."

"What about your mother?"

"What about her?" He knew he sounded evasive.

"Did you ever feel like going back to see her?"

Jerome gazed down at the tan-coloured carpet. It felt soft

under his feet and almost luxurious. "Yes, I did. I went back to see her after she'd died. It was the last journey I made. In fact, it was because of that journey that I'm here."

"Tell me about that journey back."

Slowly, which he felt allowed him to control his emotions better, Jerome recounted the full story of that Saturday evening when he made his fateful journey back.

Sarah left a respectful silence when he finished.

He explained, "I hadn't intended to tell you that story. Not because I want to hide anything, but…"

"I understand," she replied quietly.

Sarah put down her pen in a deliberate manner, clenched her hands together and brought them close to her face. "Jerome, may I put a supposition to you?"

"Of course." He nodded thoughtfully.

"From our conversations over the weeks, I've formed the view that you're a thoughtful, truthful person, who's not given to flights of fancy. I also feel you are a rational person, and if someone else were to present you with your story about time travel, you just wouldn't believe them." She raised her eyebrows, seeking in vain for confirmation. "And so let me suggest a possible, rational explanation for your episodes. I believe they may be connected directly to the deaths of your grandmother and mother; two people you obviously loved very deeply. When someone very close to us dies, we go through a whole gamut of emotions, including terrible sadness, often anger and sometimes guilt. Even though it may be completely illogical that we should feel guilty, we still do. Occasionally, these feelings can be so profound that we almost stop functioning. We're unable to cope in a normal way with the tragedy of the loss. It can be in situations like this that our mind can resort to unusual or irrational ways to deal with the situation. That can be by way of distracting or blocking out the event, and that can mean that the normal process of grieving and accepting the loss finally is hindered."

Jerome noticed that, as she spoke, she had begun to move her hands in an expressive manner, unlike her usual measured movements.

She went on, "I think, in your case, this has manifested itself in the creation of these journeys back in time. But I sense that, on a rational level, you know they can't be real. Does that make any sense?"

Jerome rested his head against the back of the chair. "But these journeys began years before the deaths of my grandmother and mother."

"You may have been having these episodes before your grandmother died or you may now believe that to be the case. But, either way, I believe it is the grief from these deaths that has brought matters to a head."

Jerome shifted forwards in his chair. "But if these journeys weren't real, why would I learn different languages?"

"Well, I suspect you could always speak German."

"And Aramaic! Why on earth would I learn an obscure language and travel to Israel at the exact time of my mother's death?"

Sarah gave a gentle shrug. "It could be the mind creating the story after the event to meet the circumstances, Jerome. For example, if you were in France instead of Germany when your grandmother died, the mind could create a very believable story that you travelled back to visit, say, Napoleon; or if you were in Italy, maybe Mussolini. The mind can adapt very quickly."

"Even if I accept your version of events – which I don't, by the way – it still doesn't explain why I would spend almost a year learning the Aramaic language on the off-chance of being in Israel when my mother died. It just doesn't make sense."

"I can't explain that, Jerome. And I will bring in the Dictaphone next week, I promise." She paused and breathed out audibly. "But I feel like you're asking me to present an alternative explanation for everything that you've experienced, and that may not be possible.

There may be no eureka moment when I can point out some glaring flaw in your story, or when I'll accept that what you're saying is real all of a sudden. We may just have to accept that I can't prove your story is false in the same way that you can't prove it has actually happened. We often think of the subconscious mind as a kind of unstructured part of the brain that deals in emotions, but it can be extremely thorough and logical and cunning. I believe in your case that it has very cleverly created a set of rules for your time travel, which means that no one can prove or disprove that you travel in time, and that includes proving or disproving it to yourself.

"I feel you have not got much joy or happiness from these journeys, and I wonder if you can let them go. If you can accept that, irrespective of whether they are real or not, they do you no good. Then I would hope, as time goes by, your desire to make these journeys would wane, and you may be able to grieve properly for your mother and grandmother. There may come a time when you will accept that they never really did happen, but even if that point is never reached, you would have adjusted to living without these journeys, and can get on with ordinary, everyday life." She sat back in her seat and slowly interlocked her fingers. "I know I've thrown a lot at you over the last few minutes. Have you any initial thoughts?"

"Sarah, I appreciate fully that you are only considering my well-being, but nothing you have said surprises me. The supposition you put forwards and the alternative explanations are things I have also considered, maybe not with the clarity you have expressed, but I haven't been unaware of these possibilities. I haven't tried to block them out, but there remain too many things that just don't add up. In some ways, I'd like to accept your version. It would make life a lot simpler. But, at the moment, I just struggle to do so."

"I understand that. This will be a gradual rather than a sudden process. That's just the way the mind works."

Jerome nodded. "I think you feel I'm on the road to accepting that the journeys are not real." He gave a tired smile. "But that's not where I am."

She returned his smile as the tension of the previous minutes began to dissipate. For the rest of this session, they restated their positions tentatively, with neither seeming to convince the other.

"Will you think about what I have said over the next week?" she asked as the session drew to a close.

"Of course I will." As he got up to leave, he turned again. "Don't forget the Dictaphone."

"I won't," she confirmed with a laugh.

***

Sunday, 20th August 2017

It was early evening, and Jerome was alone in the house. Pieter had just gone out to visit a friend and would not be back for at least an hour. Jerome was enjoying the unusual solitariness of being alone at home – and, on this occasion, it suited his purposes.

During the three days since he had last been with Sarah Wine, Jerome had reached two definite conclusions. The first was that the sessions with her had run their course. They had reached the impasse that he had suspected from the beginning was inevitable. His second conclusion was that he would have to travel back to see Jesus to deal with his unanswered questions. There was no other way. Only by asking Jesus face-to-face could he get closure. But, before that, he wanted to close the loop with Sarah properly. He had promised her he would not use the oxygen while the sessions continued and, in a way, he felt bound by that promise. Nevertheless, in his mind, the sessions had already ended and so travelling back in time then would not be breaking his word. However, his next journey back would not be to meet with Jesus;

it would be to visit Sarah. He went to his room and pulled the oxygen cylinder out from under his bed.

**

10th August 2017; 8.55am

Jerome climbed the four stone steps, pushed open the heavy front door and entered the familiar waiting room, which he knew would be empty this morning. It was the occasion of his fourth session with Sarah, when the receptionist was late. Walking quietly down the corridor, he knocked softly on the door of Sarah's room.

"Yes," came her enquiring voice.

He opened the door slowly and drew his head into view. "Hi Sarah, I'm sorry I'm a little bit early. May I speak to you for just a few minutes?"

She looked at him quizzically over the top of her reading glasses. "Erm, yes, sure."

He sat down in his usual high-backed chair. Sarah remained behind her desk.

"Do you remember when I explained to you about transitory time? The time when I travel back but no one except me remembers?" questioned Jerome.

She removed her glasses before replying. "Yes, of course I remember."

Jerome looked directly at her. "Well, this is transitory time. This is not real time."

Sarah appeared to stiffen in her seat and made no reply.

He continued, "I have just come from Sunday 20th August, which is ten days in the future. I'm sorry if I'm alarming you in any way. I don't mean to, and there's nothing to be worried about."

Jerome paused, but still she said nothing, although he was relieved that she appeared to be looking at him with curiosity rather than trepidation. He glanced at his watch. "In just under ten minutes, at around 9.10am, there will be a knock on this door. It will be me. The transitory time will end, and you will remember none of this. The reason I have come back to see you is mainly a selfish one." Again, he paused.

This time, she did reply. "I'm listening, Jerome."

"I would like you, please, to tell me something about you that no one could know." He raised his hand to try to pre-empt her unnecessary concern. "And I don't mean something personal. Just something trivial that no one else could possibly know. I want to be able to tell you about it at our final session. I know it's selfish of me, but I feel the need to prove to you the truth of what I'm saying."

Sarah moved back slightly in her seat and swallowed. She looked at Jerome, who gazed unthreateningly at the floor. A full minute passed in tense silence. There were no disturbing or comforting sounds intruding from the outside.

Jerome looked at the clock on the wall. "In less than eight minutes time I will be gone, and you will remember none of this. So, if at 9.10am there is no knock on the door, you will have what you will subsequently call a eureka moment when you will be able to say to me, 'See, these time-travel journeys aren't real after all.' Please…" He paused and then looked at her pleadingly. "Indulge me on this. What difference does it make? I have very little time."

Sarah joined her hands together and rested them on the desk. "Well, this is against my better judgement, Jerome. But when I was a child, my mother used to put a rug on my bed in the winter. It had red and green squares, like a picnic rug, and was fairly threadbare – at least, that's how I remember it. Sometimes it smelled of our dog, who would lie on it when he got the chance. And I used to send myself to sleep by rubbing the material of the rug between my thumb and forefinger."

"Thank you very much," said Jerome. "You've been very kind."

The healthy flush on Sarah's cheeks had returned as she turned slightly to glance at the clock. She raised her eyebrows as she looked at Jerome. "So, what happens now?"

"There will be a knock on the door shortly, and it will be me. The laws of my time travel decree that I can never meet myself, so this transitory time will end, and you will remember none of this."

"So we only have a few minutes to wait?"

"Yes."

"You seem very confident of this, Jerome."

"Yes, I am."

The subsequent stillness was broken by the soft tread of footsteps in the corridor. Sarah tensed slightly. Someone stopped outside. They knocked on the door: three quick, gentle raps.

She stared at Jerome then gave a small cough before enquiring, "Yes?"

"Oh, hi Sarah, it's Jerome Black here," came the unassuming voice from outside.

Jerome, noticing the look of shock on her face, rose immediately from his chair and opened the door, to bring this journey to an end.

Chapter 44

Glasgow;
22nd August 2017

He couldn't tell his brother. Karl just wouldn't understand. Throughout his sessions with Sarah Wine, Jerome had been upbeat about them in the very brief conversations he had with his brother on the subject. It just seemed easier to tell him what he wanted to hear. At this point, if he were to inform Karl about his plan to go again to Israel and travel back in time, it would create sadness, worry and possibly anger in his brother. There was no point in causing that. So, once again, Jerome made his plans alone. It was Tuesday evening when he informed his father that he would be gone for a few days.

"I'll be away from Thursday to Saturday this week. Will you be OK on your own?"

His father put down his newspaper and looked at him with a slightly confused expression. "Aye, I'm sure I'll be fine. Where you going?"

"I'm meeting up with Chris in Amsterdam for a few days."

"Oh, that sounds like it could be enjoyable." Pieter returned to his newspaper, but he couldn't concentrate. He turned again to look at his son. "Will you be coming back home, Jerome?"

"What?" It was then Jerome's turn to look confused. "Will I be coming back home? Of course I will. What made you think that?"

Pieter gave a small shake of his head. "I don't know. Probably a wee notion I had. Anyway, ignore me. You enjoy Amsterdam, and I'll see you on Saturday."

***

Thursday, 24th August 2017

On Thursday morning Jerome went into Sarah's room for the final time. He sat in the only chair he had ever occupied and watched as she rustled busily in one of her desk drawers. He looked around the room, as though locking in fond memories of a place he would never revisit. Jerome was apprehensive about the upcoming conversation but tried not to show it.

"Here it is." Sarah held up a small, black, oblong Dictaphone. "I do keep my promises and I've even put new batteries in." She moved purposefully to her seat and handed the Dictaphone to Jerome. "Just press the front two buttons, and it will start recording."

Jerome had not been expecting this and took the Dictaphone with some hesitation. "What would you like me to translate?" he asked uncertainly.

"Oh, anything; you choose."

"No, you have to choose. It wouldn't be a proper test otherwise."

"OK." She opened the Manila folder and took out the pages describing Jerome's journey to meet Jesus. "Here, translate the first couple of paragraphs."

He turned the top page on the table so it faced him and

looked thoughtfully at the words: his words. Then, pressing the two buttons, he began translating.

"Well," she said after he had finished. "I honestly didn't know what to expect, but you are certainly a linguist, Jerome."

He held the Dictaphone out, and she took it gently.

"Sarah, I'd like to say a few things to you now, if you don't mind?" he requested.

"Absolutely." She placed the Dictaphone carefully beside the folder and looked watchfully at him.

"This will be our last session together."

"Oh, why is that, Jerome?" She glanced at him, sharply but protectively.

"Please hear me out." He joined his hands and pointed them downwards. "I want to thank you for your patience and concern, which I believe to be totally genuine. But I feel we've reached the end of our road together, and I need to travel another road to find answers to the questions we've both asked. I told you I wouldn't use the oxygen while our sessions were continuing, and, like you, I prefer to keep my promises. On this occasion, however, I've had to break that particular one." Jerome looked at her face. It was intense with concentration; her eyebrows curved downwards, giving a slightly worried appearance. "I travelled back in time to see you. It was in this room, a couple of weeks ago, just before one of our sessions."

She cocked her head slightly and appeared on the point of asking a question, but didn't.

Jerome went on, "It's become very important to me that someone believes me. In fact, it's become very important that you believe me and believe my story. So I travelled back in time and asked you to tell me something about you that absolutely no one else could know. And you very kindly did. You indulged me, even though you said it was against your better judgement."

"And what did I tell you?" she asked slowly.

"You told me that when you were a little girl, your mother would put a rug on your bed in winter time. It had red and green squares, like a picnic rug, and you recalled it as being threadbare. You said it sometimes smelled of dog because your dog would lie on it if it got the chance. And you used to rub the rug between your thumb and forefinger to send yourself to sleep."

Sarah looked at him, her face still. Slowly, her eyes narrowed challengingly. "How do you know that about me?"

"You told me. You were sitting over there…" He indicated the seat behind the desk. "And I was here."

"Have you been speaking to my mother?"

"No, Sarah. I don't know your mother. I only know this story because you told me."

She looked away, breathing audibly. "I don't know how you found this out, Jerome, but I don't like it at all. In fact, I find it disturbing. Have you been stalking me?"

"Is that what you really think? That I would stalk you?" Jerome looked genuinely shocked. "Really?"

"Well, what else can I think? You come into my room and start revealing personal information that you didn't get from me."

Jerome rose quickly. "I'll go now. I'm sorry I've caused you alarm. I never intended to, but… goodbye and thank you again." He walked to the door where he paused briefly. "Maybe now you'll understand better why I'm so reluctant to talk about my powers to anyone."

***

Jerome caught the late morning train to London and travelled on the early evening flight from Gatwick airport to Jerusalem. He sat in a window seat, sometimes reading from his Kindle, but, being easily distracted, he spent much of the journey gazing out at the clouds, and the occasional distant patches of green and brown land below.

As usual, Jerome had booked the cheapest option for the flight, but, even so, he was aware this trip would largely exhaust what remained of his grandmother's inheritance. Karl had offered to pay for his sessions with Sarah, but Jerome had insisted on meeting the cost. He was glad he had, even though his coffers had been getting low. And, in a way, it seemed appropriate that – as he approached his final journey back in time, for he felt sure it would be so – it was only made possible by using the last of Helga's gift.

He felt a grim determination about undertaking this journey back in time. That morning's meeting with Sarah had reinforced his resolve. Her hostile reaction to his story confirmed that he should expect no belief or help from his family, friends or anyone else with regard to his time travel. He was on his own on this subject, and it would always be so.

Jerome reflected on the strange comment from his father: "*Will you be coming back home?*" Did his father know or sense something, or was it really "*just a wee notion*"? However, of most concern to Jerome was the possibility that his travelling back so far in time could again result in the death of someone close. It was a genuine fear and the one reason he had considered not embarking. But he sensed that the alternative was to go through life without making this trip, and he could not do that. So, he suppressed his worries, and returned to his Kindle and reading about the garden of Gethsemane.

Chapter 45

Jerusalem, Israel;
Thursday, 24th August 2017; 10.00pm

He arrived, feeling calmer than he had expected, in the not unfamiliar surroundings of Ben Gurion airport. Once outside the terminal building, he caught a taxi to his hotel, which was the same one where he had stayed on his previous visit. He checked in and then went to a nearby cafe to get a late snack. Sitting outside in the warm evening breeze, he sipped a small glass of beer and checked his map again for the route to the garden of Gethsemane. He had planned to wait until daylight before reconnoitring the place, but he changed his mind and walked briskly up a steep hill close to the eastern wall of the old city. On reaching the top, he came across a beautiful church with onion-shaped, gold domes, reminding him of the famous St Basil's in Moscow. By consulting his map, he confirmed it was the Church of Mary Magdalene on the Mount of Olives, and a Russian Orthodox church. From there, he could see down to another church and beside it was his destination: the garden of Gethsemane. Jerome toyed with the idea of descending immediately and exploring the garden, but the light was poor.

Tomorrow; he would wait until tomorrow. And, in the meantime, he gazed down at the shadowy outline of the garden and thought again of meeting this man and of what Jerome would say.

***

Friday, 25th August 2017

The early morning sunshine had a watery appearance, reflecting the heavy rain Jerome had heard fall during the night. After a quick breakfast, he retraced his steps to the church at the top of the hill, finding the climb a bit more tiring than the previous evening. The garden was clearly visible below. He descended the Mount of Olives to another church at the bottom of the hill: the Church of All Nations, according to his map. He did not enter it but instead walked slowly and thoughtfully around the nearby garden: Gethsemane. Groups of tourists accompanied by their guides meandered around the marked paths in various states of interest. An elderly Franciscan monk in his grey habit was standing on his own, staring placidly at a gnarled olive tree, both bent over with age. There was little shelter here from the increasingly hot sun. Looking away from the monk, Jerome shaded his eyes and scanned the garden as sweat trickled down the back of his neck. He checked his watch. It had taken him thirty-five minutes to reach the garden from his hotel.

Security in this area, while not overwhelming, was still obvious. Policemen and women, in their short-sleeved, navy-blue shirts and baseball caps were walking around casually, but very visibly, and these were just the ones in uniform. He was sure there were other security personnel around, whose *modus operandi* was not to be seen. Taking out his oxygen container and putting on the mask in this environment would have its risks. Indeed, even getting here carrying his rucksack could arouse suspicion, though he had passed no security checks on his journey here from the hotel, which gave him some reassurance. He watched the Franciscan monk shuffle down the path, with the low layer of dust stirred up by his sandaled feet marking his slow progress.

Jerome made his way quickly back to the cool of his hotel room. He decided that the security position made it too risky to try using the oxygen in the garden in daylight. He would therefore undertake his final journey later that night. Initially, he thought he would pass the intervening hours in his room, but restlessness set in quickly, and he left the hotel at 11.30am, heading north towards where the Muslim quarter was marked on his map. The bustle and noise of the streets and markets were welcome distractions, and the sheer exuberance and liveliness of the people surprised him. He didn't buy anything, despite the numerous entreaties, and learned quickly to look, smile, say no and move on, past the clothes, jewellery, perfumes and wonderfully aromatic stalls offering both fresh and cooked food.

The narrowness of the streets gave an additional vibrancy to everything, and not in an uncomfortable or unpleasant way. He noted with interest that some of the men wore *dishdashas*, though most didn't. All around him, other ordinary, less hectic activities were taking place.

He came upon three elderly men sitting around a small, rickety table, which was made more precarious by the unevenness of the cobbled street, playing a board game that looked like dominos. All were dressed in Western suits, but were also wearing the traditional Arab headdress, unfolded and stretching down to the smalls of their backs. Their chatter was almost nonstop and, judging by the intermittent bursts of laughter, good-humoured. They never took their eyes from the table, except to turn every so often and shout something at the children who, Jerome assumed, were their charges for the day. The scene resonated with a warm, relaxed sense of family and friends together in a secure place, without worries or fears. He could have watched them for hours.

At one point, a football rolled towards him. Instinctively, he put his foot on it and, after looking up, flicked it accurately into the arms of the young boy who was running to retrieve it.

"Are you a real footballer?" asked the child in accented-but-clear English.

"Yes," replied Jerome as two other children moved towards them, "the best in my country."

"Really?" queried the wide-eyed child.

"Yes." Jerome nodded, feigning a smug expression.

"Do you want to play with us for a while?"

"No, I can't." He smiled warmly at the dark-haired boy. "I'm busy today; maybe tomorrow."

"You won't come tomorrow."

"How do you know?" asked Jerome, amused at the boy's certainty.

The child moved his head from side to side by way of explanation. "If you do come tomorrow, could you bring us a new ball? This one's very old."

Jerome laughed in response. The men continued to play their board game seemingly oblivious to this brief encounter.

Although he realised he had seen only a small part of the city, Jerome was surprised it was so pulsating. Somehow, he had expected a sombre serenity in a city sacred to Christians, Jews and Muslims – a holy counterbalance to the secularism of Tel Aviv – but it was not so. He stopped at one of the food vendors, attracted by the smells and by the entrepreneurial spirit evidenced by pricing a falafel wrap in six different currencies, "All gratefully accepted". He watched the woman, in her dark clothes, prepare his wrap with considerable care and, despite the heat, encouraged her to put in more chillies. He also bought a bottle of water and paid for everything in shekels.

As he walked slowly through the early afternoon crowds, wrap in one hand and water in the other, he spotted a stall with footballs on offer, hanging in a net from a horizontal pole. He bought one, strolled back to where the boys had been and, without saying anything, tossed it into the gleeful arms of his young recent acquaintance. As he turned to go, Jerome noticed one of the men at the table look at him with indulgent surprise.

Chapter 46

Jerusalem;
25th August 2017

Jerome had intended to start his journey to the garden at 9.00pm, but he was ready at 8.30pm and decided not to wait any longer. After tightening the cord of his *dishdasha*, he lifted the blue-black rucksack containing the oxygen cylinder and closed the door to his hotel room quietly behind him. Once outside in the warm night air, he walked at a deliberately leisurely pace, gripping the handle of the rucksack in his left hand. He climbed the steep hill for the third time in twenty-four hours, holding his head high and keeping to the centre of the pavement, so as not to appear suspicious.

On reaching the top, he began the descent of the Mount of Olives immediately. It was dark, and the noise from the city was fading gradually away. He knew if he were to meet any security personnel just then, he would almost certainly be stopped, though he felt confident that it would not happen. Picking his steps carefully in the gathering gloom, he could hear his increased breathing as the silence descended further.

He halted at a spot about fifty metres above the garden and, squinting through the murkiness, he scanned the area below watchfully. Parts of the garden were illuminated by what looked like ground-based lights marking some of the paths. Other sections were much darker and more useful for his purposes.

He moved cautiously to the garden's entrance and, seeing no one around, walked in quickly. Hurrying past this well-lit front section, he left the path and glided stealthily among the olive groves. He ducked down to avoid the low-hanging foliage and then stopped beside an old tree, possibly the same one the Franciscan monk had been observing earlier in the day. Hunkering down, he listened alertly for any hint of sound, but he heard only distant traffic sounds and some insect calls nearby.

He unzipped the rucksack and lifted out the oxygen cylinder gently, placing it beside him on the dry soil. Jerome placed the mask on his face and pulled the elastic holding strap over his head. He hesitated for a few more seconds, his senses alert for the possibility of anyone being close by, before switching it on and breathing deeply.

At that moment, a male voice from the path twenty metres to the left of Jerome shouted, "Stop! Put that down immediately."

Jerome did not move.

The voice belonged to a policeman who moved slowly into Jerome's line of vision. He was crouching down and pointing a gun directly at him. "Put that down immediately or I'll shoot."

There was still no movement from Jerome as two other police officers appeared on the path, both also pointing guns at him. As Jerome pulled off the mask, a shot whizzed past him.

"Put your hands in the air immediately, and don't make any other move or you'll be shot dead." It was a female voice this time. "Do you understand that?"

Slowly, Jerome raised his hands. Suddenly, he found himself on the ground, his face pressed down into the gritty soil, and his arms jerked painfully backwards. There were voices, one in particular asking abrupt and – with hindsight, he accepted – reasonable questions: "Do you have any weapons or explosives? What were you doing? What is your name? Where are you from?"

There were other questions, and he tried to answer them all, all that is except what he was doing. He passed on that initially, but they were persistent, so he told them. He also remembered revolving lights from two police cars on his left, the direction in which his face was pointing, which kept going as the noise subsided gradually.

He was handcuffed, taken to a police station and interrogated further for three hours. But the questioning lost its menacing edge gradually as his story was checked, his relatives contacted and his hotel room searched thoroughly. Eventually, they placed him in a cell, and gave him a bar of chocolate and a bottle of water; their glares of anger having been replaced by glances of annoyance.

It was 9.00pm the following evening when Jerome was let out of the cell. He was taken into a small, brightly-lit room where two officers awaited him; the younger one was seated behind the desk and the other was standing at his right shoulder. Jerome was asked to sit in the one unoccupied seat in front of the desk.

"Well, Mr Black. You are very lucky young man." The seated speaker looked surprisingly young, possibly no older than Jerome. "You could have been killed last night with your crazy behaviour. Do you know that?"

Jerome looked at him in a tired, distant way and made no response beyond raising his eyebrows and giving a gentle nod in acknowledgement of the suggestion.

"I think you might be suffering from Jerusalem syndrome. Have you ever heard of it?"

"No," replied Jerome.

"Well, might I suggest you look it up when you get home?" He looked at Jerome as he scooped up the pages from his desk. "Because, yes, Mr Black we are letting you go home. Your brother and psychiatrist are waiting to bring you home this evening."

"They're here?" Jerome looked animated suddenly.

"Yes, they're waiting outside. And, Mr Black, please don't come back to Israel. We may not be so indulgent the next time. Your belongings are in your suitcase over there." He indicated towards the corner of the room. "Sign this form before you go."

Jerome signed the form without reading it. "May I change into fresh clothes?"

The officer gave a reluctant nod.

***

Karl and Sarah were sitting side-on to Jerome as he approached them in the foyer of the station. They saw him at the same time and stood to embrace him gently.

"How are you?" asked Karl softly.

"I'm OK," confirmed Jerome.

"You've got some scratches on the side of your face," said Karl, indicating the same area on his own cheek.

Jerome touched the scratches. "Yes, that was from when they arrested me, I guess." He looked anxiously at his brother. "Karl, is everyone OK at home?"

"Everyone's fine, Jerome. We're all just worried about you. But, don't worry, everyone's fine."

"That's great." Tired relief settled on Jerome's face. Then he looked at Sarah as they left the station. "That was very kind of you to come over. You didn't need to."

"Well, I felt I did, Jerome," she stated.

They hailed a taxi and drove to the hotel to collect Karl and Sarah's belongings. Jerome had his suitcase minus the oxygen cylinder, which had not been returned.

"I won't need it again, anyway," he said on the way to the airport. "Those journeys are over."

"I'm glad," replied Karl without elaborating further

They then sat largely in thoughtful silence for the rest of the taxi trip.

**

On the plane, they were seated together, with Jerome (he suspected by design) occupying the middle seat.

It was only when the plane was in the air that Karl, stretching back in his seat, seemed to relax. "Were they hard on you?" he asked turning towards Jerome.

"The police?" questioned Jerome.

"Yes."

"Ah, not really; I guess they were doing their job. When did you guys get here?"

"I got a call from the British Consulate in Jerusalem late last night. They explained the situation. I spoke to Sarah, and she decided to fly out with me. We arrived at around 5.00pm this evening, checked into the hotel and then went straight to the police station."

Jerome nodded thoughtfully. "Thank you both very much." He looked at Karl and then at Sarah. "Did they give *you* a difficult time?" asked Jerome looking again at his brother.

"No, not at all," replied Karl, dismissing the notion. "They suggested you might be suffering from something called Jerusalem syndrome."

"Yes, they said that to me too. Do you know what it is?"

Karl nodded in the direction of Sarah, who said softly, "It's where some people have religiously themed dreams or visions triggered by being in Jerusalem."

"Anyway, you're safe now. That's the important thing," Karl declared with finality, as though he didn't want to discuss anything about Jerome's trip to Jerusalem. His brother was coming home and that was all that mattered.

As the flight entered its second hour, Karl fell into a gentle sleep, his head turned away from his brother.

"I'm sorry I reacted the way I did, in our last session. It wasn't very professional of me," apologised Sarah. Her perfume seemed refreshingly cool to Jerome compared to the cloying heat of the prison cell.

"Don't be daft. You reacted the way any normal person would have. I shouldn't have done it. It was selfish."

"Well, I must admit it did spook me. I even rang my mother who, of course, had never heard of you."

"Everyone back home really is OK, aren't they?" He seemed anxious suddenly.

"Yes, they are." She rested her hand on his right arm. "Everyone's fine." After a short silence, Sarah removed her hand and then asked quietly, "You went to Jerusalem to visit him again?"

"Yes."

"That place you were in last night, Jerome, one of the policemen told me it was the garden of Gethsemane, where Christ prayed on the night the Roman soldiers took him away to be crucified. Were you trying to get back to him there?"

Jerome felt emotion well up inside. "Yes."

"And did you?" Her voice was gentle.

Jerome stared at the seat in front of him. "No, I never got the chance."

Chapter 47

Gethsemane, Israel

But Jerome did go back that night in Gethsemane, although he has never spoken to anyone about it.

When he first arrived, cold was the initial striking feature. The temperature had fallen by at least fifteen degrees Celsius. Shivering suddenly, he blew warm air into his cupped hands as he stood up slowly. The artificial light from the city was absent, although it did not seem much darker. One light was shining from a lone fire on top of the Mount of Olives; silhouetted in front of it stood three figures, possibly soldiers. Above them, the sky seemed stunningly bright, with dazzling stars and a crescent-shaped moon hanging low in the north.

As he adapted to his new surroundings, Jerome saw the garden nearby was full of young olive trees. Whether any of these were the ancient ancestors of the gnarled versions he had left behind, or perhaps even the same trees, he did not know. He moved unhurriedly in the direction of some open space, his footsteps sounding loud and clumsy. The crackle of the fire was sharp, clean and clear, despite being so far away, and the distant sound of sporadic laughter carried in the still night air. He could hear breathing close by, his first indication that there were others in the garden. The sound was gently rhythmic and came from more than one person. He assumed they were sleeping. Carefully, he moved towards the noise, placing his sandals gingerly on the ground, trying to avoid the dry leaves or twigs that could alert them to his presence.

He soon came upon three sleeping men, lying on the ground on the far side of a rough path and wrapped tightly in their light-coloured cloaks. In the darkness, he could not distinguish beyond that. He stood very still, trying to eliminate the noise of his breathing, and watched them. Their heads were all partially hidden, and he could not recognise any of them with certainty. Jerome looked along the path in both directions and chose to go right. It was a winding path that soon took him out of sight of the sleeping men.

On rounding another bend, he saw the outline of a figure standing beside what looked like a small stone building. The person had their back to Jerome and was not moving.

As he moved stealthily forwards, he could hear words spoken softly and entreating in tone coming from the figure.

Slowly, Jesus turned around. "You!" A look of fear changed abruptly to one of astonishment.

"Yes," replied Jerome. "Do you remember me?"

"I thought you were a phantom. Are you real?"

"Yes, I'm real." Then it was Jerome's turn to sound surprised. "We've met before."

"In Galilee, on the mountain; I thought that was just a dream."

"No one remembers me. You are the only one."

"Who are you? Are you an angel?"

"No, I'm not an angel. I'm just an ordinary man with a gift to travel back in time."

"You have a message for me?" Jesus's eyes widened with expectation.

"No." Jerome, confused, shook his head. He could see that the small building behind Jesus looked like a shed of some kind. The warm breath from an animal on the floor drifted out through a wide opening in the wall.

"But why have you come to me at this time?" He stared intensely at Jerome.

"I don't know. I'm not sure why I chose this time. I just wanted to speak to you. When we met before, I told you about my strange powers to travel back in time, but I didn't understand why I had these powers or how I was meant to use them. You said I should follow my destiny, but when I tell people in my own time, they refuse to believe me. They treat me like a simple fool, as though I am mad." Jerome paused and continued less hurriedly. "And when I journey far back in time, someone close to me dies at that exact moment. Why would that happen?"

There was no response. The night air remained cool and still, except for the intermittent chirp of a solitary cricket.

Jerome moved towards him. Up close, he noticed the changes in Jesus's appearance. Apart from the tiredness around the eyes and mouth, his cheeks were red and showed signs of inflammation. The black facial hair had acquired strands of grey; his hair and eyes looked dull.

"Why do you come to me with these questions?" asked Jesus, with the hope ebbing from his face.

"Because I feel certain you're the one person who might know the answers," clarified Jerome.

"If the Father has given you a special gift, it will be for a reason. If you need to know why, he will tell you."

"But I feel that *you* know something; I sense that *you* can tell me."

"You expect too much from me," Jesus said harshly. "Don't

you know that I too have many unanswered questions? Whom do I speak to? Who answers *me* when I ask? You choose a cruel time to come to me for help." The anger passed quickly and was replaced with a look of sadness without reproach.

Jerome felt suddenly unconscionably selfish for having burdened this man at this time. He dropped his gaze and stared at the stone-strewn ground.

"When we met before," began Jesus, "I said I felt that we would meet again before I die. Are you a harbinger that my end is very close?"

Slowly, Jerome raised his head. He felt he couldn't lie. "Yes." He nodded reluctantly.

"This night?"

"No," replied Jerome. "Tomorrow."

For the first time, Jesus looked at him with real compassion. After a moment, he said softly, "I do not know why people close to you should die when you journey back. It seems unjust, but..." He paused and looked into the shed at the thin donkey lying beside a large, circular stone. "They all think I have physical courage to match my brave words, but I have not. I have a dread fear of physical suffering. I am a coward in that way. And I fear I will show cowardice when the time comes and shame everyone I care about. I cannot overcome this premonition.

"I have always known my destiny, but I had hoped that, when this time came, there would be legions and nations of people accepting the word of God gladly and that I could pass quietly through this final gate to my Father." He looked back to where the sleepers lay. "I have no more than a handful of followers. I fear I have disappointed my Father and have no time left to change it."

Jerome, shaking his head, looked piercingly at him and began talking with great conviction. "No, no, that's not right. Your message does live on. Two thousand years from now there are hundreds of millions of people who follow your teachings."

Jerome paused and added softly, "You do die but with no show of fear and with great dignity. It is an inspiration to your followers and future generations."

Jesus raised his head gradually. "I am tired, very tired. Perhaps this is the last time I will see the moon or stars. I just want to reach the far shore and fall into the welcome embrace of my Father, and to sleep safely in his arms, knowing I didn't let him down." Jesus looked at Jerome. "I have never seen him, my Father, but I know him." He placed his left hand flat on his chest. "His heart beats here."

Silence returned to the garden before Jesus spoke again. "Every message has its time, and perhaps mine is not now. Or maybe it is the understanding and acceptance of the message that require patience. We will see. I have done what I believe was asked of me." An unusual, quizzical look had come into his face as he turned to Jerome and again asked, "*Do* you have a message for me?"

"You asked me that before. I don't understand what you mean."

"Have you been sent to me by my Father?"

Jerome was stunned. "No." After a few moments and with less conviction, he added, "I don't think so." And then, with slowly dawning realisation, "Have I?"

The shocked silence was broken by the approaching sound of Jewish men and Roman soldiers, and, suddenly, Jerome was gone.

Epilogue

I arrived back to see a policewoman pointing a gun at me.

"Put your hands in the air immediately, and don't make any other move or you'll be shot dead." She looked serious but calm.

They said later that it was the effect of the oxygen that clouded my senses and contributed to my inability to act rationally when I removed the mask. That's not the case. My arrival back had been a shock to me. I had left Jesus suddenly, but not at my instigation or at the expiry of the normal time period. I had been sent back.

As time passed, and I went through the interrogation at the police station and the subsequent flight home, my mood remained one of weary confusion. I had received no answers to my questions on this journey back, but I had provided comfort to Jesus. He had remembered me from Galilee, so, presumably, he would remember this occasion too and that would comfort him in the hours leading up to his death. Had the purpose of this journey been to let him know, at his moment of despair, that everything would be all right, and that he would handle his death with courage and dignity? And had I been sent back sooner because my job was complete and my usefulness at an end?

As well as feeling confused, I also experienced huge relief that no one else had died. And I was certain I would never again use these powers. There was a sense of finality about this journey, which I couldn't really explain at the time. Maybe it was just exhaustion at the thought of having to go through this again. Anyway, I was happy to convey the message to Karl and Sarah that my journeys were over. Back home, there was a general sense of tired relief, tinged with ongoing concern from my family, which my reassurances only partly dispelled.

***

It was the third day after my return from Jerusalem. I was in my bedroom looking through my emails when I saw one from Rachel Berger; the subject was Angelic. I opened it.

> *Dear Mr Black,*
> *Unfortunately, I have to tell you that my mother, Angelic Berger, passed away last Friday. I had spoken to her about you and she remembered you warmly.*
> *Yours sincerely,*
> *Rachel Berger*

I reread the email with a growing sense of shock and anger. My initial reaction was not to respond further, but I had to know more. So I emailed this reply:

> *Dear Rachel,*
> *I am very sorry to learn about your mother's passing. She was extremely kind to me on the two occasions I met her.*

*This may seem like a strange request, but could you please
let me know what time of the day your mother died?*
Kind regards,
Jerome Black

I knew my journey back had been at around 9.00pm. That was
7.00pm London time. I sat in front of the screen, and the response
arrived about one hour later:

Dear Mr Black,
*Mum passed away peacefully at just after seven o'clock in
the evening.*
Yours sincerely,
Rachel Berger

I stared at the screen for a long time. To be honest, I've no idea
how long; finally, I was awoken from this trance by my father
bringing me a cup of tea.

I recall him saying, "There you go," as he placed it on the
bedside locker.

I remember answering, "Thanks", but not much more.

***

That was six weeks ago. I'm now in the north of Scotland, on the
Isle of Iona, where I once went as a boy with my parents. Fled,
you might think, but I would prefer to look on it as a retreat, in
both senses of the word: a retreat in order to fall back and mentally
regroup, and also to reflect on my life, encouraged silently by the
old, monastic surroundings. Karl wasn't too keen on the idea. I
think he feels I shouldn't be left alone, but he accepted it reluctantly.

I must confess that my overwhelming emotion in the days
after learning about Angelic's death was anger. If the objective

of giving me these powers was solely to make that journey to Gethsemane, then why all of the other stuff? Why the journey to Hitler? Why the charade with the oxygen? Why the unnecessary suffering caused by the journey to see my adored mother? Why the early episodes as a child and the diagnosis, and the necessary misdiagnosis? And, above all, why the deaths of innocent people?

In my mind, there is only one explanation: the purpose of all these events was to ensure I would never be believed. The fact that I could be destroyed in the process was incidental and irrelevant. No, it was more than that; it was necessary. A greater cause was being served. I wonder if Judas came to the same conclusion. At times, I do feel some empathy with him, although when I emerge from my darker moments, I am grateful there are so few trees on this island.

I had thought of showing the emails on Angelic to Sarah. Slapping them down on her desk and pointing to them saying, "See, I told you she existed. And, look, she died at the exact moment I travelled back. I am telling the truth." But the need for her to accept my story seems a lot less important now. I'm not sure why.

Perhaps now, as I emerge gradually from the shadows, things do not seem so dark. If this story is never to be told, then why didn't I die at the spot? That would have been the cleanest and the safest way of dealing with me. And why allow me to write this story? No one has seen it yet, so there could be a final twist, but I doubt it. I sense whoever gave me these powers is not malicious. And I was given the opportunity to comfort Jesus in his hour of need. Surely that is a memory worth cherishing?

Karl arrived unexpectedly and walked over the shale beach towards where I stood tossing pebbles into the cold bright sea.

"I couldn't reach you on the phone, so I decided to come up and visit you," Karl explained.

"Yes, I'm sorry about that. The battery's dead in the phone. It's good to see you," I told him.

"So, has your head cleared a bit?" He picked up a handful of pebbles and began throwing them into the sea.

"Yes, it has, thanks. It has."

"Sarah rang to ask me how you were getting on. She said to tell you that she got a linguist to listen to your tape and that you were right. She said you'd know what she meant."

I smiled and continued to throw the pebbles. I noticed Karl's were travelling further. "How's Dad?" I asked.

"Dad's fine. Think he's getting more comfortable living on his own. Oh, and that reminds me, that girl... what's her name?" he continued nonchalantly, "Stancia. She called round at the house looking for you; seemed very keen to see you, according to Dad." He let the remaining stones drop to the ground and rubbed the sand off his hands.

I turned and looked fondly at my brother.

"Let's go home, kid," he suggested.

"Aye," I replied, "let's go home."